Born and brought up in Lanarkshire, PAT MCINTOSH lived and worked in Glasgow before settling on Scotland's west coast, where she lives with her husband and three cats.

Also by Pat McIntosh

Crow

Pat McIntosh

Constable • London

Constable & Robinson Ltd
55–56 Russell Square
London WC1B 4HP
www.constablerobinson.com

First published in the UK by Constable,
an imprint of Constable & Robinson Ltd, 2012

First US edition published by SohoConstable,
an imprint of Soho Press, 2012

Soho Press, Inc.
853 Broadway
New York, NY 10003
www.sohopress.com

A copy of the British Library Cataloguing in Publication
data is available from the British Library

ISBN: 978-1-78033-163-8 (hardback)
ISBN: 978-1-78033-165-2 (ebook)

Printed and bound in the UK

1 3 5 7 9 10 8 6 4 2

US ISBN: 978-1-61695-158-0
Library of Congress Cataloging-in-Publication Data is available

MIX
Paper from
responsible sources
FSC® C018575

This one is for my brother.

Ever since it became a kingdom, Scotland has had two native languages, Gaelic (which in the fifteenth century was called Ersche) and Scots, both of which you will find used in the Gil Cunningham books. I have translated the Gaelic where needful, and those who have trouble with the Scots could consult the online Dictionary of the Scots Language, to be found at http://www.dsl.ac.uk/dsl/

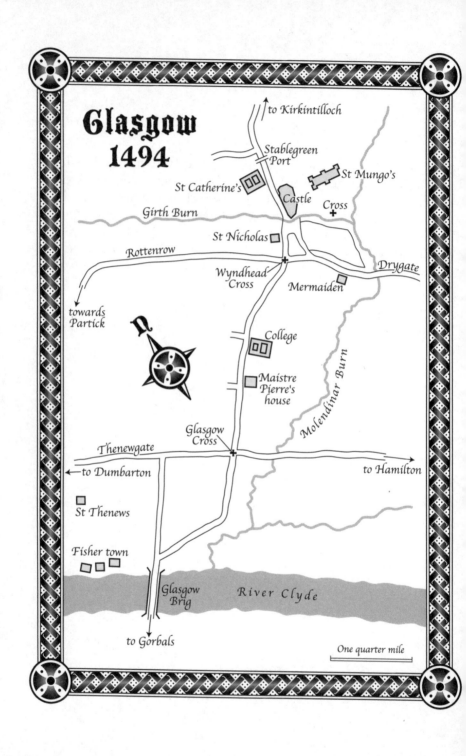

Glasgow
1494

to Kirkintilloch

Stablegreen
Port

St Catherine's

St Mungo's

Castle

Cross

Girth Burn

St Nicholas

Rottenrow

Wyndhead
Cross

Drygate

Mermaiden

towards
Partick

N

College

Maistre
Pierre's
house

Molendinar Burn

Glasgow
Cross

Thenewgate

to Dumbarton

to Hamilton

St Thenews

Fisher town

Glasgow
Brig

River Clyde

to Gorbals

One quarter mile

Chapter One

She was quite certainly dead.

Without realising it, he had taken a great leap backwards, away from that hideous face where it lay at the edge of the shadows. Now he stood as if his feet had taken root, staring at the moonlit horror. A great trembling overtook him.

Nothing else seemed to move in the night. A cloud slid over the moon, shrouding all in darkness, and then passed, and with the returning light it was as if she raised her head a little to look at him. With a muffled yelp of terror he turned and fled, down the hill, towards safety.

'There's someone bound to St Mungo's Cross,' observed Gil Cunningham's new assistant as they rode back into Glasgow through the August evening, rounding the high red sandstone walls of the Archbishop's castle.

'Now what would anyone be doing that for?' wondered Euan Campbell, from behind them. 'Surely somebody would set them free?'

Gil turned in the saddle to look at his two very dissimilar henchmen. Lowrie Livingstone, aged nineteen, recent graduate of the University here in Glasgow, was fair and good-looking, with an easy cultured charm which would stand him in good stead in any occupation, particularly that of notary in which Gil had contracted to train him, although just now, with his face, his broad straw hat and the narrow sleeves of his blue woollen gown powdered with reddish dust from the roads, he looked nearly as disreputable as the gallowglass at his back. Euan on the

1

other hand, dark haired and black browed with the crooked Campbell mouth in a long narrow face, simply looked what he was: a man who hired his sword arm for a living.

They had all three spent the August day out in Strathblane, attempting to straighten out the ownership of two portions of land on the flanks of the Campsie hills. It had been a pleasant day for the task, warm and serene, with birdsong in the thickets and a clear view out over the Clyde valley and down into Renfrewshire and Lanarkshire, but talking to witnesses, many of whom spoke Ersche rather than Scots and required Euan's unreliable help as a translator to make their statements, had proved wearisome, and he was glad to be nearing home.

Young Maister Livingstone had observed correctly: away to their left, just inside the low wall of the kirkyard, Gil could see the tall stone cross which stood by the Girth Burn, the most important of the several crosses which marked the boundaries of the sanctuary area. There was certainly someone bound to the massive upright, writhing and shrieking and securely roped, surrounded by a crowd of grinning spectators. Small boys ran in and out, throwing handfuls of water from the burn at the prisoner and anyone else who was not quick enough to get out of the way.

'*They bringis mad men on fuit and horss,*' he quoted, '*and bindis them to Sanct Mungos Corss.* Did you never see it before?'

'Oh, that!' said Lowrie. 'No, I never saw it, but I heard of it a few times. How often does it happen?'

'Maybe once in a quarter, perhaps more often in the summer months. You'd not leave even a dog outside without shelter over a winter's night, after all. It's a great entertainment for the multitude, you can see that.'

'And does it cure them, to be spending a night tied to the cross like that?' asked Euan, staring at the crowd. 'More like to send them even further mad, I would be thinking.'

'I've never heard.' Gil heeled his horse onward. 'The dinner will be waiting.'

'I wonder who he is.' Lowrie followed his master past the

kirkyard gates and into the vennel which led to the Drygate. 'Poor devil. Likely Madame Catherine will know.'

'Indeed it is likely,' agreed Euan. 'Madame Catherine is knowing everything, and her not having a word of Scots, neither.'

Seated over a late dinner in the house called the Mermaiden, Gil reflected on the recent changes in his circumstances. In the last few months he had acquired a house of his own, a household, an assistant, and, more particularly, the means to support all these. He felt slightly dizzy with the speed at which it had all happened, and he was not looking forward to the next quarter's bills, but he relished the feeling it gave him to look down the long board from his chair at its head. On his right, his young wife Alys showed her pleasure in his return from a day's journey into Stirlingshire; on his left, Alys's aged duenna Catherine consumed sops-in-wine with toothless dignity; at his feet his wolfhound Socrates lay hoping for crusts and crumbs. Beyond Catherine, Lowrie was just reaching for the ale-jug, Euan had returned from stabling the horses and was addressing his supper with eagerness, and further down the table the maidservants who had followed Alys one by one from her father's house, Jennet, Kittock, Annis, and his small ward's nurse Nancy, were chattering companionably. We need to find a serving-man or two, he reflected; I need a body-servant, and Euan is not my first choice for the task. Or even my second.

'*Mais non,*' Catherine was saying in French, 'I had not heard of another poor soul at the Cross.'

'They were saying at Vespers at St Nicholas' it's a lassie,' offered Jennet, overhearing Lowrie's question. 'Out of Ayrshire, so I heard, maister, though I never got her name.'

'A lassie!' said Alys. 'Oh, poor soul indeed. I wonder if she knows where she is? Does anyone watch, Gil, while someone is tied up like that? It must be terrifying, to be exposed the whole night alone.'

'I've no idea,' he admitted.

'Likely St Mungo himsel oversees all, mem, seeing it's his

cross,' suggested Jennet. 'I've aye heard it's the custom just to tie up the poor madman and go off to St Nicholas' chapel for the night, his friends I mean, to keep out the night air.'

Alys's father, the French master-mason, paying a late call after the supper was cleared, agreed in part with this.

'I had to chase both my laddies away from her,' he said with disapproval. 'Her friends were present, but they kept apart from the crowd once she was bound. Surely they would have done better to wait until it grew dark and the town was quiet before they put her there. She is quite young, no more than five-and-twenty, too young for such treatment.'

'Did you speak to them?' Alys asked. 'Who is she? What form does her madness take?'

'She is an Ayrshire lady named Annie Gibb,' said her father, accepting the glass of wine which Lowrie handed to him. They had repaired to the solar at the back of the house; the sun had struck the two windows of the little chamber for most of the day, and it was still pleasantly warm. Maistre Pierre stretched his feet out comfortably and added, 'Her servants would say little more, not even what part of Ayrshire she is come from, but I should say she is melancholy-mad. Much of her raving was of how she wished to be let die.'

'Ah, poor soul,' said Alys, as she had done before.

'Gibb,' said Gil reflectively. 'Likely from Kyle, then, at least by origin. Well, no doubt we'll hear in the morning. And how does our good-mother, Pierre?'

'Ah.' Maistre Pierre looked sideways at his daughter, and Gil braced himself inwardly. Another of the changes of the last few months was about to confront them. Two women could never agree under one roof, that was widely known; it looked as if Alys and her new stepmother would never agree in one burgh. He should not have asked the question, and yet civility required that he did.

They had first met Angus MacIain the harper and his sister Ealasaidh two years since, when the harper's mistress, the mother of his son, had been murdered in the building

4

site at the side of the Cathedral. By the time her killer was uncovered Gil and Alys were betrothed and the baby was Gil's ward, but it was only this spring that Pierre and Ealasaidh had come to an understanding. It was now two months since their marriage, and it did not seem to Gil as if Alys was any closer to accepting the idea than she had been when it was first mentioned.

'Élise,' said his father-in-law now, 'wished me to ask you where is the linen for the great bed?'

'I left it where it has always been kept,' said Alys without expression, 'in the kist at the bed-foot. I touched nothing in your chamber.'

'Ah,' said Maistre Pierre uncomfortably. 'The kist with the brass lock, you mean?'

'Yes, that kist. Is it not there? Has *madame mère* moved it? Or mislaid the key? Perhaps one of your new servants has taken it.'

Lowrie, the ready colour sweeping up over his neck, turned away and began to riffle through a stack of music on the windowsill beside him. Following his cue, Gil opened the lid of the monocords and tapped at the first few keys of the little instrument. Maistre Pierre ignored the spidery notes.

'*Ma mie*, she is mistress of my house now,' he said sternly in French. A mistake, thought Gil.

'Then she may run it herself,' said Alys, still without expression, 'without referring to me.'

'What, after you removed all the maidservants who know where everything is?'

'I took only Jennet and Nancy, Father,' Alys said. 'The other women left of their own accord.'

This was unanswerably true, Gil knew. Kittock was still complaining about what 'the new mistress' had ordered done in her kitchen.

'Shall we have some music?' he suggested. Alys set aside her handwork and rose.

'You may have as much as you please,' she said. 'I have matters to see to. Good night, Father.'

She bent her head for his blessing, which he delivered reluctantly. As the door closed behind her Gil said,

'Have you managed to find servants yet?'

'Élise has hired a crowd of women. They all speak Ersche,' said Maistre Pierre glumly. 'I thought Alys would have been more generous. She should be obedient to her new mother.'

Gil kept silent. He liked and admired the harper's sister, a handsome strong-minded woman who had not had an easy life, but his perception had been that it was Ealasaidh who was ungenerous; she could never have run a household before, let alone one as large as that his father-in-law kept, and Alys had offered advice. It had been refused, without gratitude.

'Well, no doubt she will come round,' said Maistre Pierre after a pause, though it was not clear which contender he referred to. 'Do you tell me this woman at the Girth Cross is from Kyle? From the middle part of Ayrshire?'

'It's where the surname comes from,' Gil agreed in relief. Lowrie turned back towards them, holding several sheets of music.

'Ockeghem?' he said hopefully.

'There is a family named Gibb who own a quarry,' said the mason, 'beyond a place called Cumnock. Good blond freestone, a valuable resource. I wonder are they her kin? Yes, why not Ockeghem,' he went on, before Gil could answer, 'though I must not stay too late.'

Having seen his father-in-law off the premises an hour later into the quiet August evening, Gil locked the front door and paused to admire the incised and painted mermaiden now on the inside of the heavy planks. Even with the door reversed so that this well-known symbol of sexual licence was not shown to the street, they still had the occasional caller who had not heard that the bawdy-house was closed. He grinned, put the sturdy bar in place and set off through the house, checking shutters and hearths as he went. The dog paced after him, his claws clicking on the wide boards. Here on the ground floor, as well as the little solar beside the back door there was the lower hall where they had eaten their supper, with another three smaller chambers opening from it. In one, a narrow stair led up, eventually, to the great bedchamber, a resource which Gil had not so far made use of. In the next, Catherine was probably still at her devotions, which he knew were extended; in the third, Annis and Kittock were already snoring. Kittock had wished to sleep in the kitchen as she had always done, but the kitchen here was a separate building, and Alys had preferred that all the household were under the one roof at night. He had supported her in that.

Climbing the principal newel stair he checked the shutters in his own spacious closet, then paused again to survey the wide upper hall. Its painted walls were lively, the allegorical figures in their flowery alcoves bright even in the fading light. Despite the previous tenant's occupation, only one of the images required to be concealed by the plate-cupboard, which was fortunate, he reflected, given that they did not have many other large pieces of furniture yet.

He went on up the main stair. At the top, the dog nudged one door open and clicked away into the shadows. Behind the other door, along the short enfilade of chambers above the painted hall, Lowrie spoke sharply and Euan answered. Following the dog, Gil stepped quietly past the sleeping child in his cradle and the shut-bed where Jennet and Nancy still murmured together, and went into his own bedchamber. The house was settled for the night.

Alys was also at her prayers, the candlelight gleaming on her hair where it fell in sheets across the shoulders of her bedgown, her head bent intently over the prayer-book which had been a marriage-gift from her father. She did not look up, even when Socrates nudged her hands with his long nose.

Sighing inwardly, Gil said his own prayers and readied himself for bed, reckoning up the tasks of the morrow. Two contracts to draw up for different tradesmen of the upper town, one set of sasine papers to compose for Lowrie to write, a report to compile for his master the Archbishop of Glasgow. A quiet day, he thought with some relief.

He woke from a dream of thunder and falling rocks, to realise that the noise was a knocking at the house door. The dog was barking, away below stairs.

'The back door!' said Alys, as he tugged open the curtain at the side of their box bed. 'Who— Is it light yet? The servants are not stirring.'

'Barely.' He had scrambled into his shirt, and now flung open the shutters on the window which overlooked the yard and the approach to the back door. To his left, the dawn was turning rosy over the Dow Hill. To his right, at the other end of the house, Euan was already leaning out into the chilly morning, bare chested, black hair tousled. Socrates was still barking.

'Who's knocking?' Gil called.

'It iss one of the clerks from St Mungo's,' offered Euan, drowning the first answer from the ground. 'I think it iss Maister Sim.'

'Who is it?' he repeated. 'Quiet!' he shouted at the dog.

'Gil, is that you? You're wanted up at the Cross!' A figure stepped away from the door far enough to see and be seen from up here. One of the songmen from the Cathedral, as Euan had said, one of his occasional partners at Tarocco or at tennis.

'Habbie!' he said in some surprise. 'What's amiss? Bide there, man. I'll come down.'

'Never you worry, Maister Gil,' said Euan cheerily. 'I'll be letting him in, just let me be finding my shirt.'

'Maister Sim?' said Alys as Gil drew his head in. 'Is someone dead?'

'I don't know yet,' he answered, knotting the cord of his drawers. 'But at this hour it must be something urgent.'

Maister Sim agreed with this assessment.

'Oh, aye, she's dead,' he said, pacing up and down the lower hall, Socrates watching him suspiciously from the cold hearth. 'A dreadful sight, and all. We've managed to

8

keep them from moving her, but you'll need to come now, Gil, afore it gets any busier at the Cross.'

'Let me get my boots,' said Gil, stepping aside as Kittock emerged from the end chamber blinking and hooking up her gown across her broad bosom, her apron over one arm. 'Would you cut me a bite of bread and cheese?' he asked her. 'I doubt I'll be home afore the porridge is eaten up.'

'What's amiss, maister?' she asked, shaking out the apron. 'Is it the English at the gates? Will you be wanting your jack and helm? For I'm not right sure where we put them when we flitted you.'

'I don't know yet,' he confessed. 'Habbie? Who's dead?'

'It's the woman that was at St Mungo's Cross,' began Habbie Sim.

Within the small chamber, Annis shrieked in alarm.

'Christ amend us, is she got loose? Is she dangerous? Are we all to be murdered in our beds?'

'No, no, you're safe enough, lass,' said Maister Sim, pausing to rub at his arms as if he was cold. 'It's the woman hersel— She's dead. Someone's slain her where she was bound.'

'Our Lady save us all. Murdered, you mean, maister?' said Kittock intelligently, over another shriek from Annis. She crossed herself, and muttered a prayer. 'Right, Maister Gil, I'll get a piece and cheese put up for you, and you be sure and eat it, now. Annis, you can stop that noise, hen. The poor soul will be led straight to Paradise by St Mungo himsel and Our Lady, I've no doubt.' She set off towards the back door, followed by a reluctant Annis, just as loud footsteps on the main stair proclaimed the arrival of Euan, now decently clad and waving Gil's boots.

'Here's your boots, maister, you'll likely be wanting them,' he said unnecessarily, 'and Maister Lowrie's on his way down, and Jennet's getting the mistress up, and the wee fellow's still sleeping, praise be to Our Lady, we'd not want him running about hearing all what Maister Sim has to tell us, would we now?'

'Away out with Kittock,' Gil ordered, accepting the boots,

9

'and gie her a hand to get the fire going.' He sat down on the nearest bench and kicked off his house shoes. 'Go on, Habbie, tell me what's amiss. Who found the woman? Is it certain it's a violent death?'

'Oh, aye, certain. It was two of her friends found her,' said Maister Sim, as Lowrie slipped quietly into the room, fully dressed and booted. 'Her servants, I suppose. They came out to get her afore the dawn, and here she was dead, which distressed them greatly a course, and they cam up to St Mungo's to fetch someone. It was only when we found the cord about her neck they realised she hadny just up and died of her own accord. And when the light grew they recognised she'd been beaten and all, a dreadful sight, Gil. You need to see her.'

'A cord?' Gil repeated. 'I see why you've come for me.' He stood, tramping his heels down into the boots, and bent to fasten the straps which held the soft leather in place about his calves.

'Aye. So will you come now, afore they shift her? I've heard you often enough about what's to be learned from a corp afore it's shifted.'

The light in the chamber was increasing, and the full glory of Maister Sim's garb was visible. Always a showy dresser, he had risen this morning in a short gown of tawny velvet faced with gold-coloured silk, which contrasted nicely with a red cloth doublet and bright blue hose. Boots of a different red and a round green felt hat completed the outfit. Beside it, Gil's habitual, well-worn black appeared quite drab. Used to this effect, Gil ignored it, lifted his plaid from the peg by the back door, nodded to Lowrie and snapped his fingers for the dog.

'The hunt's up,' he said. 'Let's go. Tell me more as we go, Habbie. What did her friends do when they found her?'

'Set up a hue and cry,' said Maister Sim, following him out of the house. 'One ran to St Nicholas', another to St Mungo's and found us just assembling for Prime. So Will Craigie and I went to see, since we could be spared, our parts are both doubled in this morning's setting, and when we found the cord I came down to fetch you and he stayed to offer up the first prayers, which was only right in the circumstance.'

Gil nodded, pausing at the kitchen door to take the scrip Kittock had ready for him, and glad his friend could not see his expression. Most of the songmen were in minor orders at least, though possession of a good singing voice was the more important criterion. Maister Craigie was one of the few who were fully ordained, but his private life was not what one might hope for. He cheated at cards to Gil's certain knowledge, there were other tales to the man's discredit, and Gil's uncle Canon Cunningham had admitted that the Chapter of St Mungo's was occasionally exercised about his behaviour. Not who I would wish to offer prayers at my death, Gil thought, striding out onto the Drygate.

'And who are her friends? Who's she, indeed? I heard she was from Ayrshire.'

'Well, you ken more than me, if that's so,' admitted his friend. 'These were two of her servants, I think. They called her Annie, and said her sisters were in the guest-hall at St Catherine's. Likely they've been tellt by now.'

There was a small crowd in the kirkyard near the tall stone cross, exclaiming in shock and amazement above a rich bass drone which became recognisable as the prayers for the dead. Gil made out William Craigie close by the Cross as its source, with two bareheaded men standing white faced and stricken next to him. One of the St Mungo's vergers in his blue gown of office stood by radiating indignation; the rest of the dozen or so spectators seemed to be servants of the Upper Town and other early workers, attracted to the scene on their way past. He recognised the livery of St Nicholas' hostel, but nobody from St Catherine's seemed to be here yet.

'Get all these names if you will,' he said to Lowrie as they approached. 'Likely the most of them have nothing to do with the matter, but you never ken.'

'Will I be sending them all away, Maister Gil?' offered Euan helpfully behind him.

'No, you will not. Stand back and keep out of it,' Gil ordered, and shouldered his way in next to the tall cross.

'Maister Cunningham!' said the verger as he reached it. 'What are you going to do about this? She canny stay here, we canny have this! I told the woman we couldny take an eye to her, and now see what's come o't!'

Gil considered him for a moment.

'A drop of compassion would be becoming to a servant of Holy Kirk, Barnabas,' he observed. The man coloured up, but said defensively,

'It willny do for St Mungo's, and any road Canon Henderson's no going to be pleased. We're no wanting this kind o thing on our ground!'

Abandoning the matter, Gil moved round him to touch the body where it hung slumped and stiffened in its bonds.

'She's long gone, maister,' said one of the men beside her. 'But sic a way to go! Who'd ha done that to a poor mad lassie?'

The woman was quite certainly dead, there was no doubt about it. She had been bound to the Cross with a stout new hemp rope, no cheap item, which in happier circumstances would have been gifted to St Mungo's altar by now, to be sold on later to pay for lights. It had been tied with care, though not particularly tightly, perhaps leaving her enough room to flex arms and legs to prevent cramp, and as a result she now leaned forward and sideways, her head bent. Unkempt mud-coloured hair was trapped under the cord which Maister Sim had mentioned where it crossed the nape of her neck, but more locks fell free, hanging below her waist, and obscured her face. She was clad in a peniten- tial sacking gown, a surprisingly threadbare woollen plaid bundled over it, her bare feet visible below its bedraggled hem. There was a strong smell, not merely of stale urine as one might expect, but of a ripely unwashed body. He felt her hand and then her neck; the dead flesh was quite rigid. The dog nosed at the body, and turned to look up at his master's face.

'She's deid, maister,' said the man who had spoken

before, while Maister Craigie switched from *Requiem aeter-nam* to *Pater noster*. 'She's cold and set, and I thought she was sleeping.' He spoke quite calmly, but his hands shook.

'Was it you found her?' Gil asked, moving a hank of hair aside to look at the dangling ends of the cord. They seemed as new as the rope. Who would use a cord like that, he wondered, and for what?

'Aye, it was. Rab and me.' The man indicated his silent companion. 'We was watching in St Nicholas', over yonder, seeing St Mungo's was locked for the night, and I keeked out every hour or so, cam across to the kirkyard wall wi a lantern to see that all was well, she spoke to me a couple o times and asked me to set her free, and I wish I had, mais-ter, I wish I had. And then I cam down and it was, it seemed, it was all quiet, she'd ceased her raving and fell asleep, and there was the moonlight, and the laddies that were about had all went hame by midnight and— When we cam down to loose her afore dawn I still thought she'd fell asleep, I— I thought she was sleeping,' he repeated, 'till I spoke her name and she never stirred, and then I seen— I seen—' He crossed himself, tears springing to his eyes. 'It's no just that she's deid. Look at her face, maister, look what's come to her! Who could ha done that?'

Gil lifted away the rest of the dangling hair, and flinched. Maister Craigie's steady murmur checked at what was revealed, and flowed on with extra fervour. The woman had been beaten, and savagely. Blackened eyes, pulped nose, a swollen and purple cheek, torn mouth, were all caked in blood, which had run across her chin before it dried.

'Sweet St Giles!' he said. 'I take it she never looked like that when you left her.'

'We left her hale and healthy, maister, save she was mad,' the man assured him. 'Who could ha done this to her, bound as she was, the poor lassie?'

'Nobody from St Mungo's!' said Barnabas indignantly.

'And you heard nothing from where you were?'

'Nothing, maister! And we were awake the whole night, so we were, the both of us. Surely she'd ha screamed if she

was— Could she no ha cried out? We'd ha heard her, maister, we would that!' The man swallowed hard. 'Poor lass,
she never wished— She bade us take her away as many
times, she never felt it would do her good. I wish I'd listened.
I wish I'd watched at her side.'

'Have you been with her long?' Lowrie asked, fetching
up at Gil's elbow, tucking his tablets back into his purse.
Much of the crowd had evaporated rather than have its
names written down, as Gil had hoped, and the remaining
handful had retreated to a safe distance, Euan among them.
He caught the words *Blacader's quaestor* passing around.

'I followed her fro her faither's house,' said the man.
'And Rab here's been wi her near as long. Maister, who
could ha done this? She was under the saint's protection,
she'd never ha been a harm to anyone, we bound her only
to prevent her running off. Why throttle a lassie that
canny— And to treat her like that and all—' He turned
away, his hand going to his eyes. Lowrie patted him on the
shoulder, and looked at Gil.

'What do you see?' Gil prompted, as Maister Craigie
embarked on another round of the prayers for the dead.
'Anything useful?'

'Ground's too dry, even this close to the burn,' said
Lowrie, 'and there's been too many feet around here in any
case. No tracks to recognise. No marks on the gown or
plaid, I'd think she hasny been stabbed at all, just beaten
and strangled.' He grimaced. 'It's like what they tell of the
Inquisition, isn't it, maister?' He prowled around the high
carved cross, tugged at the rope which bound the woman,
peered at the hemp strands as Gil had already done.
Socrates followed him, sniffing carefully where he looked.
'These knots haveny been untied, have they?'

'I don't know,' said Gil. Socrates sat down at the feet of
the more talkative servant, nudging his hand. The man
stroked the soft ears, smiling crookedly at the dog, and Gil
said to him, 'Do you mind how she was bound last night?
Would you say all was as you left her?'

The man looked at him, startled, then at the restraints

which held the corpse upright. He appeared to count the loops which circled the skirts and torso, then stepped behind the cross to check the knots.

'It looks like it,' he agreed. 'You can see, we put plenty good knots in it, Rab and me. She'd never ha got them undone, maister, we— We took good care o that.'

'Well it was nobody from St Mungo's,' declared Barnabas officiously. 'I tellt the woman, I tellt her plain, it's naught to do wi us what happens down here at the Cross, there's nobody to spare to have an eye to her. It was nobody from St Mungo's untied they knots.'

'Sawney,' said Rab suddenly. He glanced beyond his colleague, beyond the cross, just as Gil became aware of a commotion approaching the kirkyard gates, of raised voices and women weeping.

'Oh, Christ aid us all, it's the lassies,' said Sawney. 'Maister, it's her good-sisters, we'd best head them off, she isny a sight for young lassies, no till she's laid out, if then.'

'I'll go,' said Maister Sim, who had stood by silently until now. 'Will, come wi me, I think the living need you.'

Maister Craigie, finishing the prayer he was reciting, crossed himself, looked round and nodded. Maister Sim was already hurrying towards the group of women. As the priest followed Gil said,

'Barnabas, if you would fetch Euan a board or the like we can cut her down, afore it gets any busier here.'

'A board?' repeated Barnabas, as if he had never heard the word before. 'Oh, no. The boards we've got are all accounted for, it's more than my position's worth to let them out my hands.'

'There will be something there that would not be missed for an hour or two,' said Euan. 'Come and show me what you have.'

'But where'll we take her to, maister?' asked Sawney helplessly. 'I've no— I canny— Our maister's no fit to direct me, and it's no a matter to take to Dame Ellen.'

This was the first Gil had heard of a head of the household. He set the point aside for later and said, 'If you're lodged at St Catherine's, we should take her there. They'll put her in the chapel for now. I want to see her afore she's laid out.'

'Better to wait till she's washed, maister,' said Sawney, watching Euan making for the Cathedral, the protesting Barnabas beside him. Several of the spectators were following, possibly in the hope of learning more. 'She's pretty ripe. See, it's been since her man dee'd,' Sawney expanded. 'What wi that and she'd lost the bairn he gave her, she fell into a great melancholy, poor lassie, and she vowed she'd live single all her days, and never wash, nor be combed, nor anything of the sort. Nothing her sisters said would budge her from it.'

'Sweet St Giles!' said Gil, but Lowrie was nodding.

'I've heard of that. There was a woman away beyond Stirling did the same, so my mother once told me. It's in a song, too. *Sall neither coif come on my head, nor kaim come in my hair, Nor neither coal nor candlelight come in my bower mair,*' he quoted, and added thoughtfully, 'doesn't say anything about never washing.'

The group of women had been persuaded to retrace their steps, though one of them kept looking over her shoulder. The two songmen were going with them, gesturing past the rose-coloured sandstone walls of the castle in the direction of the pilgrim hostel.

'Tell me about her,' said Gil. 'Who is she?'

She was, as Maistre Pierre had said, Annie Gibb, daughter and heiress of a gentleman of Kyle, one James Gibb of Tarbolton. Wedded at fourteen to Arthur, son of Sir Edward Shaw of Glenbuck, a bonnie lad a year younger than herself, she had lost a bairn at seventeen, by which time her husband was already racked by the coughing sickness which killed him a year later, shortly after her own father died.

'So he never gave her another,' said Sawney, 'and here she was a widow at eighteen, poor lass, and by then she was over ears in love wi him, and fell into a great melancholy like I said. And given that Sir Edward's got his death and all, he was hoping to see her cured so he could wed her safe afore he dees hissel, and not leave her a charge on his lassies or their husbands. There's no other heir,' he explained.

'How old is she now?' Gil asked.

'Near one-and-twenty,' said Sawney, 'and her faither's dead these two year and all,' he repeated.

Gil looked at the corpse's bent head and unkempt hair with pity. *My deth I love, my life ich hate,* he thought. Alys would be nineteen at midsummer; his youngest sister Tib, married a few months ago, had just turned twenty. This girl's life had taken a very different turn from theirs, and now it was over, and violently. He could not imagine either his wife or his sister succumbing to such a melancholy, but he could see why it might happen.

'Will we be cutting yon good rope?' Euan had returned, some of his eager entourage behind him bearing a wattle hurdle. 'It seems a shame, it does, though I would not be wishing to use it myself after this—'

Gil was not very familiar with the two pilgrim hostels of Glasgow, and had never been inside St Catherine's, though he had encountered its Master once or twice in the course of his legal practice. The hostel, he discovered, was a series of timber-framed buildings off the Stablegreen, with its own small stone chapel in the outer courtyard and guest halls for male and female pilgrims flanking an inner one. In the Master's modest dwelling Sir Simon Elder met Gil with concern.

'They're all in great distress,' he said. 'None o them making much sense, and small wonder. Did you ever hear the like, Maister Cunningham? I've broke it to Sir Edward, seeing his lassies were in a right state and Habbie and the other fellow had to get back to their duties.'

'How did he take it? His man Sawney said he's sick to death. I hope this won't hasten his end.'

Sir Simon grimaced.

'I'm not certain he took it in, to tell truth. Nodded and thanked me for bringing him word, but when I offered to pray wi him he said, No, he'd need time to it. Then his doctor put me out of the chamber, and then the lassies needed comforting.'

'How big is the party?'

'Oh, a good number. There's Sir Edward himsel, poor soul, and his doctor, and his sister, and his own lassies and the husband of one of them, and this poor lass who's in the chapel now, and all their servants. Fortunately, Sir Edward's well able to make us a generous donation, or I'd have to be asking them to leave as soon as their three nights was up, no to mention all their beasts out-by in the stables, and I'd not like to do that in the circumstances. And we're quiet the now, we'll not get busy again till nearer the Assumption, we've a few days yet.'

'What ails Sir Edward?' Gil asked.

Sir Simon made another long face. He was a tall, angular, lantern-jawed individual with a thick ring of white woolly hair round his tonsure, a sharp and tolerant eye for human failings, and a sardonic smile which was notably absent just now.

'Trouble in his water, or the like,' he divulged. 'Times it pains him right bad, poor soul. How he managed the journey I couldny say. Sawney's got the truth o't, you've only to look at the man to see he's near his end.' He considered Gil a moment longer across his cluttered chamber. 'Were you wanting anything more?'

'I'll need a word wi Sir Edward, if I can,' Gil confirmed. 'And wi the good-sisters, and the servants as well, if I'm to find whoever did this and see him brought to justice. Or her,' he added. 'I'd say one woman could strangle another if she was bound fast the way Annie Gibb was, though the beating she had before that might be another matter.'

'You wouldny think,' said Sir Simon without much hope, 'it was some passing ill-doer, someone wi a grudge at madwomen, or the like? Or the prentice-laddies? They had one o their games last night, could some o them— She hadny,' he said in alarm, 'she hadny been forced, had she?'

'No sign of that. Her skirts were bound all about her knees. As for someone wi a grudge, I'd say whoever did it knew what he was doing. It was very deliberate.'

18

'You mean,' said the other man after a short pause, 'I've maybe got a murderer under this roof?'

'Aye,' said Gil baldly.

'Then I'd best get to my prayers,' said Sir Simon, 'for him and for the rest of us.'

Chapter Two

'I count it a merciful release,' pronounced John Lockhart of Kypeside.

Do you, indeed, thought Gil. And I wonder if Annie Gibb would agree?

'She's prayed for her death these three year,' continued Lockhart, as if he had heard Gil's thoughts. 'Or so my wife tells me.'

'And your wife is?' Gil prompted.

A request to speak to the family of the dead woman had brought this man out of the guest hall in a protective rush; he was a plump, self-important fellow about Gil's age, with the fair, wind-reddened skin of a man who farmed his own land somewhere around the headwaters of the Avon.

'Mistress Mariota Shaw,' Lockhart announced. 'The eldest daughter. We were wedded the same year her brother died, God rest him.'

'Is your wife of the party?'

'Oh, no, no.' Lockhart smiled tolerantly. 'She could hardly bring the bairn, after all.'

'So who did come to Glasgow? Will you sit down and tell me about it?'

There was the sound of weeping in the women's hall. They were in the inner courtyard of the hostel, a cobbled space lined with tubs of flowers, with several benches placed so that weary pilgrims could enjoy the sunshine when there was any. Today, early though it was, there was not only sunshine but plenty of warmth; Gil had no real need of his plaid. Alys had grown flowers in tubs like these in the courtyard of her father's house, away down the High Street. He wondered suddenly whether Ealasaidh would keep them growing, and whether Alys would set more flowers round the House of the Mermaiden next spring.

Lockhart had settled himself on the bench, booted feet stretched out before him.

'Well, there's Sir Edward himself,' he expounded, 'and my wife's sisters, that's Nicholas and Ursula. Two very bonny lassies,' he admitted, 'and I believe they're well taught to hold a household, but I had the better bargain. My wife's a sensible lass. There was Annie, poor girl, and me myself, and a course there was the doctor. Doctor Januar. He's attending my good-father, you understand.'

'Doctor Januar,' Gil repeated. 'Aye, Sir Simon mentioned him. I never heard there was a doctor out in Avondale. Is he a Scot? Where did he study?'

'You'd need to ask him that yoursel,' said Lockhart, suddenly uncomfortable. 'I've no understanding o such matters. Seems to me he's a foreigner o some kind, but I've never heard either way.'

Gil nodded, setting this aside for later consideration.

'That's six of you so far,' he prompted. 'Any more?'

'Poor Annie, a course, no I mentioned her, did I no,' Lockhart sighed, and crossed himself. 'Who'd ha thought we brought her to her death, maister! What a thing to happen, dreadful. I had my doubts about leaving her bound the whole night, but Sir Edward was set on it, and see, I was right, it was too much for her. And then there's Dame Ellen, who's Sir Edward's sister and has an eye to the lassies. That would be the whole of us that's lodged here, though a course there was Dame Ellen's two young kinsmen and all, that left us here. A great procession it was, what wi Sir Edward in a horse-litter and the rest of us on horseback, and poor Annie raving.'

'And servants?'

'Well, naturally.' The other man paused to reckon on his fingers. 'Five all told, one woman and four men. Oh, and the man that serves Dame Ellen's kinsmen, a decent

21

fellow, went off wi them a course. And then the grooms for the horses.'

'No steward? Nobody to see all as it should be?'

'I suppose you'd say the doctor was acting as steward,' said Lockhart, a little reluctantly. 'For certain it was him ordered all when we halted for the night.'

'A useful fellow,' said Gil.

'Aye, you could say that.'

'Whose idea was it to bring Annie here?'

'You'd have to ask some of the household that. I wasny party to the decision, since it was haying-time, I was over at Kypeside. Likely Dame Ellen will tell you.' Lockhart turned to look at Gil, frowning. 'Why are you asking these questions? What's the Archbishop's questioner to say to the matter, any road? The lassie's dead instead o cured, what need o a hantle o questions?'

'Have you looked at her?' Gil asked. Lockhart shook his head, and Gil rose. 'Come and see her. Was she bonnie?'

'No latterly,' said Lockhart, following him through the passage into the outer courtyard, his voice echoing momentarily under the vault. 'I mind when I first set eyes on her, when I first courted Mariota, she was right bonnie, wi blue eyes and hair like ripe corn. She still wore it bride-like, ye ken, wedded so young as she was. And then Arthur died, poor fellow, and she'd lost the bairn, and she made her vow, and after that, well!'

'I can imagine it,' said Gil, pulling off his hat as he stepped into the little chapel of the hostel. 'She's far from bonnie now, poor soul. Did the men not tell you? She never died of her own accord, or of being bound to the cross, she's been beaten, and then she was throttled. By someone else.'

Lockhart, hat in hand, looked sharply from Gil to the linen-draped mound on the bier before the chancel arch. Of course, a pilgrim hostel would likely have regular need of a bier, Gil thought irrelevantly, as the other man moved forward and drew the cloth away. The candles at the corpse's head flickered with the movement, and at the sight which met him Lockhart rocked back on his heels, almost winded by shock.

22

'Deil's bollocks, man! Sawney tellt us, but I took it for a serving-lad's supersaltin. Her own mammy wouldny ken her.' He drew a deep breath, steadied himself and contemplated the battered, swollen face, the red and purple bruising and the caked blood, then made the sign of the cross over it and pulled the linen up. Passing a hand across his own face, and surreptitiously wiping his eyes as he did so, he turned to Gil and said resolutely, 'Maister, nobody deserves sic a death, least of all Annie Gibb. She never did anyone any harm, she was a dutiful daughter and a faithful wife afore she ran mad, she was a good Christian lassie.' He gestured at the figure of the saint next to the altar. 'St Catherine be my witness, if there's aught I can do to help you track down whoever did this, I'll do it.'

'Well spoken, my son,' said Sir Simon Elder, emerging from the shadows of the little chancel. 'Where does he start, Maister Cunningham?'

Back out in the sunshine, Lockhart was less immediately helpful than Gil had hoped.

'I suppose it was the doctor arranged it, like all else,' he said. 'We rode into Glasgow yesterday, two hours or so after noon, and after we'd dined here and I'd fetched the penitent's gown and a new rope from St Mungo's, the women had Annie into her sackcloth and the whole household save Sir Edward over to the High Kirk afore Vespers, to hear a Mass and be confessed—'

'Annie was able to confess?' Gil queried. 'She knew what she was saying?'

'Oh, aye, indeed. She was rational enough, save for wishing to dee, she spent the most of her time at her prayers. She's— She was aye a good Christian. And then once she was confessed and the ashes put on her brow, and the rope was blessed, the doctor and her two men took her over to the cross and bound her there, and we left her.'

'And none of you had an eye to her, apart from the servants,' said Gil.

'No,' said Lockhart rather sharply. 'Do you think we don't regret it?'

Gil paused for a moment in acknowledgement of this, then said,

'She must have had property of her own. Who inherits it? How would it be left?'

'I've no knowledge of how her fortune lies,' Lockhart admitted. 'It never concerned Mariota, or so I thought, so I never asked. She was James Gibb's heiress, his only surviving bairn, though I believe there were others that never made it out their cradles. She brought Arthur a good stretch o land in Ayrshire at their marriage, and more when her father died, but as to how it was left to her or what happens to it now, I never heard.'

'What about her mother's land?' It seemed a reasonable guess that Gibb would have wedded land himself, which Annie would have inherited, but Lockhart shook his head.

'I've no knowledge o that either. Her mother's long dead. She wasny a Kyle lady I think, though I don't recall her name.'

'Why did your good-father not find a second marriage for her? I'd have thought an heiress like that would be easy enough to place.'

Another shake of the head.

'Sir Edward's— He's aye been right fond of her, as if she was his own lassie. He'd not see her forced to marry against her will. Besides,' Lockhart added realistically, 'who'd wish to take a lassie that spends her days mourning her first husband, even with the land to sweeten the bargain?'

'I think Sir Edward's nearing his own end,' Gil said delicately. 'Have you any knowledge of how he'll arrange his affairs? He has the three daughters, I think? Was Arthur the only son?'

'Aye, the lassies are co-heirs.' Lockhart looked embarrassed. 'I'm no certain, you'll understand,' he went on after a moment, 'and he'll need to change it all now, a course, but at one time he was speaking as if he'd divide all equally among the four lassies, Annie and his own three. That is,' he qualified, 'my wife would get as much as to bring her portion equal wi what the other lassies would get.'

'And how did his own daughters feel about that?'

'They were pleased enough, I'd ha said. They've all been like sisters since ever Arthur was wedded to Annie, they seemed happy enough to share wi her.'

'And the rest of his will? Has he much to leave beyond the heritable land? Bequests to his other kin or to Holy Kirk?'

'You'd need to ask him that yoursel,' said Lockhart, 'or else his man of law. I've little knowledge of what he decided, and that at third hand.'

'And he is?'

'Maister William Dykes,' said Lockhart promptly, 'to be found next St Nicholas' Kirk in Lanark.'

'The arrangement would have left Annie a wealthy woman,' Gil observed, making a note of that, 'what with her own portion.'

'Aye, and the conjunct land from her marriage.' Lockhart turned to look at Gil in dismay. 'What, you think that might be behind it? That someone slew her to prevent her inheriting her fourth part?' He swallowed. 'But there's none of us— I was agreeable, and so I tellt Sir Edward at the time, and it was long afore the younger lassies was betrothed, it was written into their contracts that way. And to beat her like that and all! I took it it was some madman,' he swallowed and grimaced at his own words, 'some fellow wi a grudge at St Mungo, or the like. Surely never one of her family, maister!'

'I concur with that predicate,' said a serious voice in Latin. Gil twisted to look, and found a short, richly dressed man just emerging from the men's hall.

'Oh, it's you,' said Lockhart.

'It is,' said the other in Scots, moving forward from the doorway. 'Could you keep your voices down, or go elsewhere? Sir Edward's sore afflicted.'

'You could close the shutters,' said Lockhart.

'You must be the doctor,' said Gil, rising. The newcomer bowed.

'Chrysostomus Ianuarius, of Ghent and Salerno,' he said, returning to Latin. 'Do I address the Archbishop's quaestor?'

'If you're to patter away in the Latin tongue,' said Lockhart, finally getting to his feet, 'I'm away. I'll be about if you're wanting any more from me, maister,' he added to Gil, and strode off towards the gate which led out to the stables.

Gil let him go, and studied Chrysostom Januar with some interest as the man straightened up from his formal bow. He was a striking figure, robed in a bag-sleeved gown of crimson and yellow silk brocade which would surely draw Habbie Sim deep into the sin of covetousness if he set eyes on it; worn over this, in faintly academic fashion, was a black cloth hood with a deep, tight shoulder-cape, its lining of squirrel showing to advantage where it was folded down about his ears. A fat purse and an astrologer's vade-mecum hung from a green leather belt shod with silver. The brim of the bright blue velvet bonnet which he had just clapped back onto a head of dark, luxuriant curls was pinned up with an enamel brooch, and under it, Gil realised with some embarrassment, the man's equally bright blue eyes were studying him.

'You'll ken me again, maister,' he said in faint amusement. His Scots was rapid and accented, with the harsh consonants of the Low Countries.

'More than likely,' agreed Gil in Latin. 'I ask your pardon. I had not expected to find a doctor of Ghent and Salerno in Glasgow, much less in Avondale. How did you fetch up there?'

A faint grimace crossed the doctor's face.

'The wheel of fortune turns,' he said sententiously. '*Magister*, I do not think this death can be ascribed to one of the family.'

'What makes you say that?'

'My patient is unable to leave his bed,' replied the doctor carefully, 'the man who has just left us was asleep at the other end of the hall within my sight throughout my vigil, and the women likewise shared a chamber in the other hall. I saw this when I was called to administer a calming draught to the two girls. None of the family left the place in the night.'

But what about the servants, Gil wondered. And what about these two kinsmen of Dame Ellen's?

'And Annie herself,' he said. 'She too was your patient? She was in a poor case. *Sorewe and siche and drery mod Bindeth me so faste.* The melancholy was of long standing, by what I'm told.'

'In part.' The doctor turned and strolled away across the courtyard after Lockhart, inviting Gil to accompany him with a jerk of the head. 'I had hardly begun to treat her.'

'What would your treatment have been?'

'Not this, at any rate. I advised most strongly against it.' Doctor Januar considered briefly. 'Company, music, good wine – as good as one might obtain in Ayrshire, at any rate – a diet both dry and warming, all of these. Confession, in order to obtain release from her ridiculous vow as soon as she began to wish it, and someone to talk to about her dead husband.'

'What good would that do?' Gil asked, surprised. 'I'd have thought it would make her the more melancholy.'

'It would encourage weeping,' pronounced the doctor, 'and thus the release of the moist humours which promote the state, and besides it would affirm that she has cause to mourn. Certain of the family have not been—' He cut off the sentence and fell silent.

'And Sir Edward?' Gil asked after a moment. 'What can you tell me of his illness?'

Doctor Januar glanced at the guest hall, shook his head, and turned to pace across the further side of the courtyard, well out of his patient's hearing.

'A tumour of the bladder primarily,' he said quietly, 'with secondary afflictions in the bowel and lung. He is aware of it, otherwise I would not divulge so much. He is in great pain, which I am managing, from day to day at first and now from hour to hour. I expect to bury him here in Glasgow.'

'Why did you move him, so near his end?'

'He was determined. It would have hastened the end, I think, to gainsay him.'

'So it was his idea to bring his good-daughter to St Mungo?'

The doctor contemplated this question for a moment, without interrupting his measured pace.

'I think,' he said eventually, 'it may have been Dame Ellen who suggested it to him first. However, she is a clever woman, and led her brother to believe it was his idea.'

'How did she do that?' Gil asked, amused.

'Oh, by crying it down at every turn. It is how she deals with him.'

'Tell me about Annie's life in his household. Was she well regarded?'

'Why do you ask me?' asked Doctor Januar, looking up at Gil. 'Why not her sisters?'

'You are the observant outsider. Are they truly sisters? Lockhart certainly seemed to think they were all very fond.'

'Lockhart does not live with the family.'

'And you do, I think.' This was not answered. 'Did she have her own apartment? Her own servants?'

'Yes.' The doctor looked disapproving. 'She has dwelt for nearly three years in two chambers at the end of one wing of the house, with all her own furnishings and some few things which belonged to her dead husband. Her own maidservant oversees all for her, brings in her food, carries messages, she has two men who deal with her share of the outside work. Her good-sisters visit from time to time, the parish priest calls on her regularly – I will say, *magister*, he is a good man – Dame Ellen attends her daily to exhort her to repent of her vow and wed where Sir Edward might direct.'

'And where would that have been?'

'Probably not where Dame Ellen thinks. Sir Edward's affection is real.'

'No life for a girl of twenty. She never went out of doors?'

'Rarely. As you say, no life for a girl of twenty.'

'Nevertheless, the family's intentions have been good,' Gil suggested.

'I would not say so,' replied Doctor Januar after a little. 'In fact I have seen no evidence of that.' Gil raised his eyebrows. 'Oh, they speak of how much they hold her in affection, but they do little to improve her situation.'

'Are their intentions evil?'

'I cannot say.' Cannot, not would not, Gil noted.

'Will you come and view the body?' he asked. 'My friend the mason has experience in dealing with the dead, but a medical man's opinion would be—' He stopped. Doctor Januar was shaking his head.

'No,' he said firmly. 'Perhaps later I will do so. I must go to my patient. Already I have been away too long.'

He bowed, with a sweep of the blue velvet hat, clapped it back on his head, and squaring his shoulders turned away and marched towards the guest-hall. As he reached its doorway, heavy footsteps sounded in the passage from the outer courtyard; he checked for a moment, then resolutely pushed open the door and stepped inside.

Gil stood staring after him for a moment, then turned as his father-in-law emerged into the sunlight, Lowrie on his heels. Socrates hurried past them to thrust his head under his master's hand in greeting.

'What is this young Lowrie tells me?' demanded Maistre Pierre. 'The woman at the Cross murdered where she stood? And under the saint's protection, too! A bad business!'

Back in the chapel, the linen drawn aside, the mason scrutinised the dead woman with pity at first. He studied the fingernails, tested the stiffness of the jaw and neck, tweaked at the cord where it was lodged in the flesh of the neck.

'Bad,' he said again, working his way down the corpse to check the rigidity of the feet. 'And she was still tied where we saw her last night.'

'Yes,' said Gil, snapping his fingers at Socrates, who obediently left off sniffing at the hem of the sacking gown and came to sit at his side. 'And her men say she was not beaten like that when they left her.'

'No, no, I agree,' said Maistre Pierre. 'I had a good sight of her face last evening, and she looked nothing like this.' He returned to the head of the bier, touching the bruised face. 'Her death is not as it seems, is it?'

'Exactly my thoughts,' said Gil.

'The ground was too hard and too much trampled to pick up any sign,' said Lowrie, 'and the dog found nothing to interest him.'

Maistre Pierre nodded, unfolding the checked plaid which still lay round the dead woman's shoulders. Gil stared at her, considering what he saw.

Hunched over as she was, her build and stature were not easy to make out, but she seemed to be about Alys's height, perhaps five and a half feet high. The neck and wrists exposed by the sacking gown were thin, the shoulders bony. Not a well-nourished girl, he thought, despite the family's wealth. Perhaps, in her melancholy, she picked at her food.

'There is no mark on this gown,' Maistre Pierre observed. 'We cannot be certain what killed her until she is stripped.'

'I took it it was the cord,' said Lowrie in surprise. 'Though it's clumsy work, both ends at the front of the throat like that. Surely you'd work from behind—' His voice trailed off as Gil shook his head.

'Not while she stood tied to the cross like that. You would cross your arms, with the ends of the cord in your hands, and cast it over the victim's head,' he mimed the action, 'and pull hard, whether from before or behind. It's a professional's trick. But that wasn't what killed her.'

'No, I agree,' said Maistre Pierre. 'She was already dead when the cord was used.'

'What? She was throttled after – after she was dead?' said Lowrie incredulously. 'Why? Why would anybody do that?'

'Not long after,' conceded Maistre Pierre. 'She had barely begun to stiffen. See, the cord has sunk into the flesh a little way, but there has been no swelling round it.' He lifted one dangling end as he spoke, and began to ease the length of hemp away from the thin neck, working with difficulty round under the jaw. 'I suppose she hung on those ropes?

Her head is so far bent I am surprised this comes free, even without being sunk in the flesh.'

'And when did she die, I wonder?' said Gil. His father-in-law shook his head.

'No certainty, though it was probably within an hour of midnight, a little earlier, a little later.'

'I spoke to the men,' said Lowrie after a moment. 'Sawney and Rab. It was just as Sawney said while you were there, Maister Gil. Their task was to bind her to the cross, and keep an eye on her through the night. They thought she'd be safe enough, and St Nicholas' chapel was handy and out of the night air.'

'No way to go about their duty,' said Maistre Pierre disapprovingly, 'and see what has come of it. Why could they not stay with her, to keep her from harm?' He coaxed the last length of cord from its seat and studied its length, then wound it round his hand and handed the tow-coloured loops to Gil.

'It's usual to leave them alone at the cross for the night,' said Gil. 'But it's mostly men that are treated like that, and I do wonder at anyone leaving a lassie alone. She was tied there in the dark, her friends out of sight in St Nicholas' chapel, and someone came along, beat her senseless or near it, slew her in some way we've not yet discerned, and only then throttled her. It makes no sense of any sort.' He bent over the girl's battered face again. 'Pierre, can you see any ashes on her?'

'Ashes?' His father-in-law came closer. 'What, on her brow? As for Ash Wednesday?'

'Lockhart said they applied ashes when she heard Mass, before she was put in place at the Cross. I don't see any about her now.' He touched his own forehead involuntarily. 'It's fine stuff, it doesny come off readily, save you use soap and water. I wonder how she got rid of it?'

'That is strange indeed. There is more,' said Maistre Pierre. 'When I saw her in the evening she was bound so,' he stood upright, his arms at his sides. 'Her hands were not free.'

'That's how she was before we took her down,' agreed Lowrie, 'though she was hanging on the ropes by then, as you said, maister, just the way she's set now.'

'Then tell me how she has managed to scratch her attacker.' The mason cradled one of the corpse's stiffened hands in his big one, pointing at the fingertips. 'There is blood under her nails, and two are broken. She has fought. How did she do that, bound as we saw her?'

There was a brief silence.

'The ropes,' said Lowrie cryptically. He turned and darted out of the chapel. Gil remained, studying the dead woman.

'Something else I wonder at,' he said, 'is the family. So far I've spoken to the good-brother, and we've met two serving-men. Where are the rest of them? If they're all as fond as the man Lockhart gave me to understand you'd think someone would be here to see her, to order her laying-out or the like, or to pray for her.'

'Perhaps they wait until she is washed,' said Maistre Pierre. 'For which I should not blame them.'

On the word, footsteps sounded in the courtyard outside, and the mason pulled the linen up over the hunched shoulders and hideous battered face, just before a woman entered the little chapel, tall against the light for a moment. She checked at sight of them, then came forward, saying,

'Well, sirs. That must be you that's put the fear of God into Lockhart, then?' She stepped aside to let a sturdy maidservant past with a basin of water. 'Aye, lass, set it all down there, we'll get to work soon enough. I'll have to ask you men to leave us, till I get my poor niece made decent.'

'Dame Ellen, is it?' said Gil.

'And what if it is? Who's asking?'

Gil bowed, and introduced himself and his father-in-law. She heard him out, nodding, and smiled thinly at them both by the light from the doorway. Her front teeth were large, and crossed, giving her mouth a kissable shape greatly at odds with the rest of her expression.

'Aye, you have it right, I'm Ellen Shaw, that's run my

brother's house and raised his lassies these twelve year.' She considered Gil. 'A Cunningham, are you? You'll be Gelis Muirhead's laddie, I suppose. I mind her when we were young. You've a look o her.' She unbuttoned the tight sleeves of her kirtle and began to roll them up. 'Now I'd ask you to leave, sirs, till Meggot and I get to work, and you can take that great dog wi you.'

'I need to inspect—' Gil began.

'It can wait. She was aye a modest lassie, even in her melancholy, and we'll just maintain her modesty now she's dead. Away ye go.' She made shooing motions with her large bony hands.

'Have you been told what happened to her?' Gil asked. She looked more intently at him and nodded, her face grimly set. 'Beaten and then throttled, or so we think. We need to know if you find any more injuries, anything at all, and if anything seems out of place or not right about her clothes or her body.'

'I'll keep a look out, maister, you can be sure o that, and so will Meggot, but we must have your room afore we begin.'

Gil went, not very hopefully. Out in the yard Maistre Pierre was already kicking gloomily at a clump of grass growing between two cobbles.

'The world is full of high-handed women,' he complained.

'Certainly Scotland is,' agreed Gil.

'And where did young Lowrie go? That is a useful fellow, you were wise to take him on, Gilbert.'

'Alys suggested it.'

'Hmm,' said Alys's father, but said no more, as Lowrie entered from the street with his arms full of a great tangle of rope.

'Euan had it,' he said. 'Deil kens what he was planning to do with it. Look at this, Maister Gil.'

He dropped most of the tangle, in order to hold up one length. Euan, or one of his helpers, had cut the loops of rope to free the dead woman from the upright of the cross, and the knots were still present. But clearly to be seen were the kinks and curves of a previous knot, unpicked with care some time before the dead woman was bound in her place.

'So was she freed, beaten, and tied up again?' speculated Lowrie.

'*Mon Dieu!*' said Maistre Pierre. 'Or was it not a new rope, perhaps?'

'We need to check,' said Gil. 'It's usually a new rope. This one has certainly been tied and untied once at least, I agree, Lowrie.'

'Would the family tell us?' Lowrie asked, colouring up at the commendation in Gil's tone.

'Lockhart, or the men—' began Gil, and was interrupted. There was a sudden outbreak of shouting within the little chapel, the two women's voices raised, one in anger, one protesting, the sound of a hearty slap. Gil, striding towards the discord, collided in the chapel doorway with the maid-servant Meggot backing out.

'I swear it, mistress!' she was protesting, one hand nursing her ear, 'it's no her, it's no our Annie! It's some other woman, Our Lady kens who it is, but it's never her!'

'Fool of a lassie!' Dame Ellen was in pursuit, hands reaching for her shoulders to shake her, 'who else could it be? Barefoot in a sacking gown and bound to the Girth Cross, a course it's Annie! No matter if her own mammy wouldny ken her face!'

'What's this?' demanded Gil, and they both stopped to stare at him. 'Is there some doubt about the corp?'

'This gomeril—' began Dame Ellen, and visibly controlled herself to assume her thin smile. 'This foolish lassie tries to tell me—'

'No, mistress, I swear it!' said Meggot again. 'It's no her! It's no Annie Gibb!'

Beside the bier, despite the indignant comments of Dame Ellen, she offered more reasoned argument, lifting a lock of the corpse's elbow-length mud-coloured hair.

'Our Lady kens who she is,' she said again, 'but her hair's away too long, maister, my mistress's hair never came ablow her shoulder-blades, and see here,' she pulled the hem of the penitential gown aside to expose the small bare feet, twisted sideways by the way the body had sagged in its bonds and somehow very pitiful, Gil thought. Meggot seemed to feel the same way, for she curved a gentle hand round one instep as she said, 'See, this lassie's gone barefoot the most o her days. Her feet's hard as neat's leather. Annie wears hose and shoon, I took them off her yestreen afore she— Afore she— What's come to her, maister? Where is she? Is she deid, or hurt, or—?'

'The lassie's run mad like her mistress,' declared Dame Ellen. 'Who else could it be but Annie? Maister Cunningham, I think we need hardly trouble you wi this nonsense. We'll get on wi our duty to the dead, if you'll just leave us.'

Gil considered the two women. Dame Ellen stood by the head of the bier, tall and indignant in the light of the candles. She was probably past fifty, dressed like any country lady in a plain gown of good woad-dyed homespun over a kirtle of a lighter blue, her head covered by a black Flemish hood. Wisps of grey hair escaped at her temples, and her face was lined and bony. Under his gaze she crossed her arms, hitching up a substantial bosom, and said, with an attempt at a complicit smile,

'I've raised the lassie since she came into my brother's house, how would I not know her when she's come to be laid out?'

'And I've served her and dressed her and put her stockings on these six year,' retorted Meggot. She was shorter than Dame Ellen, a round-faced comfortable young woman in a side-laced kirtle, her shift rolled up over its short sleeves to expose capable hands and forearms, her hair hidden under a kerchief of good linen. She had not partaken of her mistress's vow, Gil concluded. 'I ken her feet from a stranger's,' she was saying, 'I ken what length her hair was. These are no her hands, this lassie worked, and just look at these nails! I tell you, maister, it's some other poor lassie, and what can have happened to my mistress?'

She paused to wipe tears from her eyes. Socrates padded

forward, his claws rasping on the tiled floor, to sniff at the corpse's feet, and Maistre Pierre said,

'Did you both see her bound to the cross?'

'I did indeed!' said Dame Ellen, as Meggot nodded. 'I stood by and watched while the two lads led her over there and bound her secure. And our good doctor oversaw all.'

'Oh, he did?' said Gil.

'It suited my poor brother to gie him that duty, sir. Now are you to leave us about our business? It's a sad day enough, without unseemly arguments like this.'

Meggot drew a breath, found Gil's eye on her and remained silent.

'Someone must stay and watch,' pronounced Maistre Pierre. 'We are both married men, madame, we will not demean the dead. What has happened must be determined.'

Gil turned away for a moment, to find Lowrie still standing watching the discussion in fascination, the lengths of rope dangling from his hands.

'Go and find those two lads, if you will, and the other servants too,' he said. 'Talk them through what happened to Annie after the party arrived in Glasgow, see if you can find how often they looked at her and how close they went to the Cross. Don't mention this,' he cautioned. 'And here, ask them if they'd ever seen this before.' He held out the coil of cord Maistre Pierre had removed from about the dead woman's neck.

'Of course,' agreed Lowrie. Gathering up the rope he set it in a bundle on the stone bench which ran round the wall, took the cord from Gil and made for the inner courtyard. Gil turned back into the chapel, to find Meggot already working at the ties of the sacking gown, her mouth set in a determined line, while Dame Ellen was still trying to argue the point with Maistre Pierre. Joining the maidservant by the bier, he said quietly,

'This lassie has no ash on her brow.'

'No,' she said shortly.

'Is all this as you last saw it?'

She paused to look at him, her eyes glittering in the candlelight.

'I canny mind how I left it. All I can think on's how Annie begged us no to leave her there, to take her home and let her dee. What's come to her, maister?'

'You were fond of her,' he said. She nodded, and went back to her task.

The garment she was working on was cut loosely, designed to fit almost any size of supplicant and to be easily put on by his or her attendants; it was secured down the back by linen tapes, which were now in tight knots.

'Take a knife to them,' Gil suggested.

'Aye, you're right, maister,' she said, and paused to loosen the strings of the purse at her belt. 'This isny how I left these, you're right there and all. I fastened it all neat and secure, but so's I—' She clapped the back of her hand across her mouth, tears starting to her eyes again. 'So as I could easy take it off her this morning,' she finished.

Gil drew his own dagger and sawed through the first of the tapes. By the time he had dealt with all five of the knots Meggot had recovered a little and Dame Ellen had abandoned her argument.

'What are you doing there?' she demanded, hurrying over. 'Have you any idea what the hire of that gown cost my brother? We'll ha to return it to St Mungo's in good order! That will come out your wages, my girl. Maister, I beg you no to encourage her!'

'St Mungo's should ha took better care o my mistress, then,' retorted Meggot, and turned back the two sides of the gown to reveal the shift beneath it. She drew a sharp breath. 'Oh, that settles it, it's never Annie! This is none of our linen, I'd think black shame o mysel to send my mistress anywhere in a clout like yon. It's not fit for a floor-cloth!'

Gil had to agree. As well as the stains from her death, which had not transferred themselves to the outer garment, the dead woman's shift was torn and dirty, marked with sweat under the arms, and rubbed blue from a woad-dyed gown at the neckband and seams; it had probably not been washed in several months. He could not imagine any of the women he knew wearing such a garment, other than in the direst need.

'She herself is no less ill used,' observed Maistre Pierre. Reaching past Gil he pulled the neckband of the shift down to display a dark bruise and several scars on the thin back. 'Her life has not been kind.'

'Now do you see?' demanded Meggot of Dame Ellen. She eased the gown away from the hunched shoulders, down over the rigid arm. The older woman stared at the bruises thus exposed, her expression grim. 'I've never a notion who it is, but it's no more my mistress than the Queen of Elfland.'

Chapter Three

'She what?' said Canon James Henderson, Sub-Dean of St Mungo's Cathedral. He stared at Gil over a laden table; he had been interrupted breaking his fast on smoked fish, white bread and new milk, with a dish of quince marmalade and another of raisins set by his elbow. 'How can she be so sure? If the face is unrecognisable—'

'A course she's sure o't, if she's going by the shift,' said the plump maidservant at his elbow. 'There's no a woman in Scotland wouldny ken her own linen from another's. I'd pick your shirts out anywhere.'

'Be silent, woman,' ordered Canon Henderson. He broke off another piece of bread and buttered it with irritable, jerky movements. 'I don't like the way you keep turning up corpses – female corpses, at that – on St Mungo's land, Gil. We'll ha no more of them, if you don't mind.'

Gil preserved a careful silence in the face of this injustice; there had been one other female corpse, two years since in rather different circumstances.

'But what's come to the lassie that was there?' entreated the maidservant. 'Surely St Mungo never carried her away to Paradise?'

'Will you be quiet?' demanded her master. 'Where has that woman gone, Gil? What's her name again, Annie Gibb. I could see this nonsense wi the Cross far enough, it never does them any good, and now see what's come of it!'

'I'll set up a search,' said Gil. 'I need to let the Provost hear of this, since we'll have to have an inquest on the dead woman, try to find a name for her, find out how she came to

39

be at the Cross. Will I borrow some men from him, or will we use Cathedral servants to search?'

'To search?' Canon Henderson frowned. 'What kind o a search did you have in mind? Rattling at doors, or looking under bushes, or searching outbuildings?'

'All three, I'd say.'

'Aye, you're right, I suppose. She could be anywhere in Glasgow, and dead or alive come to that. Better see what the Provost can do, our men haveny the same powers outside St Mungo's land.' A child wailed, elsewhere in the house, and the Canon glanced at the maidservant and gestured at the door. 'Away and deal wi that bairn, Kirsty, and see if you canny keep it quieter.'

'Takes after his faither,' retorted Kirsty with a toss of her head, but left the room with reluctance.

'Tell me it again,' said the Canon. 'Annie Gibb was bound to the cross wi a new rope, and it's been untied and tied again, you say.' Gil nodded. 'So someone freed her, and throttled this woman to put in her place.' He crossed himself. 'Wickedness! What would make anyone act that way? And her friends never saw a thing?'

'Not till they came to untie her in the morning,' agreed Gil. 'It makes little sense. We've two problems, I think. Who is the corpse, and how did she die and come to be bound to the cross, and where is Annie Gibb and who freed her?'

'That's more than two,' Henderson said fretfully. He took a draught of milk, emerging from the beaker with a white moustache. 'Well, you sort it out, Gil. If you need folk to help you, likely some o the songmen would be glad o a change of duties. Sim and Craigie are already involved, you can ask them. And the vergers are aye useful men in a stushie, the younger ones at least, though I hope it'll no come to that.'

'So do I,' agreed Gil.

'Away and speak to the Provost. He'll need to hear about it all, I suppose.'

'I was looking for you to call by,' said Maister Andrew Otterburn, depute Provost of Glasgow, waving at a stool beside his desk. Gil raised an eyebrow. 'Aye, I've heard about it. Andro brought the word in earlier. Did you ever?'

'Extraordinary business.' Gil sat down. Socrates sprawled at his feet, grinning up at Otterburn.

'Tell me about it, then. What have you discerned?'

'Very little. The women have the corp stripped now. She's much of an age with their kinswoman, thin as a lath, has probably borne at least one child so Dame Ellen says. How do they tell that?'

Otterburn glanced at him, but said only, 'Likely some women's knowledge. Ask at your wife, I should.'

Perhaps not, thought Gil.

'We've no idea yet what killed her, unless the beating,' he went on, 'let alone who she is or how she came to be there. As for where Mistress Annie Gibb might have got to, that's anyone's guess. St Mungo's isny best pleased about the matter.'

'I'll wager.' Otterburn glanced out of the window at the cathedral towers, visible above the warm sandstone outer wall of the castle. He was a lanky man in his forties with a long gloomy face and a wry sense of humour; he was not fully appreciated in the burgh, but Gil had found him easier to work with than his predecessor. 'Let Walter have a description of the corp—' His clerk looked up from the end of the desk and nodded, his pen pausing in its eternal squeaking progress. 'He'll get her cried round the town, see if anyone's missed her. Now tell me what you've found, maister, and what you're doing about it.'

Gil obeyed, summarising the little information they had gathered so far.

'I've yet to speak wi the rest of Mistress Gibb's family or friends,' he ended. 'I thought you'd as soon hear about it now rather than later. Young Lowrie's talked wi the servants, but all he's learned so far confirms what the family says. They all arrived together, they seem to ha stayed within the hostel walls, other than Mistress Shaw's two young kins- men and two fellows that were sent out on an errand for the doctor and were back within the half-hour, until Mistress

41

Gibb was led out wi the whole household, save Sir Edward and his man, to go to St Mungo's for confession. I'll set Lowrie to track down the bystanders from this morning and find out if they know anything, and my man Euan's away to talk the vergers into searching St Mungo's, but I'm not hopeful.'

'Aye.' Otterburn turned the sand-pot on his desk, frowning at it. 'So the one we have was beaten till she's beyond recognising, and slain some way we don't know yet. Could the beating ha killed her?'

'It might,' said Gil cautiously. 'Pierre found no trace of a head injury, but we won't know for sure till she softens. There's no sign she was stabbed or the like.'

Otterburn grunted.

'And then she was throttled, but no till after she was dead, and then she was tied to the Cross. Why? It makes no sense! And where's the other one got to?'

'I'd say she was tied to the Cross first, and then throttled,' said Gil. 'The hair at the back of her neck was caught under the cord, but the rest hung free. And at some point the sacking gown Annie Gibb was wearing was put on her.'

'Is it the same one?'

'I need to check wi St Mungo's.'

'So is Mistress Gibb running about Glasgow in her shift? She'll be easy enough recognised if that's so. How mad is she? Is she a danger?'

'Her friends say not. She seems to be melancholy rather than wood-wild. And she may well be in her shift, I got her maidservant to check and her clothes are all in the pilgrim lodging where the lassie put them last night, naught missing.'

Otterburn grunted again.

'Give Walter her description and all. We'll get the two o them cried through the town and see what that turns up, and you can ask at Andro for any help you need. The men should enjoy searching for a stinking lady in her shift. Have you any more to tell me?'

'Not yet,' admitted Gil, 'but I've another question.' He

drew from his purse the coil of cord, and laid it on the Provost's desk. 'This is what was used to throttle the dead woman. The Shaw servants never saw it afore, so far as they can tell. Can we learn aught from it, do you think?'

'Cord's just cord, surely,' said Otterburn, lifting a honey-pale loop. 'This doesny look anything out of the ordinar.'

'A barrel's just a barrel,' countered Gil, 'but I once learned a lot about one barrel by speaking to its maker. Most crafts-men can make their own cordage if they're put to it, but this looks like a specialist's work. Do we have any spinners of twine and cord in the burgh?'

'Walter?'

'You might ask at Matt Dickson the rope-drawer, mais-ter,' suggested the clerk. 'It's mostly heavier stuff he turns out, so I believe, but he'd likely ken where that came from.' He assessed Gil's blank expression. 'Away out the Thenewgate, almost at Partick. A great long shed o a place, been burned down two-three times. You canny miss it.'

Like most major offices around a great cathedral church, that of Almoner to St Mungo's was a sinecure, a post whose holder was not expected to take more than a perfunctory interest in its duties. These were carried out by the Sub-Almoner, a depressed individual who inhabited a cramped, sour-smelling chamber up a stair in the north-west tower, surrounded by piles of neatly folded clothing and blankets. When Gil found him there, Sir Alan Jamieson was just dismissing the last of his morning's supplicants, a surprisingly well-nourished boy of eight or nine.

'No, no, wee Leckie's fit enough,' he said when Gil commented. 'He's the laddie that's paid of the burgh to lead old Jeanie Thomson, that's been blind these ten year. He was fetching another head-rail to her, to keep her decent, seeing her last one blew away when her neighbour laid it out to dry.' He pulled a face. 'That's their tale, any road. I just hope they got its worth at the rag market. What can I do for you, Gil? I take it this isny a call on my duties?'

'Maybe no directly,' admitted Gil. He set the bundle he

carried on the table beside the almoner's great ledger. 'You'll have heard what happened at St Mungo's Cross, then, Alan?'

Sir Alan crossed himself.

'Aye, poor lady, her servant came up to the vestry just as we were about to sing Matins. She's free o her troubles now, right enough, but no in the way she—' He paused as Gil shook his head. 'What d'you mean, no?'

'There's more happened than that,' Gil said. 'The lass that was found dead at the Cross this morning wasny the same one that was bound there last night.' Jamieson gaped at him. 'She was wearing this,' he nodded at the bundle, 'and I'd like to hear if you reckon it's the same gown you gave out yesterday, or another. It was me cut the inkles,' he added hastily as the almoner reached for the folds of sacking. 'I'll pay for the repairs.'

'Aye, you did,' said Sir Alan, inspecting the ragged ends of the tapes. 'Made a thorough job of it, and all.' He shook out the light brown folds. 'Let me see now, where's the— Aye, this is the gown I lent out to Mistress Gibb's kinsfolk yesterday afternoon. There's the mark.' He pointed to a row of neat red stitches just inside the neckline. 'Six red lines for gown number six. There's a dozen,' he enlarged, 'but we've never needed that many, even when thon band of penitents cam here two summers ago, hoping to flagellate theirsels the length o the High Street. Canon Henderson soon put a stop to that, I can tell you.'

'He did that,' agreed Gil, recalling the occasion with faint amusement. It had provided his uncle with food for shocked discussion for days. The parade of the High Street had been reduced, in short order, to a procession round the Upper Town and a vigil by the patron saint's tomb in the crypt; the weather had been unkind, and the fiddler the group had brought with them had refused to risk his instrument in the pouring rain, so the singing had been doleful indeed. When last heard of the group of penitent pilgrims had been riding out of Glasgow, back to wherever they came from (Arbroath, was it?) quarrelling bitterly about whose idea it had been in the first place. 'So you'd swear to this being the same gown?'

'Let me mak certain.' Jamieson clipped his spectacles onto his nose and drew the great ledger towards him. 'A plaid to Hoastin Harry, a woad-dyed gown to Maggie Bent, aye, aye, here we are. Penitential gown number six, to the kin o Annie Gibb.' He turned the great book about so that Gil could read the entry. 'Clear enough, I'd say, and I'll just mark it returned.' Drawing the book towards him, he reached for his pen.

'Clear enough,' Gil agreed. 'Thanks for this, Alan.' He dug in his purse for a couple of coins. 'Will that cover the repairs? Is it just clothing and blankets you give out here? I'd thought you'd some provisions to supply the poor and all.'

'Oh, I do, I do.' Jamieson shook sand on the new entry and wiped his pen on the blotched rag at his elbow. 'Such as there is the now.'

'What, are donations running low? I'll tell my wife.'

'No, no, donations is no bad, though we can aye do wi more. The poor we ha aye wi us, after all. No,' Jamieson straightened up on his stool, shaking his head, 'it's hard to keep hold o the stuff the now. It's all stored next the dry goods for the Vicars' hall, round the north side o the kirk, and there's as much vanishing from both dry stores, the last six month or so, it's a right worry.'

'Theft, you mean? How secure is the store?'

'Secure enough, I'd ha said, till now. Aye, it's theft. There's aye the odd cup o dried pease or handful o meal goes astray, but this is a half-sack at a time just walking off when naeb'dy's watching.' The Sub-Almoner pulled a long face. 'You don't see folk at their best in this post, Gil, you'll believe me, but to my mind that takes the bell, thieving from the poor. I've got the vergers warned to look out for it, but it wouldny surprise me if they were in the game and all.'

'I'd not heard of that,' Gil confessed. 'You've changed the locks, I take it.'

'Oh, aye, and a new padlock at my own expense. That walked off and all, I'd to get a second.'

Thinking it was little wonder that the Sub-Almoner was usually afflicted with melancholy, Gil took his leave of the man and returned to St Catherine's, where the nameless corpse was now laid out in the little chapel under Annie Gibb's own shroud, with Sir Simon murmuring in the shadowed chancel. Drawing back the linen he studied the dead woman with care, counting the scars and bruises on her thin body, considering the rough skin of her hands and feet and the broken nails. Meggot had washed these as thoroughly as the rest, and had cleaned under the nails with the point of a knife, extracting dirt and blood and fragments of skin.

'She's marked him, whoever he was,' she had said darkly. 'And I'd say,' she twitched her nose fastidiously, 'she's lain wi him or wi some man at least, no long afore she was slain. But there's no sign she was forced, maister, that I can see from here, even wi all these bruises.'

'Aye,' agreed Dame Ellen, 'though we'll maybe make certain o't when she softens and I can get a wee look at her—' She bit off the next words. Curiously, the term which Gil's unruly mind supplied was French, and not one which Alys used.

Examining the nail-scrapings, he had concluded that there was nothing more to learn there; he had hoped for some clue to the woman's identity, or at least her trade or profession, but the dirt appeared to be grease from cooking, something nearly all women came into daily contact with.

Now, contemplating her battered body, he reflected that the violence it revealed was also something many women met daily. Who was it? he asked her silently. Who bloodied your mouth and blacked your eyes? Was he your husband, your father, a client? Does he know where his last beating has put you?

'So what happened, maister?'

Sir Simon had left his prayers again. Gil blinked at him, collecting his thoughts.

'It's none so easy to read,' he admitted.

'Poor lass,' said the Master, bending to peer into the

corpse's downturned face, 'she's had her troubles, but she's free o them now. Who must you speak wi next? Your laddie's away to ask round about if anyone heard anything, and the good-brother, Lockhart, he's away over to St Mungo's to complain of their lack of care, but if you're wanting any of the women I'll fetch them out.'

'Aye, if they're fit to talk to.'

'I'll get the lassies out to you, they're a wee thing calmer now.'

If Annie Gibb's sisters-in-law were calmer now, Gil was glad he had not attempted to speak to them earlier. Led out into the sunshine they proved to be rather younger than Annie or the dead woman, perhaps fifteen and seventeen, two sturdy girls neither pretty nor plain but something between, with curling brown hair and eyes swollen with weeping. The older one had the hiccups, which provoked increasingly hysterical giggles in the other girl. Their names, it seemed, were Nicholas and Ursula, and like Dame Ellen they had watched from a distance while Annie was bound to the Cross and then had left her.

'She protested, I think,' said Gil, sitting down on the opposite bench. The sisters looked at one another, and one nodded.

'She never wanted it,' said the other. 'She wanted just to be left alone.'

'But it wasny right, living the way she did,' said her sister, and hiccuped. Blushing, she covered her mouth, and said behind her hand, 'No company, and never meeting anybody, and we couldny be with her that often, we'd duties about the house.'

'Had she none?' Gil asked.

'Aye, but she renounced them,' said the hiccuping girl, Nicholas he thought. 'We'd to see to them all atween us. Feed her hens, take her share o the sweeping and cooking.'

'Fetch her food,' said the other, who must therefore be Ursula.

'Did her maid or her waiting-men not do that?' It hardly made sense, he thought; he had seen several servants already, and the householder was described as a gentleman and his daughters as heiresses. His own sisters had had their duties certainly, but they hardly amounted to cleaning and kitchen-work.

'Meggot had enough to do trying to keep her chamber clean.'

'Tell me about the household,' he suggested. 'How many are you?'

They looked at each other. Beyond the outer courtyard, beyond the walls of the hostel, Gil heard the burgh bell-man ring his great brass bell and begin the description of Annie Gibb.

'Well, there's us,' said Ursula, counting on her fingers, 'and Faither, and our aunt, and Annie. And there was Mariota till she wedded Lockhart, and times there's Henry and Austin—'

'Who are they?' Gil asked.

'Cousins?' said Nicholas.

'No, they areny cousins,' said Ursula. 'Only by courtesy. They're no blood kin o ours, Nick, they're Ellen's nephews by her first man's sister Margaret Boyd, they're Muirs, the both o them.'

Outside, the bellman had dealt with Annie Gibb and was now describing the unknown corpse, inviting any who might know her to visit the chapel of St Catherine's hostel. A mistake, thought Gil. We'll be overrun. Reckoning his mother's Boyd kindred in his head, he located Margaret Boyd and her sons. They were perched on a very distant branch of the pedigree, but the connection with Dame Ellen could be useful.

'They might as well be cousins, the way Ellen carries on,' said Nicholas. 'Making them ride into Glasgow wi us, keeping on at Annie how handsome they are,' she added darkly, and hiccuped. Ursula bit back more giggles, and continued,

'And there's that doctor the now, and then there's Meggot, and Gillian that waits on my aunt.' She proceeded to list a good half-dozen indoor servants before she lost count, looking helplessly from her hands to Gil.

'Most of those have stayed at home, I think,' Gil said. Nicholas nodded. 'Why did you come to Glasgow?'

'Well, for the miracle,' said Ursula reasonably. 'It wouldny work tying her to the farm gatepost, after all.'

'No, I meant you two in particular.'

They looked at each other again. Nicholas hiccuped, Ursula giggled.

'To see the High Kirk?' suggested Nicholas, trying to ignore her sister. 'And all the vessels on the Clyde, and the market, and that. All the things the chapman tellt us, that was through Glenbuck last month.'

'We've only seen St Mungo's so far,' said Ursula. 'Might as well ha stayed at home.'

'Ellen wouldny ha left us at home,' said Nicholas sagely. 'Where we go, she goes, and where she goes, we go, till we're wedded. And Ellen had to come wi Annie,' a shadow flickered across her face, 'and Faither.'

'Tell me about Annie,' he suggested. 'What like was she before she fell into her melancholy? Was she a good sister?'

'Oh, aye,' said Nicholas, and hiccuped. Ursula ducked her head, suppressing more giggles, and her sister went on, 'She was a good laugh, she was aye fun to be company wi, she'd lend all her gowns and her jewels and borrow yours.'

Gil nodded; his sister Margaret had summed up this sharing as *First up, best dressed*.

'Then she lost the bairn,' said Ursula, sobering. 'She was right melancholy after that.'

'And then Arthur died,' both sisters crossed themselves, 'and she vowed she'd never cease mourning him, and all the rest of it.'

'Sitting in the dark, aye at her prayers, no singing or joking or bonny clothes.'

'She'd locked her jewels all in her kist,' said Nicholas resentfully.

'She must have loved him very deeply,' said Gil.

'Aye,' said Ursula, 'and the deil knows why, it was just Arthur.' Her sister hiccuped explosively, and she gasped and turned her head away, biting back the giggles.

'Has she any friends in Glasgow?' Gil asked.

'Just us,' said Nicholas blankly. 'Who would she have? She's never been in Glasgow in her life afore this.'

'So she's adrift in a strange burgh,' said Gil deliberately, 'barefoot in her shift. What d'you suppose has come to her?'

'She'll be safe enough,' said Ursula, on a sudden uncontrollable burst of giggles. 'The way she stinks now, nobody'd go next or nigh her!'

Her sister drew breath looking shocked, hiccuped resoundingly, and collapsed in equal laughter. The door to the women's lodging was flung wide, and Dame Ellen stalked out.

'What a way to comport yoursels! Your sister missing, a dead woman in the chapel, your faither the way he is. Sit up straight and behave yoursels decent, or the Archbishop's man will send in sic a report of you, you'll never be wedded this side o Doomsday.'

Both sisters rose, scarlet with mingled laughter and embarrassment, and collected themselves enough to curtsy briefly to Gil before fleeing past their aunt and into the shadows. He could hear them, still laughing within the hall, and Dame Ellen turned a bony simper on him, the rather dreadful coquetry of her mouth by no means matched in her eyes.

'What a pair of lassies!' she was saying. 'You'll accept my apologies for their behaviour, I hope, maister.'

'They're very young,' Gil observed. The simper vanished bleakly.

'Aye, well, if they're old enough to be wedded, they're old enough to behave theirsels like modest women. What my kinsman at St Mungo's would have to say about them I canny think. Have you learned aught yet? That doctor says my brother's—' She broke off, her expression softening as voices rose in the outer yard, Sir Simon's among them. Feet sounded in the passageway, Socrates growled quietly, and two young men burst into the sunshine.

'What's this yon fellow says?' demanded the first of her, as Gil checked his dog. 'Annie vanished and some dead woman in her place? What have you been at here?'

'Now, Henry, mind your tongue afore Blacader's quaestor!' chided Dame Ellen. 'These are my nephews, maister, that rode into Glasgow wi us and are lodged wi their kinsman along Rottenrow. Henry and Austin Muir.'

Her gestures identified them: Henry fair and ostentatious, Austin tawny and diffident, both sturdy, handsome and expensively dressed in identical short velvet gowns which did not conceal Austin's low-necked shirt of fine linen or his brother's embroidered doublet of crimson silk, its high collar caked in silver braid. That must itch, Gil thought irrelevantly.

The brothers stared, taken aback, until Henry recalled his manners and made a swaggering bow, sweeping his jewelled bonnet above the cobbles. Gil returned the courtesy, saying,

'Aye, Mistress Gibb is vanished away. Have you any knowledge of where she might have taken shelter or hid herself?'

'*Hid* herself? Why's she done that?' said Austin, still staring.

'We'd looked to find her here,' said Henry. 'Is there truly no trace o where she's at?'

'What brings you here to find her?' Gil countered. 'Had you business wi her?'

'Business?' repeated Austin. 'Us? No, we—'

'What else would bring them but civility? They've called in the hopes o finding her cured o her madness, a course,' said Dame Ellen, smiling fondly. 'And the wish to see their old aunt, I hope.'

'But what's happened?' asked Henry, ignoring this. 'Have you no set up a search? Why was there another woman in her place? Who is it, anyway?'

He was speaking to Dame Ellen, but Gil answered him:

'The Provost's men are searching for Mistress Gibb, and we've got both women being cried through the town. We'll see if anyone kens the corp we have. Someone must ha missed her.' He paused, considering the two. 'Where were you last night? '

51

'Where were we?' Henry bristled. 'Are you saying we had aught to do wi it?'

'If I ken where you were and whether you saw anything useful,' said Gil patiently, 'it would help me trace where the dead woman came from. In fact, I'd be grateful if you'd take a look at her now.'

'And then you can join the search for Annie, the both of you,' announced their kinswoman. Henry gave her a sharp look, but said,

'Aye, well, we were in our cousin's house all the evening, getting the news o Glasgow and telling him the news o Ayrshire.'

'Together?'

'That's right,' agreed Austin, nodding.

'So what about this corp?' demanded Henry. 'Are we to look at her, or no?'

'One thing,' said Austin, 'she'll ha stayed this side of the Girth Burn.'

'Who will? What are you on about now?' demanded Henry, turning to follow Gil to the outer courtyard.

'Annie, a course. She'll ha stayed up here atween the two burns.'

'How d'you make that out?'

'They canny cross running water. Everybody kens that.'

'That's witches, bawheid! Annie's no witch, just melancholy.'

There was a handful of local people in the chapel, arguing briskly about who the dead woman might be, their speculations hindered only slightly by the fact that none of them could recognise her. The bier was now attended by two of the hostel servants; a man in blue livery stood at its head and a woman in a blue gown and grey cloak knelt at the foot, her beads sliding through her fingers. Near them, leaning negligently against the chancel-screen, was Lowrie. His attention was on the arguing townsfolk, but when Gil stood aside to let the Muir brothers enter first, he straightened up, watching them approach. Gil, watching his assistant in turn, was warned by the way the younger man's expression went blank, a fraction before Austin

Muir stopped in his tracks and dropped his hat to seize his brother's arm.

'Henry! Is that no— Is it no—' He swallowed, and his brother turned a furious face on him, as the group of neighbours paused to watch. 'Aye, it is, surely!'

'It's no Annie, bawheid, they've tellt us that,' Henry said savagely. 'Hold your tongue, and let the rest o us decide what's to do!'

'No, it's no Annie, I ken that,' argued Austin, 'it's surely— It's that— It's awfy like—' He took in his brother's expression and fell silent. Henry freed himself and stepped forward to the bier, bending to look at the dead girl's damaged face, then straightened up.

'Never saw her afore,' he said. 'I've never a notion who she might be.'

'And you, Austin?' said Gil deliberately. Austin jumped, looked over his shoulder at Gil, and back at his brother.

'I, I— I never saw her neither,' he averred.

'Likely she's some hoor from away down the town, from the Gallowgate or the like,' said Henry easily, crossing himself as he moved to join Gil. 'Poor soul.'

'That's a good thought, maister,' said one of the neighbours, a stout woman with a basket full of purchases from the market. 'You never ken what they folks down the Gallowgate will get up to, beating lassies to death would be nothing to them.'

This met with agreement from two more of the group, but one man shook his head and the other woman present said,

'It's right far to carry her once she's deid, Agnes, to bring her up here to St Mungo's. Did the bellman no say she was bound to the Cross? Why would anyone do that?'

'So they wouldny get the blame for it away down there, a course!' said the basket-carrier triumphantly.

'There, you see,' said Henry to Gil. 'Make sure the bellman cries her down the town, or better still carry her down there and show her, the most of them'll not trouble themselves to come up here for a dead lassie. Likely someone down the Gallowgate'll name her for you.'

'But how would they do that, Henry?' asked his brother in perplexity, 'when they—'

'Will you be quiet, bawheid that you are?' demanded Henry. 'Hold your wheesht and let those of us that can think do the thinking.'

'No, I never met them before this,' said Lowrie, accepting a share of bread and cheese with gratitude. 'I doubt Austin can sign his name, let along con his books, and Henry doesny seem like a college man. Certainly he's no Glasgow man.'

'He never came to visit your friend Ninian when you were at the College? Ninian Boyd, I mean,' Gil expanded, without much hope. Lowrie shook his head.

They had repaired to the inner courtyard; Gil wanted to consider what he had learned so far, and it seemed a good moment to consume Kittock's dole. Now he continued, 'I reckon they'd be some kind of kin of Ninian's, third or fourth cousins maybe, closer than they are to me. The two of them are lodged wi Canon Muir on Rottenrow, who Dame Ellen said was another kinsman. I need to get a word wi him, confirm that, confirm what they were doing last night. I'm not at all convinced they gave us the whole truth.'

'Austin knew the corp, or thought he did,' Lowrie agreed, 'he was struck wi horror at first sight. It could have been her bruises, but it seemed to me he recognised her.'

'Henry was very quick to silence him.'

'I liked his suggestion of the Gallowgate.'

'A nice piece of misdirection. It could even be true.'

Gil extracted the cheese from between the remainder of his bread and ate it. Lowrie was watching him intently and chewing hard, and after a moment swallowed and said,

'I had another word wi the servants here, both the guests' household and the hostel folk, now it's known Annie's missing.' Gil made an interrogatory noise. 'The two that guarded her kept a good eye on her till about midnight, it seems, because there were folk about till that hour. The man Sawney says she spoke to him then, asking him to set her free, addressed him by name, so I think we can assume she was there and unharmed at that point. I've a note of who slept where here in the hostel, which should help if we're checking movements, and that pair in the chapel the now, Will and Bessie, are man and wife and dwell by the gate here, and they mentioned there were comings and goings in the night.'

'Oh, there were, were there?' Gil gave his crusts to the expectant dog and took another hunk of bread from the linen wrapping. 'Did they name anyone?'

'No, it seems the door was left unbarred a-purpose, in case they brought Mistress Gibb back earlier than the dawn. The woman, Bessie, heard the door go an hour or so afore midnight, so she reckoned, and looked out assuming she'd be needed to help Annie back to the women's hall, but the courtyard was empty.' Lowrie dug in his purse for his tablets, found the right leaf and scrutinised his notes. 'And twice more after that she heard footsteps and the door closing, and voices in the courtyard. Seems it shuts wi a thump that shakes their bed, no matter the care that's taken. She never looked out the later times, she said she took it if she was needed they'd bang on the lodging door. Likely she was too warm to move by then,' he added in faint amusement.

'Three times the door went,' said Gil thoughtfully.

'Three times after they were in bed,' Lowrie qualified.

'A good point. And yet none of the folk we've spoken to referred to being out of the hostel. You'd think they might have mentioned it.' He considered the final portion of bread and cheese, then broke it carefully into two large pieces and a small one, handed the small one to the dog and gestured to Lowrie to take one of the others. 'Did her man hear anything?'

'He says he heard the door go but never roused enough to take note of how often.'

'Hm,' said Gil. 'Did you get anything from the others? From the Shaw servants?'

'No more than I've told you already. So do we need to start asking who was about in the night?'

'That can wait.' Gil brushed breadcrumbs from his person, gathered up the linen cloth and shook it out. Several chaffinches flew down onto the cobbles, keeping a wary distance from the dog, but flew up again when the two men rose. 'I want to get another look at the Cross, and the ground about it, if Andro and his men haveny trampled it into dust. The amount of movement there must have been, they'd surely have left some trace.'

'Who?' Lowrie followed him across the outer yard. 'Whose traces are you thinking we might find?'

Gil nodded to Sir Simon at his chamber window and strode on, out of the gate, before finally saying,

'At the very least, Annie herself and whoever released her from her bonds. Depending on what came after that, it could be as many as five or six people we're trying to track.'

'Do you think she went willingly?' Lowrie asked after a moment.

'A lot turns on that,' agreed Gil. 'And on precisely why she was released.'

Lowrie was silent while they skirted the high sandstone walls of the Castle and approached the gate of St Mungo's kirkyard. Finally he said, counting off the points on his fingers,

'Marriage by consent, whether for love or money. Marriage by capture. Simple compassion.'

'As a hostage,' Gil supplied. 'To get control of her land or her money, even without marriage. Any of these.' He paused on the slope that led down to the Girth Burn, looking about him. Off to their left the building site which was Archbishop Blacader's addition to his cathedral church showed signs of life, with the clink of metal on stone and the creak of wooden scaffolding; as Gil turned that way Maistre Pierre's head showed above the wall. Seeing them, the mason waved, and vanished down into the structure.

Between the Fergus Aisle and the burn which formed the boundary of the kirkyard was a clump of hawthorns, their berries just beginning to show in still-green clusters. Taller trees beyond them threw a thick-leaved shade. Crows swirled about their tops, cawing, and the long blades of bluebells grew thickly in the dappled spaces between the glowing sunlit trunks, the flowers long faded and the green seed-cases ripening on the curved stems. A sudden memory assailed Gil, of hunting among the bluebells for a harp-key while the harper's mistress, small John's mother, lay dead in the Fergus Aisle, of finding a wisp of woollen thread from her plaid on one of those same hawthorn bushes.

'So again we search the kirkyard,' said Maistre Pierre at his elbow.

'Aye. Have Andro's men been here?'

'No, they have tramped the other bank of the Girth Burn, through the gardens, but did not enter the kirkyard. I suppose they have no jurisdiction on church land.'

'There's been nothing bigger than a fox through those bluebells,' said Lowrie.

'Not in the last day and a night,' agreed Gil. 'Let's take a look at the Cross itself.'

Chapter Four

They approached with care along the path, all three men scrutinising the ground about their feet as they went. The Cross was not a cross, but a tall stone with the shadows of ancient images still visible on all four sides; it could easily date back to Kentigern's time. If it had ever had arms they were long since broken off, but Gil thought he could make out a cross carved in relief on one uneven surface, with the ring, or nimbus, or symbol of the infinite Godhead, or whatever it was, circling the juncture.

'It takes more than one man,' observed Maistre Pierre, 'to tie someone to that, unless the subject is willing.'

'Did you say you saw them bind Mistress Gibb?' Lowrie asked.

'I did. It took three of them. I was rounding up my men like a sheepdog, you understand, and young Berthold was right at the front of the crowd. I had a good view. Two were servants, I should say, and one man in a gown worth a baron's ransom who held her in her place while the men bound the ropes about her. And one of the clergy, was it that fellow Craigie? offering up prayers.'

'So was the other woman, the one in the chapel now, still alive when she was put here?' Lowrie stood still to contemplate the idea. 'Why would she consent? Or was she already dead, or in a great swoon from the beating, or what? I wouldny think it any easier to bind a dead woman here than a live one.'

'We're looking for traces of at least two people, then,' said Gil.

'There were more than two about here last evening,' declared Maistre Pierre.

Gil stepped cautiously over to the Cross and stood with his back to it, looking about him.

'Unless they crossed the burn,' he said slowly, 'whoever released her came down the slope from the gate, and the ground's by far too trampled to tell how many they were. I wonder, was she awake, expecting them?'

'Like Maister Craigie,' said Lowrie. Gil, who had already seen the songman making his way towards them, made no comment, but Maistre Pierre tutted audibly. 'It makes less and less sense, doesn't it?' Lowrie went on.

'It never has made sense,' grumbled the mason. 'Everything we have learned so far has made the matter more confusing.'

'Well, well, Gilbert,' said Craigie in Latin, coming close enough to speak. 'And what have you learned so far? A sad matter, a sad matter, and not good for St Mungo's.'

'The Sub-Dean is very displeased,' agreed Gil, accurate but uninformative.

'Very sad,' repeated Craigie. 'I little thought, when I offered prayers for Mistress Gibb's healing, that this would be the consequence of her petition to our saint.'

'It was you offered prayers?'

'It was. Her family wished it, and I was free. And now this has happened.'

Gil considered him. He was a handsome, stocky man with a wide grin, dressed with less flamboyance than Maister Sim in a fashionably cut long gown of dark green cloth faced with black velvet. His belt was shod with silver, the brim of his round felt hat was pinned up with a bright enamel brooch, and altogether he was the image of a prosperous, modest cleric. Now, becoming slightly uncomfortable under Gil's gaze, he said, switching to Scots,

'Is that right, what the bellman's crying? Does it mean someone throttled a complete stranger? Surely not! I canny believe it!'

'She is certainly a stranger so far,' said Maistre Pierre. 'We have not yet a name for her.'

'But what was she doing here? Where is Mistress Gibb?'

'If I knew that I'd be rattling at her door,' Gil observed. 'What did you see when they called you down here this morning, William?'

'What did I see? Well, her men were here at her side, and there the woman was bound to the Cross. You saw her yoursel, Gil. How did the men no recognise her? That's gey strange!'

'You saw her too,' Gil pointed out. 'You must mind how badly she was beaten. Her men saw what they expected to, I suppose. Nobody else was about?'

'No at that moment, though a good few gathered once they saw us.'

'Which of the men came up to St Mungo's? How did he get in? What did he say?'

'Oh.' Craigie paused to consider. 'Well, we were all in the vestry robing up for Prime, and this fellow came in from the nave wi one of the vergers on his heels, likely he'd got in at the west door, crying that his mistress was dead. I've no idea which of them it was, likely the one that spoke to you when you got here. And seeing there was only us songmen and Canon Muir in the place, Adam Goudie told off Habbie and me to go and deal wi the matter. We could see at once there was naught to be done, she was cold and stiff, so I began an act of Conditional Absolution and Habbie went to fetch you.'

'Who found the cord about her neck?'

'Oh, that would be Habbie. He was for trying to revive her, patting her face and the like, and here were the ends hanging.' He crossed himself. 'A bad business, a very bad business. And no good for St Mungo's,' he repeated.

Gil dug in his purse for the coiled cord. Shaking it loose he said,

'This is what was about her neck. Have you seen the like before? Have you any idea where it might have come from?'

'What, an ell and a half of stout cord?' said Craigie. 'Just about anywhere, I'd have thought. Try the candlemakers, they use string and cord, all sorts.'

Gil nodded, and wound the cord about his fingers again, turning back to the Cross. Its massive sandstone pillar gave nothing away, and the trampled grass around it showed no useful signs, as Lowrie had commented earlier. There was a long silence, into which Maister Craigie finally said,

'Well, I'll let you get on. But tell me if you learn aught, Gil, so I can put it in my prayers.'

'Do that, William,' agreed Gil. He turned to raise his hat politely, but Craigie was already on his way up the slope towards St Mungo's. Maistre Pierre, staring at the man's green cloth back, remarked in French,

'Does he think we suspect him?'

'He seems concerned,' Gil agreed. He waited a moment longer, till Craigie was well out of earshot, then said to Lowrie, 'So what have you got there?'

Lowrie rose from where he had hunkered down in the shadows twenty yards along the bank of the Girth Burn. Socrates, who had been sitting beside him looking where he looked, splashed into the water and waited hopefully for a stick to be thrown.

'Someone cut across there to the waterside,' said Lowrie, pointing upstream of where he stood. 'And I wonder if this is why? It looks like a garment, blue woollen cloth any road. It's caught under the other bank here, where the Provost's men would likely ha missed it. Could it be her gown? And someone came down this way to throw it into the burn?'

'Ah!' Maistre Pierre made for the burn, avoiding the line Lowrie had indicated. Gil followed him more slowly, picking out the signs the younger man had found. They were slight, a matter of bent and flattened grasses, the print of a heel in a softer patch; whoever left them had contrived to avoid the bluebells' juicier, more easily damaged leaves. Was that luck, he wondered, or good judgement? 'Or was it daylight by then?' he said aloud.

'No,' said Maistre Pierre firmly. He was calf-deep in the burn, fending off the interested dog and gathering up the waterlogged cloth which Lowrie had seen. 'Not if this was put in the water at the same time as the body we have was bound to the Cross. Lend a hand here.' Lowrie sprang to help him, with a quick apology. 'She was put there within perhaps an hour of her death, and then she was throttled, and left to stiffen like that. After midnight, but long before dawn, I should say.'

'Someone who kens the kirkyard well?' Lowrie offered. He and the mason splashed out of the burn with the heavy wet garment between them and began to spread it out.

'This has been cut off her,' said Maistre Pierre, unfurling a ragged sleeve. 'See, cut the whole length from cuff to neck, and the braid at the elbow too.'

'And the other sleeve,' said Lowrie, unfolding it to match. 'The laces are cut and all.'

'So likely she was dead already when she was brought here,' said Gil. He stared about him, then moved carefully back to the Cross and began quartering the trampled area about its foot. Socrates joined him, and after a moment so did Lowrie, while Maistre Pierre continued to arrange the folds of wet blue wool.

'It is a working woman's kirtle,' he said at length, 'with such short sleeves, and in this cheap woollen stuff, though this bit of braid at the sleeve may help us to identify her. The hem is much worn and stained. And also— Pah! Full of insects. The seams are thick with their eggs. Lice, I suppose. I wonder where she worked.'

'A flesher's? One of the cookhouses?' Gil suggested. 'Somewhere the floor is wet and dirty, at any rate, and not in the better parts of the town either.'

'*Peut-être*. Do we seek her in the alehouses, perhaps?'

'That would certainly account for why nobody has come forward yet to name her.' Gil was crouched, peering at the ground. 'We might learn more once they open up for the day's trade. Lowrie, come and tell me what you see here.'

Lowrie obeyed, elbowing the dog aside to study the scraps of colour caught under the flattened stems.

'That's it,' he agreed. 'That must be it. She was cut out of the gown here.'

Gil used his fingernails to extract one wispy blue thread, and laid it on his palm, trying not to breathe on it.

'Or at least, the gown was cut,' he amended scrupulously. 'She was probably still in it, but we have no proof.'

'Here's a bigger bit,' said Lowrie, now on hands and knees. He pinched something up from a mat of grasses, and turned back to Gil. 'Look, Maister Gil, it's a bit of the weave, not just an odd thread.'

Gil took the fragment, turning it over carefully.

'How did that happen?' he wondered.

'He used shears,' said Maistre Pierre. 'One sleeve has been cut using shears, quite small ones such as a needle-woman carries, and the other using a knife.'

'Two people, then,' said Gil.

'Mistress Gibb herself, with the scissors from her hussif?' Lowrie said in surprise, and answered his own question. 'Hardly, she had naught on her but that sacking gown I suppose. Unless whoever freed her brought her clothes to her. No, the tirewoman said her clothes were all in the hostel.' He looked down at the wisps of cloth in Gil's hand. 'I wonder they never kept this whole for Annie to wear, at least till she found shelter.'

'Not so easy,' said Maistre Pierre, 'to strip a corpse in the dark. I suppose it was quicker this way.'

'Nonetheless,' said Gil, 'it fits. We have our two people at least, as we reckoned it would take to bind the corp to the Cross, and one of them carried a pair of small shears. Our corp was dead when she was brought here, and then stripped of that blue gown, the sacking gown put on her, and I suppose one held her up while the other tied the ropes.'

'Well, that is clear enough,' agreed Maistre Pierre, straightening up cautiously. 'It only leaves the one question, and that greater than all the rest together.'

'Well, I think there are others we've not asked yet,' said Gil, 'but that is certainly the biggest one right now. Why? What did they gain by it? Why that lassie in particular, why any corp at all, why change her dress? What was the purpose?'

'Time,' said Lowrie, sitting back on his heels. 'Did the man Sawney no say he came down to the gate wi a light every hour or so? If he'd found nobody here he'd surely ha raised the alarm immediately. They must have won several hours that way, between making the exchange and Sawney and Rab finally coming to free their mistress.'

'And if we knew how long that was,' said Gil, 'we'd have some idea how far afield we'll need to search for Annie Gibb. I think you must be right, Lowrie.'

'Do we seek her?' asked Maistre Pierre, still studying the wet kirtle. 'It is not against the law to run from friends and family.'

'Mistress Gibb, or whoever freed her,' said Gil deliberately, 'kens more than we do about the lassie in St Catherine's chapel and how she died. I want a word wi her and her friends.'

Lowrie nodded. Maistre Pierre cocked his head, and said,

'Well, for now you may seek her on your own. It is more than time I went back to work if those pillars are to be set up this side of Judgement Day. I have not heard a chisel for the quarter of an hour. Moreover,' he added, 'that boy Berthold is no use today. Boys will be boys, I accept that he and Luke went out last night after supper, but Luke came home at a reasonable hour, just before midnight indeed. Saints alone know when Berthold came in, and this morning he cannot lift so much as a mell without dropping it. I wish you joy of him when he serves you, young Lowrie.'

'The good Doctor Chrysostom has told me the news,' said Sir Edward in the thread of a voice. Chrysostom Januar, fingers on his patient's pulse, nodded encouragement, and a man in the decent plain clothing of an upper servant, presumably a body-servant, stood by watching jealously. Sir Edward breathed carefully, in and out, in again, and went on, 'Maister, I couldny say where Annie might be. I hoped,' another cautious breath, 'to meet her again freed of her ills, though no as I shall be of mine afore long.'

Gil studied the sick man with sympathy. This was the wreckage of a warrior, he thought; the flesh had fallen away from a broad frame with a sturdy ribcage and big-boned hands. Silver scars on the yellowish flesh of neck and brow below the linen nightcap told their own story.

'She never said anything to you about friends in Glasgow or hereabouts?' he asked. Sir Edward considered briefly, but answered a soundless *No*. 'Did she speak of her future at all?' Another *No*. 'What had you intended for her, sir? Lockhart thought you planned to treat her the same as your own lassies when you divide the property.'

This time the answer was *Aye*. Sir Edward collected himself, lifted a hand slightly and added, 'My will. Show him.'

'In the small leather kist, I think,' said Doctor Januar, and received an infinitesimal nod.

The men's hall was a big, open chamber with two rows of beds, wide troughs of Norway pine set on short legs against the long walls. Most of them were bare but one opposite and three at the far end held straw mattresses which now, by daylight, were humped up like caterpillars to air, with a clutter of bags and boxes on the floor round them. Here, nearest the door and the light, Sir Edward lay on good linen, propped on a mound of pillows, a feather-bed under him and a fine woollen blanket about his shoulders. More kists were stacked on either side of the bedhead; there was a tray with spoons, a beaker, a jug of water on top of one pile.

Turning away, the servant extracted a leather-bound box from the other stack. He searched briefly in it and drew out a folded parchment, which he handed to Gil, returning to his post. Gil unfolded the document and tilted the writing to the light. It was not the original, which was presumably lodged with the man of law Lockhart had mentioned, but a full copy.

'This is well drawn up,' he said after a moment. Sir Edward's thin mouth twitched in a faint smile. 'It makes matters quite out of doubt.'

The will was also very wordy, but the testator's intentions were unmistakable. There were bequests to the servants, to Dame Ellen, to the parish kirk and its priest; then in a long preamble Sir Edward's affection for his daughters and his good-daughter were set out in terms which could only gratify the four women concerned, and the quite significant property which Sir Edward held was allocated, feu by feu, with reasons given for each bequest.

'Would you by any chance,' Gil asked, still perusing the list, assembling the blocks of land in his head, 'would you by any chance have any of Annie's papers wi you? Her contract, the lands from her own faither, that sort of—' He broke off, as Sir Edward signalled with one finger and pointed at the kist again.

The servant, searching through it as if he knew what he sought, extracted several documents which he bundled together and handed to Gil. Over his head as he did so the doctor met Gil's eye with a significant look. Significant of what? wondered Gil, preserving a blank expression. He turned to the papers, skimming through them. Anna Gibb, daughter of James Gibb and Mariana Wallace his spouse, was a wealthy woman, that was immediately obvious; she had no need to live in one room like an anchorite. These documents were the originals, and seemed to be the complete set of her titles to everything that was hers outright, along with a short copy of the deeds to several conjunct fees and a number of properties in which she had the life interest. He raised his eyes to the three men watching him, and met another of those intent looks from the doctor.

'Well, that all seems very clear,' he said after a moment, and Januar looked away. 'I'll make some notes, if I may.' He drew his tablets from his purse and began a careful list of the properties and their respective values. The doctor moved quietly about while he worked, pouring a spoonful of something from a flask, something else from a jug, into the glass beaker on the tray by his side. The servant lifted the glass and stepped to the bedside, and the sick man accepted the dose gratefully, drinking it in small cautious sips.

'Who has a mind to Annie's property?' Gil asked eventually, stacking the documents into their bundle again. 'There must be more than one family would be glad of the alliance. Who have you turned away?'

Sir Edward gazed at him unreadably for a long moment. Eventually he said, in that thread of a voice,

'Most of Ayrshire. Half Lanarkshire. Boyds, Muirs, Somervilles.' One of those faint smiles. 'Lost count a while back.'

'None of them seemed more determined than others? More persistent?'

A soundless *No*. Whether that was the case or not, Sir Edward was clearly not the one to ask. Gil was considering his next question when hasty feet sounded in the courtyard, Socrates wuffed a greeting beneath the window, and Lowrie entered, rattling at the pin as he opened the door.

'Forgive me, maisters,' he said, bowing briefly. 'Maister Gil, I think we have a name for the dead lassie.'

Out in the yard he was a little more explicit.

'One of the alehouses out near the Stablegreen Port. Seems the bellman stopped there to wet his thrapple, and cried his tale by the door as he came and went, and naturally they all came up here to see the sight, and recognised her kirtle where we've spread it out to dry on the grass.' Gil nodded, acknowledging his dog's salutation. 'They think it's one of the lassies from the next tavern, just inside the Port. Someone's gone out there to tell them, fetch her man, maybe get the alewife here too. I thought you'd wish to witness that.'

'You're right,' said Gil. 'What is her name, then? Assuming they're right, and assuming the dead lassie is the owner of the kirtle,' he qualified.

'Peg, they called her. Peg Simpson. She works at the sign of the Trindle, so they thought, and her man's a porter in the town.'

In the chapel, a small group who might or might not be

different from the previous group was discussing this, while the woman who had been praying earlier sat on her heels, her beads wrapped round her hand, listening to the comments. Her husband had vanished, presumably to his duties about the hostel.

'Likely one o their regulars tried it on a bit far,' said a man in a cowhide apron as Gil entered. 'You ken what the place is like, after all.'

'I don't know it,' said Gil. 'Tell me about it.'

All the heads turned, and the man in the apron, taken aback, swallowed once or twice and then said,

'Aye, well, it's no the most— It's no a— It's no like the Mitre that Ep Davison keeps, that's a clean house and well ordered.'

'A true word, Willie,' agreed a woman in a striped kirtle. 'Eppie keeps a well-ordered house, right enough. Her lassies are all decent folk, a woman can take a drink in there and never be troubled by other folk's husbands. Unless she wants to be,' she added thoughtfully.

'Jean Howie's ale isny the wonder o the town neither,' said a man with a bright green hood rolled down on his shoulders. 'That's her that keeps the Trindle,' he added.

'Aye it is,' contradicted someone else, 'it's a wonder that folks goes back there after they've tasted it once.'

'That's no what they go back for,' said another voice.

'I heard that, William Pringle,' said a stout woman at the chapel door. She pushed past Gil without apology, taking her beads in her hand as she went. 'Now what's this about Peg? She should ha been at her work hours since. What's she doing here, and dead wi it?'

'Here she's, Jean,' said the man in the hide apron. 'That's if it is her, she's been beat that bad you wouldny ken her.'

Mistress Howie halted at sight of the dead woman's face, crossed herself, and went forward more slowly.

'Oh, in the Name,' she said after a moment. 'What a beating she's taen. The poor lass. I'll wager it's that man o hers, raised his fist to her once too often.'

'More than his fist, I'd ha said,' offered the woman in the

striped kirtle. 'She's black and blue, head to foot. Take a look, Jean.'

Bessie, the hostel servant, got to her feet and raised the shroud, glaring at the male bystanders. Mistress Howie cast a cautious glance under the linen at the hunched length of the corpse, and nodded grimly, pursing her lips.

'Have you sent to take him up?' she demanded of Gil, unerringly scenting authority. 'Her man. Billy Baird. Makes his living carrying other folks' goods on his back, such as doesny fall into his pouch on the way to where he's going. Scrawny black-haired creature wi a scar across his lug.' She raked one finger across the folds of her linen headdress, over her ear and down her cheek. 'It's hardly murder, if a man slays his own wife wi his fists, but he should face the Provost for it any road.'

'They've sent after him, Jean,' said the man in the hide apron. 'Likely he'll be here to gie a name to her.'

'Aye, but who did ye send?' she said sceptically.

'Where do they dwell, mistress?' Gil asked. 'Have you any notion where the fellow Baird might be working this morning? Have you seen him the day?'

'No to say seen him.' Mistress Howie folded her arms under her substantial bosom, slightly relieving the strain on her red kirtle. 'When I threw out the night's stop-overs, maybe an hour afore Prime, I seen him keeking out at their door, but he ducked back as soon as he seen me look at him. They dwell on our back lands,' she enlarged, 'got a room in one o the wee sheds. Right handy for . . .' Her voice tailed off, and she glanced at the corpse and crossed herself. 'Poor lass,' she said again.

Gil, listening to what was not said, could only agree with her. How did the man Baird feel if his wife brought her clients home, he wondered. Indeed, was she his wife?

'Would you swear this is Peg Simpson?' he asked.

She gave him a sharp look, then made another inspection of the shrouded corpse, obviously seeking something.

'Aye, I would,' she said at length. 'She's got the mark o a burn on her arm, that I recall her getting at my fireside last

Yule. That's Peg. But her man should ken her and all,' she added, changing her tune slightly.

'And when did you see her last?' Gil persisted.

'I seen her yesterday afternoon,' said the man in the hide apron. 'I seen her in that blue kirtle that's lying outside on the grass, fetching a basket of bread home to your tavern, Jean.'

'Aye, that would be right,' said Mistress Howie after a moment's thought. 'I sent her for bread, maybe an hour after noon. She was ower long about it—'

'Aye, she would be,' said the man with the apron, 'seeing she was standing at the Wyndheid watching the procession come in, all the fine folks and their braw clothes on horseback coming here, and the horse-litter for the poor man that's on his deathbed, quite an entertainment it was.'

'Aye, it would be,' agreed Mistress Howie. 'So that's where she was, right enough? She denied it to me. Wait till I get a word wi her . . .' Her voice cracked as she realised what she was saying, and she suddenly pulled the tail of her linen headdress up across her face. 'Och, the poor lassie,' she said from behind it, muffled. 'She never deserved this.'

'Come away, Jean, and get a seat.' The woman in the striped kirtle drew her aside, and the hostel servant Bessie drew the shroud with care over the dead woman's face. Gil waited till Mistress Howie was settled on the stone bench at the wall-foot and then asked her again:

'When did you last see Peg Simpson, then? You saw her when she brought the bread back, I take it.'

'Oh, aye, for I'd to get the change off her. Then she was about the tavern, her and the other lassies, all the evening I'd ha said, though she took a couple trips out the back wi one fellow or another, her regulars they were,' Mistress Howie sniffed, and swallowed hard, 'but as to when I seen her last, it would ha been when we closed up, put the shutters up. After Compline, that would be.'

'Oh, well after it,' said the man in the green hood helpfully. 'Near midnight, it would ha been, Jean.'

'Nothing o the sort,' she said repressively.

'She was about at the end of the evening?' Gil persisted. 'You're certain you saw her then?'

'Well, I must ha done, for I never missed her. You could ask at the other lassies, if you're—' She paused, staring up at him. 'Are you saying maybe it was one o her regulars that's put her here? Is that why you're asking?' Gil nodded. 'Oh, I wouldny say that, maister. They're wild enough lads, but none o my customers would—'

'Someone did,' observed the man in the hide apron. Mistress Howie would have answered him, but there was a disturbance at the door of the chapel, where more spectators had gathered; a pushing and elbowing, a rising tide of indignant comments suddenly swallowed, heralded the arrival of a scrawny man with lank black hair and a scarred face, his blue bonnet clamped to his head by a stiff leather hood with a short cape. He dragged both these off as he emerged from the crowd, looking round desperately.

'Peg!' he said. 'Where is she? What's come to her?'

'You ken well enough what's come to her, Billy Baird,' responded Mistress Howie tartly. 'There she lies, dead and cold, covered in the marks you laid on her. You'll not raise your hand to her again, you ill-doer.'

'Peg!' said the newcomer again, ignoring all of this but the most significant point. He flung himself at the bier and pulled back the linen, stared for a horrified moment, and turned to the crowd.

'Who the hell did this? I swear by all the saints, if I find who's treated my Peg like that I'll have his lights for garters. Who did it?' he demanded, as if someone present was concealing the information.

'Listen to you!' said Mistress Howie scornfully. 'You'll be telling us next you never put a bruise on her yoursel!'

'I never put these on her,' said Baird fiercely. 'I never did more than show her what was right. A man can chastise his own woman, I suppose. Look at that, she's taen a vicious beating, way ayont what's reasonable!'

Gil, trying to imagine how one might find beating one's wife reasonable, said,

'When did you last see her?'

Baird turned dark eyes on him.

'Who're you?' he demanded aggressively. Several voices told him, with varying degrees of triumph, that this was the Archbishop's quaestor. He considered Gil with contempt, scratched at his codpiece, then said, 'Aye well, I hope you're on the trail of whoever slew her already.'

'I'm still trying to pick up the trail,' said Gil. 'So when did you see her last?'

The dark gaze slid away from his.

'That would be last night,' he said. 'No long after the alehouse closed.'

'Oh, the leear!' said Mistress Howie. 'When she slept at home wi you!'

'She never!' said the man desperately. 'She never, she went away out, and I wish she hadny! I tried to stop her!'

'A good tale that is,' said the man in the green hood.

'When did she go out?' Gil asked.

'After the alehouse closed. I said.' Baird brushed something from his eye. 'She came down the back to our place, and then she went out again.'

'Why?' Gil asked patiently. 'What took her out again, in the dark, after an evening's work?'

'He's having you on, maister,' said the woman in the striped kirtle. 'He's slew her himself, no doubt of it. Ask them 'at dwells down the same pend.'

'No I never!' protested Baird. 'I never did! She left me, she left our house, and I looked for her to come back, and she never did, no afore I had to go out to my work afore Prime. I never saw her again, till.' He stopped, staring at the bier, and scratched behind his codpiece again. 'Till now.'

'Why did she go out?' Gil asked again.

'She said she had to see someone. She wanted a word wi someone.'

'At that hour?' said the man in the hide apron. 'When decent folks are all in their beds? What was she about?'

'Maybe in someone's bed and all,' suggested another man, grinning. Baird lunged at him, roaring, and was restrained with difficulty by the man in the hide apron and his fellow with the green hood.

'Let me go!' he shouted, writhing in their grip. 'Let me at him, he'll no— Let me at him!'

'Who was it she went to see?' Gil asked him. 'What did she tell you about where she was going?'

'Nothing!' he said rather desperately. 'Just it was— She said something about he was back in town, she would get a word wi him.' He paused in his struggles and stared at Gil, and added, 'She didny sound as if he would enjoy it, but.' He read scepticism in Gil's face, and offered, 'Maybe she said more to the other lassies?'

'Likely she did,' agreed Mistress Howie with another of her abrupt changes of direction. 'You could ask at them, maister. I'll bid them tell you the truth.'

'Aye, where are your lassies, Jean?' asked the man in the green hood. 'I'm surprised they're no here and all, to see the show. Pay their respec's,' he corrected himself.

'I tellt them to get the house swep' and the day's kale on the fire, that's how they're no here,' retorted Mistress Howie.

'So are you going to take him up, maister?' asked the man in the hide apron. 'I'd say he slew her, myself, he should come afore the Provost for it, though I suppose he'll no hang.'

'Whoever killed her tied her to the Cross in place of Mistress Gibb,' Gil said. 'That could be seen as attempting to conceal it, which makes it secret murder—'

'Secret? Out in the open at the Cross like that?' said the woman in the striped kirtle, laughing.

'At the Cross?' repeated Baird incredulously. 'Are you saying that was my Peg they were talking about? Bound at the Wyndheid and left in the midnight? Will you two let me go?'

'No the Wyndheid,' several voices contradicted him. 'St Mungo's Cross in the kirkyard,' added the man in the green hood. Baird stared at him, then looked at Gil, who nodded confirmation.

'She was tied to St Mungo's Cross in place of the mad lady,' he agreed.

'What was she doing in the kirkyard?' Baird asked blankly. 'She hated the place, she'd never ha gone there in the daylight, far less in the dark, no for any money. She was feart for bogles, ever since someone tellt her some daft tale about a hand coming out a grave. What would take her there, maister?'

'That's right,' affirmed Mistress Howie. 'She'd never go near the High Kirk, aye worshipped in St Thomas' wee chapel out ayont the Port.'

'She'd ha been feart to death,' said Baird, his voice sounding constricted. 'Bound there and left to die. St Peter's bones, if I find who did that to my lassie I'll throttle him mysel, I'll no wait for the hangman to do it.'

'You stop that, you filthy leear,' said the man in the hide apron, shaking him. 'Right, maister, will we just take him round to the Provost the now while we've got our hands on him? Saves hunting for him later on.'

'No,' said Gil. There were indignant exclamations. 'No, let him go. I need a right word wi him, and I'm not doing it here with half the upper town looking on.'

'He'll run as soon as he's loosed,' said the woman in the striped kirtle.

'I will not, Agnes Wilkie,' said Baird, 'for that I'll be hunting for him that did that to Peg.'

'Let him go,' Gil repeated, and was obeyed with reluctance. 'And leave me wi him.'

Lowrie began to clear the chapel of the various bystanders, eventually persuading them that there was no more excitement to be had. When all that remained were Gil and Lowrie himself, the hostel servant Bess, and the man Baird, Gil led the porter over to the head of the bier and deliberately turned back the sheet to show the dead woman's face.

'Tell me when she went out,' he said. Baird looked down at the battered countenance, his mouth twisting.

'No much to tell,' he said, with fractured bravado. 'She cam round fro the alehouse when they'd put up the shutters, lifted her plaid and said she'd be away out.'

74

'Her plaid?' Gil repeated. 'What like is her plaid? You're certain she took it?'

'Well, it's no in the lodging, I'd to sleep cold. Just ordinar. Kind o brown checkit thing. Aye, that's it.' He nodded at the bundle Gil lifted from below the bier. 'That's hers. Can I get it back, maister? I was— I was right cold last night.'

'And what did you say when she said she would go out?' Gil prompted.

'I said, *Away out? At this hour?* and she said, *Aye. There's someone back in the town I need a word wi.*' He paused, scratching at his groin again, his face sour as if the memory tasted bad. As well it might, Gil thought. 'So I says, *Who would that be?* and she says, *Nobody you ken, Billy, though he's afflicted the both o us.* Then she goes away out. *Don't wait up,* she says, *I'll likely be a while.* And I never,' he dashed impatiently at his eye, 'I never seen her again. Till now.' He put out a hand and touched the bruised cheek with surprising tenderness. 'Peggy, lass, who was he? What did you do that he slew you this way?'

'She didny tell you who he was?'

'No a word.'

Gil went back over the man's statement in his mind.

'She said there was someone back in the town,' he repeated, 'and someone who had afflicted both of you. What did she mean by that? Your landlord, maybe?'

'No likely,' said Baird dismissively, 'it's Jean Howie rents us the place, or rents it to Peg any road. Likely she'll want me out o there now,' he added, 'seeing I canny bring in custom to her alehouse.'

'You think it might have been a matter of picking a fight with this man? Of having something out wi him?'

'It looks like it, doesn't it no?' retorted Baird with grim humour. 'No, I canny add aught to what I've tellt you, maister. The lassies 'at worked wi her might have more to say, she maybe told them whatever it was that was eating at her.'

'You're saying she was worried about something?'

'No worried,' contradicted Baird. 'More like annoyed. Something wasny right. I never asked her,' he said a little desperately, 'I thought she'd tell me when she cam in, maybe wi money in her purse. I'd naught but those few words wi her afore she went off into the night and I never seen her again till this. It's no right, maister! It's no justice!'

Following Gil out into the sunshine again, leaving Baird standing in baffled anger by the bier, Lowrie said quietly,

'Was she maybe putting the black on someone? Is that why she was killed?'

'It's possible,' said Gil. 'I wonder how this fellow had afflicted them both? And when he came back into the town?' He glanced at the sky, and snapped his fingers for Socrates, who obediently left the doorpost he was inspecting and came to his side. 'I think we need a word wi the lassies at the Trindle, and then it's high time we went home for the noon bite.'

Chapter Five

Jean Howie's alehouse presented itself much as Gil expected. It stood with its sagging stone gable facing the street, at the top of one of the long narrow tofts north of the Castle walls and just within the Stablegreen port. Tumbledown thatch lowered over the doorway, a similar building stood just beyond it, and a straggling line of sheds and shacks further along the path must include the lodging Billy Baird had shared with Peg. Beyond the fence at the far end of the toft was a stretch of common ground, and then the foot of the gardens of Vicars' Alley, where the songmen of St Mungo's dwelt. There was a sound of women weeping, and two gloomy men standing outside the house.

'Is this it?' said Lowrie doubtfully.

'The sign says it is,' Gil answered. The younger man looked at the weather-worn board hanging crookedly over the door; just recognisably it depicted a trindle, one of the long candles matched to the donor's height and coiled into a spiral which were pledged to one saint or another in return for favours granted.

'They aye make me think of dog-turds,' he remarked, following his superior along the path. 'Trindles. The way they curl round about.'

'Thank you for that,' said Gil. He nodded to the two men at the door, and rapped smartly on the doorjamb. Socrates returned from a brief jaunt down the path and sat down grinning at his feet.

'You'll get no assistance, neighbour,' said one of the

bystanders. 'A man could die o thirst in there the day, if he wasny drowned first wi them weeping.'

'Aye, well, they're a' owerset,' said his companion. 'One o their hoors is deid,' he explained to Gil, 'strangled to death at Glasgow Cross in the night so they're saying. It's only natural they should be out o sorts.'

Inside, the alehouse was dark, the fire burning low. The room seemed to be full of sour-smelling bodies huddled together in sobbing groups, but as his vision improved Gil made out Mistress Howie moving about by the two barrels of ale on their trestles, and no more than four other women, three at the single window with their arms about one another and one on her own by the hearth, stirring something in a pot. This one rose and came forward, wiping her eyes.

'You'll ha to forgive us, friend. Maister,' she corrected herself as she assessed Gil's clothing in the dimness. 'We're no serving the now, for we've just had bad news—'

'I ken that,' he said, raising his hat to her. Lowrie had taken up position by the door, the dog at his feet. 'I was hoping for a word wi all of you that worked beside Peg Simpson. It's possible she said something yesterday that might help me track down the man that slew her.'

'You found us, then,' said Mistress Howie from the tap. 'Aye, Sibby, answer his questions, and if you ken aught that would help, tell it him straight out.'

'It was that man o hers, for certain,' said one of the group by the window. 'Question him, why don't you, or just take him up afore the Provost—'

'I still need to know why she died,' said Gil. 'Did she tell any of you why she went out last night? Or where she was going?'

'I seen her,' said another woman by the window. She disengaged herself from the group and came nearer, rubbing at her arms as if she was cold. The sleeves of her kirtle were decorated with braid like Peg's. 'She went off down the road wi her plaid about her. You seen her and all, Mysie.'

The one who had spoken before nodded, saying, 'Aye, so I did.'

'What time would that be?'

'Just when we closed,' said Mysie. 'We'd put up the shutters, the mistress was barring the door ahint us.'

'It wasny full dark,' said the woman with the braided gown. 'Maybe ten o' the clock?'

'Had she said where she was going?' Gil asked.

There was general agreement that she had not.

'Never said much all afternoon,' contributed the fourth girl, and scratched at her belly through her gown.

'I thought she was in a strunt,' said Sibby, stirring her pot again. 'She was civil enough wi us, but she seemed right annoyed about something.'

'No just annoyed,' said Mysie. 'Spoiling for a fight, maybe.'

'I asked her what was eating her,' said the fourth girl, 'and she said, *Same thing as all of us. But I'll get him for it*, she said. That was all, Richie Allen wanted her out the back then and we said no more of it.'

'And is something eating all of you?' Gil said. What had she meant by that, he wondered. Surely not the lice which infested her gown, those were a hazard of everyday life against which respectable people waged continuous war. The women looked at one another, but Mistress Howie said briskly,

'No, indeed. My house is a happy house, maister. Well, the most o the time. The lassies all gets on well enough, don't you no?'

'Aye, we do, mistress,' agreed Sibby.

'What put Peg in a strunt?' Gil asked. 'Was she in a mood when she rose in the morning, or was it something through the day?'

'No, she was great in the morning,' said the scratcher. She seemed to have infected the others; the girl next her was rubbing uncomfortably at her apron. 'We'd a good laugh ower the last night's crocks, her and me.'

'No, I thought it was after the mistress gave her into trouble for being as long wi the day's breid,' said Mysie.

'She said naught to me,' said Mistress Howie, coming forward with a cup of ale in each hand, 'but then likely she wouldny.' She handed one of the cups to Gil, and drank to him from the other. 'Your good health, maister, and here's to a ready solution.'

'And yours, mistress, and all within here.' Gil raised the cup in turn.

''At's kind, maister. No, she took what I said to her quiet enough, seeing as I'd the right o it, and set about her tasks as she should. Never gave me no back-answers or nothing.' Gil preserved silence, and she sniffed, and wiped at her eyes with the tail of her headdress. 'Poor lassie, nobody deserves that.'

'I'm for the privy,' said one of the two still by the window, moving suddenly towards the back of the room. 'Canny wait any longer.'

'Good luck,' said somebody else under her breath. She grimaced, and slipped out into the daylight.

'What else was Peg speaking of in the day?' Gil asked

They looked at one another blankly. Heads were shaken in the dim light.

'Just ordinary things,' said Mysie. 'Nothing special. What like the day's broth was, what the baxter's lad said when she fetched the breid, that kind o thing.'

'She mentioned her bairn,' said Sibby. 'Said it would ha been its name day soon.'

'Lowrence, was it called?' said Lowrie, speaking for the first time.

'Aye.' She glanced at him. 'Said it was in a better place, she did, and then went on scouring the crocks.'

Ah, yes, thought Gil. The feast of St Lawrence would fall in a few days, name day of all called for the saint, when every Lawrence, Lowrence, Lowrie in Glasgow would be at the saint's altars; Peg Simpson would likely have found a penny for a candle in her baby's name.

'I suppose that might be why she was in a strunt, if that vexed her,' he suggested. More shaking of heads.

'She aye said Our Lady would look after it,' said Mysie. 'She wasny one to brood.'

And yet she went out to pick a fight with someone who had done her some sort of ill turn, Gil thought.

'And what about the customers? Was she speaking to—' He broke off, as a heartfelt, pain-filled wail reached his ears. It seemed to come from beyond the back door of the house. Lowrie, by the door, tensed and looked sharply at Gil. Mistress Howie ignored it; the other women looked at one another, one shrugged her shoulders, and another said,

'Go on, maister. What were you saying?'

The sound had stopped. He swallowed, gestured to Lowrie to relax, and continued, 'Was she speaking to any in particular? Who did she take out the back?'

'Out the back?' repeated Mistress Howie indignantly. 'Now that's atween me and them and poor Peg, maister, I canny tell you that, you must see!'

'Given that anyone else in the place would ken who she took wi her,' he retorted, 'no, mistress, I canny see.'

'He's right, at that, mistress,' said Sibby. 'And she might ha said something to one o them.'

This was not entirely Gil's meaning, but he let it pass.

'Richie Allen. Daniel Shearer,' said Mysie, 'I seen her wi him. And then wi Tammas Syme. Was there another one, Dorrit?'

'Never seen.'

The fourth girl slipped back into the house, moving uncomfortably, as if she was afraid she would break, and joined the group. Dorrit put an arm round her, and Mistress Howie said irritably,

'Aye, well, it was Will Thomson if ye must ken.' Gil looked over his shoulder to check that Lowrie was making a note of the names. 'But I'll no have my regulars harassed. If you go asking them in front o their wives what—'

'I'd never dream of it,' said Gil politely, 'unless they refused to answer me.'

Mistress Howie snorted, and turned back towards her barrels.

'Well, if you're done asking questions,' she said, 'ye

can either leave, or start paying for your ale. I've a house to run here.'

'I was never in a bawdy-house before,' said Lowrie diffidently, making down the hill past the rose-pink walls of the Castle. 'At least, I was in the Mermaiden when it was still—' He paused. 'That one was very different.'

'It was,' said Gil rather grimly. 'And no the kind of place I'd hope you'd frequent, save in a matter of the law. Long Mina takes better care of her girls, though I believe her prices reflect it. We'll go round by the Castle the now. I'd better warn Otterburn or his man Andro, for I'll wager their men use that place, handy as it is.' He looked round, and saw Lowrie's surprise. 'Those four all have the clap.'

'Oh.' Lowrie followed him a few paces further, then asked, 'How can you tell?'

'Later,' Gil said, very aware of the busy street. Half of Glasgow was going home for its midday meal, and this was no moment to discuss the signs of the afflictions of Venus: the privy itching, the burning water. It occurred to him that he had not foreseen this aspect of educating a young man when he took on an assistant.

Andro, the captain of the castle guard, was crossing the outer yard when they emerged from the gatehouse. He received the news with resignation, and promised to put the Trindle out of bounds to his men.

'No that it'll make much difference,' he said. 'Once that's abroad in a town there's only one way to avoid it, and they're never all going to take that road.' He eyed Gil. 'Where have you got to wi this missing woman, maister? Or the other one?'

'That's what took me to the Trindle. The dead girl is one of theirs, Peg Simpson, last seen last night when they closed up. I need to find who she went off to meet. As for the other, I was hoping you might have something for me.'

'No a thing.' Andro shook his head gloomily. 'We tramped all down the Girth Burn to the mill-burn, we've looked in sheds and outhouses and cellars and all, we've had as many sweirings from kitchen-wives. They're still out searching, but we're far enough fro the Cross now that if she was carried there to be hidden, you'd wonder why they bothered going so far. If you ken what I mean.'

'You think she's alive, then?'

'Or hid somewhere right cunning. Tell you truth, I think she's run off wi her lover. She never got untied fro the Cross hersel, somebody helped her and took her off. Likely she's at Edinburgh by now, though how she got out o Glasgow's anyone's guess, for she never passed the ports this morning, I've checked wi all my lads.'

'And the other lass? The dead one?'

'No, that's your problem, maister, none o mine.'

'Just the same, if any of your men was in the Trindle last night, I'd like a word.'

'You'll get it,' said Andro. 'And I'll get a word wi him too, whoever he is.'

'So you have one lassie vanished away without trace,' said Alys in her accented Scots, 'apparently in her shift, and another lassie who left her . . . her place of work to speak to someone unknown, and turns up beaten to death, tied to the Cross, and strangled. In that order?'

'In that order,' Gil confirmed.

'But are these the same matter?' She clasped her hands together, then spread them apart, looking from one to the other. 'Or are they separate?

'You tell me,' said Gil.

They were in the little solar at the back of the house, where they had retired after the midday repast along with small John and his toy horse, the last of the ale and a dish of sweetmeats. Now Lowrie handed the pewter dish to Catherine, who took a lozenge of apricot leather and said in disapproving French,

'The girl who has vanished must have been melancholy indeed, to make such a vow as you describe, *maistre*. I do not know why her priest permitted it.'

'But why?' said Alys. 'I can understand if she wished to

live without candles, though doing without coal in Scotland in winter seems to me a great folly, but why would she vow never to wash or comb her hair? She must have been crawling with—' She made a fastidious movement as if crushing something.

Lowrie offered,

'The Provost's captain was certain it would make her easy to trace, but I'm not so sure. She only has to wash herself and find some clothes, after all, to alter all that.'

'She must also be absolved of the vow,' Alys observed, 'or be guilty of perjury.' She withdrew her feet as John's little wooden horse galloped over them, and went on, 'Where would she find a priest for that? And would he see it as a moment to break the seal of confession and inform her friends?'

'This is the upper town,' Gil said ruefully. He seized John as the boy came within reach, and hauled him onto his knee. The harper's son, Ealasaidh's nephew and Gil's ward, was a handsome child nearing three years old, tall for his age with sparkling blue eyes and a mop of dark curls. 'Sit quiet a moment, John. She needny trouble the Cathedral or St Nicholas', she just has to rattle at the nearest door to find a priest behind it.'

'*C'est vrai, maistre,*' said Catherine. 'And his servant would not be bound by the seal of confession.'

'John *down*! No cuddle!'

'A good point, madame.' Gil let the child go, and looked at Lowrie. 'A task for you, then. Work your way out from the Cross, talking to servants, asking a different lot of questions. Not, Are they hiding Annie Gibb, but, Have they seen a woman in her shift at all?'

Lowrie pulled a face.

'Andro and his men will have crossed that trail,' he pointed out.

'I've every confidence in you.'

'But,' persisted Lowrie, reddening at the comment, 'you mind we thought they put the other lassie at the Cross to gain time. Is it worth hunting for her close by, or do we look further afield? Could she have left the burgh?'

'How would one get out of Glasgow in the night?' Alys wondered. 'The ports would all be barred, but I suppose some of the vennels lead out where one could get onto the Dow Hill or the Stablegreen.'

'In the dark,' said Lowrie. 'Here, John, horsie could run along the windowsill.'

'Someone that knows Glasgow, and well, could do it,' Gil said as the horse's wooden legs clattered on the sill. 'I don't think that applies to any of the party at St Catherine's, but I need to check. The brothers Muir might be more familiar wi the place, I'd say, given their kinsman's office at St Mungo's. I'd best get a word wi them and find out where they spent the night.'

'She might also have left by boat, or on a horse,' Alys said. 'But surely, if she has spent the last year or two dwelling in one chamber, not taking even her share of the work about the house, she has no strength to walk any distance.'

'That's a good point. Aye, I think we make sure of whether she's still within the burgh,' Gil said, 'afore we start looking outside.'

'Much depends,' said Catherine, 'on just how much help the lady had, as well as where it came from.'

Gil nodded, and downed the last of his cup of ale.

'I'll get a word wi Otterburn,' he said, 'and call on Canon Muir. Then I'll go and trouble St Catherine's some more. I'm not convinced the whole answer's there, but some of the questions lead back there, at least. Oh, and I need to find this ropewinder out towards Partick, and ask him about the cord.'

Alys rose, holding her hand out to the child. 'Come, John, shall we see if Nancy has finished helping Kittock with the crocks? You could take Euan out with you,' she added hopefully. 'Kittock finds him no use about the kitchen.'

'There's a coincidence,' said Gil.

'Och, indeed I was working hard on Maister Cunningham's behalf all the morning,' protested Euan. He nodded towards

85

the honey-coloured bulk of St Mungo's where it loomed above the houses on the north side of the Drygate. 'We was making certain, me and the vergers, that the lady was not hid about the High Kirk anywhere. I was never searching so big a building afore,' he added earnestly. 'You would be having no idea how many corners and stairs and chambers there are about the place, it is nothing like St Comghan's wee kirk at home.'

'Did you search the towers and all?' Gil asked, irritation giving way to amusement.

'Indeed we did. That Barnabas was saying there was no need, so naturally I would be making certain,' said Euan virtuously. 'Maister Cunningham has no need to concern himself wi St Mungo's now, the lady is never hidden there.'

'Thank you,' said Gil. He took a wide course round a tethered pig, with the dog adhering to his heels, and looked up and down the Drygate. Chickens and another pig or two foraged in the street, children were playing, a few stragglers were returning to work after their midday meal. Little knots of women made their way to call on one house or another for the afternoon, many with spindle or sewing or other handwork bundled in an apron. The conversation Gil caught was mostly about Annie Gibb, though the dead girl was mentioned.

'Away down to the Clyde,' he said to Euan, with sudden inspiration, 'and get a word wi the fisher-folk. See if any of them took a passenger anywhere out of Glasgow in the night.'

'You think she might ha sailed away out of Glasgow?' said Euan intelligently. 'Och, the cunning! Never you worry, maister, if that's what she did I'll be tracking her down.' He touched his blue felted bonnet and loped off towards the Wyndhead. Gil watched him go, suppressing relief. Euan had made himself moderately useful a few weeks since, when Gil had been summoned on the King's hunting trip to the Western Isles, but now he seemed to have attached himself to the household where he was a great deal less help.

Wondering what to do with the man, Gil followed him more slowly, to turn up along Rottenrow towards Canon Muir's manse.

He knew all the resident members of Chapter, having encountered them often enough in his uncle's house. As the Official of Glasgow, the senior judge of the diocese, David Cunningham had a certain level of state to keep up, and entertained his fellow-clerics regularly. While Gil had been his pupil, learning those secrets of the notary's craft which he was about to transmit to Lowrie, he had assisted at many such occasions, and recalled Canon Muir as elderly, slightly foolish, and a little too fond of his wine.

This was still the case.

'My cousin Dandy's boys,' the Canon agreed, smiling indulgently. 'Are they no the dearest laddies, Gilbert? And so handsome as they both are.' He sighed. 'They used to tell me I was bonnie-looking, but I'm sure I was never the equal o those two. They ought to be wed by now,' he went on, 'indeed Will Craigie's been quite urgent wi me on that head, to promote a marriage wi some kin o his for one or other, but as I said to him, you canny force a young man, it takes time to these things. I think they're ower fond o their freedom yet.'

Gil, seated on an uncomfortable carved wooden back-stool with the dog at his feet, preserved silence, and after a moment Canon Muir went on,

'And what was it you wished me to tell you? You think they're connected wi all this at St Mungo's Cross? No, no, I hardly think it. Two sic sweet-tempered laddies, they'd never be mixed up in the likes o that.'

'They're connected wi it already,' Gil pointed out, 'seeing they escorted the missing lady into Glasgow, and they claim kinship wi her aunt.'

'That's very true. There's much in what you're saying.' The Canon took refuge in his glass of claret. Emerging after a moment he said triumphantly, 'But they're no true kin o Ellen Shaw's, only by marriage. I think Will Craigie's closer kin to her. No that she hasny been a good friend to the laddies, looking about her for aught she can do for them, a good friend. Any road, Gilbert, they lay here last night, and I saw them to their bed mysel. Will you have more o this wine? It's right good, I had it from John Shaw at the College. And a wee cake, maybe?'

'They've a servant wi them, I think,' Gil said. 'Your kinsmen, I mean.' He accepted more of the claret, admiring the colour in the little glass.

'Aye, that's so. A good fellow, keeps those bonnie clothes right well, though I think, to tell truth, he might be a wee bit fond o his ale. No that I like to criticise a good worker, but my man William said he'd the deil's own task to rouse the fellow this morning.'

'He didny share the brothers' chamber, then?'

'Oh, aye, but William went in to waken him, that he might fetch the laddies their hot water to wash in, and a bite o bread and ale to break their fast. We ken well how to keep guests in this house, Gilbert. And they were all asleep, their man on his straw plett and Henry and Austin like mice in a nest in the shut-bed, so William said, so you needny suspicion they were out in the night snatching a lady off the Cross in the kirkyard. Beside,' concluded Canon Muir triumphantly, 'where would they put her? There's no lady hidden about this house, I assure you, son, and nowhere to put one if they tried.'

Gil had to admit to the truth of this. The manse was commodious, but the upper floor contained only one large hall and two small chambers. One of these was clearly Canon Muir's bedchamber, since his prayer-desk with two books propped on it and the corner of his box bed were visible round the open door. The other was the guest chamber in which the brothers were lodged, to judge by the way the Canon had gestured towards it. Here in the hall was one of those great beds which in Gil's experience were rarely used and never comfortable, its hangings of green dornick elaborate and rather dusty, and also the set of carved backstools and the benches and trestles for the long table where the household ate. The plate-cupboard at the far end of the hall bore a decent array of silver, including a large and very ugly salt, and a tall press in the corner suggested stored linen for the table. On the ground floor, the servant who admitted him had said, there was one huge storeroom and the kitchen from which the rather stale little cakes had emerged. Canon Muir's benefice was a rewarding one, Gil concluded.

'So Henry and Austin were here, were they,' he said, 'from when they arrived in Glasgow to the time they came out this morning, to ask after Annie Gibb's health? The lady that was tied to the Cross,' he elucidated, seeing the old man's blank expression.

'Oh! Oh, I see what you're asking me. Aye, a course they were, for they'd all the news o Ayrshire to let me hear, and word o our kin, and so forth, so they sat and talked wi me after dinner a long time afore they went out to see their friends. But the lady wasny there to ask after, was she? She'd been snatched away. Is that no a strange thing? Who'd want to carry off a mad lady? Is she very wealthy?'

'I'd say so.'

'Likely that's it, then. Someone will wed her out of hand and shut her away while he gets the benefit of her lands. Well, so long's he takes good enough care o her, I suppose it's an act o Christian charity to keep the poor soul safe. But is her kin no all out hunting for her? Surely,' said Canon Muir, putting his finger accurately on what troubled Gil, 'surely they'd want to keep hold o her lands for theirsels, they must want to fetch her back.'

'You'd think so,' Gil agreed. 'What friends are those that the two of them went out to meet? Henry and Austin, I mean.'

Canon Muir paused for a moment's thought, then shook his head. 'They never said. Likely some of the young fellows about the town.'

'And did you hear them come in?'

'Oh, aye, I was still about the place. I saw them to their bed myself, I told you, Gilbert. I never sleep much nowadays,' the old man confided improbably, 'it's hardly worth

89

my while lying down afore midnight, so a course I was still up when they came in.'

Dissatisfied, Gil refused another glass of claret and took his leave, following Rottenrow out along its length, past the port at the end of the street where the guard dozed in his shelter, and onto the land called the Pallioun Croft. The roadway ran along the brow of a steep slope here, and quickly deteriorated into a muddy track, which shortly angled down towards the river and joined the Thenewgate to head for Partick and then out towards Dumbarton. It was not much frequented; he paused on the crest of the slope to survey the scene, but saw nobody about, and there were few footprints and only the marks of one light cart in the mud. Birds sang in the bushes, some of the burgh cattle grazed on the grassy slopes. Otterburn's clerk had described the ropewalk as being *almost at Partick*. It was a pleasant day for a walk, he decided, and set off.

Socrates launched himself from his side with delight, running in great loops through the grass and bushes, appearing over the roadside dyke from time to time to grin at his master, then vanishing again. Gil found himself grinning in return at his dog's pleasure, but the grin did not stay in place. The problems which confronted him were bewildering indeed. He knew better than to expect to identify Peg Simpson's killer this soon, but Annie Gibb's disappearance perplexed him. She could hardly be hiding out here, he thought. *My bed schal be under the grenwod tre, a tufft of brakes under my hed.* Hardly likely for a gently bred, reclusive girl. Canon Muir, like Lowrie, had hit on the likeliest explanation for it: someone had carried her off hoping to lay hands on her wealth. But in that case, who? Why had he, or they, not contacted the girl's kin already to ask for her title deeds? Why had Sir Edward, or even Lockhart, no idea who might be responsible? No, that's unfair, he thought, when I spoke to Lockhart we still reckoned it was Annie who was dead. I need to speak to him again. But if she went willingly, why did she do it this way? Why not simply agree to someone's proposal of marriage, get absolution from the ridiculous vow, and wash? Perhaps her pride would suffer too much if she did that. And why did she not tell her friends, the servants who knew her since she was a child? I need to talk this through with Alys, he thought, as he forded one of the many small burns which ran down through the grazing-lands to the Clyde. Socrates splashed through the stony shallows behind him and paused to shake himself, the drops flying from his rough coat glittering in the sunlight.

Matt Dickson the rope-drawer proved to be a sturdy man in his forties, in a sleeveless jerkin and patched hose, his shirtsleeves rolled well up. When Gil entered the long, low shed by one of its many doors he was measuring off a new rope in armspans, counting aloud as he worked, a raw-boned journeyman coiling it down beside him.

'And twelve. I'll be a moment longer, maister,' he called. Gil nodded, and stood quietly, looking about him with interest. He had vaguely imagined something like a huge spinning-gallery, with hemp instead of flax or wool, but this was quite different. On a floor of beaten earth, a long groove showed the track of the rope-workers between a thing like a child's windmill toy, mounted on a solid trestle, and a second smaller trestle on two wheels, with a large hook which could clearly turn by means of a handle. How did that work, he wondered. Other tools stood about or leaned against the walls – surely that was not a hay-rake? Hanks and balls and bales of the product of the craft were all about, hung from the rafters or stacked in neat heaps ready for baling, and over everything a cloud of dust, presumably hemp dust, danced thickly in the beams of sunlight which leaned in at the doors.

'And twenty-one – and twenty-two – and three,' said Maister Dickson finally. 'And if four spans is seven ells, then that's,' his lips moved silently for a moment, 'forty ells near enough. Aye, tie it off, Patey, and put it by. Maister Mason's man was to come for it the morn.'

'A rope for my good-faither?' Gil said, surprised. 'I suppose he must use rope, like most of the trades.'

'Our Lady love you, a course he uses rope,' said Dickson, laughing indulgently. 'Cord by the bale for his scaffolding, rope for his hoist, twine to tie off his sacks o lime to keep the rain out. Just like near every craftsman in Glasgow. There's other folk laying rope about the burgh,' he conceded, 'but it's all small stuff. If Patey and Andy and me,' he nodded at an equally scraggy apprentice who was sorting hanks of flax nearby, 'wasny at our trade the whole town would come to a halt. That rope's for a new hoist your good-faither's about to put in where he's working at the High Kirk, to lift the stone up to where it's needed.'

I should have mentioned this to Pierre, Gil thought, and saved myself the walk. But would Luke, much less Berthold, ask the right questions?

'I know what rope is, but what's the difference between cord and twine?' he asked.

'Cord's corded, maister, and twine's no but twined. Andy!' The apprentice jumped up from his work and went to his master's high desk where the order-book lay almost submerged in small balls and hanks of cordage. He brought two of these, and Maister Dickson nodded approvingly. 'Show it all to Maister Cunningham, then, laddie. Let us hear what you've learned.'

Listening to the boy's hesitant exposition of the stages of ropemaking, Gil compared the samples he was showing him with the ell-and-a-half of cord still in his purse. It was cord rather than twine, he could say now, since rather than being a simple twist of many fibres of hemp it was made up of several such strands twisted together, but its use was still unclear. Young Andy was gesturing at the instruments in the middle of the floor, describing rather incoherently how they worked; Gil had already lost track of left-hand and right-hand twists. One probably had to know what the boy was talking about to understand him.

'Aye, very good, laddie,' said Dickson as the stumbling description ground to a halt. 'Well said. So that's the difference, Maister Cunningham. So was it cord or twine, then?

Maybe a bale o twine for the garden o yir new house? Needs a bit work, so I've heard.'

'Neither, in fact,' said Gil, irritated by this. 'I've no doubt my wife will order what she sees needful. No, I came out here to get an expert's view on this.' He opened his purse, slipped the boy Andy a penny in reward, and held out the coils of cord. 'What can you tell me about it, maister?'

'*Tell* you?' Dickson glanced at him curiously, and took the hank. Shaking it out he measured its length, inspected the ends, separated the strands to test how tightly it was twisted, picked with a chewed fingernail at the fibres of each strand. The journeyman came to join him, doing much the same with the other end of the cord.

'It's no ours, is it, maister?' he said at length.

'I'd hope no, Patey,' said Dickson sternly. 'It's no evenly twistit, the strands is no equal, it's a mix o hemp and flax. Andy there could lay a better cord. Where did you come by this, maister? I hope you didny pay out good money for it?'

'No,' Gil admitted. 'Did you hear about the lassie at St Mungo's Cross ?'

They had not. It was too far out of Glasgow for someone to come simply to bear gossip, and quite likely they carried their own noon bite with them, rather than walk home and back again. Gil gave as moderate an account as he might of how the length of cord had been found, but the facts themselves were enough to make Patey's eyes pop out.

'This very cord, maister?' he said with relish, his grasp on the loops tightening. 'And put about her neck to throttle her?'

'After she was dead,' Gil confirmed. 'So I'd like fine to ken where it came from, what sort of use it might be sold for, since I doubt whether it was sold for strangling lassies.'

'Oh, very good!' said Dickson, laughing. 'The idea!' He studied the loops of cord again, picked at the neatly lashed end he held, and peered at the other end still clutched in Patey's bony hand, while the apprentice stared longingly from a few feet away. 'It's been cut out o a greater length, see, and bound off both ends. It's the exact length it needs to be and it's to be put to use a good few times, whatever use that is, and that's as much as I can say.' He considered a little longer, and added, 'Aye, well, it's no unlike the cord George Paterson lays, off the Drygate. He's about the longest walk in the burgh, maister, can put up thirty ells, works alone wi his oldest boy. You could ask at him if he kens this quality.'

Prising the evidence with difficulty from Patey's grasp, Gil took his leave, whistled up his reluctant dog and set off back into Glasgow. He had no idea of a cordage-spinner on the Drygate, but no doubt Alys would know where he lived.

Sir Simon was in the outer yard of the pilgrim hostel, deep in Latin discussion with the doctor, their gowns contrasting vividly in the sunlight. As Gil entered at the gate, Doctor Januar looked up in some relief and said,

'Perhaps Maister Cunningham can tell me. Is there to be a quest on the dead woman, *magister*? When will it be?'

'Not before tomorrow,' Gil said in the same language, 'or even the day after. Is it a problem?'

'No,' said Januar unconvincingly.

'And how's your patient?' Gil asked in Scots. The doctor bent his head.

'Sinking,' he said gravely. 'I would estimate he has two days at most.'

'Our Lady send him a quiet end,' Gil said. 'I suspected as much, when I saw him earlier.' He looked hard at Januar. 'I'd like to be able to bring him news o Mistress Gibb afore his end, if that's possible—'

'Surely nothing could ease his last hours better,' offered Sir Simon. 'Supposing it's good news, a course.'

'—so I need to ask more questions of the rest of the party here.'

'I have told you all I can,' said the doctor after a moment.

'Na'the less, I've questions for you and all.' Gil looked about. 'Sir Simon, might I use your chamber? The other courtyard has too many windows and doors onto it.'

Seated in the paper-strewn chamber, a jug of ale from the kitchen at hand, Gil studied Chrysostom Januar and said in Scots,

'You're gey reluctant to be questioned, *magister*. It makes a man wonder what you might be hiding.'

'We doctors dislike answering questions.' The Latin was professionally inscrutable. 'The patient never asks the ones to which we have an answer.'

'I know how that feels,' Gil said ambiguously. 'Now, I've heard that the outer yett to the hostel, which is through the wall from the bed the two St Catherine's servants sleep in, went three times in the night.'

'*Three* times?' The doctor's bright blue gaze flicked up to his face, and away again. 'How strange. One might expect twice, or four times, but three times suggests that someone left and did not return, or entered and did not leave.'

'Or, I suppose, two people went out together and came back at different times,' Gil said. 'Would you maybe like to reconsider what you said, about nobody being out o the hostel in the night?'

'None o those that slept in the men's hostel left their beds,' said the doctor in Scots after a moment. 'I suppose Sir Edward's daughters might ha slipped past Dame Ellen, though who they would go out to meet I canny imagine.'

'Were you out of the hostel yourself?'

'I had a patient to care for,' said Januar, the blue gaze very direct this time.

'Has any of the family ever mentioned a connection in Glasgow? Anyone Annie might turn to?'

'No that I recall. But mind, *magister*, I have little conversation with the most part of the household. My patient, obviously, and his manservant, some of the outside servants when I have need of herbs from the garden, but otherwise the rest of them come little in my way.'

That isn't what you said earlier, Gil reflected.

'Mistress Gibb is abroad in Glasgow,' he said, 'barefoot in her shift. Are you not concerned for her?'

'Aye,' said the doctor, 'concerned indeed, but I'm also

concerned for my patient, and I'm a stranger here. You and the Provost's men can seek Annie Gibb more effectively than I can.'

'Not noticeably, this far,' said Gil wryly. 'Very well, maister, I'll let you back to your patient. Have you any idea where John Lockhart might be?'

Chapter Six

Lockhart, despatched from the men's hall, appeared less formally clad than he had been this morning, his shirt cuffs rolled up over the short sleeves of a leather doublet.

'I've had the men out, searching the green out there,' he said, waving a muscular arm. 'What d'ye call it, the Stablegreen? And asking questions all up the street here as far's the port ayont the Castle. I ken it's no much, but it's about all we can do, seeing we're no familiar wi the burgh.'

And muddying the waters for anyone seeking Peg Simpson, Gil thought resignedly.

'What have you been asking? Have you learned anything?'

'Nothing useful,' admitted Lockhart. 'One or two folks saw a lassie on her own coming down Castle Street, but that was well afore midnight. There's no woman been seen coming away from St Mungo's kirkyard in the night, and those that were seen this morning were all kent faces, folk could put a name to them.'

'Who saw the lassie on Castle Street?'

'Oh, I couldny tell you. Just folk we asked, I never made a note. Why?'

'Because that might ha been the lassie that's lying dead in the chapel here,' Gil said patiently. 'I need to trace her, find where she went.'

'That's little enough o my concern,' said Lockhart.

'Oh, I think you're wrong,' said Gil very politely. 'I'd say it's likely that whoever loosed Annie Gibb from the Cross tied Peg Simpson to it afterwards, so if we learn more about the one, we'll ken more about the other.'

'Oh!' Lockhart digested this. 'I see what you mean. I'll ask at the men, see if they recall who it was.'

'Did you find anything else? What were you asking, anyway?'

'No that I mind.' The other man screwed up his face in an effort of recollection. 'We were saying to folk, had they been abroad late yestreen, or early the day morn, or even looked out at door or window, and had they seen aught unfamiliar. And none had.'

It could be worse, Gil thought, and drew out his tablets.

'Give me a note o where you asked, who you spoke to if you can recall it. No sense in me going over the same ground.'

Listing these took some time, but eventually Lockhart ran to a halt, blew out his cheeks and said,

'I canny think where or who we spoke to more than that. Oh, maybe a couple houses round into, is it the Drygate? And we did tell folk, if they minded aught after we'd gone on, they should bring it here. So likely if there's anything useful, it'll turn up at the yett.'

'Very likely,' said Gil, concealing scepticism. He closed his tablets and put them back in his purse. 'Let me know if you mind anything else that might help. And another thing you might tell me – was anyone out of the hostel in the night?'

'Out of the hostel?' Lockhart stared. 'Why would— What, you think it was one of us? What would we do that for, after all the trouble it's taken to get the lassie to St Mungo's?'

'Nevertheless, the hostel door went three times, I'm tellt. More than one person was out, and if they were nothing to do wi Annie or the dead woman they might still ha seen something to the purpose.'

'Well, it wasny me, or any from the men's hall,' asserted Lockhart, 'for I was right by the door, and I'd ha heard any leaving, and I'll never believe that any o the lassies got past Dame Ellen, she takes right good care o my good-sisters and the rest o the household.'

'Did all the servants sleep in the guest-halls?' Gil asked. 'None in the stables?'

'Aye, we're all in the two halls.' Lockhart stared at him a little longer, then said, 'No, I canny think that any o the men would ha got by me either. I heard the doctor moving about, and the like, he was to be my bedfellow but I think he never lay down all night, though he did at least change his clothes, he's in his second-best gown the day, that red-and-yellow, no the gold. Looks like a papingo, does he no! I think he let the man Doddie get his rest after seeing to my good-faither on the journey. I'd ha noticed the hall door opening.'

Gil nodded.

'Would you ken,' he asked carefully, 'whether Mistress Gibb had any friends or kindred about Glasgow? Anyone she could turn to? Someone must ha taken her in, if she's not lying under a dyke somewhere.'

'No that I ever heard mentioned,' said the other man firmly. 'But I'd little conversation wi the lassie hersel, y'ken, and never a lot wi her good-sisters. I'd not say my wife has spoken of it either.'

'Or any who've asked Sir Edward for her, that might have gone this length to make certain of her and her lands?'

Lockhart stared at him, blew out his cheeks again, and said,

'Well! That's a thought, maister. I'd need to chew on it a bit, there's been one or two folk hoping for her hand in the past year, by what my wife has heard.'

'Sir Edward hinted as much,' Gil agreed, 'though he's not fit to recall names.'

Lockhart grimaced, and nodded.

'I'll think on it, try if I can mind who it was. It was all Ayrshire names my wife mentioned, you understand, smaller lairds, no folk I'd ken well. As for who she might turn to, you'd do better to ask at Dame Ellen, or at Nicholas or Ursula. They'd likely mind if she mentioned sic a thing when she was first living in that house, for I think she was more inclined to speak o hersel then. Or her woman might have some knowledge. Aye, you should talk to them.'

Dame Ellen was not inclined to be helpful.

'Oh, no, maister. None of the lassies left the hall in the

night,' she stated, in a tone that invited no discussion. 'Neither Meggot nor my nieces. By Our Lady's mantle, I'd ha known the reason why if any had tried it. Ask at Sir Simon, why don't you,' she added, with another dreadful simper, 'maybe it was him on some errand. Priests ha calls on their time the rest o us areny troubled wi. No, I've never a notion o friends Annie might turn to round here. Her mother? Why are you asking me about her mother? She's long deid, poor lass.'

'I'd like to know where she was from.'

Dame Ellen gave a little thought to this, eyes cast piously upward.

'I believe she was a Renfrew woman. Long deid, as I say. Was she a Wallace, maybe?' She shook her head. 'If she wasny a Wallace, I've no idea who she was. Sir, you'd surely be better out hunting for the lassie, instead o harassing me wi questions I've no answer to?'

'I need a word wi Meggot,' said Gil, 'and maybe wi your own woman.'

'Oh, no, maister, you'll ha to go into Ayrshire for that, then,' she divulged, 'for I never brought her wi me, daft piece that she is, I reckoned to do better without her. I'll fetch Meggot out to you.'

But interviewed across the courtyard from Dame Ellen's watchful eye and tapping foot, Meggot could add little to this.

'I think her mammy was a Wallace,' she agreed, 'though no from Elderslie. Somewhere else in Renfrewshire, I'm sure she said once. I'm sorry, maister, I canny mind clearer than that. As to friends around Glasgow, no, she never mentioned any. Her daddy was an Ayrshire man, had no kindred in these parts, nor her mammy neither that I recall.'

'Meggot.' Gil looked directly at her. She held his gaze for a moment, then blushed and looked away. 'You're fond of her, you said that.' She nodded, tightening her lips. 'She's adrift in a strange place, wi no clothes to her back. I want to find her. Can you tell me nothing that would help her?'

She shook her head, whispering,

'No, maister, I canny.' Tears sprang to her eyes. 'If I knew aught I'd tell you it, so I would. I—' Her glance slid sideways, to where Dame Ellen still glared attentively. 'It seems to me, sir,' she went on, still whispering, 'she must ha had help, maybe she had plans made, but who it was helped her or where she's gone I canny think, it was none o the household that Sawney or me can discover.' She looked up earnestly at Gil. 'Wherever she is, I hope she's safe, the poor lass.'

Gil dismissed the woman, thanked Dame Ellen without real gratitude, and looked at the sky. The sunny morning had changed into a cloudy afternoon with a brisk, chilly wind; it would probably rain before dark, but meantime he could tell that it was getting towards dinnertime. If he could track down the cordmaker on the Drygate, he might just catch the man before his day's work ended.

George Paterson's ropewalk was easier to find than he expected; the second passer-by he asked directed him onto the back-lands behind a sagging wooden house not far down the hill from the House of the Mermaiden. Rounding the crooked gable he found himself looking down a long toft, with the trees lining the Girth Burn at its foot and – could that be the back of the Sub-Dean's house opposite?

'Oh, aye,' agreed Paterson himself when he located him. 'Tell truth, that's how I got the St Mungo's trade. If you don't ask, you don't get, see, and I just took a couple hanks a good cord ower the burn and showed it to Dean Henderson, and he tellt me to take it to the Almoner, and Almoner Jamieson was pleased wi't as a donation, and said he'd take more as a purchase. Three year syne, that was, three year at Michaelmas next. No, lad, leave that bale sep'rate, I haveny proved it yet.' He scowled at his son, and said aside to Gil, 'Him and his friends were up to some mischief last night, he's no use to me the day. Laddies, eh?'

They were in the ropewalk itself, a long shed like the one out towards Partick, though narrower and less cluttered. The machinery was less ponderous as well; presumably this reflected the fact that Paterson made cord rather than

101

rope. His son obediently put down the bale of raw hemp, and pulled the canvas wrapping over the fibre. He was a gangling, slow-moving boy of fifteen or so, all hands and feet and elbows, but would be very like his father when he stopped growing; both were tall for Glasgow men, though shorter than Gil, with ragged mouse-coloured hair and well-worn working clothes.

'You deal wi St Mungo's?' Gil said.

'Oh, aye. They take all the twelve-ply and most o the six-ply we can make. I ask a fair price, maister, and the Almoner gets fair value, we're all satisfied wi the outcome.' Gil nodded at this, and produced the length of cord from his purse. Paterson looked sharply at it. 'That looks like some o my six-ply.'

Gil handed the coils over, and the man studied it much as Matt Dickson had done, untwisting the tight spirals, picking at the fibres, inspecting the lashed ends.

'Aye, I'd say it's mine,' he pronounced at last. 'The colour's gey like the last batch o hemp we had, that I'd to put some flax to a cause it was that coarse. Here, is this what they used to throttle that lassie at the Cross? Some o my cord?' His son looked round, then hastily back to his work when his father glared at him.

'It was,' Gil admitted. 'So I'd like to ken where it came from. Did you send all that batch to St Mungo's, or did some of it go elsewhere?'

'Well, this has been to St Mungo's, for certain,' observed Paterson, 'for that's how they finish it when they've to cut a length, bound off wi some o my single twine so it willny ravel. See, most folks just ties a knot, but if you're wanting your length to last a while and do you duty you need to finish it off right. Jamieson understands that, and so does his vergers, those that help him in his office.'

'So I should have shown it to Alan Jamieson when I saw him,' Gil said. 'How d'you deliver it?' Paterson looked puzzled. 'In hanks, of course, but do you take it to Maister Jamieson himself, or to the Vicars' hall, or just leave it at the tower door?'

'Oh, I see! No, the lad takes it round to the hall, time when we ken the Almoner's going to be there, so he can mark the tally for him. Given into Alan Jamieson's hands, it is, maister. George!' The boy looked up from the cord he was winding. 'Mind this lot? You gave it to the Almoner hissel, did you no?'

The youngster came closer and touched his blue bonnet to Gil, peering at the loops of cord in his father's hand.

'Aye,' he said. 'Likely.'

'Did you or no?' Paterson demanded. His heir shrugged.

'Likely,' he said. 'I canny mind, Da!' he protested as his father drew breath to remonstrate.

'Do you ken Maister Mason's boy Luke?' Gil asked. Young George considered the question, and shrugged again.

'Likely,' he admitted. This time he was not fast enough to avoid his father's hand.

'You be civil to Maister Cunningham, that's our neighbour and a freen o the Almoner!' commanded the elder George.

'Aye,' said the boy, sulkily rubbing his ear. 'I ken him,' he expanded. 'He's wi the High Street band, in't he no?'

'Ah.' Gil considered this aspect of burgh life, recollections of his student days rising in his memory. The apprentices of the burgh banded together by street, High Street against Gallowgate or Thenewgate, Drygate against the small Upper Town group; the younger students of the College formed another, larger band. In general the rivalry confined itself to chanting, thrown stones and the occasional scuffle or game of football, but from time to time it exploded into violence. Several apprentices seemed to have been abroad yesterday evening. 'Was it a battle?' he asked. 'Last night, I mean. The moon was, what, well past the quarter, there would be plenty light.'

Another shrug and a, 'Likely.'

'Who was it? The Drygate and who else?'

'Answer Maister Cunningham,' ordered Paterson. After a moment his son mumbled something which might have been,

'High Street. Stablegreen.'

'I hope the Drygate won.' This earned a reluctant grin, delivered sideways under the mouse-coloured thatch. Encouraged, Gil went on, 'If you mind anything more about this cord, you can let me hear it, or bring it to my man Lowrie. Or aught else you think of that might help me. I want to find who killed the lassie at the Cross.'

'Aye, wi some o our cord!' said the elder Paterson energetically. 'Aught we can do to help, maister, we'll do right willingly, me and the boy both!'

'And what did the Almoner say?' asked Alys.

'He agreed it was likely some of his,' Gil said, carving a slice off the roast before him. 'When it comes into the store, one of the vergers, a fellow called Matthew, cuts it down into lengths of an ell or an ell and a half, and whips the ends. It's kept on a shelf in the dry store, a box for each length, very methodical. The piece we have is gey like the longer lengths that Jamieson uses to bind up the great sacks of donated goods, though I'd not say he knew which one it came off.'

'That would be too much to expect,' said Alys gravely. She accepted a second slice of meat, and held her platter while Gil spooned gravy from around the roast. 'And what have you learned, Lowrie?'

'Some new oaths,' said Lowrie ruefully. 'Nobody had seen a lady in her shift in any of the houses near the kirkyard, much though some of them might have wanted to.'

'So we can discount that idea, and give thought to something else,' said Gil. 'Good work.'

'*Maistre le notaire, votr' valet n'est pas rentré,*' observed Catherine as Gil helped her to a share of the gravy to savour her platter of pounded roots.

'Euan knows when the dinner goes on the table,' said Alys. 'Gil, surely the woman at the Cross is not connected with the theft from the Almoner's stores? It did not sound as if she had any means at all, much less what she should not have had.'

'No, I agree.' Gil served Lowrie and then himself with slices of the roast. 'She may be connected, but not because she was involved in the thieving.'

'So what do we know, maister?' asked Lowrie.

'I've told you often enough,' said Gil, 'use my name. We're both sons of the College of Glasgow, whatever else is between us.' He used his eating-knife to cut the meat on his platter into smaller pieces, while Lowrie muttered something in embarrassment. 'We're still at the stage where we have a great handful of facts which might or might not be related, and no idea how they join up. One lassie was freed from the Cross in the middle of the night, by one or more people, and then vanished in her shift. Nobody seems to have heard of any friends she might have hereabouts, and nobody admits to having seen her.'

'Why?' prompted Alys.

'We don't know that either.'

'The reason,' said Catherine in her elegant toothless French, 'that the girl was freed and has vanished may indicate the person who freed her.'

'Very true, madame,' agreed Gil, and translated quickly for Lowrie, 'but I'd be grateful for hearing anything at all about her.'

'And the other lassie,' said Alys. 'Peg, is that her name?'

'Last seen about ten o'clock leaving the Trindle, turned up dead and bound to the Cross wearing Annie Gibb's sacking gown and her own plaid—'

'Then Annie had more to wear than her shift,' said Alys. 'Or she would have kept the plaid, rather than leave it with a dead woman.' She chewed thoughtfully for a moment, swallowed, and said, 'What time did you think Peg had been left there?'

'Not long after she died, your father reckoned.'

'I thought that was the cord,' said Lowrie.

'Aye, you're right,' agreed Gil, running the conversation through his mind again. 'He said the cord was in place before she began to stiffen.'

'Could it have been,' Alys checked, grimaced, and went

on, 'could she have been throttled before she was tied to the Cross?'

'Mai— Gil thought not,' said Lowrie, 'because of the way her hair was caught under the cord.'

'So she was killed, and then stripped and tied to the Cross, and then throttled,' said Alys, 'all before she began to stiffen, although not necessarily all in one set of actions.'

'If the woman who is dead,' pronounced Catherine, 'was killed merely in order to distract the demoiselle Gibb's friends, that is a great crime. If she was killed by another person, for some other reason, then the demoiselle was fortunate not to encounter the killer herself.'

'The town must have been going like a fair last night,' Gil said wryly. 'The prentices had a battle appointed and all, High Street, Drygate and Stablegreen.'

'Could some of them have killed Peg?' Alys asked. 'Or spirited Annie Gibb away?'

'I'd not ha thought it,' Gil said. 'The night battles aye used to be a matter of stalking, of pursuit and capture. We never involved the townsfolk if we could help it. Lowrie, was it the same when you were a bejant?'

'It was,' agreed Lowrie, his first year at the College much more recently behind him. 'Is it worth speaking to Maister Mason's fellow Luke? Or to young Berthold?' He checked, his eyebrows going up. 'Did Maister Mason not say Berthold was useless the day? That sounds as if he was abroad last night, for certain.'

'Then you may both go down there after the dinner,' said Alys, 'and speak to them.'

Opposite her, Catherine looked disapproving, but said nothing. It was useless, Gil knew, to suggest Alys came too. They had both visited formally since the marriage, but Ealasaidh did not encourage dropping in.

The household at the White Castle had apparently dined later than that at the Mermaiden, and was still at table when Gil knocked on the broad planks of the door. Luke opened it, and greeted them with a wide grin.

'Come away in, Maister Gil! That is—' He looked over his shoulder, but his master endorsed the invitation from his great chair at the head of the board.

'Yes, yes, come away in, Gilbert, take a seat! We have eaten most of the food, but you will take an oatcake and a mouthful of ale? Usquebae? Lowrie, you will take something too?'

Gil bowed to Ealasaidh where she sat tall and forbidding at Maistre Pierre's right hand, and flourished his hat in a general greeting to the rest of the household ranged along the great board. Apart from Luke, now waiting to take their plaids, young Berthold and the mason's older man Thomas were the only familiar faces; four women in various forms of the dress of the Highlands stared at him with what seemed like faint hostility. Berthold, on the other hand, was looking terrified. What has the boy been up to, thought Gil, accepting a beaker of ale and a buttered oatcake.

'What progress have you made?' his father-in-law was asking him. 'Is there no trace of the missing lady?'

'And is that right,' said Ealasaidh disapprovingly, 'that she does not wash herself nor comb her hair since her man died?'

'Little progress.' Yet again, Gil summarised what he had learned that afternoon, while the four Erschewomen whispered in their own language and Luke and Thomas craned to hear him. Both Maistre Pierre and his wife exclaimed over the thefts from the Almoner's stores.

'But does he not guard the place?' the mason wondered. 'How do the goods vanish?'

'Is the one who died the thief, perhaps,' suggested Ealasaidh, 'or was she maybe meeting them at the wrong moment, the way they were killing her?'

'That was what Alys thought, too,' Gil said, and saw her face darken. What was it between the two of them, he wondered. 'I don't think there's any connection, myself, but I'll keep an open mind. What I would like, Pierre, is a word wi Luke.' Further down the table, the boy's expression changed. 'I think he was abroad last night, and Berthold too. I'd like to hear if they saw anything – or nothing, for that matter.'

'Willingly,' said their master, 'though I must still translate for Berthold, unless you think you may understand him, Lowrie?'

'I'd be grateful, maister,' said Lowrie. 'He's grasped a few instructions by now, but I'd not ken where to start asking him something like this.'

Luke, summoned from his place at the board to talk more privately by the hearth, looked apprehensive but admitted readily enough that he had been part of the night's battle.

'Who else was out?' Gil asked. The boy considered, tugging at his untidy thatch of hair, his blue knitted bonnet clamped under the other arm.

'There was all the High Street,' he reckoned up, 'and the Drygate, and the Stablegreen. There's no so many of the Stablegreen,' he expanded, 'they mostly allies themselves wi the Drygate when we've a battle. It wasny serious, see, it was just a chase. There was rules.'

'What were they?' Gil recalled the distinction from his youth. A chase with rules usually meant there was no fighting, or at least no serious fighting; there might be a target to defend or capture, or some territory to be crossed without being caught, but always there was the Watch to be avoided.

'We was to start at the Bell o' the Brae and take the Girth Cross up at the Wyndhead,' said Luke, 'seeing there was a moon, but honest, Maister Gil, none o us saw aught o a lady in her shift, and she'd ha showed up in the moonlight, sure she would.'

'Did you see anybody at all moving about the Wyndhead?' Luke shook his head. 'Not on the Drygate, Rottenrow, the Stablegreen?'

'It was late, Maister Gil. Folk was a' gone hame by then. I got a glimp' o two fellows,' the boy admitted, 'came out o Rottenrow, turned up by the Stablegreen. Quite old, I'd say, maybe past twenty.'

Gil, who had turned twenty-eight last January, did not comment, but asked, 'How were they clad?'

108

'Och, they both had short gowns and boots on, and hats wi feathers. Gentry, for sure. We let them by, they were none o our mind.'

'Anyone else abroad in the night?' And that was likely the Muir brothers, he thought.

'I've no notion,' said Luke, 'for we took the Cross just after that, and the Drygate was trying to get us off it.'

'And Berthold was wi you the whole time?'

The boy looked uneasy, and glanced at his fellow where he still sat at the long board.

'I couldny say that,' he confessed with reluctance, 'for it's hard to keep track o one face in a scuffle. He was at my back afore we took the Cross, I ken that, but after they knocked us off I lost sight o him. He cam home a wee while after me,' he added more confidently, 'and gaed straight to his bed, but he's maybe had a fright, or no liked the fighting, or something, for he's no been great company the day, hardly had a word to say for hissel. Look at him now, like a coney in the heather.'

Berthold, summoned in his turn, did indeed resemble a cornered rabbit, all huge eyes and trembling limbs. He was about fourteen, a slight blond boy with fine features and short-sighted blue eyes. Gil surveyed him with sympathy; it was only a few months since the boy's father and uncle had been killed, leaving him stranded here in a strange country, without protection, unable to speak Scots. Currently he was supposed to be learning the language under Maistre Pierre's auspices, though Gil thought most of the teaching came in fact from Luke. Now, questioned in High Dutch, he answered hesitantly, shaking his head.

'He says he was at the battle,' Maistre Pierre reported, 'beside Luke, but saw no person who was not involved in the game.' He posed another question, and Berthold shook his head again. 'He says he was with Luke the whole time, and saw what he saw.'

'These answers are not compatible,' Gil said thought-fully. 'Why did he come in after Luke? Where was he just before that?'

A quick glance towards Luke, now helping the Ersche maidservants take down the table, and a muttered answer. 'Nowhere,' translated Maistre Pierre sceptically.

'Ask him, what did he see?'

Berthold understood that. Gil understood his answer, mostly from the tone of panic fear: '*Nein, nein, ich habe nichts gesehen, nichts!*'

'Does he ken what happens to boys who tell lies?' asked Lowrie. Berthold bent his head, crossing himself with a trembling hand, muttering that he did know.

Gil paused, considering what to ask next, and was fore-stalled by a knocking at the door. Startled, he looked at Maistre Pierre, who shrugged his broad shoulders. Thomas was already lifting the latch.

'Is Maister Cunningham within?' A strange voice, a glimpse of a blue gown of office. 'They tellt me at his own house he was here. He's sent for, to St Mungo's. Another death. One of the vergers.'

'Sheer chance that I found him,' said Maister Sim.

'Gil, you have to find what's doing this,' expostulated the Sub-Dean. 'It's no good for the kirk!'

'Tell me again.' Gil looked down at Maistre Pierre's head, bent over the recumbent body of the irritating Barnabas at the foot of the steps which led down to this cross-aisle. Candlelight leapt round them, chasing the shadows between the arches, glittering on the water pooled round the verger's booted feet and the skirts of his gown. 'He was *in* the well? Here inside the Cathedral? How far in?'

'No that far down,' admitted Maister Sim. 'He'd wedged on the bucket, see. We'd the Deil's,' he bit off the phrase and crossed himself, with an apologetic glance at the Virgin and Child on their pillar near the door of the lower church, 'we'd a deal o trouble to haul him out, and at first we took it there'd been an accident o some sort, and then we saw—'

'This,' agreed Maistre Pierre grimly, his big blunt fingers going to the corpse's neck. He lifted the end of the cord which hung over the high blue collar, and began to ease it away from the swollen flesh. 'I think it the same kind as was used on that poor girl last night, and this time it is certainly what killed the man.'

'So the same person?' said the Sub-Dean. He was striding about the arcaded space at the top of the steps, his dark red gown swirling round him, slapping at the honey-coloured pillars with the pair of embroidered gloves in his right hand; Gil estimated they had cost as much as he could earn in a week, but Henderson was oblivious to the damage he might be doing to the stitchwork. The head verger, a spare foxy sensible man, stood grimly by. Two more vergers were keeping out of the way by the Chapter House door and the Dean's secretary, scrawny and nervous in black, lurked anxiously in the shadow of a pillar. 'Sim's right, we have to put a stop to this, Blacader willny be pleased at all. Fast as you like, Gil, fast as you like.' He paused in mid-swing, mouth open. 'Was he throttled here in the Lower Kirk or was he brought in from elsewhere? Do we ha sacrilege? Do we ha desecration? Tell me that, Gil, answer me now! Where should he ha been, Galston?'

'He was assigned to the Sub-Almoner this afternoon, Dean,' said the head verger impassively.

'He was dead before he went in the well, that much I can say,' pronounced Maistre Pierre firmly. 'His head was wedged in the bucket, which held water, Sim tells me, but he has not drowned.'

'How can you tell?' Lowrie asked from the shadows. Maistre Pierre glanced up at him, then pressed firmly on the corpse's chest. Small bubbles gathered at the nostrils and the corners of the empurpled mouth.

'There is yet air in his lungs,' the mason said, 'not water. His last breath—'

'Euch!' said Henderson; the gloves flapped as he crossed himself. 'So he might ha been slain outside the kirk?'

'He might,' conceded the mason. He reached up and dislodged one of the fat creamy candles from the pricket-stand by his head and held it closer to the corpse, tilting it so that the wax dripped onto the tiled floor rather than his hand and ignoring the sharp intake of breath from all three vergers. 'Where should he have been this past few hours?'

'Right, so he was slain outside St Mungo's,' said the Sub-Dean with determination, 'but we still owe it him to find out who slew him. No to mention who put him down our well. Let me hear as soon as you've sorted this, Gil,' he said, and left, his secretary scurrying after him. Fading daylight flooded in as he hauled the heavy door open, diminished as it swung behind him. The latch clinked down as the secretary reached it with a faint bleat of dismay, and all the candle flames ducked and leapt up again, those in the pricket-stand as well as the banks of lights round the Lady Chapel and the tomb of St Mungo away among the treelike columns. Galston the head verger signalled to his minions, and one of them moved to check the lights, pinching out those which had begun to gutter.

'Helping Alan Jamieson, by what Galston says,' offered Maister Sim, going back to Maistre Pierre's question, 'if he was still on duty.' Galston nodded, without comment.

'Tell me how you came to find him,' Gil said again. His friend waved a hand at the well in the southeast corner of the wide vaulted space.

'By chance, Gil. I cam in here from the Chapter House, seeing as,' his voice trailed off, and he swallowed. 'Aye. We'd sung Vespers and Compline, and we were tidying up in the Sacristy above there, and one of the other vergers—'

'Which one?' Gil prompted, aware of Galston's disapproving scrutiny.

'The useless one. What's his name, Robert? *Oh, I dinna ken, Canon,*' he mimicked, waving his hands jerkily. 'Never gets a thing right. That one. Had left the small candle-box down here in the Chapter House, so he said, so I cam down the wheel stair to seek it seeing it was easier than sending him, and a course it wasny there. So I cam out here to take a look in the several chapels,' he waved a hand again, more cogently, at the row of small chapels off this cross-aisle at the eastward end of the lower church. 'Found it laid on Bishop Wishart's breast and was just coming away when I saw the well-cover standing open, came in to shut it down and, well, found I couldny.' He grimaced, and kicked the candle-box at his feet. 'Just as well it was me seeking this rather than Robert.'

'It is unusual to find a well within a kirk,' Maistre Pierre observed. 'I know one such at Chartres, in the crypt, where one must sleep to obtain a cure, and also at St Pierre in Lisieux, but otherwise they are rare. This is not a healing well, I think?'

'Never heard that of it,' said Maister Sim doubtfully. 'It's John Baptist's chapel, he doesny usually do healing, does he?'

'He must ha been seeing to the lights,' said Gil, looking at the effigy of Bishop Wishart on his tomb-chest between the two middle chapels, 'Robert I mean, and laid the box down. When was he here, d'you suppose? Galston?'

'Robert's duties should ha brought him down here three hours afore Vespers,' returned Galston promptly. His tone was wooden, but conveyed very clearly all that he would not say. Sim said it for him.

'Aye, very like. But he'd never ha noticed whether Barnabas was head down in the well or no, Gil, it would tell you nothing even if you got the right time off him.'

'He must surely have noticed if the killer was here at the same time,' suggested Maistre Pierre. 'I think it was not long since, a matter of an hour or two, three at most. Gilbert, I should say this has been a matter of opportunity. Many people come down here to the Lady Chapel—' he paused, and Galston turned his head, frowning, as an argument floated down the stair from the Upper Kirk where another verger had been placed like Cerberus to prevent access. 'Also many come past the *chantier* to come in by that door, we see them go by.'

'I suppose you saw nobody from there,' said Gil.

'This has happened since I and my men all went home, I think. No, this fellow and his killer must have simply chanced to be in here at the one time, and nobody with them, rather than his being enticed here to be killed. Too much danger of someone entering at the wrong moment.'

113

'You think it was here in the kirk?' said Galston, frowning.

'If he was killed outside,' said Maistre Pierre, 'there are many places to hide the corpse more easily, without bringing him in here and heaving him into the well. I think he was killed here and hidden in the nearest spot out of immediate sight.'

'I agree,' said Gil. He looked down at the corpse, sprawled in the candlelight, the fading daylight from the traceried windows making no impression on the scene now. 'So you came in here, Habbie, found him in the well. How was he placed? He'd wedged on the bucket, you said.'

'Aye, head in the bucket, which I think must ha had water in it, and his bum in the air. Feet jammed further down either side the bucket. He was pretty well wedged in the width of the well, he'd ha gone no further down I'd think, whoever put him there must ha kenned he'd be found soon or late.' Maister Sim, like Gil, considered the corpse, and grimaced. 'I'm glad it was sooner.'

'There is no other injury on him.' Maistre Pierre got to his feet, straightening his back with care. 'Only the mark of the cord. I would say he was taken by surprise. It will have been quick.'

'Thank Christ for that,' muttered Maister Sim, crossing himself. 'And then,' he went on, 'I called for help, and these two lads,' he jerked his head at the two men still standing by the Chapter House doorway, 'Matthew and Davie here cam down and lent a hand to get him out o the well. Wasny easy, I can tell you. And then Matthew went for Galston, and found Dean Henderson on his way, and he cam down and offered Conditional Absolution while we waited for you, though I think he was almost that angry he couldny speak. It isny good for St Mungo's, Gil, another death.'

'No,' agreed Gil. He found Lowrie in the shadows. 'Go and find Alan Jamieson, if you will,' he requested, 'let him know what's happened, ask him when he last saw Barnabas.' The younger man ducked his head in a bow and left by the same door the Sub-Dean had used, and Gil lifted the pricket-stand with its remaining candle and turned to the chapel of

John the Baptist. It was a small rectangular space, bounded on two sides by the south and east walls of the building, on its north side by an arcaded partition wall which separated it from the next chapel. The well, its cover standing open, was a dark shadow on the wall-foot bench in the south-east corner, surrounded by wet patches where the corpse had been dragged out. The bucket, still tethered to its rope, stood forlornly by. Gil took the candle over and peered into the well; past the glow of the light he could see a faint glitter of its reflection, a pale glimpse of his own face cross-lit. The water was not far down.

'Sheer luck he wedged on the bucket rather than going right in,' said Maistre Pierre grimly at his elbow. 'I know this is not a well for drinking, but nevertheless—!'

'What happened?' Gil said aloud. 'Some kind of encounter here in the Lower Kirk, whatever Dean Henderson thinks, and the man strangled with a cord and then thrust into the well for concealment.'

'He was not a big man,' said his father-in-law, 'but nevertheless I should think it needs another grown man to lift him and put him in there. Or perhaps two people.'

'Two?' said Gil in dismay. 'I suppose it might be. Some kind of conspiracy, maybe.'

Chapter Seven

He turned away from the dark cavity and took the candle into the next chapel. Wooden in the carved altarpiece, St Andrew supported his white-painted cross on one shoulder and raised the other hand in blessing; Bishop Wishart, that warlike man of God, lay austerely under the arch of his tomb between this chapel and that of Saints Peter and Paul beyond him. Nothing which might be of any help showed up in the leaping light.

'But why?' asked Maister Sim from where he still stood near the corpse. 'He was a right scunner, never did aught you asked him without arguing, and times no even then,' Galston stirred; Sim glanced at him, and went on, 'but that's no reason to throttle the man. He must ha done something to provoke it!'

'Did anyone know he was here?' asked Maistre Pierre. 'Did you fellows know?'

'He should ha been off duty by now,' said Galston, 'seeing he's on early this week.'

The two vergers still standing by the Chapter House doorway looked at each other in the candlelight.

'Aye, he was here first thing,' said one of them, 'he was, it's— It was his turn to open up this week, he was here afore the songmen cam in for Prime.'

'That's right,' said Maister Sim. 'He was.'

'He'd ha been free to get off home an hour or two since,' Galston continued, 'unless Maister Jamieson had work for him. When did you see him last, Davie?'

'Afore Vespers?' the man offered.

'And who of the clergy should have been down here?' Gil moved past the two men into the chapel of St Nicholas next to the Chapter House door, holding the candle high to look about him. Nothing seemed to be out of place here either. 'There's these four chapels, there's Our Lady, there's St Mungo himself.' He nodded towards the other two shrines, placed in the middle of the pillared space, their banked lights showing gaps now as the candles set by the faithful burned out. 'Which of the canons or their vicars is responsible for these altars? I'll need to ask them when they said Mass, though I suspect none of them would be late enough in the day to be any help.'

'I could do that,' offered Maister Sim, 'though maybe no till the morn's morn now.'

'Indeed,' said Maistre Pierre, 'surely the most of them will be under their own roofs, thinking of retiring for the night by this.'

Or of going out to start the evening's drinking, thought Gil, not meeting his friend's eye in the candlelight.

'Aye, Habbie, if you would,' he said with gratitude, and would have continued, but beyond St Mungo's shrine hasty feet sounded on the north stair, the stair which led out to the Vicars' hall as well as the main church.

'Maister Gil?' Lowrie's voice. 'Here's Maister Jamieson. He's something to tell us.'

'Indeed aye!' Jamieson was right behind Lowrie as they threaded their way through the forest of stone, to emerge in the candlelight beside the corpse. 'What's this? Is the man deid in truth? How can that be? I was speaking wi him no an hour since! Galston, is that right?'

'Aye, deid right enough, Alan,' said Maister Sim.

'An hour since?' said Gil, hastening to join them. 'Are you certain, man?' Behind him he could hear his father-in-law rumbling dissent, and was aware of relief. An hour was hardly possible, given all that must have happened here. Jamieson, bending to look closer at the body of his henchman, said,

'Aye, aye, Gil, it canny be longer, I'd stake my— How is

117

he all wet like this? What's come to him? Has he had Conditional Absolution?'

'Tell me when you last saw him,' Gil said. Jamieson straightened up, crossed himself, muttered a brief prayer and turned away.

'No that long since,' he said, frowning. 'Let me see, it was afore Vespers I'd say, but no so long afore it.' So at least two hours since, thought Gil. That's more like it. 'We'd been telling the dry stores, him and me, and trying to account what might ha gone missing this week. And it seems to me,' he frowned, 'as if something he saw, or something one o us said to the other, put him in mind o a thing, for he suddenly up and said, *It canny be! It canny be!* Like that, ye ken, all astonished. *Surely no*, he says. What canny be, Barnabas? says I, but he stood there like a stock wi one o the sack-ties in his hand, and then he says, *Forgie me, Maister Jamieson, I'll no be long*, and starts out the door. I cried after him, Where are ye going, and he says ower his shoulder, *I'll no be long, I see it now*, and that's the last I saw him.'

'What did you do?' Gil asked, fascinated.

'Oh, I gaed on wi the task. The poor we ha aye wi us, after all, I need to be sure o how much I can gie out in alms. To tell truth,' Jamieson looked down at the corpse again and crossed himself, 'I forgot about him, and about the time. It gied me quite a start when your man here chapped at the almonry door, let alone what he had to tell me.'

'The length of cord, the sack-tie you called it,' said Maistre Pierre. 'Did he take it away with him?'

'Aye, for I'd to find another to the second boll o barley. Canny leave it lying open all night.' He bent to touch the corpse, tracing a cross on the darkened forehead. 'Poor fellow, I canny believe it. Talking wi me, he was, no an hour since. I canny believe it. What came to him, Gil? You've no tellt me yet. He's dreadful to see, he looks as though he's been throttled, but he's wringing wet forbye. Was he in the Girth Burn, or something?'

'He was in the well,' said Maister Sim. 'St Mungo's own well, yonder in the corner.'

Jamieson looked at him in astonishment, then turned to Lowrie who was watching quietly from the top of the steps.

'You said that!' he said. 'I mind now. Throttled and put into the well, you said that, I mind it. Why? Who'd ha done that? It makes no sense!'

'We need to find out,' said Gil. 'By what you say, it looks as though he left you to find someone. Given that he's been dead well over an hour, I think it's likely that person killed him, probably throttled him wi the sack-tie he was carrying. Aye, that one,' he added as Maistre Pierre produced the cord he had unwound from the corpse's neck. Pausing to acknowledge Jamieson's shocked identification, he went on, 'Can you mind anything more about when the fellow left you? What were you talking of? Did either of you say something that set him thinking, or was it something you handled, or—?'

'No, no that I can think,' said Jamieson doubtfully.

'Maisters,' interrupted Galston, 'maisters, would you maybe take your questions away somewhere else?' Gil looked round at the man, startled, and he bowed politely. 'We'll ha to shift Barnabas out o here, Maister Cunningham, and get tidied up, all afore locking-up time, and there's no denying it would be a help if you clergy wasny here.'

'I can see that,' said Gil. He looked about him. 'Aye, I think we're done here, but I need a word afore I leave the building.'

Galston nodded.

'We'll be in the vestry,' he said, and gestured his minions forward.

Lighting the way out to the Vicars' hall, Gil was suddenly aware of the empty spaces round him, of the echoes from the upper church, the air movement between the squat pillars. The atmosphere of the place was tense, watchful, as if the whole building was waiting for him to move, to ask the right questions, to find the truth of what had just happened. As if its patron himself was looking for an answer. He paused as he went under the arch to the stairs, and glanced over his shoulder at the brightly painted shrine within its wrought-iron fence. Blessed St Mungo, he said to the saint in his head, I'll do what I can, but you'll have to help me. I need to know what to ask, who to speak to.

Just for a moment the shadows shifted in the elaborate vaulting above the shrine, like a stirring of tree branches in the wind.

The Sub-Almoner led them into the undercroft of the Vicars' hall, and picked his way between the pillars and the stored ecclesiastical bibelots to the far end, where he unlocked a padlock which fastened a sturdy door.

'This is the dry store, you see,' he said, 'and there's the Vicars' store alongside it. I've the key here, but there's still goods walking out when my back's turned, and out the Vicars' store and all, so they tell me.'

'Alan?' Gil turned at the voice. It was William Craigie, descending the stairs from the hall above. 'What's amiss, Alan? The vergers is all at sixes and sevens. They should ha locked up by this.'

'Oh, William!' said Jamieson. 'Plenty's amiss. There's no wonder the vergers is in disarray, here's Barnabas dead and drowned in St Mungo's own well.'

'*What?*' Craigie's rich bass rose a couple of octaves. 'In the *well*? What's he doing there?'

'Not drowned, in effect,' said Maistre Pierre, sounding annoyed, 'but strangled with a cord, a sack-tie—'

'A sack-tie? Like the girl at the Cross?' Craigie came closer, into the circle of their several lights. He looked shaken, his eyes huge with astonishment. 'Here, is that someone slain within St Mungo's? That's— Does the Dean ken?'

'The Dean is very clear that it happened outside St Mungo's,' said Gil without inflection.

'But how did it happen? Who? When?' Craigie shook his head. 'I canny believe it.'

'And I was talking to him no an hour since,' said Jamieson.

'It's been some time afore Vespers,' Gil supplied, 'maybe a couple of hours ago.' He considered the songman. 'Where were you the now, William? Had you company? When did you last see the man?'

'Me? I've seen no sign o Barnabas since this morning. Are you certain it's him? Certain he's dead?' Gil continued to look hard at him, and Craigie's tone became defensive. 'I was in our hall the now, been there since Vespers, conning some o the morn's music. You saw me there, Habbie, I spoke to you.'

'Aye, so you did,' agreed Maister Sim.

'Are we to see inside this store, or no?' Maistre Pierre demanded. 'I wish to know what the dead man was seeking.'

The store was not large, and was uncomfortably crowded when they all tried to get inside. Lowrie backed out of the door again; Gil, thinking that it would have been more use for his father-in-law or the two songmen to withdraw, stood looking about him. The Almoner's stock was neatly set out, like that in the office in the tower where he had been – was it only this morning? Sacks of grain hung out of reach of vermin, their canvas labelled with a stencilled tree in imitation of the badge the vergers bore and a single letter, O or B or W for the contents; barrels of donated goods stood against the wall, the contents identified in chalk on the lid. *Rys, resns, aples, hering,* read the nearest few. A grey sugar-loaf hung in a net beyond the barley, the nippers wedged in beside it.

'You were checking the stores,' he said again. 'Where were you working?'

'I was down that end, see,' Jamieson waved a hand, craning to see past Maister Sim, 'and Barnabas was here, checking the level of the barrel o rice, and I said to him, gie's a hand to get this barley down. So he came and helped me lower the sack, and it was when he loosed it he held the sack-tie in his two hands, and says, *It canny be!'* Jamieson looked from one hand to the other in illustration of this. 'And then he up and went out of here, and the next I saw him, there he was stretched on the floor by St John's chapel.' He crossed himself, shaking his head sadly. 'Aye, we none o us ken when our moment will come, though there's no so many o us meet an end like that. You need to sort it, Gil, it willny do!'

'How did you raise the sack, Maister Jamieson?' asked Lowrie from the door. Jamieson looked blankly at him. 'You said you needed Barnabas to help you lower it. Did you get it back up by yoursel?'

'Oh, aye.' Jamieson gestured at the ropes. 'It goes up slow, that's no trouble. But lowering it, when you lowse the rope it can run away, burn your hands, and then the sack splits if it hits the floor. So it's best to ha someone to take a bit of the weight. Oh, I got it back up no bother.'

Beyond Lowrie, the shadows in the undercroft shifted, and he turned to look over his shoulder as footsteps approached. Keys clinked.

'Maister Jamieson?' It was one of the two vergers they had left in the Lower Kirk. 'Maister Galston sent me. Is Maister Jamieson there? Only Maister Galston thought you'd maybe better take charge o this.' The man ducked past Lowrie, peering about in the crowded little space for the Sub-Almoner. 'See, it's his keys, Barnabas' keys, and is this no the key to your bonnie new padlock? You'll want that.'

'No, no, Matthew, he never had—' began Jamieson, reaching automatically for the jangling assemblage.

'No, this one, see. I'd swear it was as like, we all said that.' The verger picked one out of the keys and held it up, the remainder of the bunch swinging from it. Jamieson checked, staring at it, then groped at his belt for his own ring of keys.

'It is,' he said. 'It's as like.' He sorted out the right key, and held it against the other one. 'It's the same key, it is.' He looked from Matthew to Gil, and back at the keys, incredulity fading slowly into stricken comprehension. 'Christ aid us all, it's surely no Barnabas has been thieving the stores all this while? The man I trusted?'

'Not necessarily,' said Gil, striding through the twilight up towards the Stablegreen Port. 'But it looks very much like it.'

'That was a rare amount of money for a man like that to have in his kist,' said Lowrie.

'Either too much or not enough,' said Gil.

'What, you think he wasny acting alone?'

'He canny have been.' Gil paused, looking about them, and dropped his voice. 'He'd been on duty since dawn, his turn to open up the building as Galston said, and that was him about to go off duty when he went to confront whoever throttled him. By what Galston told me, he's tied to St Mungo's all the hours of daylight, so when would he get the goods he's pilfered off the policies and somewhere they could be sold? He must have had a confederate.'

'Could that be who killed him?'

'No telling, for now,' said Gil resignedly. 'It might be, it might ha been somebody else. We'll see if Galston learns anything.'

'And his chamber,' said Lowrie, as they turned to move on.

Galston had listened in grim silence to the Almoner's tale, and then had accompanied Gil and Lowrie to Barnabas' lodging, a meticulously tidy chamber in the stone undercroft of one of the larger houses by the tennis court. Here he had watched bleakly while they had inspected the man's belongings, which contained some surprises. There had been the coin in his kist to which Lowrie had already referred, along with two or three jewels carefully wrapped in scraps of brocade like relics; there had been a number of garments of good quality, several pairs of expensive shoes, a pile of handsome blankets on the bed. Gil, having heard Alys lately on the subject of blankets, was well able to estimate what those alone might have cost. Clearly the man was making a good income from whatever he was doing.

'He'd kept back quite a bit, as well as selling the stuff on,' Lowrie went on. 'I saw a barrel of dried figs in his chamber, and another o apricots.' Gil grunted agreement. 'Galston did say he'd aye had a sweet tooth.'

The head verger had been burning with suppressed

anger; Gil thought it was the man's reaction to finding that one of his staff had injured St Mungo's in such a way. The two songmen, on the other hand, had been full of indignation at the abuse of privilege, and Maister Sim had been proposing an immediate stock-take of the Vicars' dry stores as well.

'It might help us to know if anyone saw him, after he left the Almoner and before he was found dead,' Gil had said as they locked Barnabas' door again. 'He might ha said something about who he was seeking.'

'If anyone saw him,' said Galston with quiet determination, 'I'll uncover it. And we'll search the building the morn first thing, Maister Cunningham, my men by threes and reporting to me every quarter-hour. I'll learn how he's been getting the stuff out o St Mungo's, if it's the last thing I do. And soon's I learn it, I'll send you word, maister.'

'Mind you,' said Lowrie now, 'those were maybe from the other store, the Vicars' store, as Maister Sim said. I canny see who'd donate a barrel o figs to the poor, and if they did it would be right conspicuous, Sir Alan would ha noticed if it went missing.'

'You can check that wi Alan in the morning,' said Gil.

They went on through the gathering summer twilight, past lit windows and raucous alehouses, and halted within sight of the Trindle. Business seemed to be brisk despite the house's bereavement; there was loud conversation inside the little building, and a group of men drinking companionably outside, under the sign.

'Who is it we're after?' Lowrie asked.

'Four names.' Gil counted them off on his fingers. 'Allen, Shearer, Syme and, er, Thomson. You can get on home, if you'd rather. It may not be easy to get them talking.'

'I can at least watch your back, unless you want me to let Mistress Alys know where you are.'

'Once was enough,' said Gil elliptically, and Lowrie snorted.

Inside the house there was firelight, the stink of tallow candles, a powerful smell of unwashed people. Mistress

124

Howie was presiding over the two barrels of ale, much as she had been that morning. Gil nodded to her, and to the girl – was it Mysie? – who picked her way over, avoiding the familiar hands of the customers, to ask what they wanted.

'A jug of ale, lass,' he said, 'and can you point out any of Peg's regulars to me?'

She gave him a sharp look, but did not answer directly.

'If you sit ower there,' she said, 'on they two stools at the wall, I'll bring your ale.'

Gil led the way obediently to a shadowy corner beyond the hearth, well aware that most of those present were watching him. He nodded to the groups on either side of the vacant stools Mysie had pointed out, getting a reluctant nod from those on one side, an unreadable glower on the other. Mysie returned, bearing a jug, accepted a coin from him, and looked beyond Lowrie at the less friendly neighbour.

'Tammas Syme, will ye be wanting more ale?' she demanded. There was a surly growl from the shadows. 'Or you, Daniel Shearer? No? Then I'll take that jug away.'

She bore the empty jug off, and Gil set his down by his feet, reluctant to drink from it when the house was so busy. The likelihood that it had been washed between customers did not seem good.

'A fine night,' he said to the two whom Mysie had addressed.

'Well enough,' said one of the men.

'Never seen you in here afore,' said the other sourly. His voice was hoarse. 'Come to see the sights, are ye?'

'I was here this morning,' said Gil. 'Getting a word wi the mistress and her lassies.' He let that hang in the air for a moment, aware of ambiguity, then went on, 'We were at St Mungo's Cross this morning. The two of us.'

There was a faint stirring of interest in the shadows.

'The lassie that worked here,' he continued, 'the one that was found at the Cross wi her face beaten so you'd not know her, left here last night to get a word wi someone.'

'I heard that,' said the less hostile of his hearers. Lowrie, beside him, was motionless.

'I'm charged wi finding who did that to her,' Gil persisted. 'We ken it was never a man from this tavern, for she said to the other lassies that someone she never named was back in the town and she wanted to speak to him.' Beyond Lowrie the silence grew deeper. 'I'm hoping maybe she'd said something to one or another of the folk that were in here last night, might give me a hint who she'd gone to meet.'

He paused, and looked down at the ale-jug by his feet. After a moment one of his hearers rose, saying, still in that sour tone,

'Well. I wish you good fortune, neighbour.'

He tramped off across the crowded tavern, stepping on any feet which were not withdrawn from his path. Nobody tried to object.

'A bad business,' said the man who had remained. He leaned forward and indicated the jug. 'Are you—?'

'Be my guest,' invited Gil.

Perhaps the length of a *Te Deum* later they left the tavern, stepping into the street to find the twilight deepened into moonlit night. The sky was clear, with stars sprinkled about where the moonlight permitted; the shadows were very black, and Lowrie stared about warily, his hand near his whinger.

'Yonder,' said Gil quietly. 'Between the two houses across the way.'

'I see him. Do we go to him, or wait?'

'We go part way.' Gil stepped into the middle of the road-way, and stood still, casually studying the sky. The man lurking in the shadows waited a moment, and then came forward reluctantly, staying in the shadows.

'I'm no coming out in the street.'

'Fair enough,' said Gil. It was the voice of the man who had left the tavern.

'You're looking for who that lassie wanted to speak wi.'

'We are.'

'Aye.' Feet shuffled. 'Mind, I'm no saying I heard this mysel.'

'A course not.'

'I never spoke wi the lassie. You understand that.' Gil nodded, then wondered if the movement would show in the moonlight and made an agreeing noise. 'But I heard. Someone said.' He swallowed noisily and then said in a rush, 'She never mentioned a name, just some fellow had been gone fro Glasgow three month, and was back, and she'd have something out wi him if it killed her.'

Lowrie made a small sound of pity. Gil waited.

'That's all,' said the hoarse voice.

'What did she call him?' Gil asked. 'She never used his name, she must ha called him something.'

'No.' A pause. 'Aye, maybe she— Maybe she said, *My fine gentleman*, or the like. Kind a sharp, as if he was anything but.'

'Thanks, friend,' said Gil.

'Neighbour,' said the hoarse voice. Gil tilted his head, waiting. 'Get him. She was just— She was just a tavern lassie, but she never deserved—'

'No,' agreed Gil. 'She never deserved that.'

Matters did not seem much clearer in the morning. Nor had Euan come home, to Gil's irritation.

'He'll be off about some ploy of his own,' he said when the breakfast was brought in. 'I'll have a word or two to say to him when he does come home. Either he's serving me or he's not, and if he's not he can take himself off. I could ha done wi his help today dealing wi Barnabas' death, to let Lowrie carry on with the other business.'

'Yes, indeed you must look into that. It seems astonishing,' said Alys, ladling porridge into the new earthenware bowls, 'that the man should have been thieving from the Almoner's stores for so long and never been found out.'

'Particularly when Alan Jamieson keeps a record of everything.' Gil accepted a bowl and horn spoon, helped himself to a generous portion of butter from the dish on the plate-cupboard and strolled off across the hall, prodding the melting butter into the greyish mass of the oatmeal. Socrates followed him, looking hopeful.

'I wonder how he got it out of the kirk,' said Alys. 'Surely he must have been seen.'

'I wondered that too,' said Lowrie. 'There must be folk in and out that hall all the hours of daylight. Ah!'

'Perhaps by darkness,' Gil agreed. 'Or perhaps it's simply that a verger moving a sack of meal or the like is nothing to remark on.'

'And he left his task, the Almoner said,' persisted Alys, 'taking the length of cord with him, and saying, *I see it now*. What was it that he saw? How the girl Peg was killed? Or who tried to strangle her?' She sat down by the little table where the crocks were laid, waiting till her own porridge had cooled.

'I thought at first,' Gil admitted, 'it was how the thefts were taking place, but it looks as if he knew all about those, even if he wasn't solely responsible for them himself. It must be something else, I agree.'

'So who did he go to meet? Or perhaps,' she dug thoughtfully with the ladle into the crock of porridge, 'perhaps we had better ask, who did he think he was going to meet? And why? Did he go to speak to his accomplice? Did he plan to accuse someone of throttling the girl who was at the Cross? And which of these would strangle him only for what he said?'

Gil set his bowl on the floor for the dog, and turned to the platter of oatcakes set on the plate-cupboard. Smearing more butter on one of these he observed,

'Habbie asked around yestreen while we were searching the man's chamber. He may not have spoken to everyone yet, but it seems plenty of folk were about. Most of the songmen, half the priests, Canon Goudie who's Hebdomader, were all in and out. All the Masses to be said in the Lower Kirk were over by Nones, in the proper way. Anyone or no one could have been down there.' He bit into the oatcake, catching the crumbs with his other hand.

128

'It was not no one, clearly,' said Alys. 'Maister Lowrie, there is more porridge. Do you wish some?'

'Galston might have learned something useful,' said Lowrie, holding his bowl out. 'Is that for this morning, then?'

'Among other things.' Gil tipped crumbs into his mouth, and reached for another oatcake. 'Ask more questions about St Mungo's. I wonder where all these goods were going to, whoever it was thieved it. I need to talk to the folk at St Catherine's again, ask again about Annie's background, who might have taken her in. I canny believe she's sleeping in a ditch somewhere, a gently reared lassie, even in high summer. I need to talk to Otterburn, and we need to ask about, see if we can track down where Peg Simpson met her death. You could see to that, if you would. Someone must ha heard her being beaten so badly, it can hardly ha been done in silence.' He bit into the second oatcake, and added through it, 'I should never ha gone chasing after the cord yesterday afternoon, I'd ha done better pursuing Peg's matter.'

'So it's Otterburn first?' said Lowrie, scraping the last of the porridge. He set his bowl down for the dog as Gil had done. 'Or d'you wish me to make a start on that immediately?'

Otterburn was in the courtyard of the castle, under a familiar striped awning.

'There you are,' he said as they approached. 'I was going to send out to you.' He nodded at the shrouded form set out in the shelter of the canvas. 'Had her moved over here early on, seeing the quest's for this morning. We ken what killed her now.'

'Oh?'

'Aye.' Otterburn pulled back the shroud, revealing the battered face. Gil winced. Some of Peg's injuries had faded as the swelling reduced, but the pallor of death was increasing and others were made more hideous by the contrast. The Provost glanced at him, nodded, and lifted the corpse's head to swivel it on the thin neck. It moved easily, and much too far.

'A broken neck,' said Lowrie. 'Poor lass.'

'Aye.' Otterburn set the head down gently and drew the shroud up. 'And the women say she'd lain wi some man or other no long afore her death, but she hadny been forced.'

'We know she was working that day,' said Gil. Otterburn grunted. 'She'd been out the back wi at least one man during the evening. No saying whether she lay with her killer or no, but I'd assume it was the same man broke her neck as left those marks on her.' Otterburn grunted again, possibly in agreement. 'We've left it a bit late, but I'd like Lowrie to see if he can find where she died. We've a sighting o a lassie on her own coming down from the Stablegreen Port about ten o the clock, and no idea where she went from there, assuming it was Peg. He can ask about, find out if anyone noticed a tussle or an argument outside their windows. Your men have heard o nothing like that, I suppose?'

'No that Andro's mentioned,' said the Provost. 'You can check wi him.'

'And Annie Gibb?'

'No a whisper. The men are saying St Mungo himsel has carried her off to Paradise, and the way things are going, it wouldny surprise me. And I'd a man Lockhart here afore Prime, wanting to hear what we've done about her. The good-brother, is that?' Gil nodded. 'Tellt him to ask you, bade him go and think what he or the rest o the party might ken that would help us.' Otterburn grimaced. 'Seems the old man's in a poor way, this Sir Edward. No long to go, by the sound o it. Here, this is the lassie's kirtle, or the kirtle you took out the Girth Burn, any road. What was it you were saying about it?'

He hauled the bundle of blue cloth out from under the bier, checked himself in the act of setting it on top of the shrouded corpse, and turned away to the mounting-block by the main door of the Archbishop's apartments.

'It's near dry,' Lowrie commented, and went to help him,

spreading the tattered garment out in the sunshine with a proprietary air. 'You see, the two sleeves have been laid open, from cuff to neck, and the laces cut and all.' He turned the folds of wool. 'And we thought – Maister Mason thought – this sleeve was cut wi shears, small ones such as a woman might have at her belt, and that one wi a knife, or at least a single blade. You see how different the cuts are?'

'Aye.' Otterburn bent to examine the frayed edges. 'I see it. So, if this is this lassie's kirtle right enough, you reckon it was two people stripped her, and then tied her to the Cross?'

'That's what we thought,' agreed Lowrie, with a diffident glance at Gil. He looked down at the damp wool, then leaned closer, peering at something which he picked at with a forefinger.

'What d'you see?' asked Otterburn.

'I'm no certain.' Lowrie straightened up, studying his fingertip. 'What do you think, sir? Maister Gil? It's like wee sparkles of gold.'

'Of gold?' Gil bent to look. Otterburn craned over the mounting block, but shook his head.

'I canny see that close,' he confessed. 'What's he found?'

'He's right. Spangles, or powdered gold, or something.' Gil touched his forefinger to Lowrie's and inspected the result, a couple of minute gleams of colour. 'Where on earth has that come from? Peg was hardly like to have gold dust about her, poor lass. The braid on her sleeves is coloured floss, no gilt there. I'd ha thought if she came by such a thing as a scrap o gold braid she'd ha sold it on the rag market.'

'It's only here, on the one sleeve,' said Lowrie, turning the ragged cloth carefully, tilting his head to see where the bright specks caught the light. 'I can see none on the other sleeve, nor on the body.'

'Has it come off whoever cut her out her gown?' suggested Otterburn. 'Who goes about shedding gold dust?'

'That would fit,' said Gil. 'If whichever one wielded the knife was scattering flakes of gold, that would explain why it's only on that sleeve. But where's it coming from? Off his hat? Off his clothes?'

131

'Could be.' Otterburn nodded gloomily. 'Could be either. Is there any in the case clad in gold so far, Maister Cunningham?'

'No that I've noticed,' said Gil. 'Silver braid on a doublet, but no gold braid so far.'

'This is certainly gold,' said Lowrie, still peering at the folds of cloth. 'What about brocade? Could it be off a gold brocade sleeve?'

'It could as easy be off a cope or a vestment, I'd ha thought,' said Otterburn, 'given she was found in the kirkyard.'

'What, you're suggesting it was one of the clerks stripped her?' said Lowrie, startled. 'But they'd never be wearing gold vestments out in the kirkyard?'

'And she was certainly stripped in the kirkyard,' Gil concurred. 'We found the scraps of cloth in the grass.'

Otterburn grunted sceptically, and stepped away from the mounting-block.

'Well, maisters,' he said, 'I'll bring these specks o gold to the assize the day, but I doubt they'll no see it as important. I'm hoping to bring it in persons unknown, for I'm inclined to agree wi you, her man's no the one that's broke her neck. He maybe knocked her about a bit but he touched her corp afore me willingly enough. Mind you, it's going to confuse them,' he added thoughtfully, 'if I start talking about folk wi gold brocade sleeves. We'll need to see who we get for the assize. Here, you better get on, if you're to be back here for the quest.'

Leaving Lowrie to ask along the length of the Stablegreen whether anyone had heard an argument in the street on the night Peg Simpson died, Gil made his way to the cathedral, and tracked Galston to his covert, not in the vestry which was the domain of the Vicars Choral and the clergy but in the base of the north-west tower, on the floor below the Sub-Almoner's office.

Here, under the vaulted ceiling, surrounded by stacks of lumber, a broken altarpiece, the benches for the college meetings in the Chapter House, the planks and beams for the seating before the west door at Pentecost, the vergers had made themselves comfortable. Several suspiciously ecclesiastical chairs had been padded with folds of elderly brocade, two lamps and a row of candle-stands were lit by wax candles, a brazier of glowing charcoal contested the chill of the ancient stones. The ropes for the cathedral's three bells descended through a suitable aperture in the vault, and were gathered up to one side of the door.

There were only two people in the chamber, the useless Robert sitting with a cup of ale which must have come from the barrel set up under one of the narrow windows, and Galston, moving counters about on a cloth spread on a tall desk beside another candle-stand. When Gil tapped on the heavy door of the chamber Robert clambered to his feet, bleating some sort of welcome, and Galston looked up and came forward immediately.

'Maister Cunningham,' he said, raising his hat.

'Finish your accounts,' Gil recommended, 'or you'll lose your tally.'

'Not accounts, maister,' said Galston, 'but the week's duties to be rearranged.' He crossed himself, frowning, and Robert said something faint about *Aye, poor Barnabas!* 'I've questioned the men,' Galston went on, 'and put the fear o God into them, no to mention the fear o Tam Galston, and I have to say, maister, I've learned little enough to aid you, save that Robert here caught sight o Barnabas hastening through the kirk.' Robert nodded eagerly. 'He'd the cord in his hand, so he says, and when he spoke to him he said he couldny wait, he'd to catch someone afore he left the kirk.'

'Did he say who it was?' Gil asked Robert directly. The man nodded again.

'Oh, aye, he did, poor Barnabas, at least he said, *Where is he? I've to catch him afore he leaves the place.*'

'Did he name the man he was seeking?'

'Oh, no, he never said a name.'

Gil met Galston's glance over the blue-clad shoulder.

'Did he say aught else, Robert?' asked the head verger.

'No, no, I doubt it,' said Robert amiably, 'he was in that much of a hurry, that was all he said. *Where is he, I've to catch him, him and his sack-ties*, he said, *now see what's come o't. He'll need to deal wi't*, he says.'

Gil caught Galston's eye again, and said carefully,

'What did he mean about the sack-tie, Robert, do you suppose?'

'Why, that was what he was holding, was it no?' said Robert, surprised. 'Likely he was seeking him to gie it back to him.'

'And did he say who he was seeking, to give the sack-tie to?' Gil asked patiently. 'Or what he had to deal with?'

'No, no,' said Robert with regret. 'He never. But it was one o the clerks,' he added.

'What makes you say that?' Gil prompted, while Galston rolled his eyes, his impassivity broken.

'Well, we was all in here, the rest o us,' Robert said, 'and he'd ken that, we're aye in here at that hour, getting a bit bread and ale that Maister Galston sees us, afore we set up for Vespers and Compline and then see to all for the morning. We waited for him a while, but he never came, so we just ate his share and all.'

'Is that right?' Gil raised his eyebrows at Galston, who nodded a little reluctantly. 'And you were all in here? All the vergers but Barnabas, and Robert till he joined you?'

'Aye, that'd be right,' said Galston after a moment reckoning on his fingers, and Robert emitted a faint bleat of agreement.

'That's very helpful,' said Gil. 'My thanks, Robert.' He dug in his purse and found a coin for the man, who accepted it gratefully, glanced at his superior and hurried out with an indistinct remark about the candles for Sext.

'He's truthful enough,' said Galston drily. 'He's too much o a fool to make a good leear. We're still searching the place, maister. We've found naught to interest you this far, but there's still both the towers and the Vicars' hall to go, there's a few wee neuks in all o them might hold a barrel or a sack wi nobody noticing.'

'Would he have access to the Consistory tower?' Gil said. 'The vergers go all over the building, I ken that, but he'd have no duties there, I'd ha thought anyone that saw him could question why he was there.'

'That's true, maister, but we'll check just the same,' said Galston, reverting to his previous manner. 'One o my men has stole fro Holy Kirk, there's nobody will say I was remiss in finding how it was done or in putting it right.'

Chapter Eight

Carefully not looking at the row of fat beeswax candles which lit the chamber, Gil settled down to question the man about the vergers' duties. He was surprised by how extensive they were. He was aware of the cathedral servants, always moving about the building in their blue belted gowns, the embroidered badge on the breast displaying St Mungo's tree and bell, but he had never had cause to list how many things had to be done in such a big, important kirk.

'Oh, aye, maister,' said Galston. 'And if it's no done by the clergy, it's done by my men.' Gil raised an eyebrow, and Galston expanded: 'So if it doesny mean going about in a procession, it's a vergers' matter, and if it does mean a procession, there's one or maybe two o my men there wi the rod or the mace, put a bit dignity into it.'

'And the watch and ward of the building?' said Gil, keeping his own counsel about that. 'How is it kept secure by night?'

'Aye,' said Galston, a little uncomfortably. 'See, maister, we've aye jaloused if there was to be trouble, it would be someone after the treasure, which is kept well under lock and bars by the Thesaurer, or after the holy relics, or the altar-furnishings out there in the kirk, or maybe after the Body o Christ itself,' he crossed himself, 'where it's kept in the tabernacle. So it's the kirk itself we keep watch on, and we do that by me sleeping in here.'

'In here?' repeated Gil, startled. He looked about him, but could see no signs of permanent residence. Galston nodded at the nearest stack of lumber.

'I've a straw plett and some blankets stowed ahint the Easter Sepulchre yonder, maister. I get them out when the place is barred for the night. It's warm enough in here, wi the brazier going, and if I were to hear anything I'm right handy for the bell-ropes.'

'You are that,' Gil agreed, recognising the wisdom of this. One man could hardly hope to defend a building this size, but he could raise the alarm. 'It's a big building, mind, for a man to guard on his own.'

'I'm no on my own, maister,' said Galston with a simplicity which rebuked. Gil nodded in acknowledgement of this point, and went on,

'So you'd say Barnabas has never shifted aught out of here by night?'

'No out o the main building. The Consistory clerks sees to locking up their door,' Galston nodded towards the south-west tower, 'and I lock the outside door to this tower after the Almoner and them has gone.'

'Which leaves us,' said Gil deliberately, 'the Vicars' hall and its undercroft.'

'It does,' agreed Galston. He eyed Gil in the light of the candles, then lifted a snuffer and began extinguishing the nearest. 'You reckon the goods have left here by night, then, maister?'

'It seems likeliest.' Gil found another snuffer and started at the other end of the row. 'Given that Maister Jamieson's been aware of a shortfall for a while now, he'd ha noticed if anything was being shifted by daylight, you'd think.'

'Aye, Canon Jamieson would notice,' agreed Galston, still intent on the lights. 'So it might no ha been Barnabas, right enough.'

'All things are possible under God,' Gil observed. Galston changed hands to cross himself, and gave Gil a wry look by the remaining light.

'That's the kind o thing the clergy says,' he remarked. 'It's well seen you'd a narrow escape fro that yoursel, Maister Cunningham.'

Locking the tower door behind them – 'There's as many

holds keys to this, you might say there was little point,' observed Galston, replacing the jangling bunch at his belt, 'but there's less point still in inviting Jockie Pick-Purse to make a profit on his confession' – they made their way through the hum and bustle of a morning in St Mungo's. Sext was just ended, so the Masses were beginning again at the many lesser altars in the nave, and the devout were making their way to hear their favoured saint commemorated. As the Hebdomader and choir, led by Robert with the verger's silver-tipped wand of office raised high, emerged through the massive archway of Archbishop Blacader's choirscreen, another three vergers appeared on its walled top, casting about the casing of the Cathedral's smaller organ, their lanterns throwing dim, leaping shadows onto the smoke-darkened sandstone walls of the nave. Across the church, three more were engaged in a hissing argument with one of the clergy about who should have access first to St Moloc's altar.

'I'm surprised it's business as usual,' Gil commented, 'considering what happened in St John's chapel last night.'

'Aye, well,' said Galston. 'Barnabas wasny slain inside St Mungo's, Dean Henderson was very clear about that. He's permitted me to put a rope across, keep folk out St John's at the least till it's cleansed and censed, but he's no for shutting down the whole kirk. The faithful need to get in, he says.' His gaze slid sideways to meet Gil's. 'Them and their pence,' he added softly.

Reckoning a day's probable revenue from the various collecting-boxes about the building, Gil saw how this position could appeal to the Dean. Himself, he was very uneasy about it; he had no way of telling where the verger had died, but the treatment of the body alone must surely amount to sacrilege within St Mungo's. Perhaps the Archbishop would have a different view. He waited for the last brocade folds of the Hebdomader's procession to vanish along the north choir aisle towards the vestry, and made for the doorway to the Vicars' hall.

'Robert's maybe no the wisest man in the place,' remarked

Galston, following him, 'but he's well able to conduct a procession.'

Behind the heavy door the undercroft of the Vicars' hall was not, as Gil had expected, busy with blue gowns and lanterns. There was a buzz of conversation away round to the left; picking his way among the pillars, the vaulting leaping over his head in the lantern light, he discovered a group of six or ten of the vergers arguing over something. He would have approached quietly, but Galston stepped past him and advanced on the assembly exclaiming,

'Now, lads, what's this about! Why are you no searching this place like I tellt you to?'

'We have done, Maister Galston,' said one of the nearest. Gil recognised Matthew, and Davie beyond him. 'Only we've found this, see, and we was wondering if it's what we was seeking.'

'And what is it, then? Stand back and let me look.' Galston put Matthew bodily aside and plunged into the gathering. Gil, following, saw him check in surprise. 'The handcart? That's nothing new, you daftheids!'

'No, but this, see,' said someone else.

In the pool of light from the lanterns, under a wing of the vaulting and surrounded by more stacked lumber, the St Mungo's handcart stood slightly aslant in what was obviously its designated niche. A bundle of pale brocade had been opened up on the flat bed of the cart, revealing linen lining and a row of black metal hooks, and within the folds a fat leather purse and a small wooden box which was oddly familiar.

'It was stood like that, the cairt,' said the verger Davie, 'and I came ower to set it straight, see, and found this laid on the top o't. So we opened it up and this is what we found,' he waved at the bundle, 'and the worst thing is, look at the wheels!'

Galston stepped back, almost treading on Gil's foot, to inspect the wheels, and Davie swung his lantern down so that the shadows sprang up the walls around them. The wheels were caked in mud, and even in the lantern-light the scratches on the paint of the spokes were clear to see.

'Well!' said Galston. 'And who's had this out wi'out permission?'

'And that's it, Maister Galston,' said one of the men. 'We were just trying to work that out, and there's none o us has had the cairt out in weeks, no since the Pentecost benches was put by, and it was washed and stowed away proper then. You seen it yoursel, and approved all. So we were just goin' to come and find you, seeing it was a thing out o place like you said, and then we thought to look at this bundle on the top o the cairt, and then you cam in that door.'

'Aye,' said Galston in a sceptical tone. 'And what is the bundle, then?'

'It's a man's short gown,' said Gil. Galston looked over his shoulder and then back at the folds of cloth in the lantern-light. 'I'm more interested in the purse and that box, but they're all three strange things to find hidden in here.'

'They might no ha been hid,' argued the man Matt fairly. 'They might just ha been forgot.'

'Aye, but whose are they?' said Galston, putting his finger on the nub of the matter. 'Maister Cunningham, will you take charge o these?'

'I will,' said Gil after a moment, 'if you'll study them wi me before they leave St Mungo's.' Galston met his eye, and nodded. 'Is there aught else?'

'Nothing else,' he said to Otterburn an hour or so later. 'They'd searched the building thoroughly enough, I'd say.'

'And these,' said Otterburn, prodding the purse as it sat on his desk. 'Did you learn whose they might be?'

'The gown,' said Gil, loathing the taste of the words in his mouth, 'and the box, which has a set of Tarots in it, are Maister Sim's.'

'What, Habbie Sim the songman?' Gil nodded, and the Provost stared at him inscrutably for a moment, then said, 'Awkward for you. Will I question him on it?'

'I've spoken to him, in Galston's presence,' Gil said. Otterburn's expression flickered with – was it surprise? Respect? 'He agrees the gown's his, a good one o yellow brocade faced wi green taffeta, says he's not seen it for four days or so, likewise the cards. I can confirm,' Gil went on carefully, 'and will swear to it, that the last time we met for cards Habbie wore a green checked wool gown, and said he had mislaid his cards. He was asking if any of the fellows had picked them up by mistake. We'd to use someone else's set that evening.'

'And this?' Otterburn prodded the purse again. It chinked faintly. 'Have you counted it?'

'Five merks and fourpence ha'penny. Habbie says he has never seen it. I thought he was telling the truth,' said Gil, still speaking with great care, 'but I'd be glad if you'd question the Head Verger as to what he thought.'

'Ah.' Otterburn nodded approvingly. 'It's a useful thing, is a legal training.' He glanced at the open window, where the noise from the courtyard entered increasingly loudly. 'And now, I've a quest to direct out there. Is that lad o yours back yet from talking to the Stablegreen folks?'

'He is,' said Gil. 'I met him in the yard. I think he has news for you, though it maybe takes us no further forward. One or two of those he spoke to mentioned a man who had heard a scuffle outside his window, the night we are concerned wi, and looked out to see a woman arguing wi two men. But it seems the fellow walked to Kirkintilloch the day, about a dog he wished to purchase. He might be back the night, he might no. Lowrie needs to go back when he's at home.'

'Wi two men?' repeated Otterburn. 'And you thought it was two men cut her out o her gown and bound her to the Cross?' He rubbed his hands together. 'Ah-hah! That would fit, that would fit, maister!'

'It might,' agreed Gil cautiously.

'Aye. Well, come and we'll see about this quest. I bade the Serjeant be sure and pick me a biddable assize this time, the last two he's found me have been packed wi fools.'

* * *

'They did what?' said Alys incredulously, and set the ladle back in the kale-pot. 'They brought it in—?'

'Against Annie herself,' agreed Lowrie, his eyes dancing. 'The Provost was quite displeased.'

'It is a thing most extraordinary,' said Catherine. Further down the long board, small John shouted as his little plate was set in front of him.

'And what of Annie's kin? What did they say?'

'They were none of them present.' Gil spooned kale, and frowned at it. 'I'm surprised Otterburn never cited any of them as witnesses, at the very least to swear to the time Annie was last known to be at the Cross.'

'That does seem strange,' Alys agreed.

'I think he sees the two matters as entirely separate,' Lowrie observed.

'But what did he do? He could not let it stand, surely?'

'He directed them again,' Gil said, grinning at the recollection. 'It was as much his own doing as the assize's. He should never have tried to get the cuts in the cloth past them.'

'What cuts are these?'

'Lowrie discovered them.' Gil gestured at the younger man to explain, and addressed himself to his meal.

The scene in the courtyard had been one to relish; the assize, duly sworn and cautioned, had listened to the evidence placed before it, inspected the cuts on the blue kirtle, asked some questions about Annie Gibb which had alarmed Gil, and retired to consider its verdict. Less than an hour later, it had filed out into the courtyard again, and the spokesman, asked if he had a verdict to pronounce, had squared his shoulders and said importantly,

'Aye, Provost, that we do.'

'And what is it, man?' demanded Otterburn. 'How do you find this woman met her death?'

'We find,' said the spokesman, a well-built man whom Gil recognised as the keeper of an alehouse on the Briggait, 'that Peg Simpson met her death by being unlawfully killed by this woman Annie Gibb—'

'What?' said Otterburn sharply, his colour rising.

'And then bound to St Mungo's Cross after she was dead, and then throttled wi a sack-tie stole from the almoner, which was a most sacrilegious thing to ha done,' continued the spokesman. 'And we find Annie Gibb guilty o murder, and she should be put to the—'

'You'll find no such thing in my court, Dandy Greenhill!' said Otterburn. 'The lot o ye, get back in that chamber and stay in it till ye've decided what I tellt ye to decide! It's clear as day, persons unknown, two o them!'

'See, I tellt ye,' hissed Greenhill at one of his fellow-assizers. 'Provost, we've talked it through—'

'Well, ye'll just ha to talk it through again,' said Otterburn. 'Walter, you've never wrote that down, have you? I'm no having that stand as a verdict.'

'He got his verdict the second time, *persons unknown*,' said Gil now, helping himself to another slice of the sausage which went with the kale. 'The bystanders seemed to agree wi that,' he added. 'I heard more than one saying the assize was trying it on, maybe hoping for another wee refreshment for their second session. They were disappointed, if so, Otterburn sent in a jug of water from the Castle well.'

'And these two men who were arguing with a woman,' Alys said, smiling at this. 'Is there any description?'

'Several,' said Lowrie, 'none compatible with any other, from folk who'd heard the tale. Big men, wee men, in armour, in hodden grey, wi swords, wi cudgels. I'll need to get a word wi this man Johnson when he gets back from Kirkintilloch. He dwells right on the Stablegreen, so he could well ha heard something useful. I spoke to his wife, but she'd seen nothing, and couldny recall what he said yesterday about it. Oh, and the folk at the Trindle had never heard o the man Barnabas. I described him, but they were certain there had never been one of the vergers in the place.'

Gil nodded.

'Barnabas showed no sign of recognising Peg when we

took her from the Cross, though a course we all thought she was Annie at that point. I asked his fellows, and none o them had ever heard him mention a woman, or the Trindle itself. That bears that out, then.'

He paused to consider the afternoon, as the women cleared away the kale and sausage and set out a dish of little almond tarts. Alys handed the dish round; when all at the head of the table were served she sent it further down, where it was greeted with a shout of 'Pie! Pie John!' Catherine began cutting her pastry into little pieces with her eating-knife.

'Lowrie, you can get over to Vicar's Close after we've eaten,' said Gil. 'Talk to Habbie Sim's man, see if he minds when he last saw that gown, yellow brocade faced wi green taffeta, and the box wi his Tarot cards. Oh, and see if you can make out where Barnabas had the apricots and figs from. I meant to ask them that this morning and all, but it slipped my mind.'

Lowrie nodded, colouring up. Catherine said, in French,

'I do not think Maister Sim has robbed St Mungo's. He is a good son of Holy Church.'

'Nor do I,' said Gil, 'but I'm too close to him to handle that part of the matter.' She inclined her head in agreement. 'It's a bit near even to send Lowrie, but I'm no certain any of Otterburn's men would ask the right questions of his man, and Otterburn himself would simply frighten the fellow.'

Crossing the outer courtyard of the pilgrim hostel, the dog at his heels, Gil met Sir Simon just leaving the chapel.

'Maister Cunningham,' said the priest, nodding. 'And have you aught to report?'

'Nothing,' said Gil. 'I was hoping you might have news.'

Sir Simon grimaced.

'None, neither good nor bad, maister. Sir Edward is still wi us, weaker but in his full wits. I will say, that doctor is right clever wi the medicines the way he keeps the old fellow's pain at bay and yet allows him his mind clear. And there's no sign o Annie Gibb. Were you wanting a word wi any of them? The doctor's here, a course, and I believe the women's come back fro St Mungo's, but the good-son's got the men out searching the Stablegreen again.'

'I want to talk to the two men that were guarding Annie that night,' Gil said. 'One o them said he'd come from her father's house.'

'Now, I think that's the one that's stayed behind,' said Sir Simon. 'In case there should be errands to be run, ye ken.'

Fetched from the men's hall, the man Sawney was willing enough to talk.

'Aye, I last had an answer from her just about midnight,' he assured Gil. 'She was sounding like hersel, asking me to set her free, though she said she had no cramp nor anything in her feet, we'd bound her wi good attention to that. And the next time, maybe an hour later, I thought she was asleep. I wish I'd gone closer,' he admitted, 'we'd maybe ha had a better chance o finding her if we'd kent sooner she was flown.'

'You'd kent her a while,' said Gil, letting this pass.

'Aye, from she was a wee thing,' the man agreed. 'I mind her on her first powny, wi her hair down her back. A bonnie lass, and a loving. I served James Gibb afore she was born, ye ken, maister, and a good man to serve he was and all. Deid now, a course, and Marian Wallace o Crosslee deid and all, Our Lady be thanked, and no knowing what's come to her wee lassie.'

'Her mother, you mean?' Gil said, recalling the names in the documents he had seen at Sir Edward's side.

'Aye, that she was. A good lady, and well dowered, or so I heard.'

'What was her dower? Was it lands, or money?' Gil asked hopefully, but Sawney shook his head.

'I've never a notion, maister. See, I was never out o Tarbolton till we rode to Glenbuck wi Annie. If the mistress's lands was ever mentioned by name, other than Crosslee where she cam frae, I'd no ha taken any mind, I only heard they was plenty.'

'And it all went to Annie,' Gil said.

'The whole lot went to Annie,' said Sawney, 'no matter what her kin said.' Gil raised his eyebrows. 'See, there was some talk o a bit land wi a mill, or a mine, or something o the sort, gey profitable, that James Gibb's cousin laid claim to, though he wasny even the same surname. Away ayont Cumnock, it was. His man o law tried to serve a bit paper on Annie, the cousin's man I mean, after her faither was deid, but Sir Edward and his man saw them off. That'd learn them, said Sir Edward,' he grinned at the memory, 'to take her for an unprotected lassie.'

'His man of law, you mean?' That must be land from her father's property, not her mother's dowry. Unless it was entailed, James Gibb would be entitled to leave it as he wished.

'Is that no what I said?'

'So her mother,' said Gil, trying to sum this up, 'came from Renfrewshire, this place Crosslee, and had lands about there maybe.'

'Oh, I wouldny ken about that.'

'And there was her father's land in Ayrshire, about Tarbolton and Cumnock.' Sawney nodded. 'Had Annie no connection about Glasgow? No land here, maybe an agent, any kin or friends dwelling in Glasgow? Or even in Rutherglen?'

'No that I ever heard, maister,' said Sawney earnestly. 'If her mother's lands was by Crosslee, like you said, that's ayont Paisley, or so I've heard. That's no so far distant fro' Glasgow, I suppose.'

'Was any of the people about James Gibb's house from Glasgow?' Gil persisted, clutching at straws. 'Other servants, Mistress Wallace's women, any like that?'

'No that I can mind.' Sawney shook his head. 'Maister, it's six year since I set een on any o them, and the household was all broke up when my maister dee'd, I've never a notion. What's more, if any o them had a connection wi our Annie, sent her news or the like, the rest o the house at Glenbuck would ha got to hear of it, you can be sure o that.' He met Gil's sceptical glance, and jerked his head towards the women's hall. 'Dame Ellen doesny let much stir about the place wi'out she has a finger in the matter. Or her whole hand,' he added rather bitterly.

'Aye, and it's as well somebody does,' pronounced Dame Ellen from the doorway of the hall. She advanced on Gil, simpering, her two nieces peering out of the door behind her. 'I'm sure you've more to be about, maister, than let this fellow keep you back from your tasks. Away back to the stable, Sawney, and clean that wheen harness.'

'It's cleaned,' muttered Sawney.

'I sent for him,' said Gil, raising his hat to Dame Ellen and then to her nieces, at which they giggled nervously. 'He's been a great help.' He nodded dismissal to the man, who escaped with something like relief on his face. 'Did Sir Simon say you'd gone over to St Mungo's the day?'

'We were there all morning.' She folded her arms, hitching up her substantial bosom, and jerked her head at her nieces. 'Away back to your needlework, you lassies, and Meggot can oversee you. Aye, sir,' she gave him a smile with far too many teeth in it, 'we were in St Mungo's, making our devotions at his tomb, praying for an easy passage for my poor brother. I've left coin for a couple Masses the day, to relieve his going. They're a wee bit ower-set the day, even my kinsman,' she added, her tone souring. 'Seems as if none o them can think beyond this fellow put down the well. What's a well doing in a great kirk, anyway? Just asking to have things put down it, so it is. I never heard o sic a thing afore.'

'It's said to be St Mungo's well itself.'

She gave him another of those dreadful smiles.

'So my kinsman tells me. Any road, that's where we've been.'

'I hope it gave you comfort,' he said conventionally. 'Tell me, madam, whose idea was it to bring Annie Gibb to St Mungo's? What prompted the journey? It's a long road, particularly with your brother in such a sad way.'

'Aye, my poor brother,' she said again, and crossed herself. 'Why, it was his idea, maister. Took the notion into his head to see his good-daughter cured afore he departs, and nothing would do but we must all convoy him to Glasgow town in a great procession.'

'And if she was cured? What did he plan for her then?'

'Oh, sir, I've never a notion. He never discussed the likes o that wi me.'

Did he not? thought Gil sceptically. But I'll wager you discussed it with him, even if you got no answers.

'You never thought o wedding her to one o your Muir kinsmen?' he asked.

'I did,' she admitted, with another toothy smile, 'but the lassie never favoured either o them, even had she no been melancholy-mad. A pity, they're two bonnie laddies, and well to do, at least Henry is, but there you are, lassies will be lassies.'

'Is there anyone else that came seeking her particularly?' he asked. 'Anyone that might think it worthwhile stealing her away, wedding her by force?'

'Oh, is that what you're thinking now?' She stared at him in amazement. 'Oh, no, sir, that's never what's come to her, surely! I fear the only way we'll find her now is by leaving her to lie under whatever dyke till she's stinking. I tell you, it's like to break my poor brother's heart if he's to meet his end no knowing what's come to her.'

'Lockhart's out searching, so I believe,' Gil observed. She showed her teeth again.

'If he feels he's being useful, I suppose. Well, I'll not keep you back. You've enough to do, I don't doubt.' She nodded to him, and turned away to the women's hall.

As the heavy door swung shut behind her, hasty feet sounded in the passage from the outer courtyard, and Henry Muir burst from the entry, his brother on his heels.

'Where's my— Oh, it's you,' he said, frowning at Gil. 'Where's Dame Ellen? Do you ken aught o this new matter at St Mungo's?'

'New matter?' Gil raised an eyebrow. Muir shook his head impatiently.

'Another death. One o their vergers, so the Canon told us,

bound wi ropes and put down a well. A right strange thing. He said he was strangled and all. Is it aught to do wi Annie? Or this other hoor that was in her place?'

'Aye, but Henry, that wasny—' began his brother. Muir lifted a threatening hand, and Austin fell silent.

'No connection that I can see,' Gil said. 'It seems as if the man was thieving goods from the Almoner's stores, and I wonder if his death is linked to that.'

'Oh.' Muir stared at him, frowning, and Gil studied the man in return. He was garbed today in a high-necked doublet of dark red velvet, the breast and stiff collar embroidered with silken pinks and bright green leaves, the cuffs of its tight sleeves turned back with, yes, gold brocade.

'You were out again the night Annie went to the Cross,' he said. Muir gave him a challenging nod. 'Where did you go?'

'Down the High Street.' The other man snorted in what seemed to be amusement. 'There was some kind o prentice ploy on at the Girth Cross, daft laddies all about the place and getting shoved into the burn, we'd to avoid them. We never went near Annie, if that's what you're asking. Her own servants had an eye to her, we'd no need to get involved.'

'And yet I heard you'd a notion to wed her yourself,' said Gil. 'It would ha been a nice attention, to keep watch for her.'

'Where did you hear that?' demanded Muir, but his brother was grinning and nodding.

'Oh, aye,' he said, 'Henry's right inclined to Annie, or he was, till she—' He broke off as Muir turned to glare at him.

'Till she what?' Gil asked innocently.

'Till she vanished,' said Muir aggressively.

'What were you wearing that night?'

'Wearing? Why? D'ye think I have aught to do wi her disappearing?'

'No,' said Gil mildly. 'I just wondered what sic a well-dressed fellow as yourself might wear to go out on the town.'

149

'Oh, that's easy tellt,' said Austin irrepressibly, as his brother glanced up and down Gil's well-worn black garb, 'for it was your blue brocade, and the satin doublet under it, was it no, Henry, and I had on my grey velvet. Aye, it was the brocade,' he went on, 'for you got ale on your good 'broidered shirt, Nory was right displeased at you, though it never went on the brocade.'

'Will you be quiet?' demanded his brother. 'Haud yer wheesht and let wiser folks talk. Which is just about a'body in Glasgow,' he added bitterly. Austin shuffled back a couple of steps, with what might have been meant for an ingratiating grin.

'So what time did you get back to the house?' Gil asked casually. 'I wonder if you saw anything that might be helpful.'

Muir shrugged.

'We were in bed by midnight, so it must ha been afore that.' He paused to consider. 'There was the prentice battle, like I tellt you, and a few folk going home from their drinking. Nothing I can mind.'

'There was the man wi that handcart,' said Austin, 'that I heard when we went up Rottenrow.'

'There was no handcart, you daftheid!' said his brother. 'I tell you, you imagined it, or you're making it up!'

'Aye, Henry,' said Austin docilely. 'But how did I hear it if I'm making it up?'

'Any road, I'm wanting a word wi that doctor,' Muir continued, ignoring this. 'Doctor Christian, or whatever his name is. I want to ken how does our kinsman.'

'He hasny long, I believe,' said Gil.

'Aye, but how long is that?' he demanded. 'How long does whoever's stole Annie away have to keep her hid?'

'Keep her hidden?' Gil repeated. 'Are you thinking it's someone Sir Edward would never contemplate wedding her wi? That he's waiting till her guardian's gone?'

'What else would it be, man?' said Muir contemptuously, while Austin grinned and nodded behind him. 'And if I'd thought it would work, I'd ha done the same. I just wish I'd kent who it was that was after her, I'd ha dealt wi them aforehand. All that land, to go out o the family!'

'Sir Edward did not wish to see her wedded at all, I thought,' Gil offered.

'Foolishness,' said Muir. 'Leave her property all unstewarded? Sheer waste. And what is this about the second death, then?' he demanded, with an abrupt reversion to his subject. 'The auld fool hadny a plain tale to tell, he's right stonied by it all and makin' no sense. When was it?'

'Yestreen,' Gil said. Muir frowned.

'Yestreen. So when was he killed? Who was it? One o the vergers, you said.'

'Aye,' Gil said. 'A man called Barnabas. He was found some time after Compline, and had likely been dead no more than a couple of hours.'

Muir was still frowning, working something out. Austin said,

'Oh, well, that's no a worry, Henry—' He stepped back, not fast enough to avoid the swinging backhander, and recovered himself to stand rubbing his mouth and nose, staring at his brother in dumb reproach.

'So no that long afore Vespers,' said Muir, as if nothing had happened. Gil nodded agreement. 'But why? It's a daft thing to do, put a man down a well in a kirk!'

'Daft thing to do, to throttle a lassie after she's dead,' Gil observed.

'What d'you mean by that?' demanded Muir, hackling up.

'Why, that it's a daft thing to do,' said Gil. 'No other.'

'He's right there, Henry,' said Austin, 'the one's as daft as the other. Here, d'you think it was—'

'Will you haud your wheesht?'

'D'you think it was what, Austin?' Gil asked.

'Nothing,' said Austin, rubbing at his mouth again. 'Forgot what I was going to say.'

'Henry, Austin, I thought I heard you,' said Dame Ellen in the doorway of the women's hall.

'There you are!' said Muir in the same breath. 'Madam,' he added. She gave them both a simpering smile.

'You're here in a good hour, laddies. You can escort me over to St Mungo's, till I offer another prayer for my poor brother.'

Chapter Nine

'Kittock sent these,' said Alys, setting the basket of pasties down on the bench in the masons' lodge.

This was not strictly true. When asked for a bite to offer the men Kittock had cast her eye about the kitchen and said reluctantly, 'Well, they've aye liked the cheese pasties, mem, and I could make some more for our own supper, you could take them those if you wanted.' She had then added a handful of parsley in a cloth and a dozen of the little cakes from the day's baking; Alys herself had drawn a large jug of ale from the barrel in the brewhouse. Jennet set this down now beside the basket and pushed her fair locks back over her shoulders, smiling at Maistre Pierre's man Thomas who had paused in his work to watch them.

'She had no need to do that,' said Maistre Pierre disapprovingly. 'We have gone home at noontide in the usual way.'

'An extra bite is always welcome when the men are working hard,' Alys suggested. She sat down on the bench, looking out at the busy scene beside the lodge. The men she knew, Wattie and Thomas and Luke, were working on what looked like the mouldings for a window tracery, while two more journeymen were blocking out the stones they would need next. The familiar music of chisel and mell competed with the birdsong in St Mungo's kirkyard, with the crows which swirled about the tall trees adding their own harsh bass. 'You make good progress. Is that the second window going forward now?'

'It is. Blacader has found some funds, so I begin to hope his new work will be completed in my lifetime.'

'So your marriage has brought you good fortune,' Alys said brightly. He looked hard at her, and she maintained the smile with a little difficulty. After a moment he grunted, and sat down beside her.

'Perhaps so, truly. Are you well, *ma mie*?'

'I am, Father. How does my stepmother?'

'She is well too. And your husband? How does he fare with this matter of the missing lady? I have not seen him today.'

'I think he planned to speak to the Provost about it,' she answered, 'and then to pursue the death of the cathedral servant. That is a very strange thing. I suppose you saw nothing from here.'

He gestured beyond the fence which separated his industrious men and the building site which was Archbishop Blacader's contribution to the fabric of his cathedral, from the path which ran between the kirkyard gate and the doorway of the Lower Kirk.

'*Ma mie*, there are many people on that path, a dozen, two dozen in an afternoon.' This could well be true, she recognised; there were three people visible just now, two women heading for the church, their beads in their hands, gossiping happily, and one of the canons pacing the other way. No, not a canon, it was William Craigie. 'And in any case, I think the man was killed long after we had gone home to our dinner. We talked it over here in the lodge this morning, and none of us can recall even seeing the man Barnabas, much less someone waving a strangler's cord. I think the man and his killer both went down from the Upper Kirk to where he was found.'

'The Dean is very certain that did not happen, so Gil says. That he was killed outside the church and carried to where he was found.'

'Hah!' said her father sceptically.

'What you say seems the most likely,' she agreed, thinking how much she had missed this, the talking over of events, the companionable sharing of ideas. Since they came to Glasgow from Paris, after her mother's death, it

154

had been herself and her father, and then Gil who had fitted into the family quite seamlessly. Her stepmother thought in a different way, and would not hear other points of view, which made discussion difficult, and in any case she seemed to be jealous of Alys herself.

Her thoughts paused as that idea presented itself. Jealous? Was that the problem? Why had she not seen it before?

'I have no idea what Gilbert has learned today,' her father was saying. 'They were to search the man's lodging, I do not know if they discovered anything there.'

'You could send Luke or Berthold to find Gil and ask him,' Alys suggested. 'Or go yourself.'

'I cannot leave these lazy fellows,' said her father, nodding at Thomas, who was contriving to talk to Jennet without breaking off his work. 'And I cannot spare Luke, because Berthold is at home today.'

'At home?'

Maistre Pierre shrugged.

'He is not well, one can well see, he has some kind of ague and sits about shivering and complaining of his belly, though none of the other men has taken the same ill. We have dosed him with willow-bark tea and ginger, but it does not help. Élise wished me to leave him home today, to see if a day's quiet would avail him.'

'Poor boy,' said Alys, noting this last point approvingly. 'It is strange that none of the rest of you is affected.'

Her father grunted agreement, then looked at her sideways.

'Élise has said,' he pronounced deliberately, 'that she sees shadows about him. Shadows, and also crows.'

'Shadows? What does she mean? And why crows? Crows such as these in the treetops, or metaphorical crows?'

'I do not know,' he said, though she did not believe this. 'That is all she has told me. So I have no time to pursue your husband about the town, and no time to sit here longer talking to you, pleasant though it is, *ma mie*.'

She rose obediently when he did, and looked about for Jennet, finding the woman at her elbow.

'If I see Gil in the town, I will tell him you are kept here.' She put up her face for his kiss. 'Will you send Luke to bring the jug and cloths home at the day's end? I should like a word with him.'

'Where now, mem?' asked Jennet as they crossed the stoneyard. 'Are we to go into St Mungo's? I'd like fine to see where that verger was put down the well. It's pity, so it is,' she went on, following her mistress towards the door of the Lower Kirk, 'they none of them saw whoever did it go to and fro on the path, it would ha made our maister's work a sight easier.'

'Did Thomas say anything about the boy Berthold?'

'Him? No, he never mentioned him. Save he said the laddie's no weel,' she amended, 'complaining of his belly. Likely it's the change from his foreign food that's disagreed wi him, he'll be right when he's accustomed hissel to kale and oatmeal.'

Alys, curtsying to Our Lady, small and ancient on her pillar inside the door, made no answer. She reached up to touch the little figure's blackened foot, and went past into the Lady Chapel, drawing her beads from her belt. Jennet curtsied in her turn, but made her way purposefully down the steps to where St John's chapel was firmly cordoned off with some of the blue ropes which were used to pen the multitude on feast days. Kneeling within the curtained Lady Chapel, Alys could hear her servant's pattens clopping about the east end, and a quiet recitation as if someone was saying Mass in one of the other chapels on the cross-aisle. The Lower Kirk was not empty.

One repetition of the rosary contented her for the moment. Leaving money for a second candle she moved on for a word with St Mungo himself, setting yet another candle on the bank of lights against the fence which surrounded the tomb. She murmured a section of one of the graduals concerning his miraculous life, drawing together her Latin, which was not, she suspected, as good as Gil thought it was, to petition him in a language he might understand. Though surely prayer should transcend language, she thought suddenly. The priest who had been saying Mass left by the stair towards the Vicars' hall. Had it been William Craigie? No, surely not, he had crossed the kirkyard earlier. She shut her eyes to avoid distraction. Blessed Kentigern, she said to the saint, you concerned yourself with servants, you raised your teacher's cook from the dead, whether your servant Barnabas was a thief or no he deserves justice. Help us to find his murderer. And the two women at the Cross, both the one who is vanished and the one who was found dead there, they deserve your care too. What should I do to help them? How can we find Annie and bring her to safety, how can we procure justice for Peg? Let me have a sign, blessed Kentigern.

A little current of air passed her face, as if someone moved beside her. She opened her eyes, but nobody was nearby, not even the priest.

'Jennet?' she said.

'I'm here, mistress.' Her servant emerged from the Lady Chapel, beads in hand. 'Where do we go now? Are you going to question all them at St Catherine's? Has our maister no questioned them a'ready?'

'That's right kind in you to call, mistress,' said Ursula Shaw. 'And sending your own woman out to fetch in cakes and ale.'

'A pleasure,' said Alys conventionally, and glanced beyond the two girls at Jennet, who was now sharing a portion of both with the woman Meggot.

'They feed us well enough here,' said Nicholas, 'but they's no wee extras the way there is at home.' She bit into one of the honey-cakes with evident pleasure. 'No to mention we're glad o the company. It's a wee thing tedious, what wi my aunt spending all her time across at St Mungo's.'

I wonder where, thought Alys. Perhaps she was in the Upper Kirk.

'We were thinking, when we came to Glasgow we'd get to the market,' confessed Ursula, 'and there's a velvet warehouse so I heard, the chapman said it was a right good choice you'd get there.'

'Maister Walkinshaw's warehouse,' said Alys.

'Aye, that was the name. I could just fancy a velvet gown.' The other girl looked down at her own woad-dyed home-spun, and then at Alys's well-cut tawny linen. 'Is that the sleeves they're wearing this year? Big enough for a jeely-bag?'

'Certainly in Glasgow,' Alys agreed, smoothing the deep facing of yellow silk which turned back one wide sleeve. 'I have spent all my life in towns,' she went on. 'The country-side is bonnie, especially when it is well farmed, and of course one's food is fresher by far in the country, but I should not like to be so far from warehouses, and have to rely on what the chapman brings. Is yours reliable? Does he carry a good stock?'

'What, Cadger Billy? Aye, he's no bad. Comes by every three or four month, wi a pack o stale news—'

'Cadger's news!' said Nicholas, and giggled. Her sister threw her an annoyed glance, and went on rather sourly,

'We're missing him the now, indeed, he must be out about Glenbuck wi his wee cairt, and here we're shut in here instead o viewing the merchant-goods o Glasgow that he's aye described us.'

'We'll both be wedded in homespun yet, for all Ellen cares,' said Nicholas. 'Did you say, mistress,' she went on, 'you're wedded on that man that's trying to find Annie? The one like a long drink—' She broke off sharply as if she had been nudged. 'He was here just a wee minute ago, talking wi Dame Ellen, afore she went back to St Mungo's. Is he a good man to be wedded on?'

A long drink of water, Alys thought, and repressed annoyance.

'He's very good to me,' she said. 'He tells me you're both betrothed?'

'Aye.' Ursula pulled a face. 'Though when we'll get to be wedded, wi Da the way he is—' She turned her face away briefly, blinking. 'It was to be next month, ye ken, mistress, and now there's no saying.'

'And no velvet gowns neither,' muttered Nicholas.

'Will your men not wait? It should all be signed, surely?'
The sisters looked at one another, and Nicholas shrugged.

'Likely. Hers certainly will.'

'Och, Nick, so will yours.'

'Who are they?'

Nicholas, it seemed, was to wed a neighbour of her sister
Mariota over into Lanarkshire; Alys, only dimly familiar
with the place-names they threw about, thought they might
still be too far apart for the sisters to visit easily once both
had babies to consider, but Ursula still sounded resentful
when she named her future husband's lands.

'Away down through Ayrshire,' she said, 'next to
Tarbolton, no that far from where Annie came from as a
matter of fact. A whole day's ride from her and Mariota.'

'But are his lands extensive?' Alys asked. 'Can he keep
you in style? Will you have a great household to run?'

'So my aunt says,' said Ursula, with a show of indifference.

'Was the match hers, then?'

'Aye, she promoted it. He's some kind of acquaintance o
her kin at St Mungo's, so my da said.'

'Have you met him? Is he a well-looking man?'

'Better than Lockhart,' said Nicholas. 'They both are!'

'That's no hard!'

The two exchanged another look, and giggled. Alys was
aware of Meggot, over by the other wall, glancing at the
sisters and shaking her head disapprovingly. Taking care
not to meet Jennet's eye, she said,

'I had not realised you had kin at St Mungo's. Who is it?'

'Och, none of our kin,' said Ursula dismissively. 'Some
connection o my aunt's by her first marriage, I think she
said. He's no ill looking, but he's a priest, all shaven and
shorn, though that didny stop him putting his hand about
Nick's waist when we met him.'

'Aye, and Ellen never checked him,' said Nicholas, wrig-
gling in remembered displeasure.

'But do you recall his name?' asked Alys. *He gropith so
nyselye about my lape*, she thought, reviewing a list of the St
Mungo's clergy in her mind. There were several whom she

159

would not wish to consult without Jennet or preferably Gil at her elbow, but not all of these were *no ill looking*.

'William?' said Ursula.

'William Craigie,' her sister contributed. She nodded at sight of Alys's expression, and went on, 'To hear Ellen the sun shines out his bum.'

'She wasny saying that the morn,' observed Ursula. 'Abusing him for a'things, she was, out there in the court-yard, for something he hadny done.'

'What was it?' the other girl asked avidly. Ursula shrugged.

'Never heard. She stopped when she saw me, got at me for no finishing my seam instead.'

'Just the same,' said Nicholas doggedly, 'she mostly thinks he's a pattern o perfection, but what I heard was, he'd a major penance to perform, the way he'd done something right serious against Holy Kirk.'

'Who tellt you that?' demanded Ursula. Nicholas shrugged in her turn.

'One of your man's folk, when they all cam up to sign your betrothal papers. I forget the lad's name. Meggot!' she called over her shoulder.

'Aye, lassie, what is it?' Meggot responded, pausing with another little cake halfway to her mouth.

'Do you mind that lad of Arthur Kennedy's telling us about William Craigie and his penance?'

'She does not,' said another voice from the window. They all turned, startled, to find a grim-faced woman staring in at the wide-flung shutters. Beyond her a liveried manservant slipped off towards the stable block. 'And what has it to do wi you, my girl, any road? I've brought you up better than to spend your time gossiping wi other folk's servants, Nicholas Shaw, let alone passing on whatever slanders they've spoken, and I'll thank you to keep it in mind.'

Alys, rising as good manners dictated to curtsy to the newcomer, observed the reactions in the room with inter-est. The sisters were annoyed by the interruption, only slightly embarrassed at being found gossiping; Meggot appeared to be frightened. Would this mean another beating, perhaps? Or did she fear something worse? What could be worse, Alys speculated, waiting for Dame Ellen to come round by the door of the guest-hall. Meggot might lose her place, or she might be sent back out to Glenbuck to wait alone for news of Annie, or her mistress might report badly of her to Sir Edward. No, she was Annie's servant, not Dame Ellen's, or so Gil had said; it could hardly be that.

'Good afternoon, Aunt,' said Ursula in a tone of faint malice as the older woman stalked into the hall. 'I hope you had solace of your time at St Mungo's. This is Mistress Alys Mason, that's wedded on that man that's seeking our Annie, come to offer us comfort in our troubles.'

'Indeed I am sorry for all your distress,' said Alys, curtsying again and going forward with her hands outstretched. 'Is there still no word of your niece?'

'No niece of mine,' said Dame Ellen curtly, ignoring the hands. 'No, there's no word, though it would ease my poor brother's passing greatly if he kent where the lassie had got to, deid or living.'

'It is very strange,' Alys persisted, 'that she should have vanished away so completely. Is there nobody that might have given her shelter, can you think?'

'Do you no think we've racked our brains for a clue?' retorted the older woman, bridling. 'Now we'll no keep you back, mistress, kind as it was in ye to entertain these silly lassies for a bit. And your woman and all.' Her gimlet gaze went beyond Alys, and a rustle of cloth suggested that Jennet felt similarly impelled to curtsy. 'Good day to ye, madam.'

Out in the courtyard she encountered someone who could only be the doctor, a small man with curly dark hair, in a stained cloth gown which looked as if he regularly wore it while pounding simples or concocting remedies. She curtsied to him, under Jennet's suspicious glower, and when he acknowledged it she introduced herself and asked after his patient. He shook his head sadly, and she noted the dark shadows under the blue eyes.

'I think he has a difficult passage,' she said in French, aware of watching eyes, of listening ears in the hall behind her, 'despite the prayers of his friends.'

The doctor nodded.

'Difficult indeed,' he replied in the same language. 'I can keep the pain at bay, but it is terrible to combat. There will be no poppy left in Glasgow, I suspect.'

'How long has he got? How long do we have to find the missing lady?'

'I think he will wait until he knows she is safe.'

Alys stepped forward and placed a hand on his sleeve.

'What if she is no longer living?' she said. 'The longer it takes to find her or some trace of her, the less certain my husband is that we will find her alive.'

There was a tiny pause, and Januar said smoothly,

'Why, if she is no longer living, then she is assuredly safe under Our Lady's mantle.'

Alys considered him for a moment, but let that pass.

'She seems to have no connection or acquaintance in this part of Scotland,' she said. 'If there was a house of nuns in Glasgow one might seek her there, but we can learn of nowhere else she could have turned to.'

'My concern is for my patient,' said the doctor after a moment. 'You will excuse me, madame.'

The hostel's little chapel was dark and quiet, though there were candles on the stand at the feet of the patron saint on her pillar to the left of the chancel arch. Jennet, at first wishing to exclaim indignantly about Dame Ellen's behaviour, fell silent when her mistress drew out her beads, and retreated to sit near the door on the narrow wall-bench. Alys stood before St Catherine, head bent, not praying but trying to order what she had learned just now. The Shaw sisters were remarkably silly girls, as their aunt said, she thought dispassionately, but they did not seem ill intentioned, and if they knew anything about what had happened to their sister-in-law, they would be hard pressed to conceal it. Dame Ellen was another matter; the woman was certainly

162

concealing something, but what? Was she directly involved in Annie's disappearance, or did she know or suspect who might be involved? Why did Meggot fear her?

'She's aye ready wi her hands, so Meggot said,' said Jennet as they made their way down the hill, past the high sandstone walls of the castle. 'Showed me her bruises, she did, that the old dame gied her only for saying it wasny her own mistress that lay dead in the chapel. Is that the chapel where we were the now, mem? Small wonder if they were mistook at first, it was that dark.'

'Did she tell you anything else?' Alys asked, untangling this statement. 'Does she know where her own mistress is, do you think?'

'I'd say no,' Jennet pronounced after a moment. 'She seems right concerned for her, saying she's no notion whether she's living or where she might be. What else did she say, now?' She clopped across the flagstones round the Girth Cross behind Alys, considering the matter. 'It's been a good position till now, for she's fond o the lassie that's missing, for all her strange ways. But what wi the young leddies about to be wedded, and the maister on his deathbed, though she says he's been that way for months now, she's no notion o what's to come to her, the soul.' She thought further. 'Tellt me a bit about the life. I was never in a country position, see, mem, and I wouldny fancy it, by what she says. That doctor turned up a few month ago, wi his man—'

'His man?' Alys queried, stopping to look at the other girl. 'Your maister never mentioned a manservant. Is he still there?'

'No by what Meggot says,' Jennet agreed. 'Seems he found it too quiet and all, for he vanished away one day along wi the doctor's purse wi ten merks in siller in it. Then there was the young leddies' two men cam for the betrothal, wi all their folk, and went away again, and that Dame Ellen comes and goes, and apart from the cadger they spoke o that's all the company there's been in the place since Yule. Away too quiet for me, that would be. Oh, no, I tell a lee, there was her two nephews came calling a few times, it seems, but Meggot wasny that keen to see them, by what she said. Kind o free wi their hands, or one o them is, any road.'

'That was well done. You learned more than I did,' said Alys, moving on. 'What did she tell you of her mistress's life? Did any of these visitors call on her?'

'Oh, aye. Aye pestering her, so Meggot says, to gie up her vow and come back into the world. That Dame Ellen telling her what a bonnie husband her nephews would make, even trying to persuade her wi ribbons and gewgaws off the cadger's cairt. Meggot said,' Jennet negotiated the stepping-stones of the Girth Burn behind Alys, her skirts caught up in either hand, 'Meggot said, she'd as soon see the lassie live her life like any other, but she'd not see her forced to it. She said,' she confided, 'she'd ha thought those nephews had something to do wi Annie disappearing, maybe snatched her away and hid her, save that they looked as astonished as the rest o them when it turned out it was another lassie that was dead.'

'So I thought too, by what your maister said.'

'I hope she's no to get a beating, only for talking to me.' Jennet stopped, pushing back her hair, and stared about her. 'Here, mem, where are we away to now? This is us on the High Street, no the Drygate. Are we no bound for home?'

'We're going to the old house. I want a word with Berthold,' Alys said. The other girl gave her a sidelong look, but said nothing. 'So maybe you should stay with me, rather than go off to the kitchen.'

'Och, there's nothing for me in that kitchen now,' Jennet pointed out. 'Talking away in Ersche, they are, and never a bite for a guest to eat neither. No neighbourly, I call it, no to mention the way the dust's rising in the hall, you'd think they never knew what a besom was for. I'd just as soon attend you, mem.'

'*Ich sah nichts!*' said Berthold, his eyes rolling like a nervous horse's. '*Ich kann nicht – ich sah nichts!*'

Alys reached along the bench and patted his hand. About them the garden of her father's house lay in the sunshine, the scents of lavender and gillyflowers rising from the neat plots. At least her stepmother was tending that, she thought irrelevantly.

'I know,' she agreed, and paused, mustering the little Low Dutch she knew. It was rather different from Berthold's High Dutch, but she had found it served to talk to him before now. She suspected the boy understood a lot more Scots than he would admit, but the answer she wanted was going to take some persuasion, and something approaching his own language would work better. '*Ziet u de vrouw?*' she said cautiously. Berthold shrank slightly from her. '*De dood vrouw?* The dead woman?'

The boy shuddered, and dragged his hand from her clasp. Jennet, standing by the lavender hedge, narrowed her eyes.

'That's worried him, mem,' she observed unnecessarily. 'Here, Berthold, tell the mistress all about it, whatever it is. She'll can sort it for you, so she will.'

'*Nein, nein! Ich weiss nichts!*' said Berthold, shaking his head emphatically. Alys smiled at him, and reclaimed his hand, which was sweating and trembling.

'*Waar?*' she asked him. '*Waar zij is?*' Another shake of the head. 'On the Drygate? Or on the Stablegreen?'

'*Ich sah nichts,*' Berthold almost wailed.

'*En u? Waar u was?*'

'What are you saying to him, mem?' Jennet asked. 'He's in a right tirravee about it, whatever it is.'

'I asked him where he was,' Alys said, 'the night he went out with Luke.'

'What, the night afore last? The night the lassie was slain?' Jennet looked intently at Berthold. 'Did he see it, are you thinking? Is that why he's feart, he thinks they'll come and get him and all?'

Berthold, his pale blue gaze going from one face to the other, said nothing.

'*Waar u was?*' Alys repeated. He shook his head. 'Luke

says you were not with him. Were you on the Stablegreen? By St Nicholas' perhaps?'

'*Sankt Nikolaus*,' said Berthold after a moment. Alys nodded, and patted the hand she still held.

'See, that was easy,' she said. 'Where were all the others? The prentices? Where was the fighting?' She mimed a punch with her free hand. 'On the Drygate? By the Cross?'

Berthold eyed her doubtfully, and after another pause said,

'*Das Kreuz. Neben dem Kreuz.*'

'Is he saying they were by the Cross, mem?' said Jennet. 'For that's right, that's what Luke tellt us. Been a right good battle, by the sound o't, and nobody hurt neither.'

Berthold's gaze flicked to her at the words, and his expression changed, as if he did not agree. Alys considered him thoughtfully.

'Berthold,' she said. His eyes turned to her, and she let go his hand. '*Hier ist das Kreuz.*' She drew an X on the wooden bench between them with her forefinger, and another a handspan away. '*Hier ist Sankt Nikolaus. Hier is u.*' She looked up at him, and he nodded. She waved her hand over the little scene she had mapped. '*Wat u zien*? What do you see? *De dood vrouw*?'

'*Nein!*'

'*Is hier*,' she drew a line away from St Nicholas', 'Rottenrow.' Another nod. '*Hier kom twee mensen.*' She held up two fingers, then walked them along the line of Rottenrow. '*Ja? Twee mensen.*' She mimed fine clothes, patted rich sleeves, adjusted a hat. Berthold nodded hesitantly.

'My, you're as good as a play, mem,' said Jennet, laughing.

'*Twee mensen*,' Alys said, and walked them down Rottenrow again. By the spot which represented St Nicholas' she paused. Berthold was watching her fingers; after a moment he stole a glance at her, then looked back at her hand. '*Wat u zien?*' she asked again. The boy shook his head and looked away again, staring intently at the flagstones under the bench. 'Berthold,' she persisted. '*Wat u zien?*'

His chest heaved.

'*Nichts!*' he burst out. '*Ich sah nichts!*' He sprang to his feet, bobbed a perfunctory bow, the civility heartbreaking in the circumstances, and fled towards the house.

'Well!' said Jennet. 'Did he tell you anything, mem? I canny make out his babble. It's right clever the way you can understand him, and Luke can tell what he's saying and all.'

'He saw the two brothers,' Alys said, gazing after the boy. 'The same two that Meggot was telling you about. I know Luke saw them so that must be right. But he insists that he saw nothing else.'

'He's feart for something,' said Jennet. 'Or someone, maybe.'

'So I thought,' agreed Alys. She drew a deep breath, and got to her feet. 'Come, I must be civil to my good-mother.'

Ealasaidh nic Iain, very upright on the settle in the hall, her red worsted skirts spreading round her and her dark curling hair hidden by a very new French hood which did not entirely suit her, studied Alys with faint hostility.

'Was that all you were wanting?' she asked. Then, perhaps recognising that she sounded ungracious, 'No that you are not welcome in your faither's house, lassie. Will you take another cake?'

'Thank you.' Alys took another oatcake, then offered the platter to her stepmother, who shook her head curtly. 'No, I wished a word with you as well, Ealasaidh.'

'Oh?'

They had dealt with the health and progress of small John, Ealasaidh's nephew, along with two clever things he had said, and agreed on the management of whatever ailed young Berthold with a harmonious exchange of receipts for afflictions of the spirits. Now Alys bit into the oatcake, which was smeared with some of the apricot preserve she had left in the stillroom. Across the hall, Jennet was seated primly in the window, looking with disapproval at the floor, which was certainly dusty. Trying not to follow her gaze, Alys said,

'When you were travelling about Scotland,' she met her

167

stepmother's eye and quailed at the expression in it, 'did you ever know, did you ever hear of,' she corrected herself, 'a chapman called Cadger Billy? He trades in Lanarkshire, that I know of.'

'I have heard o him,' admitted Ealasaidh remotely. 'We never played for the great houses out in Lanarkshire, you understand, they have no appreciation of the clarsadh there, but I have heard of Cadger Billy.'

'Do you know where he comes from?'

The other woman shrugged.

'They know him out by Dumbarton, and by Kirkintilloch. I never met the man.'

'That is helpful,' Alys said thoughtfully. 'His circuit centres on Glasgow, perhaps.'

'Why do you ask? Is there no enough goods in Glasgow for you?'

'He called more than once at the home of the lassie that is missing,' she explained. 'I wonder if he might have carried some word for her.'

'Very likely. Who better, indeed? Is that you helping your man again? Have you learned aught to avail him?'

Recognising the real meaning of the question, Alys recounted all that was known of the two deaths and the disappearance. As was her habit, Ealasaidh listened with many exclamations of shock and surprise, even to the portions she must have heard already, laughed heartily at the tale of the quest and the two verdicts, and finally said,

'And you are thinking our laddie might be involved?'

'I think he may have seen something. My father has told me you see shadows around the boy.' Ealasaidh's mouth tightened, but she nodded. 'Do you know what they mean?'

'No.' She waited, and after a moment the other woman went on, 'I am seeing a darkness about him, like death. It is not a death close to him, or danger of death, I am thinking, but I do not know what it betokens. And also I am seeing crows.'

'Crows,' Alys repeated. 'That is very strange.'

'Three of them,' Ealasaidh said. Her strong mouth twisted

wryly. 'As in the song, you ken it? Three crows on a wall. I am not understanding it.'

'*On a cold and a frosty morning.* Has he mentioned crows?'

'He has said nothing. He is frightened, that is very clear. Maybe I will make himself question him again.'

'I think that might not work,' Alys protested, 'for he has already lied to my father. No, leave him, we might get something from him once he has thought for longer. If Gil learns more about what he might have seen, we may be able to question him more closely.'

Ealasaidh grunted, but said after a moment, 'A shocking thing it is, all this that has happened, and all around St Mungo's too. You would be thinking the saint would be protecting his own better than that. No doubt he is revenged on the man Barnabas now. Himself was telling me of that last night.'

'He likes to talk over the day,' said Alys cautiously. Her stepmother gave her a suspicious look. She smiled, the same smile as she had shown her father, maintaining it with the same slight effort. 'He has missed my mother sorely these seven years. I am glad he has you to talk to.'

Ealasaidh's expression softened slightly.

'It is good of you to be saying that, lassie,' she said.

'Oh, yes,' Alys assured her. 'My duty is with Gil's household, after all, now he has his own roof-tree, and my father would be alone, since he has no other child.'

There was a silence, which extended beyond comfort and into an appalled chill. She felt her face solidify, and the shadows in the hall darkened and danced before her eyes. *Christ aid me,* she thought, *surely not? Not already?* Out of the darkness Ealasaidh's voice said,

'I would not have told you yet, lassie. Himself does not know, I have only now begun to sicken.'

'I wish you,' she said from a dry mouth, 'I wish you well. I wish you very well.'

A hard hand closed over hers, just as she had clasped Johan's.

'Alys.' Was that the first time the woman had used her

name? 'I take that very kindly, lassie. Are you,' the strong-featured face emerged from the dancing shadows close to hers, 'are you well? Will I call for a cordial?'

'No, I,' she rose unsteadily, 'I must go. I must call on, call on,' she swallowed, 'I must make other calls.'

Jennet was exclaiming at her elbow, concern in her tone, and her stepmother spoke again, low and intense, though she could not catch the words. Jennet said,

'What are you telling her, mistress? Get away from her, leave her alone!'

'She needs to know this.'

'Leave her, mistress, can you no see she's no well? She can hear it later. Come away, mem, can you manage the stair?'

By the time they had traversed the courtyard and the pend which led out into the street she was shivering so her teeth chattered, and clinging to Jennet's hand.

'What is it, my dearie?' her maid demanded, pulling her plaid about her shoulders for her. 'What's come to you? What will I do for you, lassie?' The girl looked about her, as if for help. 'Are you ill right enough? Oh, how will I get you home from here? Can you walk?'

'Kate,' she managed. *What shall I do, what shall I do?* went the thoughts in her head.

'Leddy Kate! A course, that's the answer. Come on, my lassie, just a few steps. Our Lady send she's home, or some of them at least.'

One foot in front of the other. Her legs like hanks of yarn, Jennet's arm strong about her waist. Voices round her, familiar and friendly.

'Mercy on us, girl, what's come to your mistress? Babb, fetch me the angelica cordial and a glass.'

'I dinna ken, mem, we called on her good-mother, then she went like this when we cam to leave. I canny get her home this way.'

'Alys? Alys, what ails you?'

'It was something the auld wife said to her.' Jennet's voice was dark with suspicion. 'My mistress wished her well, but it turned her right dwaibly, it did, for all that.'

'What did she say? Bring her here.' The familiar thumping of her sister-in-law's crutches. She was led forward, pushed onto something soft, made to lie back. 'Cover her wi this, she's cold as charity. Alys? Can you hear me?'

She nodded, and a warm hand gripped hers.

'I've no a notion what she said, mem, but my mistress was wishing her well,' Jennet repeated. There was a pause, as if the two exchanged a glance, and Kate's voice said,

'I see. Aye, Babb, bring that here. Alys? A wee drop cordial?'

'I feel a right fool,' she said.

'Rubbish,' said Kate briskly. Seated in the window-space, the cradle at her feet and her son at her breast, she peered at Alys across the hall chamber. 'I'll not ask what your good-mother told you, but if it's what I think it is, it would owerset anybody. Are you feeling better after that wee sleep?'

'I should get up the road and see to the dinner.'

'Kittock can make the dinner by herself, she's done it a few times,' Kate retorted. 'You'll leave here when I say you're fit to go. What took you to that house, anyway? I thought you wereny on calling terms?'

'That was part of it.' Alys lay back against the pillows of her sister-in-law's best bed, still feeling disorientated. 'I— We should be better friends. I thought it falls to me to make— And then she—' She swallowed, and started again. 'My father said something about Berthold, I wished to ask her more about it. And to speak to Berthold.'

'You're making little sense.' Kate objected. 'What about Berthold? He's coming on, or so John Paterson says, his Scots is no bad at all and he was out at the prentice battle the other night, it seems. A numnum!' she said to the noisily suckling baby, who ignored her.

Alys tried to gather her thoughts.

'My father said,' she recounted slowly, 'that my good-mother had seen shadows round the boy. He has been unwell for a day or two, ever since the prentice battle. We suspect he saw something that night which has frightened

171

him, and what my father said confirms it to me. I wished to speak to him myself, but it was no good, he would not tell me either.'

'Shadows.'

'And also crows. She thought, not his death, but something around him.'

Kate eyed her doubtfully, but did not comment. After a moment she said,

'Where is Gil at with this matter, anyway? We heard about the man dead at St Mungo's. Is it connected to the other death? Is someone going about the High Kirk killing folk? That'll do the pilgrim trade no good.'

'I don't know what Gil might have learned today,' she said. 'There is no trace of the missing lassie, which is strange, you would think if she has been taken to be wed by force, or for her money, her kin would have heard of it by now. I wanted to ask my good-mother something about that, too,' she added, 'but she has never met Cadger Billy, though she has heard of him.'

'Cadger Billy?' Kate repeated. 'The chapman wi the cart?'

'You know him?' Of course, she realised, Kate had grown up out in Lanarkshire. Likely Gil knew the man too, and she had had no need to ask, to get into conversation with—

'Known him all my life. He'd come by every two or three months, first at Darngaber, then after we went to Carluke, he'd turn up wi his wee cart and a great load of knick-knacks and useful things, on his way out into Lanarkshire. Pins and needles, braids and threads, belt buckles, laces, you name it, he carries it all round the West, Ayrshire and Renfrewshire as well as north of the river.'

'Where does he come from, do you know? Where is his home?'

'Oh, he's a Glasgow man.' Alys sat up with an exclamation, and Kate looked surprised. 'Why are you asking? What's he to do wi't?'

'The Shaw girls, the missing lady's good-sisters, mentioned him. I think he may have carried messages for Annie.'

'He's out on his round the now,' Kate said. 'I had a word

from Tib just yesterday, and she mentioned him, said he'd been by Carluke and went on towards Lesmahagow the day she wrote. So even if he carried word, it's none so likely he carried Annie herself off.'

'Does he have kin here in Glasgow, do you know?'

'Never a notion.' Kate disengaged the drowsy baby from her breast, leaned forward to put him in his cradle, and began to fasten her gown. 'No, wait, I think he once mentioned having taken a wife out of Renfrewshire, which disappointed my sister Margaret at the time, she'd a fancy for him. Tib and I used to tease her about it. Good-looking fellow, wi fair hair, though he doesny have as many teeth as he used to have.' She reached for her crutches, and levered herself to her feet to clump across to the bed. 'How are you feeling now? Aye, I think you're more like yourself. Were you wanting to track down Cadger Billy? Will we ask the men if they ken where he might dwell?'

Making her way home an hour or so later with Jennet watchful at her elbow, Alys picked her way along the path by the mill-burn, past the gardens of the houses on the High Street, past the tumbledown wall at the foot of the College lands, turning over what she had learned in the afternoon, though her thoughts flinched away from the one fact, the unthinkable thing, which she must not share yet with anyone, not even with Gil. Andy Paterson, steward to Kate's husband Augie Morison, had promised to ask about for Cadger Billy's lodging, though he could not see what Alys wanted with such a man, and said so.

'He's honest enough,' he admitted grudgingly, 'but you've all the warehouses o Glasgow about you, mistress, what business would you have wi him?'

Andy's nephew John had been more helpful. Aye, he minded Berthold fine at the prentice boys' battle; he had been near the Cross, and then he had slipped away, maybe no liking the tussle. John had seen him by St Nicholas' chapel, hiding in the shadows. Seeing Luke was in the thick of things, John had kept half an eye on the German laddie, and saw the two fine fellows come down Rottenrow, past Berthold, and turn up the Stablegreen, and then again later coming by the Cross, making for the High Street. They had called encouragement to the defenders of the Cross.

'Likely they was going drinking,' he said. 'And Berthold was still by the chapel then, mistress, but I lost sight o him after that, we was sore pressed by the Drygate lot, and he never cam home wi Luke and me, we took it he'd gone ahead.'

'And will you lie down on your bed when we get in?' Jennet was saying now. 'Or at the least put your feet up on the settle for a wee while—'

'It's near dinner time,' said Alys.

'I don't know,' the other girl said, 'you'd be better if you'd take a wee rest now and then, stead o running about Glasgow till you're all owerset by a wee word wi your good-mother, even if she did say what I thought she said,' she added darkly. 'And did you hear what it was she was telling you afore we cam away? No that you can set great store by what these Ersche say, great leears they are, though maybe no your good-mother, mem,' she added hastily, 'but just the same. Did you hear it, mem?'

'No,' said Alys curtly.

'Why, she was saying—'

'Mistress! I thought that was you!' said a voice. They both swung round, to confront Euan Campbell, weary and travel stained on the path behind them. 'I am back, mistress,' he said triumphantly, 'and though I never found the missing lady, I have found where she is selling all her stolen goods!'

Chapter Ten

Gil was not convinced by what Euan was saying.

'So you've been to Dumbarton,' he said, eyeing his hench-man, 'and found where someone is selling stolen goods from Glasgow.'

'Indeed I have,' agreed Euan proudly, 'all labelled with the Cathedral's stamp they are and everything.'

'Mind out the road, maister,' said Annis, 'till we set up the board.'

'Begin at the beginning,' Gil said, stepping aside while the women shifted trestles and Lowrie went to help them. 'I sent you – yesterday afternoon,' he added pointedly, 'down to the shore to see if the fisher-folk knew anything about a lady leaving the burgh by night.'

'Indeed, so it was,' agreed Euan with even more pride. 'Och, are you thinking I should have been back sooner? I could not, for I was carried all the way to Dumbarton while I found out all you were wanting to know, and I walked home today.'

Gil sat down on the bench Annis had just dragged into position.

'I sent you to the shore,' he said patiently. 'What did you do when you got there?'

'Why, I asked as you bade me, maister,' Euan avouched, 'about a lady missing from the Cross in nothing but her shift, though I never told them that bit, for decency you understand, and first one said he knew nothing and then another, and then one was telling me that the man Stockfish Tam might have something to say.'

'Maister Gil,' said Jennet beside him, 'will you raise your elbow till I put the cloth out. If you please,' she added implausibly.

'So you spoke to Stockfish Tam?' Gil prompted.

'No, no, for he was not there at that time. So I sat down and had a wee crack wi the fisher folk, seeing I ken the most o them from one time or another I've voyaged down the watter. They were right interested to hear o the goings on up at St Mungo's,' he added, 'and I made sure to tell them you'd have the murderer by the heels in no time at all.'

'And when Tam came back?' Gil asked. Sweet St Giles, he thought, what tales has the man been telling? 'What goings on at St Mungo's?' he added sharply.

'Why, the lady that was dead, as well as the verger—'

'How did you know about the verger?'

'Och, all over the town it is,' said Euan, waving one big hand.

'It was well after dinner when I was summoned,' said Gil. 'How did you know about him? When did you hear he was dead?'

'Och, it would be after dinner, likely,' said Euan. 'For Tam and me was taking a wee refreshment in Maggie Bell's alehouse, see, and we heard them talking. Tam was saying that he had no knowledge of the missing lady, but I was not believing that, for when he was hearing that the man was dead, he said he would be taking a wee trip down the river in his boatie, and would I be,' the confident voice faltered, 'would I be giving him a wee hand.'

'How much?' Gil asked.

'How much what, maister?'

'How much did he pay you for crewing for him?'

'Och, no, no, I was doing it entirely for friendship,' averred Euan. Gil watched him. After a moment the man smiled hopefully. 'Well, maybe he was giving me a penny or two. Good sailors is not so easy come by just at the drop of a rowlock.'

'No,' agreed Gil, 'particularly not on the shore where the

fisher folk dwell.' Euan gave him a puzzled look. 'Did you know which man it was that was dead?'

'Och, yes, it was the verger Barnabas, the busy one. That was what Tam was saying, that he had an errand that he, that he could complete,' Euan finished carefully.

'And the errand was?'

'Maister Gil, will you move your elbow again? Are you to sit here all the evening, maister,' demanded Jennet, 'or are we to get the board set?'

Gil looked about him. The dishes were, clearly, about to be brought in, Alys was watching him, Catherine had hobbled out of her chamber. He had already recognised that the women were upset about something, though when he had asked Alys she had professed ignorance. One did not offend the kitchen at the best of times; this was no moment to hold up the dinner. He rose and moved aside with Euan.

'Tell me quickly,' he said, 'what was the errand?'

'Why, he had a sack of grain, and two cheeses, and there was a barrel of apples and all sorts, stowed in his boat already,' said Euan, with shining honesty, 'that had come down on a handcart the night before, and all to be carried to Dumbarton and sold. So we was taking them, you see. But it was only when Tam got to haggling for the price there in Dumbarton that I saw the St Mungo's seal on them, maister, else I would never have been doing such a thing!'

Washing his hands in the pewter basin on the plate-cupboard, drying them on the good linen towel, Gil turned this information over in his mind. When he had said Grace for the meat and done his duty with the carving-knife Alys served out roast mutton with raisin sauce, turnips with ginger and more dark green stewed kale, and he contemplated the timing Euan had described. It was just possible, he supposed, that the gossip mills of the burgh had carried the news of Barnabas' death as far as Maggie Bell's tavern, across the bridge in the hamlet of Govan, before Mistress Bell evicted her customers for the night. It was certainly possible to take a boat down the river to Dumbarton before dawn if the tide was favourable, and a walk of fourteen miles on a fine day would present no obstacle to a healthy, long-legged Erscheman.

'Have you found anything useful this afternoon?' Alys asked him. Startled, he discovered that the first course was done and Kittock had just carried in a broad custard tart on its wooden board. 'I went to the hostel to condole with the ladies, and met the doctor there as well,' she said brightly, 'and I must say those are two very silly girls, but they told me some interesting things.'

He looked at her, seated at his right hand, neat and elegant in her brown linen gown with its bright facings and her black Flemish hood. She had that pinched look which meant something had upset her, so that the high narrow bridge of her nose stood up like a razor-blade. He glanced at Catherine, seated opposite her, and received an infinitesimal shake of her head.

'What have they told you, *ma mie*?' the old woman asked in French, apparently feeling his silence had lasted too long.

'A number of things.' Alys was serving wedges of the custard tart onto the painted platters which had been Augie Morison's wedding gift to them. She set Gil's before him and went on, 'Their marriages, for instance. One is betrothed into Lanarkshire, the other to an acquaintance of Dame Ellen's kin at St Mungo's, who has land by Tarbolton.'

'She has kin at St Mungo's?' Gil repeated. 'Did you learn who it is?'

'William Craigie,' she replied, sending two platters down the board. Her voice was even, but she glanced sideways at him round the black fall of her hood, acknowledging his surprise. 'I know no more than that. What is his kinship?'

'I've never asked.' He frowned. 'Habbie might— Oh.' Lowrie looked up, spoon halfway to his mouth.

'Later, perhaps,' said Catherine elliptically. 'How are they lodged at the hostel? It is a well-run establishment, one hopes. Does it compare with St Jacques at Nantes?'

Once the meal was cleared and the board lifted they repaired to the solar with the ale-jug and a platter of little cakes. Catherine joined them, contrary to her usual habit. Gil thought she was keeping an unobtrusive eye on Alys.

'We need to see where we are wi both cases,' he said, as Lowrie handed the beakers, watched intently by Socrates. 'But what's this about Craigie, sweetheart?'

'As I said. He is kin to Dame Ellen through her first marriage, though in what degree the lassies did not say. And also he has some sort of great penance laid on him, it seems.'

'A penance?' Gil repeated. 'Now that he has never mentioned. I wonder what and why?'

'Some crime against Holy Kirk, so Nicholas thought. This was hearsay,' she admitted, 'but the lassie was quite clear about who she had it from, one of her sister's future servants at Tarbolton.'

'Where Craigie comes from,' supplied Lowrie unexpectedly. 'Maister Sim's man mentioned it the now.'

'Is he now? I kent he was an Ayrshire man,' said Gil, 'but I think I never knew just where he was from. You'd think he'd ha recognised Annie Gibb by name, at least, given that's where the most of her land is situated.'

'Perhaps, if his offence was known there, he did not wish to be connected to the place,' suggested Alys. Catherine nodded sagely.

'Did you learn anything else?' Gil asked.

'Not at the hostel. I spoke with the doctor, who seems,' she paused, 'not concerned for Annie. I think that's all, except that the cadger called regularly in Glenbuck.'

'Cadger?' he queried.

'A man called Cadger Billy.'

'Oh, him. Is he still alive? Well, I suppose he must be little past forty,' Gil reckoned, recalling the man's regular visits from his childhood.

'Still alive, and still trading. It seems he goes all about Lanarkshire, Kate knows him, and Andy Paterson is to find his direction for me, for I think he is a Glasgow man.' Gil raised an eyebrow. 'I wonder if he carried messages for Annie.'

'Ah! That's very possible.'

'And I spoke to Berthold, but I can get no more from him than you. He is plainly very frightened, but he still insists he saw nothing. Oh, and Andy's nephew John confirms Luke's tale, and also saw the two men in fine clothes.'

'If Berthold is fit to be at work he must have improved,' Gil said, digesting this.

'No, I called at the house.'

He looked at her sharply, but found Catherine, beyond her, giving him a significant shake of the head. Was that what had distressed her, he wondered. What reception had she had from her stepmother?

'Lowrie?' he prompted. 'What did you get from Habbie's man?'

'Not a lot,' Lowrie admitted. 'He claims Maister Sim came home without that gown after a right good evening four days since, and the cards the same. He'd never seen the purse afore either. *Oh, no, maister, that's never ours,*' he quoted. 'Mind you, he noticed there was a lot of dust and dirt caught up in the folds of the gown, as if it had been lying about that undercroft for a day or two, maybe on the ground. He'd a bit to say about that.'

'Did he mind where Habbie had been the night he lost it?'

'No, though he thought it might ha been here. When I said, No, he had on the red one last time he was here, he began reckoning up all the other places it might ha been, but he could give me no sensible answer.'

'I wonder who had it,' said Gil thoughtfully. 'It could have been Habbie himself, I suppose, but why hide the thing and then leave it out to incriminate himself?'

'Oh, and the figs and apricots came out of the Vicars' store, as we thought.'

'So he was thieving from there as well.'

'Would he have the key for the Vicars' store?' Alys asked.

'A good question,' Gil admitted. 'Either he or his accomplice must have had.'

'It seems to me,' observed Catherine in her elegant

French, 'that there were many things happening on the night in question.'

'As ever, madame,' said Gil, 'you are perfectly right. We should fit it all together,' he added in Scots, 'starting from the time Annie was bound to the Cross.'

Alys pulled up the skirt of her gown, to reach the purse hanging between it and her striped linen kirtle. She extracted her tablets in their little embroidered bag, found a clear leaf, and drew the stylus from its socket in the hinge.

'What time was that?' she asked.

'About the time we came home,' said Lowrie. He cocked his head as Socrates scrambled to his feet, tail wagging. 'Is that someone coming to the door?'

'It is I,' said Maistre Pierre outside the window.

Drawn in, welcomed, handed a beaker of ale, he applied himself with enthusiasm to the task they had begun.

'It was eight of the clock, not later, I should say, that she was bound there,' he pronounced. Gil nodded. 'And her man said he looked at her every hour or so, yes?'

'If we can believe it,' said Gil.

'What happened next?' said Alys. 'The girl Peg?'

'The prentices,' said Lowrie. 'Say about nine o'the clock.'

'The brothers Muir,' said Gil. They looked at each other. 'I think the prentices began their battle next, indeed, though I'd ha said later than nine, more like ten, after the daylight had gone, and the Muirs walked through it, and then Peg.'

'In which direction did they go?' asked Catherine.

'The Muirs came out of Rottenrow,' said Gil, 'and claim they went down the High Street. Peg came down the Stablegreen from the port.'

'Luke saw the Muirs go up the Stablegreen,' Lowrie observed.

'And yet they did not see her,' said Alys.

'Did anyone see her at all?' asked Maistre Pierre.

'There's a man who heard a lassie arguing with someone,' said Lowrie. 'I have to go back in the morning and get a word.'

The mason nodded.

181

'But what time was all that?' Alys asked. 'It was about ten of the clock when Peg left the Trindle, I think you said.'

'The battle went on for some time,' said Gil. 'More than an hour, by the sound of it, though it was over by midnight.'

'Didn't Euan,' said Lowrie suddenly, and they all looked at him. He went red. 'Didn't Euan say the fisherman mentioned goods that went down on a handcart that night?'

'You're right,' said Gil. 'What's more, I'll wager I ken what way they went down to the shore. I saw the tracks of a handcart, out on the Pallioun Croft. *And,*' he suddenly recalled, 'Austin Muir heard or saw a handcart as they went back up Rottenrow. That's why the vergers' handcart was put away dirty!'

'So that went through the Upper Town as well,' said Maistre Pierre. '*Mon Dieu!* I have known it quieter at the Fair.'

'I wonder who pushed it,' said Alys. 'The man who died, or his accomplice?'

'And some time in all this,' said her father, 'the woman Peg was killed, and tied to the Cross instead of Annie Gibb.'

'Did you say,' said Alys, 'that Annie's man spoke to her after the prentices were finished and gone home? Was that after midnight?'

'I think so,' said Gil. 'I need to check that wi him.' He made a face. 'And Canon Muir saw his nephews to bed before midnight, so if this is right it was none of their doing that Annie was freed from the Cross.'

'A pity,' said Alys seriously. She made another note on the tablets. 'The handcart. It must have come back as well. I wonder if the Muirs saw it.'

'I wonder if Berthold saw it,' said Gil. He considered the cart and its movements for a little, while Lowrie and Maistre Pierre debated how easy it would be to push the thing down to the shore in the dark. It must indeed have been returned that night, and stowed in the undercroft. Maister Sim's gown and cards and the incriminating purse must have been put there later, but how much later? Before Barnabas was killed? After it? And why?

'And by whom?' said Alys, when he voiced the question.

'I suppose by the person who killed the verger the next day,' said Catherine in French.

'We've no proof,' said Gil, considering this, 'but it's possible.'

'And the other property left where it would cast suspicion on your friend,' the old woman continued. She gathered her skirts together and rose stiffly; the rest of them rose with her, Socrates looking hopefully at Gil. 'It is very possible, *maistre*, that if you find out who had your friend's gown you will find the killer of the Cathedral servant.' She bent her head in acknowledgement of his answer, raised her hand in her customary blessing, and headed for the door. Alys followed, to make certain she had all she needed for the night, and the men looked at one another.

'Could she be right?' asked Lowrie, when Gil had translated her comment.

'Oh, yes,' said Maistre Pierre gloomily. 'The problem is finding it out. I suppose you ask all of the songmen when they last saw the yellow gown, and decide on which is lying.'

'Something like that, I suspect.' Gil sat down again, lifting Alys's tablets, and studied the list in her neat writing. Socrates lay down on his feet with a resigned sigh. 'I must talk to Stockfish Tam. Lowrie, could you go out to the kitchen and ask Euan when Tam will be back in Glasgow?'

'So what do we have this far?' asked Maistre Pierre as the young man left.

'At midnight? We have the prentice battle lost and won and the combatants gone home, we have Annie still known to be at the Cross, the Muir brothers and all the people in the hostel blamelessly in their beds, and Peg,' he scanned the list, 'no, we have no trace of Peg save this elusive man who is said to have heard an argument.'

'And we do not know what time that was,' said Alys, coming back into the room. She sat down on the padded settle beside Gil, and tucked her hand through his arm. 'Then there is the handcart and whoever was pushing it.'

'*Vraiment*,' agreed her father. 'And after midnight?'

'Some time after midnight,' said Gil, 'Annie was freed from the Cross and Peg's body was tied there in her place. Annie and whoever was with her vanished into the night, leaving Sawney to assume that it was his mistress he saw the next time he looked. The handcart was returned, and put in its proper place in the undercroft—'

'That suggests to me,' said Alys, 'that it was the verger who put it away, not his accomplice. And perhaps,' she looked round at Gil, 'it was he who placed Maistre Sim's gown on the cart.'

'Why did he leave the coin there, if so?' Maistre Pierre objected.

'It was in effect hidden, inside the gown,' she said slowly. 'Barnabas knew it was there, but nobody else did. It was not seen until someone looked closely at the garment.'

'Hmm,' said her father. 'And if any found it, they would take it to be Maister Sim's. You could be right, I suppose.'

'There is no way to prove it,' she said, 'but it would work.'

Gil grimaced.

'I'm no judge of the matter,' he said. 'I'm too close to it. But it seems to me very odd. If it was left there by the man who pushed the handcart through the night, we could assume it was his takings from the last shipment down the river. In which case why not take it home with him?'

'Perhaps he left it for his accomplice,' said Alys. 'No, that doesn't work.'

'It could have been there for two nights and a day,' Gil said. 'Why did the accomplice not come for it?'

'Exactly,' said Alys. 'And yet . . .' Her voice trailed off as she thought about it. 'Gil, suppose it was the other man's share of the takings? If the man who pushed the handcart, whether it was Barnabas or the other, took the whole payment home with him to count and divide it, then perhaps he brought that purse back the next day—'

'Yesterday, in effect,' said Maistre Pierre.

'Yesterday,' she agreed. 'And hid it when he got the chance.'

184

'It makes the gap in the time shorter,' said her father.

'It does,' said Gil, 'though it doesn't explain the way it was hidden, unless someone deliberately wished to incriminate Habbie.'

'Sim is well regarded among the songmen,' observed Maistre Pierre.

'Quite. We need to consider that further. But returning to the night Annie disappeared,' pursued Gil, 'some time after midnight, some time after the handcart was stowed, someone came by and throttled Peg with a sack-tie, apparently unaware that she was dead already.'

'There are gaps,' said Maistre Pierre after a pause.

'There are huge gaps. And none of it makes sense. Was it the verger, or his accomplice, who killed Peg? Why was she killed? When?'

'You think it was not Annie's rescuer who killed her?'

'I hope not,' said Alys. 'To have her freedom at the cost of another woman's life!'

'Euan thinks the man will be back in Glasgow wi the tide tomorrow,' said Lowrie, returning. 'It wasny easy to get a clear answer from him, but that was about the sum of it.'

'It never is,' said Gil. 'I'll try to get down there the morn's morn, then.' He drew out his own tablets, and paused as they fell open at his list of Annie Gibb's properties. 'Ah, there is something I must ask you about before you leave, Pierre. Now, what are these gaps? What do we still need to find out?'

'Near everything,' said his father-in-law gloomily. Ignoring this, Gil drew three columns and headed them.

'For Peg, we still need to find out who she wanted to pick a fight with, and who killed her if it was not the same person, and where.'

'And when,' said Alys.

'You make it sound so simple,' said Lowrie.

'Perhaps an hour or so before she was put where we saw her,' said Maistre Pierre, ignoring this. 'No, indeed, it must be longer, for she had just begun to stiffen before she was in place, I think, from the position of her head when we found her.'

'So she might have been killed while the battle was still going on,' said Alys.

'Who had the opportunity?' Gil smoothed and re-incised a line on the wax leaf. 'All the prentices, I suppose. The man with the handcart. Peg's own man, though I think Otterburn is right, it was not him.'

'The Muirs,' supplied Lowrie. 'Anyone from the hostel that was out. The men from the Trindle.'

'Anyone, in effect,' said Maistre Pierre.

'We've found remarkably little about her, poor girl,' agreed Gil. 'Oh, and I'd like to find who throttled her after she was dead.'

'Could that be why Berthold is so frightened?' said Alys suddenly. They looked at one another. 'I wondered if it was something he had seen, but if he has encountered Peg in the shadows and—'

'Oh!' said Gil. 'He's such a wee rabbit of a boy, but Peg was hardly a sonsy wench either. It's possible, I suppose.'

'Just the same,' said Lowrie slowly, 'he keeps saying he *saw* nothing. Not *did nothing*, but *saw nothing*.'

Maistre Pierre nodded.

'I agree. It hardly seems likely. I suppose we must keep it in mind, nevertheless.'

'I need to start questioning folk again,' said Gil in annoyance. 'I've asked more questions about Annie's disappearance than about Peg's death, which isny right.' He made some more notes under Peg's name, and went on to the next column. 'Now, what do we need to learn about Annie?'

'Where is she?' said Lowrie.

'Who has stolen her away,' said Maistre Pierre.

'And we've heard nothing so far that might tell us either of those.'

'If I can find the cadger's lodging I may learn something,' said Alys. Gil looked round at her. 'I told you, I do wonder if he has carried messages for Annie.'

'But if he's out in Lanarkshire the now,' he objected, 'that's little help.'

'He has a wife, so Kate tells me.'

'So we still need to learn near everything about Annie too.' Gil made another note. 'And for Barnabas – you know, we've uncovered a lot about what the man was up to, but we're still no nearer finding who killed him either. We're no doing that well, are we?'

'No, but what do we know about the verger?' said Maistre Pierre. 'That he may or may not have pushed the handcart down to the shore and back again.'

'And that the sight of a sack-tie prompted him to go to find someone, who then killed him,' said Alys.

'Peg went out to find someone and pick a fight wi them too,' observed Lowrie. 'I suppose it wasny the same person.'

'Peg was also throttled with a sack-tie,' said Alys.

'No saying if it was all the same person,' said Gil, 'though I suspect not. It would be too simple. I think in Peg's case at least we're dealing wi two different people, one who killed her, one who throttled her. Whether either o these dealt wi Barnabas is something we need to find out.' He closed his tablets with a snap, then flicked them open them again as he recalled something. 'Pierre, you've been down into Ayrshire, I think. Would you ken aught about any of these properties?'

His father-in-law took the list and held it up at arm's length in the fading light from the window.

'You write too small these days,' he complained. 'What are these? Redwrae, Fail, no, I know nothing of these, though they are close by Tarbolton I think. Carngillan neither. Ah! Now Hallrig I have visited. That is the place where the quarry is, that I have mentioned. The tenant was very civil, though his ale was thin, and the quarry is a good one, but I thought the carriage too dear to bring the stone into Glasgow.'

'Quarry,' repeated Gil.

'Yes, yes, and a good one as I said, that blond freestone you get all over Ayrshire. It belongs to the Gibb family. Is it this Annie's property indeed, then?'

'Hallrig is hers, so likely the quarry is too, unless the feu superior retained the mineral rights. How did you come to be there?'

'Seeking stone, as ever. Why are you interested?'

'Sawney mentioned a cousin of Annie's father who felt the property should be his. I wondered if that might be a lead.'

Maistre Pierre pulled a long face.

'I have no knowledge of such a thing. I dealt chiefly with a man of law in Kilmarnock, one Maister James Bowling, and then with the tenant.'

'The man Bowling never mentioned a dispute?'

'No, never. He would hardly wish to do so,' Maistre Pierre pointed out, 'if he hoped to sell me the stone.'

Gil retrieved his tablets and considered the list for a space.

'We need to learn more about this,' he decided. 'I'm reluctant to go into Ayrshire myself the now, Hugh Montgomery is active and a single Cunningham would be a rare temptation for him, but once you've spoken to the man on the Stablegreen, Lowrie, you could go out to Kilmarnock, take Euan wi you, talk to this James Bowling. It's no more than twenty mile, you should do it in the day and back again. I'll let you have a letter of introduction and we'll talk over what you should ask him.' Lowrie nodded. 'And I'll chase Stockfish Tam.' He looked at Alys. 'I think you have plans of your own, sweetheart.'

'I do,' she said composedly. 'Though perhaps I could speak to the man on the Stablegreen, to let Lowrie leave earlier.'

'A good notion. I hope your plans don't involve being seized and held at knifepoint.'

'So do I.'

'*Et moi aussi, par ma foi,*' said her father with emphasis, and got to his feet. They all rose with him. 'I must be gone. But I wished to say to you, *ma mie.*' He looked seriously at Alys. 'Élise told me you had been to the house, and I am glad of it. Do you think you will be better friends now?'

She curtsied to him, bending her head so that Gil could not see her expression.

'My good-mother made me most welcome,' she said.

188

Maistre Pierre frowned, but did not press his question; instead he delivered a brief blessing and allowed Gil to accompany him to the back door of the house. Socrates passed them in the doorway and padded out into the evening, sniffing at corners.

'I do not know what they discussed,' Maistre Pierre said, a slight unease audible in his voice.

'Some women's matter, perhaps,' Gil suggested. Out across the yard the kitchen door opened, and the servants emerged, still chattering, heading for the main house and their beds. Seeing their master and their former master in the doorway they fell silent and waited politely while Gil bade his father-in-law goodnight and saw him walk off into the twilight, then all filed in, offering their own goodnights in turn. The dog, his patrol completed, returned with them, and Euan followed, raising his blue bonnet and ducking his head with a sheepish grin. Gil closed the door behind Jennet, who was last, and grasped her wrist before she could reach the stairs.

'A moment, lass,' he said. She shrank slightly away from him, and he let go of her, aware of faint dismay. Other men might prey on the women of their households, but it was not his way; he had thought they all recognised that. Or was it simply that all the women were upset this evening? 'Jennet, what ails your mistress?' he asked quietly. 'Was it something Mistress McIan said? Were you there wi her?'

'I've no right knowledge,' she said after a little pause. 'I was the other end o the hall, you understand, Maister Gil. Maister,' she corrected herself. He grunted agreement. 'I never heard what – what *she* said, only what my mistress answered. She was wishing her well, if you understand me.' Her face tilted in the shadows as if she gave him a significant look.

'Wishing her well,' he repeated flatly. Comprehension dawned. 'Sweet St Giles, you mean—?'

'That was all I heard,' said Jennet, equally flatly.

'Pierre has said nothing!' he said, almost to himself.

'She'll no have let him know yet, it's ower soon, when

you think when they were wed. Likely my mistress surprised it out o her, you ken what she's like for people saying things to her they never meant to say.' She put out a hand as if to touch his wrist, and withdrew it. 'Whatever it was madam told her, it turned her right kinna wavelly, she wasny fit to walk home. I got her to Lady Kate's house, and we made her rest, and she recovered a bit. But there was something else I did hear and it seems like my mistress didny catch it right, and she wouldny let me tell her it.'

'Should you be telling me?' he asked.

'I ken fine madam has what these Ersche call the Sight,' Jennet persisted, 'and she told my mistress she'd seen her, more than once she said, wi two bairns about her. One bairn, it might just be wee John, but two bairns is what she said.'

No wonder she would not hear it, Gil thought. She dare not get her hopes up.

'Away up to your bed,' he said. 'I'll unlace your mistress when we go up. Goodnight, lass. Christ guard your sleep.'

'Good night, Maister Gil,' she said gently. 'God rest you.'

She bobbed a curtsy and slipped away up the stair, and he bent to set the bar in its socket, considering this news. It sat in the midst of his thoughts like a boulder; he could hardly work out how he felt about it himself, but it was certainly what had distressed Alys, and with her the whole household of women.

He turned to go back into the solar, where light under the door suggested that Alys had lit candles. The dog suddenly growled, and left him to rush away across the hall, his claws rattling on the floorboards, to stand with his muzzle against the front door, still growling.

'What is it?' Gil asked him, and was answered by a rattle of the tirling-pin and then a loud knocking. Light grew as the door of the solar was flung wide behind him, and he strode to his dog's side. Another customer for the bawdy-house, he thought, who has not heard that the business has closed. 'Who's there?' he demanded. 'Who's knocking?'

'Maister Cunningham? Maister Cunningham?' came the

190

answer, muffled only slightly by the broad planks. 'Can ye come out, maister? It's another death!'

It was the manservant from St Catherine's, out of breath and wild with distress. Standing in the hall while Lowrie lit more candles and Gil pulled his boots back on, he gave a partially articulate account of the matter.

'It was my wife found her,' he said, pulling a hand across his face, 'poor lass, she's right owerset, after the other one, and we canny think how it happened. We're all that distracted, and the lassies weeping and all, you need to come and see, maister. Sir Simon sent me,' he added with a sudden access of coherence, 'bade me ask you to come right away.'

'But who's dead?' Lowrie asked. He kicked off his slip-slops and reached for his own boots. Alys appeared from the stair, her plaid over her arm.

'She's in the chapel,' said the man.

'In the *chapel*?' Gil repeated in dismay.

'Aye, which isny good, I can tell you, maister, it's going to take some cleaning, there's blood on all the tiles, never mind the— And the glaze wore off them a'ready, we'll maybe need to get the floor— And Sir Simon reckoning how long till we can reconsecrate, and Christ assoil me, sic a beating as she's had, it's like the other one—'

'Who is dead?' Alys asked. She had more success: the man stopped, drew a breath, crossed himself, and said more rationally,

'It's the auld wife. The dame that's wi the party.'

'Dame Ellen?' said Gil, looking up from his buckles.

'Aye, her. God rest her.'

'But what has happened? She is in the chapel, you said?' Alys came forward, drawing her plaid about her. 'Is it certain she is dead?'

'Oh, aye.' The man swallowed. 'Naeb'dy's head's that shape that isny dead.'

This was certainly the case, Gil reflected, studying the body of Dame Ellen by the light of two great racks of candles. He was glad Alys had remained in the courtyard, where the woman Bessie was still sobbing under her apron.

'What has she been struck wi?' he wondered aloud.

'Our good candlestick,' said Sir Simon glumly. 'It's all ower blood and brains, see.' He indicated the object, its pewter gleam sullied and blackened by what stuck to it. 'He's likely all ower blood himsel, the way it's spattered, whoever's done it. What a task we have ahead o us, getting this back the way it should be, let alone what Robert Blacader will have to say about it. As for when he's next in Glasgow, to reconsecrate—' He sat down again, rather heavily, on the wall-bench where Gil had found him. 'I keep thinking o other things to be done. The Blessed Sacrament to be destroyed by fire— Who'd do sic a deed in the presence o the Host, can you credit it? The vestments and hangings to be cleaned and reconsecrate. What will Blacader say?'

'This is worse than what came to Peg Simpson,' said Gil. 'Let alone the sacrilege. And that's far worse than what happened wi Barnabas.' He looked round as Lowrie came pallidly back into the little building, keeping his eyes averted from the body. 'Where are they all? The family, the servants?'

'Lockhart has them penned up in the dining hall,' said Lowrie, 'since they could hardly use the men's hall. The doctor says Sir Edward canny be told of this, he's no more than hours from his end.'

'I suppose we're certain it's Ellen Shaw,' Gil said. 'Most o her face is, well—'

'Past knowing,' agreed Sir Simon. 'We had the woman Meggot to her, she agreed it was Dame Ellen, by the teeth and the clothes, and said she kent the hands.'

'The teeth I'll accept,' said Gil, looking at the corpse. 'Did she cry out? Is that how you came to find her?'

The dead woman lay sprawled, one arm flung up and back as if she had tried to protect herself. There were injuries to both hands, and her sleeves and one shoulder of her gown were torn. Blood, black in the candlelight, soaked the crumpled white linen of her headdress; there had clearly been a fight, which had ended in the shattering blow to her forehead that had split the skull, fragmented the eye socket, laid open the cheekbone. Broken teeth, or perhaps splinters of bone, gleamed palely within the wound in the flickering light, but the crossed front teeth by which Meggot had identified her were also visible, because her mouth was wide open, as if she had died in the moment of screaming at her attacker. *Ne is no quene so stark ne stour*, he found himself thinking, *that deth ne shal by glyde*. It had certainly not glided by this woman.

'It was Bessie found her,' Sir Simon said. 'You'll want to get a word wi her yourself, I couldny make sense o her, she was that owerset. I can tell you I never heard a thing mysel, nor had any notion there was anyone in here. I suppose she could ha crossed the yard while I was at my dinner, or – no, for I'd my dinner wi the whole o them in the dining hall, and she was there right enough.'

'That was the last time you saw her?'

'It was. They were all in the hall when I left, save for Sir Edward and his man, a course, and I went to deal wi some papers, sort the accounts,' he grimaced, 'which should ha been wi St Mungo's at the quarter, and I canny get completed for lack of a docket from Alan Jamieson—'

'So she could ha come across here while you were at that,' Gil said. He hunkered down by the corpse and felt the outspread limbs, judging temperature, testing flexibility. 'She's no long gone, I'd say. What time was your dinner?'

'After Vespers,' said Sir Simon promptly. 'Maybe seven o' the clock. It would be eight when I cam away, likely.'

'Two hours since.' Gil touched the neck and jaw cautiously. 'She's been dead no more than an hour or so, I'd say, she's barely beginning to set. I wonder where she was in between.'

'Likely in here, arguing wi her murderer,' suggested Lowrie, who was casting about the rest of the small space, his back resolutely to the corpse, a tilted candle in his hand dripping wax on the tiles. Gil suddenly thought of his father-in-law doing the same thing over Barnabas' body the previous evening. He lifted a fold of the blood-soaked headdress, and said,

'Has anyone sent to tell the Muirs? I think they're kin, they should hear of this.'

'And Canon Muir,' said Sir Simon in dismay. 'He should hear o't, it's his right as patron o the hostel, but he'll want to owersee all—'

'You have to let him know,' said Gil, sharing the older man's consternation. 'And Will Craigie? He's some kind of kin to her,' he elucidated.

'Is he now,' said Sir Simon, distracted. 'I'd begun to think it. He's been here a time or two wi her, and her ordering him about like a lapdog. I heard them arguing out there in the yard this morning, you'd ha thought they were man and wife the way they were abusing one another.'

'Is that right?' Gil carefully did not look at the priest. 'What was that about, then?'

'Oh, I couldny say, my son.' Gil waited, studying the injuries to the corpse's hands. 'Well, it seemed something had gone wrong, that he expected her to ha sorted for him and it hadny gone according to plan, or the like.'

'What kind of plan? Money? Land, a position?'

'I never caught that,' said Sir Simon regretfully. 'Just by what was said he hadny kept his side o the bargain either, whatever it was. *If you'd done what you promised*, she said to him, more than once.'

'What did he answer to that?'

'He kept saying, *It's no that easy, it takes time.* Never said what, though. Oh, and, *What purpose it now, any road?* he said. To which she said, *Never concern yoursel, she'll turn up, like bad money.*'

'Something concerning Annie Gibb, then?' said Gil.

'Doesn't sound like a reason to kill her,' said Lowrie doubtfully.

'So has he been sent for?' Gil asked. 'Or at least let know his kinswoman's dead.'

'I'll send Attie round.' Sir Simon glanced at the small

dark windows of the chapel. 'Will it no do the morn's morn? It's ower late to disturb the man wi bad news. Though I suppose the Canon needs to hear, he can get the two o them wi the one lantern.'

'No, I think he should go now. And the Muirs? They're likely out drinking again, they'd never survive an evening of Canon Muir's company, someone had best hunt them down and tell them. One of the Shaw servants can go once I've spoken to them. We should let the Provost hear and all.' Gil stood up, hitching at the knees of his hose. 'He'll not be pleased, another quest.'

'No after the day's,' Sir Simon agreed, grinning sourly. 'I heard about that. Mind, he got his verdict in the end.'

'He did.' Gil looked round for Lowrie. 'Is Alys still in the yard?'

'She's gone into the hall, to the lassies. She bade me tell you, she questioned Bessie.'

Chapter Eleven

In the dining hall, at one of the long fixed tables, Alys and Meggot were attempting to bring Dame Ellen's nieces to a more balanced state of mind. One of the girls was hiccuping again, the other was simply weeping helplessly. Alys looked round as Gil entered the hall, caught his eye and shook her head. He had to agree; there was no point in speaking to either sister just now, and Meggot was as busy as Alys.

At the other table, Lockhart had a row of four shocked menservants lined up and had clearly been questioning them; he was now casting an eye over their livery, presumably looking for bloodstains.

'There you are, Cunningham,' he said as Gil sat down beside him. 'These lads were all in the hall here thegither, and then went out-by to the stables. They each speak for all.'

'You'd swear to that?' Gil asked, and they nodded raggedly. 'Did any of you see Dame Ellen go to the chapel after her dinner? Or anyone else?'

The consensus seemed to be that none of them had.

'Was any of you sent out to fetch someone to meet her? Did she send any messages at all this evening?'

Again, there was agreement: Dame Ellen had summoned nobody that the men knew of.

'What time did she leave the hall?'

The four servants looked blank. Lockhart offered,

'An hour or so after we sat down to dine? Maybe a bit more? Sir Simon excused himself to his duties when the meal was done, and she warned the lassies to bide here in company along wi Meggot, to save candles, and went out hersel, I thought she said she would visit her brother, see how he was, though the women say she spoke of going to the chapel . . .' His voice tailed off. Gil nodded.

'So none of you kens when she entered the chapel?'

The four looked at one another in the candlelight.

'No, maister,' said Sawney. 'But there's a thing.'

'What's that?' Gil asked.

'This afternoon, maister. Well, evening, it was, we was waiting out yonder in the yard, till they called us in to our dinner. This woman comes in off the street, saying she kent something about my mistress, about Annie Gibb that is. She wouldny tell it to us, said it was for our maister's ears, so I set off to fetch Maister Lockhart here, and met Dame Ellen in the other yard, and she would know where I was off to, and said she'd speak wi the woman hersel. She took her into the chapel, to be privy, see, so we never heard what the woman had to say, and she never tellt us what it was neither. Did she tell you, maister?'

'She did not. First I've heard of this,' said Lockhart, reddening in annoyance. 'Christ's nails, she was a steering woman!'

'You heard nothing from outside the chapel?' Gil asked.

'Is that no what I'm saying? Only,' persisted Sawney, 'the mistress, she cam away right annoyed and saying something about *Never a penny you'll get for sic lees as this*, and the woman sweering at her all across the yard, so I wondered maybe if it was her cam back and slew her acos she never gied her her reward.'

'Was there a reward promised?' Gil asked, disentangling this.

'Aye,' said Lockhart. 'No a great one, just for information concerning Annie.'

'What like was the woman?' Lowrie asked from Gil's side. Sawney looked at him, and shrugged.

'Just ordinar.'

'She'd a red kirtle,' said the man next to him.

'It was green,' said the one at his other side.

'An apron?' Lowrie asked. 'How big was she? Was she carrying anything?'

Some argument established that the woman had been middling sized, heavily built, wearing an apron and a good headdress and a red, blue, or possibly green kirtle with short sleeves, and had worn no plaid.

'So she hadny come far,' Sawney explained. 'I took it she was come in from the street hereabouts.'

Gil raised an eyebrow at Lowrie, who nodded.

'It could be the woman I spoke to,' he agreed. 'Agnes Templand, the name is.'

'Will I go round wi a couple of the lads to take her up?' Lockhart suggested, pushing back his stool. 'Fetch her to the Castle, see what the Provost makes of her?'

'No,' said Gil, 'but Lowrie could take your lads if you will and speak to her, see if her apron has blood on it. I'd say whoever killed Dame Ellen would be foul wi blood, and brains and all.'

'She could change it,' objected Sawney.

'If she's changed it,' said Lowrie, 'then we'll ask to see the other. Come on, man, you'll do, and you – Rab, is it?'

'A moment,' said Gil. 'Sawney, tell me something. The night your mistress Annie was at the Cross.' The man ducked his head, grimacing as if the words had stabbed him. 'When you spoke to her, after the prentices had finished their battle and gone home. Was that before or after midnight?'

'After midnight?' Sawney stared, visibly trying to recall. 'Aye, I'd say so. I canny mind right, maister, but I'd say aye, it would ha been after midnight. By where the moon was,' he reflected, 'it must ha been. Aye, aye, maister, after midnight it was.' He nodded, touched his knitted bonnet, and hurried after Lowrie.

'And your other two men,' said Gil to Lockhart, wondering how reliable this might be, 'if you'll permit it, could go out and find the Muir brothers, let them hear Dame Ellen's dead. Sir Simon has sent to their uncle, as patron, but the brothers are likely out in the town.'

'I should ha thought o that,' said Lockhart, reddening again. 'Tell truth, Cunningham, I'm right owerset by this. Steering auld witch she might ha been, but I'd thought she'd go on for ever. Certainly never thought o her meeting her end like this, deserved or no.' He jerked his head at the two remaining men, who nodded and slipped away after Lowrie and their fellows. Lockhart watched them go, then said gloomily, 'So what's happened, man? What did come to her? I saw her where she lay,' he grimaced, 'wi her brains all ower the tiles, they'll ha to cleanse that chapel all ways, let alone the sacrilege, and it seemed to me like a madman's work.' His gaze slid sideways to Gil. 'Is there any chance. Is it likely?' He swallowed. 'Could it ha been Annie?' he finished in a rush. 'Slipped back into the place and taen her revenge on the old—' He stopped. Gil waited for a moment, then said,

'Revenge?'

'Aye, revenge. For years of—' He stopped again, and shook his head. 'Maybe no.'

'Years of what?'

'No. Forget it. I never meant—'

After another pause Gil said,

'Did Dame Ellen spend much time in the chapel?'

Lockhart shrugged.

'I'd not have said so, I thought she was more ower at St Mungo's. She'd a right devotion to Our Lady in the Lower Kirk, but there's St Catherine in the Upper Kirk and all. You could ask at the lassies, they might tell you.' He glanced across the hall to where Alys was talking soothingly to Dame Ellen's nieces, aided now by Sir Simon. Nicholas still had the hiccups. 'If you can get a word o sense out them. My wife got the wits for all three o them, I can tell ye, maister. She'd not be owerset by a wee thing like this.'

'They're very young,' said Gil, as he had said to Dame Ellen.

'They're old enough to be wed,' retorted Lockhart, much as she had done.

'So how did Dame Ellen deal wi Annie?'

'Ach.' The man hesitated. 'Wi a firm hand. Aye you could say that, a firm hand.'

'Too firm?' Prompting the witness, thought Gil.

'Away too firm, I'd ha thought. Ruled her like they two heedless lassies, wi commands and duties and *Get to your needlework when I order it*. She was a— She was a steering woman, Cunningham. You ken two o her husbands hanged theirsels?'

'What? Two?' repeated Gil incredulously.

'Aye. The third one, her last, dee'd o his own accord, his heart they said, afore she could drive him to it. Small wonder she's been left on Sir Edward's hands these six or seven year. Annie's a good lass, save for this daft vow she took, and I've aye wondered if that was as much to get her out from under the auld wife's rule as to mourn her man.'

William Craigie, predictably, was the first of those summoned to arrive at the hostel. He came hurrying in, a great cloak over his plaid despite the mildness of the night, a lantern bobbing in his hand, staring nervously about the darkling courtyard as if he expected Dame Ellen's corpse to appear before him.

'What's this, Gil?' he demanded. 'What's afoot? A fellow came to tell me, there's been another death. Is that right? Is it my— Is it Dame Ellen right enough? What's come to her? Some accident, surely, she was well enough this morning!'

'Aye, Dame Ellen,' said Gil baldly. 'D'you want to see her? She's in the chapel.'

'What, is she laid out and received already?' Craigie turned to follow him.

'No, she died there.' Gil paused, hand on the chapel door, to study the other man's reaction. 'By violence,' he added.

'By violence? In the *chapel*?' repeated Craigie. He raised his lantern to see Gil's face; by its light his own expression was one of horror and deep dismay. A churchman's reaction. Was it too deep, Gil wondered; was his response genuine, or assumed? 'Who would do sic a thing? That's terrible! Here, it wasny the same as at St Mungo's? Has someone copied— Was she throttled like Barnabas?'

'No. Her death has been very different,' Gil said, pushing the chapel door open. Sir Simon, seated on the wall-bench again with his beads in his hand, looked up briefly and returned to his prayers. Craigie stepped in, halted as he took in the scene before him, and turned his face away, one hand over his mouth.

'Christ aid the poor woman,' he said, 'what an end. Here, Gil, she wasny forced as well, was she?'

'I think not,' said Gil. 'There's no sign of it, certainly. Just had her head beaten in wi Sir Simon's candlestick.'

'No mine,' said Sir Simon without raising his head. 'It's St Catherine's.'

'Aye,' said Craigie indistinctly, then hurried out of the chapel. Gil followed, and found him in the yard, heaving drily, his lantern swinging by his knee. 'You'll forgive me,' he managed after a moment, 'I canny stay in there. The smell—'

'Rich,' Gil agreed. Craigie breathed deeply a couple of times, then straightened up with a slight laugh of embarrassment.

'Never could abide the smell o blood. I couldny ha made a flesher.'

'Fortunate you went for Holy Kirk instead.' Gil considered the other man. 'What way was Dame Ellen kin to you? Are you also kin to her nieces? To the missing woman?'

'No to the lassies,' said Craigie, shaking his head, 'and certainly I'm no kin o Annie Gibb's. As for – for the depairtit, she's no true kin o mine, but a connection by way o two or three marriages. It suited her to call me kin, but, well—'

'Had you any benefit from the claim?' Gil asked casually. 'A busy, devout woman like Dame Ellen could be some assistance to a man in Holy Orders, I'd ha thought.'

'If she was, she'll no be again,' said Craigie, and clapped his round felt hat back on his head. 'You'll ha to forgive me, Gil, I'm turned all tapsalteerie wi this. Sacrilege like that, and in Glasgow. Who'd ha thought it, even after what came to Barnabas.' He took another deep breath, and let it out. 'Assistance. Aye, she'd promised me she'd put a word in for me here and there about Ayrshire and Lanarkshire. She'd a wide acquaintance, and a few o them has fine benefices to hand out.'

'Had she now?' said Gil. 'Yet I'd heard you had words wi her the day.'

'I did,' agreed Craigie, after the smallest check, deep regret in his tone. 'It shames me to admit it, I used language unbecoming a son of Holy Kirk to her. Mind you, the provocation was great,' he added. 'The depairtit called me for everything while she was reproaching me.'

'*Wantoun of word, and wox wonder wraith*? What was it about?' Gil asked.

'It's no matter now,' said Craigie, still with that deep regret. 'The plans can come to nothing.'

'On the contrary,' said Gil, 'I need to hear all she was involved in this last day or two, anything that might ha gone wrong, that might ha provoked sic a death.'

'Gilbert!' The other man took a step backwards, raising his hands as if to defend himself. 'You never— You canny think I'd—'

'Where were you these two or three hours? Since Vespers, say.'

'At John Ross's lodging, where the lad found me. Several of us had dinner sent in from one o the bakehouses after Vespers was done, and sat down to the cards. Ask at them. Ask at Habbie or John or Arthur.'

'I will,' said Gil. 'So what was it Dame Ellen expected of you? What had you planned thegither? Was anyone else involved? I think you hadny completed some task or other.'

'You're gey well informed,' said Craigie stiffly.

'Aye, well, if you have your discussion here in the yard, you'll expect to be heard. So what was your task?'

'Oh, it's at an end now, no purpose in pursuing it. Poor woman, she'll do neither hersel nor any other any good now.'

'William,' said Gil, summoning patience, 'I need to

hear what it was. Would you rather discuss it somewhere private? We could go back in the chapel, if you like, or Sir Simon would maybe let us use his chamber. Did the matter concern Annie Gibb? I think,' he said, with a sudden recollection of Canon Muir's ramblings, 'you've been promoting this match wi Henry or Austin Muir for her, am I right?'

'Aye, that was it,' said Craigie, in a kind of sulky relief.

'So how does that stand the now, wi the lass still missing and no suspicion where she might be?'

'Oh, it's all in abeyance, o necessity, though my kins-woman would never accept that, kept urging me to carry the matter forward.'

Interesting, thought Gil, recalling his own interviews with Dame Ellen.

'Where do you think she might be?' he asked casually. 'Annie Gibb, I mean. Where did Dame Ellen think she would return from, if she was still on the market to be wed?'

'No telling. No telling.' Craigie shook his head. 'I'd not think she's still in Glasgow, you'd ha found her by now, surely. Our Lady alone kens where she's got to, let alone who set her free, how she got away.'

'Who could ha done this, would you think?' Gil nodded at the chapel door. 'Who'd ha had reason to beat Dame Ellen down like that?'

'Oh, how would I know? You're Blacader's quaestor, no me. She was,' even by lantern-light it was visible that Craigie controlled his expression, 'she was a steering woman, generous though she could be, it's likely she ordered the wrong person to do her bidding.'

'What's ado here?' demanded a sharp voice. Booted feet tramped on the flagstones of the courtyard, and two dark figures emerged from the shadows. Light from Craigie's lantern glimmered on gold and silver braid, then showed Henry Muir's face, irritated and impatient. Behind him his brother grinned vaguely, and a Shaw serving-man slipped away into the hall. 'Oh, no you again! And you and all,' Henry added to Craigie. 'Yon fellow says the auld wife's found dead, is that right? Wi her head beat in? She wasny forced as well, was she?'

'No, Henry, she—' began his brother.

'What did I say?' Henry turned on him, hand raised, and Austin took a step backwards.

'Dame Ellen is dead,' Gil confirmed, 'and by violence. Will you see her?'

'No need o that, surely,' muttered Austin, and flinched at his brother's sharp movement.

'We'll see her,' said Henry grimly, and flung away towards the chapel door.

Inside the little building, he stared impassively at the grisly sight which Dame Ellen presented in the candlelight, signed himself and muttered a prayer, while his brother peered over his shoulder with a kind of prurient, timorous avidity which Gil found more distasteful than Henry's reaction.

'She's crossed someone for the last time,' said the older brother after a moment.

'Did she cross many folk?' Gil asked.

'Oh, aye.' Henry laughed shortly. 'Easy as breathing. I'll no speak ill o her afore her face,' he added, and stepped past Gil to the door. 'Come on, you.'

'Will you touch her?'

'I'll no!' said Austin before Henry could answer, 'for she'll get up and ca' me for all things if I do, same as she did on life.'

'Did she so?' said Gil. 'I thought she had a fondness for you both.'

'Never stopped her miscalling me,' said Austin, watching anxiously as his brother turned back and bent to touch one of the claw-like hands. 'Mind her, Henry, she'll up and fetch you a wallop—'

'Haud your tongue, daftheid,' said his brother. 'She's cold and stiffening. Why's she no been washed and laid out, Cunningham? It's no decent to keep her lying here in her blood. She'll be past doing anything with afore long.'

'She could be washed now,' Gil agreed. 'And the purification of the chapel can begin.'

'Oh, aye,' said Henry in a strange tone. 'Aye, it'll take a deal o purifying.'

They stepped out into the courtyard just as Canon Muir came hurrying in at the hostel door, exclaiming in agitation, wringing his hands, Attie and his own manservant behind him.

'Sir Simon! Good Sir Simon, where is he? Tell me it's no true? It canny be true!'

'There's our uncle,' said Austin unnecessarily. 'What's brought him here, then?'

'Ellen Shaw dead by violence, and in our chapel?' Canon Muir was saying, and laid hold of Gil's arm. 'Gilbert, you here! Tell me it's no true!'

'It's true, sir, though I'm sorry to say it.' Gil detached the grip on his arm, aware that the Canon's nephews had contrived to make their escape, as had Craigie. He hoped they had gone into the hall rather than leaving the place. 'Bide here, I'll fetch Sir Simon out to you.'

'But how could it ha happened? Who would do sic a thing, in a chapel, sacred ground!' The old man was right behind Gil as he opened the chapel door. 'Is she still in here? Why is she no lifted, can we no start cleansing the place? Sir Simon, how could you let sic a thing happen?'

Sir Simon rose to greet his patron. Gil stood aside, and the Canon rocked back on his heels as he caught sight of the corpse in the blaze of candlelight, and crossed himself, gabbling a prayer.

'Oh, what a thing to happen! Oh, Christ aid us all, it's dreadful, dreadful!' He clutched at Sir Simon's arm, his other hand waving helplessly. 'How did it happen? Who's guilty o sic a crime? They must be excommunicate, whoever they are! Oh, is it no dreadful, dreadful!'

'Come away out, Canon,' said Sir Simon, edging him towards the door. 'We'll get the servants in to lift her, and see to laying her out. Aye, but where?' he wondered, as the thought struck him. 'We canny put her in here.'

'The dining hall?' Gil suggested. 'I need a word wi the folk still in there, but once I'm done the place will be free.'

'What a thing to happen.' Canon Muir was wringing his hands again. 'What will the Dean say? What will Robert Blacader say? Oh, what a thing! Simon, have we enough incense? We'll need a quarter-stone anyway.'

'They'll be time enough to order it up,' said Sir Simon grimly. 'Come away, Canon, we'll get a word in my chamber while I set Attie to deal wi this.'

The women had vanished from the dining hall, but William Craigie was there, speaking solemnly with Lockhart and the serving-men; as the door latched behind Gil, the whole group turned towards the crucifix on the end wall of the chamber, removing their hats, and Craigie began intoning one of the prayers for the dead in his rich voice. Behind them, Henry Muir snorted contemptuously, lifted one of the candles and made for the nearer end of the hall.

'Well, Cunningham?' he said, hooking a stool out from under one of the long tables with his booted foot. He sat down, set the wooden candle-stand on the table, drew another stool closer to put his feet on it, and stared challengingly at Gil. 'We've been talking wi the old man all this evening, till the last hour or so.'

'And then where were you?' Gil asked, acknowledging this gambit. He tested the table for rigidity and sat on it, pushing the candle aside.

'We were in an alehouse,' said Austin, 'that one at the Wyndheid that has a bishop ower the door. Wishart's Tree, do they cry it? We kent the ale would be good, see.'

'Where yon fellow found us,' his brother supplied, jerking his head at the devout group below the crucifix. 'And you can ask at the alewife. She'll likely mind us.' He looked complacently from his own red broadcloth with its silver braiding to his brother's dark grey velvet trimmed with gilt braid and gold silk brocade.

'A course she'll mind us,' said Austin, 'for you made certain—' He bit off the words as his brother raised a threatening hand.

'Made certain?' Gil queried.

'I made certain,' said Henry, 'to gie the serving-lass a good tip, since we'd hope to go back there and good service is aye a good thing. So they'll mind us. Right?' He eased at the high neck of the red broadcloth.

'So when did you see Dame Ellen last?'

'That would be earlier the day,' offered Austin. 'When she was alive, see . . .' His voice trailed off as his brother turned to glare at him. 'Well, she was, Henry,' he persisted, recovering. 'She was.'

'Afore noon,' said Henry.

'No, it was after—' Austin fell silent at the lift of his brother's hand.

'I think she was wishing to promote a match wi Annie Gibb for one of you,' Gil said. 'Am I right?'

Henry's expression grew darker.

'Aye,' he said shortly.

'You wereny in favour?'

'We wereny,' said Austin, laughing. 'Take a mad wife that doesny wash? And no even all her dower to sweeten the match? We're no daft, either o us.'

'Why would you not have all her dower?' Gil asked, as Henry turned to look at his brother again. 'It's considerable. I'd ha thought even the half of it would be worth having.'

'But it wasny the right half, see,' said Austin.

'Dame Ellen planned an arrangement,' said Henry irritably. 'Who do you reckon killed her, Cunningham? When was it, any road?'

An arrangement, thought Gil. Presumably Dame Ellen herself, possibly Canon Muir, almost certainly Craigie, were to benefit from a share of Annie's property if the match took place, as well as the fortunate groom.

'It was after dinner, Henry,' said Austin. 'That she dee'd.'

'How do you know that?' Gil asked.

'He's right,' said Henry off-handedly. 'Must ha been. Else she'd ha been missed here at dinner, and found sooner. Is this all you wanted to ask, Cunningham? For I'll need to get a word wi Lockhart there, about where we can plant the old dame, and how this lot's to get home to Glenbuck, whether they'll need our escort or can find their own.'

'The Provost will want a quest on her,' said Gil. 'There's no burying her afore that's seen to, and the party will likely stay here while Sir Edward lives, anyway, so there's no hurry, I'd ha thought.'

'What, is he no deid yet? I took it he'd passed on by now, it's days since he was despaired of.'

'Maybe he's waiting till Annie gets found,' offered Austin. 'He's right fond o her. You said that, Henry.'

'The girls were no help,' said Alys, leaning wearily against Gil. 'We calmed them eventually, but I learned nothing from them. Meggot knew only that Dame Ellen was at dinner in the hall with the rest of them and went out after, saying she would go to the chapel. And the St Catherine's woman, what is her name?'

'Bessie,' supplied Lowrie from her other side, holding his lantern down so that its light glittered on the chattering Girth Burn.

'Bessie.' Alys gathered up her skirts in one hand, and set the other in Gil's to accept his help across the stepping stones. 'Was in the dining hall putting away the linen and the crocks, and thought none of the party left the hall other-wise, for they were telling stories and singing, pilgrim songs and the like, a family evening while the dame was out of the way. Bessie thought it was to lighten their hearts a little while they wait for the death.' She shook out her skirts, and moved on towards home. 'Meggot told me the same, when I asked her.'

'And then what?' Gil put his arm about his wife and drew her close. 'When did she find the corp?'

'After she finished her work in the hall, about the time the other household began to retire for the evening. She set out to her own lodging, by the main door, and as she crossed the courtyard she thought to go into the chapel and count the candles, having had no chance to do it before. She stepped in, and she says opened the candle-box, which dwells in the aumbry near the door, to count them by touch, and then smelled—' She broke off.

'Quite,' said Gil.

'And lighting a candle, she found – what she found, and began screaming. Poor woman, she is still much distressed. Was it very dreadful?'

'Bad enough. But there was nobody in the chapel – nobody living,' he corrected himself, 'when she went in?'

'I think she would have mentioned it.'

'And there's nowhere to hide,' Lowrie offered. 'It's a wee bare chamber, and it wasn't full dark by then. Do you think she was killed on her own account, or is it connected to one of the others?'

'No saying, yet,' said Gil. 'Did you find the woman on the Stablegreen?'

'Mistress Templand? Aye, she was there. Gown and apron clean, at least no worse than a day's wear, and her other aprons and her shoes were all free of anything like you'd expect.' He laughed. 'She would know what we were looking for, a course, and when we told her she said, *It deserves her right*, and began praying for her in the same breath. She'd been wi her neighbour the past two or three hours, telling her the tale of the argument wi Dame Ellen, so one way and another she's clear of the hunt.'

'I'd agree.' Gil halted before the front door of the House of the Mermaiden, extracting the heavy key from his purse. He could hear Socrates blowing hard at the gap under the door; about them the night was quiet, though away in the distance, outside the burgh, another dog barked. Wings swished above their heads, and a nightbird called a bubbling cry and was answered.

'Time for bed, I think,' he said. 'We can fit this together in the morning.'

The view down the Clyde from Bishop Rae's bridge was always entertaining. This morning, mild and almost windless with a steady fine drizzle, there were fewer bystanders and casual onlookers than was often the case, but there was still plenty to see. Several small boats were drawn up on the strand, their crews engaged in the mysterious occupations of mariners on land. Sails hung drying under a pent at the top of the bank, several more men were unloading barrels from a larger boat under the watchful eye of a well-uphol-stered merchant, and two further little vessels were slipping upriver on the tide. Standing on the crown of the Bishop's stone bridge, Socrates beside him with his forepaws on the parapet, Gil studied these, and concluded that the nearer, well laden with canvas-wrapped bales and boxes, was Stockfish Tam's *Cuthbert*. He snapped his fingers at the dog and strolled casually down the slope of the bridge, avoiding an oxcart full of timber and several handcarts, and fetched up on the shore just where *Cuthbert* nosed in against the sandy beach.

'Good day to you, skipper,' he said as the mariner splashed ashore bare legged, hauling on a rope. Tam checked, glanced at him over his shoulder, and went on to moor his boat, taking deft turns of the rope about a pair of timbers hammered into the sandy shore. Socrates ambled over to examine his method. 'I need a word wi you.'

'Nothin' to stop you,' said Tam. He was a chunky, fairish man of middling height, weather browned and competent with deep-set hazel eyes, not a man to mix with in a fight Gil reckoned. Now he caught a second rope flung to him by a youngster in the boat, elbowed the dog aside and cast it round another pair of timbers.

'You mind me? Gil Cunningham, Blacader's quaestor.'

'Aye.' Tam splashed back into the water and the boy assisted him to hoist one of the canvas packs onto his shoulders.

'You took a cargo down the water night afore last.'

'Did I now?' said Tam unhelpfully. He tramped past Gil, to lower the pack to the grass well above the tideline. Socrates followed him, and began a thorough inspection of the stitched canvas coverings.

'Wi my man Euan as crew,' Gil added. This got him a sharp look, but no answer. 'A sack of grain, two cheeses, a barrel of apples.' Another sharp look as the mariner passed him on the way back to the boat. 'All with the St Mungo's seal on them, to be sold in Dumbarton. What I need to learn from you, man, is who charged you to sell the goods, and who brought them to you the night afore you sailed.'

Tam plodded up the shore again with a second well-stitched pack, and set it down by its fellow. Turning to face Gil he studied him for a moment.

'Very likely,' he said. 'But why should I tell you sic a thing? Supposing I ken the answers.'

'What, you'd take delivery o a boatload wi no idea who handed it to you, nor who your principal might be?'

'Aye, Tam,' called the man in the next boat along the shore. 'You right, man?'

'I'm right, Dod,' said Tam. He looked at Gil again, snorted, and set off to fetch another bale. The boy in the boat, enough like him to be a close relation, watched anxiously.

'Or did he never tell you who the principal was?' Gil prodded. 'It was Barnabas the verger, wasn't it, who brought the cart down in the night?'

'If you're that certain,' Tam paused beside him, a box balanced on his sturdy shoulders, 'why are you troubling to ask me?'

'Was it Barnabas?'

'Him that's deid? Aye,' said Tam reluctantly. 'It was. He never tellt me his name, mind, but I asked a bit. I'll no do business wi folk wi'out a name.'

'And his principal?'

The mariner snorted again, and trudged up the slope with his burden. Lowering it to the grass where Socrates waited, he straightened up and eyed Gil directly.

'I'd got his name, I made shift to do wi'out his superior's.'

'So there was a superior? Did he never name him?'

'He tried to tell me he was alone in it,' said Tam, 'but I kent better. It was someone at St Mungo's, that was clear enough, he'd never ha got all that stuff away on his own.'

'What stuff?'

211

'All that I took down the water and sellt for him.'

'There was a lot, was there? How often did you take a boatload down?'

Tam shrugged.

'Every two-three nights? Aince or twice a week, mebbe.'

'And what did you do with the proceeds?'

'Och, I gied it back to him,' said Tam with the air of a scrupulous man. 'It was St Mungo's goods, after a', I'd never rob Holy Kirk.'

Gil paused a moment at this utterance, but contrived to keep his face straight.

'You never thought that Barnabas might be robbing Holy Kirk?' he suggested.

'What, and him one of the vergers?' Tam stepped down the grassy slope and made for the boat again. 'Is that all you were wanting fro me?'

'What will you do,' Gil asked deliberately, 'with the coin you took in Dumbarton yesterday for the last lading? Barnabas is dead, as you said. When was he to come back with another cart-load? Is that when you should ha handed over the coin?'

The mariner made a great play of getting another pack onto his shoulder, of plodding up the slope with it through the drizzle, of setting it down with care and lining it up beside the other bales. Socrates, growing bored, paced off along the shore to investigate another boat. Gil waited. Eventually the man straightened up and looked at him.

'He'd ha brought me some more the night, most like.'

'Where would you meet him?'

Tam bent his head, scratching at the back of his neck, looking from side to side as he did so.

'If you'll bide,' he said at last, very quietly, 'till I shift this load, and the boy goes to advise Mistress Veitch her goods is come home, we can take a stroll on the Green.'

Gil glanced at the sky. It was not much past Terce, he reckoned; Otterburn would be expecting him to report on the death in the pilgrim hostel, but this was more immediately useful. He nodded, whistled to Socrates, and sat down on the damp canvas-covered box.

Once the boat was unloaded and the boy had returned, panting, from notifying Mistress Marion Veitch that a stack of goods had been brought upriver out of her husband's *Rose of Irvine* and waited for her on the shore, Tam ordered the boy to watch them, jerked his head at Gil, and set off up the bank of the river, under the near arch of the bridge, towards the wide expanse of Glasgow Green.

'If our luck's in,' he said conversationally, 'the washerwomen'll be abroad. Aye good entertainment, they are.'

'So where did you meet the fellow and his handcart?' Gil asked. The mariner halted, looking about him.

'Aye, you see,' he said, pointing. 'There's the washerwomen, by the mill-burn. They're a great draw.'

He strolled in the other direction, away from the gathering of men round the three or four huge washtubs, in which the burgh's professional washerwomen, skirts kilted high above bare muscular calves, tramped the wet linen clean and exchanged edged pleasantries with their audience. Gil followed him without comment, and eventually the man halted on the bank of the river, looking morosely down at the rippling water.

'You canny sell goods in Dumbarton market,' he said. 'No if you're no an indweller or pay yir fee at the gates.' Gil, who was well aware of this, kept silence, and after a little Tam went on, 'Course they's nothing to prevent a couple o freens striking a bargain, and if the one o them's an indweller and can sell the goods on, it's nothin' to do wi the other fellow.' Gil continued to preserve silence, and the mariner prodded at the grass of the riverbank with his bare foot. 'I've aye done it,' he said. 'Goods that willny shift in Glasgow, items they're short in Dumbarton. Me and a couple o the lads has a good trade going. Ye ken?'

Thus appealed to, Gil made an agreeing sound in his throat. Tam picked a dandelion out of the tussocky grass with his toes, and stared down at it.

'I'm no saying I've done a thing that's agin the law,' he

said defensively. 'This chiel fetches up in Maggie Bell's tavern, oh,' he paused, reckoning, 'after Candlemas, it would be. Wi a tale o a poke o meal he wants to shift, and having no licence to sell in the burgh he'd as soon it went elsewhere. So we came to an accommodation, and I dealt wi it for him, and when I gied him his share o the coin he said, how about another couple o pokes? And so it went on for a week or two or more, him bringing me the goods by night and then he'd be back a night or two later for the takings. And then,' he paused, scowling at the small stook of dandelion leaves he had gathered, 'and then around Lady Day he'd a barrel o apricocks. I thought it a strange thing for one o the vergers to get his hands on, but I took it into the boatie, and it was only the next morn when me and my freen in Dumbarton was prigging over the price that I seen the St Mungo's seal on it.'

'Did you challenge him on that?' Gil asked.

'Did I no! But it was no use, he'd a long tale about it was gien him by the Almoner hissel, I could ask him if I wanted.'

'And did you?' Gil prompted, wondering if Barnabas had thought of that by himself.

'What do you think? Anyway, these last few weeks, it's come to be more and more at a time. In fact my freen was saying last week, he's no certain he can take any more, the merchants o Dumbarton are looking sideyways at him a'ready.'

'Had you told Barnabas that?'

'I did.' Gil waited, not looking at the man. Socrates came whirling back at the gallop from wherever he had been, thrust his nose briefly under his master's hand, and loped off again. Tam drew a deep breath, and let it out again. 'Daft, I was,' he admitted. 'All I got then was a sweering, language like you'd never expect fro a servant o Holy Kirk, and tellt that I was in ower my ears already, and my freen in Dumbarton and all, and I could haud my wheesht and keep the trade going. Which is all very well for him to say,' he added, 'he'd no notion o trade, that was clear, when the market's gone it's gone and no point saying Keep it going.'

Gil, who had heard rather differently from his successful merchant brother-in-law, said,

'Convenient for you the fellow's deid, I'd think.'

'Oh, aye,' agreed Tam, 'but you'll no lay it at my door, freen, I was never near St Mungo's the day he was slain, I was here about the shore all day or drinking at Maggie Bell's place. Along wi your man,' he finished pointedly.

'So Euan has already told me,' Gil accepted.

'Pit doon the well, was he, that Barnabas? No a good way to go. Oh, throttled first, do you tell me? No that that's any better.'

'So how was Barnabas to collect the coin for the last load? What will you do now?'

'That's just it,' said Tam, showing signs of discomfort. 'I'm no right sure how best to proceed. I've been turning it ower in my head, see, all the way up fro Dumbarton. He'd ha come down the night, likely wi another two-three barrels, and I canny think whether to sit out and watch, and see if his principal comes instead or maybe sends another, or whether to go to my bed and hope he doesny, or go up St Mungo's and hand this bit coin to the Almoner, or what.'

'Where did you meet Barnabas? Did he bring his cart right down to the shore?'

'No him.' Tam waved a hand downriver, then retracted it. 'No, you canny see fro here, the bridge is in the way. The far end o the shore where we haul up, there's a great stand o trees and bushes and that. It's the foot o St Thenew's land.' Gil nodded. 'He'd hurl his cairtie down the track by St Thenew's itsel, and pull it into the shadows there, so me and the laddie, or whoever I got to gie us a hand, had to carry what goods he brought down to the shore on our backs.'

'So nobody else got a look at him,' said Gil.

'Aye. So what I'm thinking, I might sit about the brazier by the sail-shed, see if anybody cam down looking for me the night. But I'm wondering, this fellow that might be waiting in the shadows, how much does he maybe ken? How much does he think I ken?'

Gil turned his head to look at the mariner. The hazel eyes met his, their expression troubled.

'I've no wife, maister,' he said, 'but I've the laddie. My nevvy. I'd no want to leave him on his lone.'

'The other fishermen?' Gil suggested.

'Maybe. I'm owed a few favours.'

Gil considered the sky again. The drizzle had stopped, and the grey clouds were lightening; it was probably nearly Sext.

'I ought to get away up to the Castle,' he said. 'Will you be about the shore the day?' Tam nodded. 'I'll come and find you, or send by one of the Provost's men. I think we could give this fellow more than he bargains for.'

Chapter Twelve

'I'm perfectly well,' said Alys. 'No need to worry about me.'

'It's not like you,' said Kate. 'Will you have some of Ursel's gingerbread?'

'I'll have some gingerbread, if I may, Mammy,' said her younger stepdaughter hopefully.

'You've had a piece already, Ysonde. Take the dish to your aunt.'

Ysonde gave a dramatic sigh and tossed her head, but lifted the wooden platter and presented it to Alys with quite a creditable curtsy. Over the row of broken gold-brown pieces her penetrating glance met Alys's, and she said significantly,

'*Dame, how does my gay goshawk?*'

Alys kept her face straight with difficulty; behind the child Kate made no such attempt, though she contrived not to laugh aloud. The older girl, Wynliane, was looking shocked.

'Maister Lowrie? He is well, Ysonde. He is gone into Ayrshire today, on an errand for your uncle.'

'Tell him his bonnie white doo was asking for him,' said Ysonde with aplomb.

'Seeing the rain's stopped,' Kate intervened, 'you and Wynliane may take John and baby Edward out into the yard, if you'll watch them carefully.'

When the children had gone outside, along with their nurses and a still-offended Jennet, Kate turned to Alys, but was forestalled by Babb, who said eagerly,

'Now what's this happened up the town, mistress? A woman murdered, they're saying, and in a chapel at that? What chapel is it?'

'Was Gil called to it?' Kate said, watching Alys's expression.

'We were both there. They sent round last night.'

'Both of you? Did you go to support those lassies you were telling me about? It's surely not one of them that's killed?'

Alys settled down to recount the events of the evening, along with what she and Gil had learned from the residents of the hostel and its various guests. Kate and the gigantic Babb listened attentively, both crossing themselves in shock from time to time as she unfolded the full extent of the sacrilege which had taken place.

'There was word from the Dean already this morning,' she said. 'There is to be a special meeting of Chapter this afternoon, to which he seems to think Gil can bring the name of the killer already, so that they may anathematise him. Does it need the Archbishop for that, or could the Chapter do it in a body?'

'What, wi bell, book and candle?' said Kate. 'D'you know, I have no idea. What a thing to happen here in Glasgow. You hear of it out among the wild Ersche, and a course there was the Bruce getting excommunicate by the Pope, for the same crime in Paisley Abbey, but that was two hundred year ago, not here and now!'

'My granny tellt me about the Bruce,' said Babb improbably. 'Her granny's granny was there and heard it, or maybe it was *her* granny, I canny mind, she'd heard all about it any road. They read the Pope's letter out fro the high altar, and all cast down their candles and shut their books, so you could say he was excommunicate twice. Cursed him north and south and east and west, so it did, and sleeping and waking, eating and fasting and a' things you could think of, and all Scotland wi him. Read in all the kirks, it was. No that we paid any mind,' she added.

'Terrifying,' said Alys.

'But who does Gil think . . . ?' began Kate, and stopped. Alys shook her head.

'No way to tell for now.'

'Yes, it's too soon.' Kate reached for the jug. 'Some more

of this spiced ale? If the anathema goes ahead we can look for someone to dwine and sicken or drop dead, I suppose, but if they'll have to summon Robert Blacader from Stirling or wherever the court is the now to issue it, it could all take a while.'

'We could,' said Alys noncommittally. 'Myself, I doubt whether someone who would do such a thing would be affected by excommunication, but there is no knowing.'

'Well, we'll see.' Kate looked round as the house door opened. 'Andy? Is all well out in the yard?'

'Oh, aye, mistress.' Augie's steward, small and bowlegged, ducked his head in a bow to both ladies, and gave Babb a friendly nod. 'It was just I seen the wee laddie out there, so I thought Mistress Mason might be wi you. I tracked the cadger's lodging for ye, mistress.'

'That was very quick,' said Alys admiringly. 'I hope it was not a great trouble.'

'No, no, was nae bother. Turns out he goes drinking when he's in Glasgow in the same howff our Jamesie's brother favours, up at the Wyndheid. So he stays up the Stablegreen, it seems, near the port, at the back o a horner's shop. His wife's cried,' Andy paused, and rasped his chin thoughtfully, 'Eppie, that was the name. Eppie Forrest. She's like to be at home even if Billy isny.'

One advantage of Jennet's bad mood, Alys found, was that the girl accompanied her without comment. She had rather expected a stream of objections to her next excursion, since the Stablegreen was a very mixed area, but Jennet was still offended by having been left at home last night and merely followed her mistress one step behind all the way up the High Street, among the groups of gossiping women and shouting students, through the Wyndhead, across the Girth Burn and past the rose-brown sandstone walls of the Castle. The street led by St Serf's almshouse, where aged voices upraised in chant suggested the residents were singing Nones, and St Catherine's, where several priests were gathered outside the gate, talking in low shocked tones. Alys avoided these, and went on to where the houses became smaller, with workshops and weaving-sheds propped against them.

Lowrie's directions were quite clear, and led her to a small cottage set end-on to the street. Under the sagging thatch a small window pierced the rubble wall near the house corner, its shutters open, and voices and a smell of stewed kale and fried onions floated out; Jennet followed as she picked her way along the muddy path to the door and rattled at the tirling-pin, the voices stopped, and there was a hoarse yapping. After a moment the door opened on a sturdy man in a sleeveless doublet, with his wife, in a blue kirtle, visible behind him restraining a half-grown dog of very mixed race.

'Will Johnson?' Alys asked over the continued yapping. 'I think our man spoke to your wife yesterday. Could I have a word? About something you heard?'

'A word?'

'And is that the dog you went to fetch? It's a very healthy beast,' she said diplomatically, unable to think of any other commendation.

'Aye, and warranted good ratters on both sides.' Johnson eyed her up and down, surveyed Jennet, and stood back civilly. 'Will you come in, mistress?'

'We're just at our kale,' said his wife. The dog barked again, and she clamped its muzzle shut with an expert hand. 'Will you hae a bite to eat? Come and sit in at the fire, mistress, and your lassie wi you. Was it about what happened yestreen? For I spoke to your man, I tellt him all,' she freed the dog, which hurried forward to check the intruders, and crossed herself, 'Christ forgive her, poor woman, naeb'dy deserves to end like that, and in a chapel and all, what's the world coming to? Sit in and eat, mistress.'

Argument was futile. Seated by the hearth before a real chimney, in the man's own chair, a bowl of kale and a lump of barley bread in front of her on a stool, the dog restrained from sniffing hopefully at the food, and Jennet beside her spooning at another generous bowlful, she allowed the couple to rehearse the events of the previous evening, offering corrections to their wilder flights of fancy but trying to give away nothing new.

'She's saying it was the Deil himsel,' said Johnson drily, jerking his head at his wife, 'but I'm thinking it wasny, they'd never a smell o sulphur or flames or the like. But who'd ha thought it, here on the Stablegreen?'

'No, indeed,' said Alys soothingly. 'It is a very proper chapel, with figures of Our Lord and Our Lady and St Catherine, and a crucifix upon the altar, the Devil could never bear to enter such a place.'

'But they're saying the woman was struck down wi the crucifix itsel,' said Mistress Templand, reluctant to abandon her theory.

'It was the candlestick,' said Alys, 'so my husband told me. But I think you had spoken with Dame Ellen, not two hours before?'

'I had that! Poor soul, and if she'd kent her end was that near, she'd ha dealt more civilly wi me, I've no doubt. Calling me for a' things, she was, and accusing me o leeing, threatened to get her men to pit me out the place,' recalled Mistress Templand, indignation rising. 'And me doing naught but tell her o what my man heard, when her household's still asking all about for news o that lassie that was throttled at St Mungo's Cross.'

'And what was it you heard?' Alys asked, turning to the man of the house. 'I think it might be helpful.'

'That night the lassie was at the Cross, Will,' his wife prompted. 'You mind, you tellt me, you looked out and there was a hoor out there arguing wi a crowd o men.'

'It wasny a crowd o men, woman,' said Johnson. 'It was two men. See, she was setting the morn's meal to soak for the porridge, and rattling crocks, and the like,' he said to Alys, 'and I was the other end o the house and about to bar the shutters and the door, and I heard voices out in the street.' Alys nodded. 'So I keeked out, and it was a lassie, I've seen her about often enough, one o the lassies from the Trindle up the road a bit.' His wife sniffed eloquently, but did not interrupt. 'She was cammellin away at two fellows in fine clothes, threapin that they awed her for something they'd gied her, which doesny make sense,' he added as if he had just thought of it, 'surely she awed them if they gied her something? Any road, it was working up to a right stushie, yir two fellows were threatening her to keep her voice down and leave them alane, but then one of them seen me keeking out, and they went off down the road, and her after them. Last I heard she was still crying out that they awed her, and threatening to take it further.'

'You must ha misheard,' said his wife. 'She'd gied them something, maybe, and that's how it was them awed her for it.'

'No, I never. *You gied me it,* she was saying, *there was never a sign afore you—*' His eyes slid sideways to his wife. 'Afore he rummelt her,' he mouthed. His wife gave another eloquent sniff, but did not comment.

'What were the men like, that she argued with?' Alys asked. 'Did you see them?'

'No that well,' admitted Johnson regretfully. 'Two well-set fellows, young enough, maybe past twenty. Fine clothes the both o them, velvet gowns,' he stuck out his elbows to show a short gown with its flaring body, 'fancy braid on their doublets, great felt bonnets. One o them had a feather in his.'

'You never saw their faces?'

'No clear. It was near dark, it was just the moon and the lantern on the corner o Tammas Tamson's weaving-shed showed me that much.' He paused to consider. 'Neither o them had a beard, nor long hair.'

Alys thought about this for a moment, stroking the young dog's soft ears.

'What time was it, do you suppose?' she asked.

'Time we should ha been in our bed. An hour afore midnight, two hour?'

Extracting herself and Jennet with difficulty from the house, Alys paused on the street to consider her next move. Jennet, thawing slightly, watched her but said nothing.

'The cadger's wife,' Alys said aloud. 'She dwells at the back of a horner's shop.'

'They's one there,' said Jennet. 'And another yonder, and two more there.'

She began by asking at the one nearest the port. Her second enquiry was more fruitful, and the workshop itself far less unsavoury. The trade clearly necessitated working with the cut horns of animals, which must be soaked and cleaned, but the stinking barrels they were soaked in did not have to be kept by the shop door, she felt. This man's green stock seemed to be stowed somewhere out of sight. She hoped it was also out of reach of his two small sons, who were squabbling over a hobbyhorse outside.

'Mistress Forrest?' said their father, a short stout man in a red doublet. 'Oh, aye. Dwells down the back yonder,' he jerked his head. 'The path's at the side o the shop. I canny interest you in a new comb, mistress? Or you, lassie, for that bonnie brown hair?'

Alys had already cast her eye over the items arranged neatly on the shelves behind the man's workbench. Beakers, spoons, combs, a stack of bowls, a broad platter, gleamed in the light from the door. A pot of water steamed on a brazier beside the bench, and a clutter of mysterious tools, knives and chisels, pincers and clamps, lay to hand.

'See, I've all sizes,' continued the horner. 'Carved wi flowers, plain as you like, long teeth or short. Best combs in Glasgow, mistress, I'll warrant you.' He lifted half-a-dozen and spread them out on a cloth with a deft movement. 'See, here's a bonny one. 'At's a good size, so it is, there's as many ladies buys that size. In fact Mistress Forrest that you're asking for, she bought one of them off me, no two days since, seeing she'd lost her old one. Or so she said.'

'Is that right?' Alys turned the pretty thing over, admiring the stripes of black and tawny colour. 'One like this, was it? She has good taste.'

'Aye, just like it, wi the wee flowers, save the raying wasny as dark. Her man buys them off me and all, to take out on his wee cairt.' He glanced at the window. 'I've no seen her the day, she's likely in the house, if you wanted to ask her how she's found her comb.'

Half an hour later, having bargained successfully for a dozen bowls, a set of beakers, and the flowered comb, and arranged for them to be sent home, Alys and a less sullen Jennet picked their way down the side of the horner's little workshop.

'The second door, he said it was, mem,' Jennet said, pausing before a sturdy, well-maintained cottage, its timber framed walls whitewashed, a tub of herbs on either side of the doorsill. Movement within suggested kitchen work, clinking crocks, chopping sounds. 'Is it this one?'

'I'd think so.' Alys paused, collected her mind and rattled at the tirling-pin.

The sounds within stopped abruptly. After a moment the door was opened, wide enough for a face to peer out. A plump, mature face, wary and apprehensive, surrounded by a decent kerchief of sparkling white linen.

'Mistress Forrest?' Alys asked.

'Aye.'

Alys waited, but there was nothing more.

'I think you've not been out to the market the day. May I come in?' she said.

'It's no right convenient.' Mistress Forrest glanced over her shoulder, into the house, and looked back at Alys. 'I'm in the midst o making, making, apple cheese.'

'In *August*?' said Alys involuntarily. 'I'd like some of those apples. I think you should let me in, for I've a word for Annie Gibb, mistress, but I can deliver it here on your threshold if you prefer.'

'Who would that be?' countered the woman. Alys, aware of Jennet staring at her, said patiently,

'I think Mistress Gibb needs to know that Dame Ellen Shaw is dead.'

Mistress Forrest began to answer, shaking her head, but behind her another voice said sharply,

'Dame Ellen dead? Eppie, let her in!'

'Let me go first!' said Jennet urgently. 'You be careful, mem, she's maybe—'

224

'Nonsense,' said Alys, stepping forward as Mistress Forrest reluctantly drew the door wider. 'She's as sane as you or me. She never was mad, were you, Annie?'

The house was small, its roof composed of one bay of rafters, but it was neat and well stocked. Its floor, of that strange mixture of ash, clay, straw and gravel, rammed down, oiled and burnished with a flat stone, which was common in the better cottages, was clean and well swept. At one end a ladder led up to a loft, where a mattress was airing, and two sturdy kists suggested enough possessions to fill them. At ground level two good wooden chairs and a pair of stools were enough to seat four women round the open hearth; a folding table against the wall, two more kists, a stack of bags and smaller boxes which must be the cadger's stock-in-trade, furnished the place well, and a quantity of cushions and hangings stitched from well-worn verdure tapestry made it easeful and suggested that Mistress Forrest was a good needlewoman.

'Dame Ellen dead,' said the girl who sat opposite Alys, for the fifth or sixth time. 'I still canny take it in.'

'And I hope she has her reward for the way she's dealt wi you, my lamb,' said Mistress Forrest. She was a comfortable woman in her forties, neatly and decently dressed in good tawny wool; her apron was as white as her headdress. She had clearly been working on the dinner, for a wooden board with a knife and carrots for chopping had been set aside, but there were no apples visible. Beside her, Annie Gibb was young and slender and bundled in what must be her host's second best kirtle, from the way it was belted in folds about her waist and exposed ankles swathed in clean but faded cloth hose. Her feet were thrust into an elderly pair of wooden-soled shoes. Her hair was fair, and cut short and curling round her head; it seemed as if her vow was set aside.

'But how did you find me?' she asked now. 'I'd ha heard the word of the death soon or late, when Eppie went out to the street or when Geordie Horner came by to tell her the news, but here you are on the doorstep to tell me it.'

'You know the whole of Glasgow is seeking you?' Alys said carefully.

'Oh, aye,' said Mistress Forrest. 'I seen the men out beating the Stablegreen, keeking under bushes, and the Provost's men asking at all the houses. But nobody kent my lammie was here, and I never said a thing, and let Geordie and his wife think I'd some woman's trouble on me and couldny talk at the door, so they've never found her. And yet here's you, lassie, come straight to my door as Annie says.'

'My mistress kens a' things,' said Jennet proudly.

'Annie's good-sisters mentioned the cadger, more than once,' Alys said. 'I wondered if he had carried some message for you. Then I learned that he was a Glasgow man, and had a wife. I thought it was worth looking here, seeing nobody else had tried it. Were you Annie's nurse, mistress?'

'I was that,' said Mistress Forrest fondly, 'and her mammy's before her. Who else would she turn to? We set it all together, her and Billy and me, so soon as the scheme of St Mungo's Cross was mentioned. And that foreign fellow that helped and all.'

'But how did you get free of the Cross?' asked Jennet, and looked from her mistress to Annie. 'I just wondered,' she added. 'Was it St Mungo himsel freed you, mistress?'

'No,' said Annie regretfully. 'Though I— No.'

'I thought it couldny be,' said Jennet, equally regretful.

'It was Doctor Januar, wasn't it?' said Alys.

Annie stared at her, her colour rising, and crossed herself.

'Who are you? You ken too much by far!' she said in alarm.

'I told you, my man is Blacader's quaestor, charged with finding you and with determining who has killed Dame Ellen,' Alys reminded her. 'I have spoken with your family, and with the doctor. He is clever, very clever, but he could not disguise that he was not concerned for you.'

'He is concerned for her,' objected Mistress Forrest. 'You should ha seen him when he brought her here, wrapped up in his gown, stinking dirty though she was. *Keep her safe*, he said to me, as though I'd do anything else, my pet.'

'Yes,' said Alys, eyeing the girl opposite her. 'Perhaps I should have said, not worried about you. He knew you were safe.'

Annie looked down, then up again, and suddenly smiled.

'How is he? And how,' her expression changed again, 'how is my good-father? Is he yet living?'

'The last I heard,' Alys said gently, 'he was still living, but very near the end, and Doctor Januar was attending him closely.'

Annie bent her head, dabbing at her eyes.

'I forgot,' she admitted. 'It was so good to be out of that, to be clean again, to be free of— I forgot how near death he was. He's been a good father to me, as loving as my own daddy. We said our farewells when we reached Glasgow, afore I went out to St Mungo's, I knew I might no see him again, but it's still—'

'Tell me,' said Alys. 'Tell me from the beginning. Was it your idea entirely, or Sir Edward's?'

'Oh, no, it was Christie's,' said Annie proudly. 'Chrysostom's. He saw how I was imprisoned, when he cam to Glenbuck, and planned it all, wi my good-father's aid, and sent his own man to Glasgow in secret to help. Our daddy was the only one could deal wi Dame Ellen, and he was right glad to see a way out for me. My sisters are betrothed already, they'll be safe enough when he's away, but neither him nor me could see how to get me out o her power, and he'd aye promised me he would see me safe.' She paused, and looked sideways at Alys. 'I've wondered often if he kent more about her than he's ever said, he was that determined I should have some protection afore he went.'

'You've no idea what?' Alys asked, curious. Annie shook her head.

'None. Any road, she's had one man or another ready for me every month since Arthur dee'd, it was clear enough she'd have me carried off by the latest in her favour afore Sir Edward was buried, and I may tell you, Alys did you say your name was? I'd not wed a man she recommended if he was the last in Scotland.'

'I can well imagine,' said Alys.

'Vicious, all of them,' said Annie, her face twisting. 'There are decent men in Ayrshire, there must be, but she—' She broke off, and Mistress Forrest patted her hand.

'There now, my lamb, you're safe now. She's gone where she'll not hurt you.'

'Aye, and how did that happen? What slew her?' Annie asked, as if it had only now occurred to her. 'Was it an apoplexy struck her down in one of her rages, or what?'

'Not an apoplexy,' said Alys. Somehow it was difficult to find the words, to form the sentence. 'She was— She has been—'

'She was murdered,' supplied Jennet, with no such qualms. Mistress Forrest sat back, exclaiming and flinging up her hands. 'Struck down wi a candlestock in the chapel at St Catherine's. My mistress was out all last night comforting your good-sisters, mem, and the whole town's in disarray wi the crime. Sacrilege on the Stablegreen!' she pronounced with enthusiasm.

'Murdered?' repeated Annie in dismay. 'And in the *chapel*? But who? Not Christie, surely! Tell me it wasny him!'

'He has hardly left your good-father's side,' Alys pointed out, 'and the servant bears this out, so my husband says.'

'But what happened?'

Alys recounted what they knew of Dame Ellen's last hours. Annie listened, frowning, and crossed herself at the end.

'Our Lord hasten her days in Purgatory,' she said. 'It sounds as though it wasny any of the household that slew her, and that's a blessing. To think of anyone I knew doing sic a thing, well, it would right scunner you.'

'So who might it have been?' Alys asked, over Jennet's murmur of agreement. 'Can you think who there might be in Glasgow who would deal with her so violently? I got no help from your sisters,' she added, 'and I think my husband learned little from the men.'

'Small wonder that!' said Annie, smiling wryly. 'They're dear lassies, but Mariota got the wisdom for all three o them. No, I couldny say,' she added, 'save she might ha summoned one or another o her freens to her, maybe started in to lecture him, and angered him beyond measure.'

Alys considered this, frowning. It seemed to link to something Gil had said, something— Mistress Forrest leaned forward with an exclamation, and drew a yellow-glazed pot away from the fire.

'I'm that caught up in what you're saying, lassie, I'm no watching this buttered ale. I'd say it was about ready. Will you take a mouthful?'

By the time Jennet had assisted in serving out beakers of the foaming, spicy stuff, the connection had vanished into the recesses of Alys' thoughts. Abandoning it for the moment, she raised her beaker and said,

'Good fortune to you, Annie, and good health.'

'Good fortune to you, Alys,' the other girl returned conventionally, 'and your heart's desire along wi it.'

Alys caught her breath a moment. Even in the midst of pursuing Gil's duties, there it was, taunting her. Her heart's desire—

'Tell me,' she said resolutely, 'tell me what happened that night. They bound you to the Cross, and left your men to keep an eye on you from St Thomas's chapel. What happened then?'

'Were you no feart?' asked Jennet curiously. 'I'd ha been mad wi fright, all on my lone like that, and tied up and all.'

'I was,' Annie said. 'It was no so bad while the laddies were at their play, out beyond the kirkyard gates, but once they went home it was awful quiet. And then there was noises in the trees, and an owl.' She shivered. 'I near dee'd of the fright when the owl screeched. But I said a prayer to St Mungo,' she went on resolutely, 'and then Christie came out from the almshouse, like we'd planned, and came to the Cross. Only, when he came to me, he had,' she swallowed, 'he had a dead woman wi him.'

'A dead woman?' repeated Mistress Forrest. 'You never tellt me that, my lammie!' She looked from her nurseling to Alys, and back. 'Is that how that poor soul came to be there? And the Provost calling a quest on her and everything!'

'Poor soul indeed,' said Annie. 'He'd found her lying in the roadway, stark dead. I asked him why he'd carried her there, and he, he, he suggested that we bind her to the Cross in my stead, so my men would think it was me.'

'Could you no ha trusted them, mistress?' asked Jennet. 'Seemed to me they was all gey fond of you, Meggot and the fellows too by what she said.'

'Ellen. That was why. If they knew nothing,' Annie said, 'Dame Ellen could get nothing out of them. She'd ha beaten the lights out of them if she suspected they knew where I'd gone.'

'So you cut the dead woman's gown off,' said Alys, 'and threw it in the burn, and bound her to the Cross.'

Annie nodded.

'Christie had his wee shears on him, and his knife, and the two o us—' She grimaced. 'Poor lassie. I canny forget the way she rolled about as we worked.'

'What about the cord round her neck?'

'Cord? What cord? No, her neck was broke, Christie said, that was what killed her. He'd no notion who she was.' She crossed herself. 'I thought, well, whoever did that to her flung her down in the road like rubbish on a midden, maybe if we left her at the Cross St Mungo would take her under his protection.'

'You tied no cord about her neck?'

'No, have I no just said that? What are you talking about?'

'Some time before dawn,' Alys said deliberately, 'someone came by and throttled the dead woman with a cord. Someone who thought they were killing her.'

Annie stared. The beaker fell from her hand, rolling across the beaten-earth floor and spilling foam. The blue eyes rolled upwards into her head, and she collapsed bonelessly sideways, onto Mistress Forrest's broad bosom.

'Oh, my lamb! Annie!' the older woman exclaimed. Jennet scrambled to help her. Alys rose to snatch the plaid hanging on a nail at the back of the door and spread it out, and they lowered Annie to the ground. She was already beginning to stir, her hands twitching as if she was fighting

230

something off. Mistress Forrest, still exclaiming, began patting her cheeks and chafing at her arms.

'She'll be better in a moment,' Alys said, observing Annie's returning colour. 'Have you spirits in the house, mistress?'

In half an hour or so, sitting up again and sipping cautiously at a small amount of usquebae in a tiny beaker, Annie protested,

'No, I've never a notion who'd ha done that. It's just the thought of the escape I had that turned me dizzy. What if I'd no— Or Christie had been late— Oh, it doesny bear thinking on!'

'Well, don't think on it,' said Jennet robustly. 'Maybe the saint was watching out for you indeed, I'd say you owed him a candle, mem.'

'Aye, you're right, lass,' said Annie, though her teeth chattered on the rim of the beaker. 'Two candles, at the least. But no, Alys, I canny think, I've never a notion who might have tried to, to, who might want rid of me that bad. Our household's all good people, Meggot hasny an ill bone in her body, my sisters are fond enough I'd ha said.'

'Dame Ellen?' Alys asked.

'No, no, she was at me to accept one or other of the Muirs. I think she was to share some o my land wi them if the match went ahead, by what Meggot hearkened one time when they thought they were all alone in the yard. So that wouldny be like, she'd still be hoping I might come round.'

'Is there no still that cousin o your faither's, my lamb?' said Mistress Forrest, straightening up from the hearth. 'What was his name, now? I canny mind.'

'What cousin?' Annie stared at her nurse.

'Och, him that made all the outcry when your faither gied you the land, at your marriage, Our Lady grant him rest. Specially for the bit wi the quarry on it.'

'Hallrig, you mean? I don't mind that. I wonder if Sir Edward and my own daddy dealt with it all?'

'Aye, Hallrig. Likely they did, you were naught but a wee lassie. Any road, he made a great stushie, this kinsman, about the land going out the Gibb family, which was a right laugh as we said at the time seeing he wasny a Gibb neither. Just afore I was wedded and left the household, that was,' said Mistress Forrest sadly, 'and the most o them I've never seen since.'

Alys murmured in sympathy, and set this aside for later consideration.

'Once you left the Cross,' she said, 'and Peg tied to it, poor woman—'

'Is that her name?' Annie crossed herself, and murmured a swift prayer.

'Did you come straight here?'

'Aye, they did,' said Mistress Forrest, 'all arranged, it was, your doctor man had sent a laddie to warn me, so I kent it was for that night, and I was sitting up watching and waiting for them. Right quiet it was, and all, by that time. There was all the outcry the prentices made in their battle, and then all the folk going home from the alehouses, and then it was silent as the grave after that, till I heard them on the path, and then Annie said my name at the door.'

'Did you see anyone?'

Annie shook her head.

'There was none stirring. We went from shadow to shadow, you understand, once we were out of the kirkyard, and both of us wi our ears stretched for the Watch and anyone else we might need to hide from, but there was none afoot.' She shut her eyes, the better to remember. 'One or two dogs barking, here and there a bairn waking inside a house. Some fellow wi a handcart. A couple arguing ahint their shutters.' She opened her eyes. 'And then we were here, and Eppie had hot water and shears and comb waiting.' She ran a hand through the short curls. 'I'll ha to find me a priest, to seek absolution from the vow, but Our Lady kens, it's good to be clean.'

'Och, it was foolishness,' said Mistress Forrest comfortably. 'You'll be easy let off it, they should never ha let you swear such a daft thing. It's no as if you washed yoursel, after all, it was me got you clean, just as I did when you were still in tail-clouts, and clipped your hair and combed out all the wee louses.'

Alys met Annie's eye, but did not comment. It was clear the other girl was aware, if her nurse was not, of the serious nature of her position: a broken oath was perjury, no matter what the circumstances of its breaking.

'What did the doctor do?' she asked.

'He went back to the hostel, to his duties.' Annie drew a deep breath. 'Alys, what do I do now? Should I go to them, to the household? My sisters will be needing me, and I'd like— I'd like a last word wi our daddy if he yet lives. Forbye easing their concern for me.'

'Och, my lamb—' began Mistress Forrest.

'You could come wi me, Eppie. I'd be glad of it, in fact.'

'I think you must,' Alys said. 'And I'll come too, if I may. There are things I need to ask them all.'

Chapter Thirteen

'I'd looked for you afore Terce,' said Otterburn. 'What's all this at St Catherine's? It's got St Mungo's going like a spilled byke. I've had the Dean sending to me afore I'd broke my fast, bidding me find the murderer by this afternoon, and a special despatch from my lord, the Stirling road must ha grooves in it by now, and you nowhere to be found.' He pulled a sheet of paper towards him and unfolded it, to display a passage of William Dunbar's neat secretary hand, with Blacader's crabbed signature below it. 'He's to be in Glasgow this afternoon for the same meeting I've to find the murderer for, Christ aid us, and then he'll pronounce the anathema and see to the reconsecration at the hostel. The most o that's St Mungo's concern, I hope he's sent to the Dean as well, and our folk here ken how to prepare for my lord, but he's expecting the King to follow him, which is no so good. Where were you, any road? Sit there and gie me your tale, and I hope it's a good one.'

'I was down at the shore.' Gil drew up the stool the Provost indicated. Socrates sprawled across his feet with an ostentatious sigh. 'Getting a word wi Stockfish Tam. Can you lend me three-four men the night? We might take the St Mungo's thief if we're careful.'

'Oh, is that what you've been at? Aye, likely. That would be a good thing, and something to silence the Dean. We'll get a word wi Andro about that directly. First let me hear about St Catherine's. It's a bad business, this, Cunningham. The woman's lying in my storeroom, waiting till I call a quest on her. The family wants to get her in the ground, and I want to get her out my lord's way.'

Gil summarised what he had found at the hostel. Lockhart listened attentively, his long gloomy face becoming even gloomier.

'Inside or outside?' he said at last.

'Outside, I suspect,' Gil admitted, 'which is tiresome. It would be simpler by far if I thought one of the household was responsible, but they all speak for one another.'

'Do they now?'

'I think it's genuine,' said Gil. 'The lassies in particular are too foolish to take their part in a plot.'

'So who is there outside?'

Gil shrugged.

'I'd ha said the Muirs were a good choice, but Henry tells me they were talking wi Canon Muir all evening till well after the time she died. Will Craigie's another, but he seemed as shocked as any o the clergy by where she was killed, as well as being right squeamish over how it happened. Someone must ha come into the hostel, but who it was I canny guess.'

'And nobody heard this door go? This door that makes an almighty thump when it closes?'

'Door.' Gil stared at the Provost, his mouth falling open. Closing it, he shook his head. 'That was it. That was certainly it. Something was troubling me last night, something out of frame, you ken? We were standing in the yard at St Catherine's, and the door was going like a weaver's shuttle, and never a thump or a bang to be heard.'

'So anybody could ha been in and out of the hostel at any time,' said Otterburn intelligently.

'I'd say so.'

'I've had a look at her – this latest corp. Seems to me someone lost their heid wi her,' Otterburn said, playing with one of the seals on his desk. 'Had she other acquaintance in Glasgow?'

'I need to establish that the day, no to mention what else she was up to, what her intentions were concerning Annie. I suspect she believed the girl was hiding somewhere and would turn up again unharmed, whatever she said when she spoke to me.'

'It's my belief and all,' Otterburn admitted. 'The lassie must ha had accomplices, they've carried her off somewhere secure.' He set the seal down on the desk with a click. 'Where will you hunt next? We're short o time, Cunningham, you realise that I hope.'

'I might call on my uncle,' said Gil. 'He'll take offence if I don't keep him abreast of the tale anyway, and he might have useful information.'

'I heard it was well chewed through at Chapter this morning,' said Otterburn obliquely. 'No to mention this special session, this afternoon.' You're well informed, thought Gil without surprise. 'Now what's this about down the shore? What's Stockfish Tam up to now?'

Stepping in at the kitchen door of Canon Cunningham's house stone house on Rottenrow, Gil found his uncle's housekeeper Maggie Baxter inspecting a vast sausage which she had just hauled dripping from its cauldron of broth. Several other members of the household stood about the kitchen table admiring the object on its platter and savouring its rich aroma. Shining pools of fat gathered about it, reflecting the firelight.

'Aye, it's done,' pronounced Maggie. 'Away up the stair and set the table. Is that you, Maister Gil? Set another place, Matt.'

Canon Cunningham's taciturn body-servant raised a hand in acknowledgement as he turned towards the stair. Gil made for Maggie and kissed her broad red cheek in greeting.

'Away wi you,' she said, elbowing him off. 'How are you, Maister Gil? How's Mistress Alys? Away wi you and all,' she added to Socrates. 'Here, William, cut me a crust for the big dog, there's a good laddie.'

'She's well.' Gil watched as the kitchen boy obeyed, and signalled to his dog to accept the offered hunk of bread. 'That's a magnificent pudding, Maggie, but will it go round one more? I could do wi a word wi the old man.'

'Aye, there's plenty kale to sup wi it. What, is it about this business at St Catherine's? I should think so. He's right put out you haveny been round afore now asking his advice.'

This proved to be true. Once Grace had been said and the pudding cut into rich, spicy portions, the whole matter of the three deaths and Annie Gibb's disappearance had to be gone over, in minute detail, before Canon Cunningham was mollified. Conversation down the table was stilled while the whole household, Maggie, Matt and the other servants, listened avidly to Gil's account.

'A very bad business,' said the Canon when it was ended. He set his spoon neatly in his bowl. 'Indeed, it amounts to a series of attacks on Holy Kirk itsel. Chapter was extremely difficult this morning, even without taking the matter of the sacrilege at St Catherine's.'

'I can imagine,' said Gil. His uncle shot him a sharp look, but went on,

'But are all these separate? We have,' he enumerated on long fingers, 'theft from the Almoner's stores, apparently by one of St Mungo's own servants, and the death of the same servant somewhere about the Cathedral lands. We have the loosing of a supplicant to St Mungo, a very dangerous matter, and her replacement by a dead whore. Whatever the Dean thinks of that form of supplication,' he added, in a tone which gave some insight into the way in which Chapter had been difficult, 'these are both serious offences. And finally, and worst of all, we have a woman, whom we can assume to have been defenceless, done to death by violence in a consecrated place. These are all crimes against Holy Kirk, but are they separate crimes, or all part of one campaign?'

The conversation further down the board had turned to an argument about whether the procedure required at St Catherine's was exorcism or not, and Gil realised that his uncle had switched to Latin.

'I don't know, sir,' he answered, in the same language. 'I had assumed they are separate, because I see no way in which they are all connected, other than in time. That is, they have all happened in the past—' He stopped in amazement. 'The past two days. They may be connected, but I don't see how.'

His uncle considered the empty platter before him for a time, then said,

'The man Barnabas was presumably killed by his accomplice.'

'My thought too.'

'But who was that?'

'I suspect it was one of the songmen, but I have no way of knowing which. They all live beyond their means, and all those I have spoken to were indignant about the theft from their stores as well as from the Almoner's. I don't even know for certain where the man was killed.'

Canon Cunningham nodded, his lean face below the black felt coif still intent on the congealed fat on the platter.

'And the St Mungo's Cross matter,' he said. 'How are Steenie Muir's young kinsmen involved? Poor fellow, he is much distressed by the events at St Catherine's, feeling he is in some way responsible for the death of the woman.' His tone spoke volumes about the idea. 'I remember his cousin Dandy, the father of these boys, who was a wild fellow in his youth. I believe Steenie had hopes that one of them might wed the missing woman.'

'That appears to be so,' Gil agreed. 'Will Craigie the song-man has been promoting the match. I believe there is some agreement to mutual profit if it goes ahead.'

'I can well believe it,' said his uncle. 'I have observed that William is perennially short of funds, and for good cause.'

Gil waited a moment, but when the Canon said no more he went on, 'I do not think the brothers abducted Annie themselves, though I suppose they could have ordered it done. Canon Muir tells me he saw them to bed in person, after spending the evening talking with them.'

His uncle surveyed him with an eye as grey as St Columba's.

'Steenie Muir,' he said with care, 'fell asleep in Chapter this morning, in the midst of the discussion of the matter. The Dean was explaining to us how we felt about the custom when he began snoring. If he can sleep through the

238

Dean explaining something on which he feels strongly, he can sleep through two young men leaving the house to go drinking.'

'Oh,' said Gil, and felt the case shift round him like ice on a half-thawed pond. 'Oh!'

'Precisely,' said Canon Cunningham. He glanced at the windows. 'Here, is that the time?' he said in Scots. 'I'll be late for Chapter. You ken Robert Blacader's to be there?'

'His first outriders were arriving as I left the Castle,' Gil began, and was interrupted by a furious knocking at the house door.

'Maister Cunningham!' a voice was shouting. 'Are you there, Maister Cunningham? That lassie's turned up! The stinking lassie's come home!'

'We sent straight to the Provost from here,' said Alys. She tucked one hand into Gil's, and stroked Socrates' head with the other. 'He must have sent his man out direct to find you. I wish you had seen them,' she admitted, watching the Shaw household reunited on the other side of the hostel dining hall. 'You'd be in no doubt but they were pleased to see her. Look at them now.'

Gil nodded. It had begun to rain again, heavy drops rattling on the shutters and the horn upper panes of the hall windows, but the mood inside was sunny. Even Lockhart was smiling, and looked as if a part of his burden had been lifted. His sisters-in-law were still almost hysterical with relief and delight, and Annie Gibb herself, in her ill-fitting borrowed garments, clearly felt this was a homecoming. The woman Meggot was mopping at her eyes with the tail of her linen headdress, the serving men were grinning, and Sir Simon, summoned from his darker considerations, was reciting a *Te Deum* before the crucifix. Well, he could hardly go into the chapel to give thanks, Gil thought grimly, and was startled to recognise their own maidservant Jennet at Meggot's elbow, part of the rejoicing.

'Has the doctor been told?' he asked. 'Can he leave his patient?'

'Not yet,' Alys said. 'That is, he knows, and he came to the door of the men's hall and spoke, but he is waiting until Sir Edward sleeps a little before he comes away. I think they are very much in love,' she added.

'What, Sir Edward and—'

'No!' She was laughing, realising he was teasing her. 'Annie and her doctor. They hardly spoke, only looked, and then she came away.'

'And you tell me he knew where she was?' Gil reviewed the several conversations he had had with Doctor Januar. 'Aye, he never lied to me, he simply concealed the truth.'

'And when I spoke to him too,' she agreed.

Behind them the door of the dining hall opened. Annie broke off what she was saying and turned; Doctor Januar smiled at her, faintly, reassuringly, and bowed to Gil.

'I think you must have questions for me,' he said. 'I'll take Annie to my patient, and come back here.'

By the time he returned, Lockhart was in low-voiced colloquy with Sir Simon and Alys was caught in conversation with the girls. Gil drew the man to a seat at one of the long tables, looking hard at his face. Sir Edward's deathbed was clearly an ordeal for those who watched with him as well; the blue eyes were shadowed and heavy with disquietude.

'I'll apologise first, before I say anything else,' said the doctor, and once again Gil realised he was staring. 'Her location had to be a secret. If Dame Ellen had guessed that any of us knew where she was—'

'I understand,' Gil said, 'though the Provost may take a different view. I imagine he'd have been round here by now in person, if he hadny to deal wi Robert Blacader.' He thought for a moment, and said carefully, 'I need to know what you saw or heard when you went out of here that night. Annie has told my wife what she knows, which is little enough. What's your version?'

'My version.' Doctor Januar considered for a moment in his turn. 'I left this place about midnight.'

'Hold hard,' said Gil. 'Lockhart and the others were certain nobody had left the men's hall.'

'I made certain they slept soundly,' said the doctor simply. 'As well as my patient. I left about midnight, and made my way down this street here.' He waved a narrow, elegant hand towards the hostel gate. 'I may tell you, *magister*, that the door does not make a loud noise, or at least it did not when I closed it on my return.' He frowned, and turned the blue gaze on Gil. 'That is curious. It slammed behind me when I left, though I tried to close it quietly, but not when I returned. I had not thought of that before.'

'Did it, now,' said Gil. 'It was quiet last night. I wonder if it has been greased recently. Go on.'

'A little way down the street, I fell over a dead woman.'

'How dead? I mean, how long had she been dead?'

'She had barely begun to stiffen about the neck and jaw. I could still determine her neck was broken.' Doctor Januar bent his head. 'I am not proud of what I did next. It occurred to me that this poor soul could give us some time, that if Annie's men—'

'Yes, I know that bit. So you took her along with you. In a sense,' Gil admitted, 'you did her a favour, for it meant her death came to my attention. I haven't yet tracked her killer, but I hope we'll find justice for her. There was nobody about when you found her?'

'Nobody. The place was silent, save for an owl over by the Cathedral.'

'And you heard nothing stirring when you came back with Annie?'

'We heard and saw one man,' said the doctor precisely, 'with a handcart.'

'Ah! Where was he?'

'He came out of Rottenrow, I think you call it, and wheeled the thing towards St Mungo's.' Januar grimaced. 'We had hidden in the same shadow where I found the dead woman, and he did not see us. I heard him go in at a gate, and then a door opened and closed, and I heard the wheels no longer. It was dead of night, every sound carried.'

'And that was all you heard.'

'All I heard. Except—' He paused, and bit his lip. 'I'm not certain, you understand. I was weary. I thought I was weary,' he corrected himself, 'though now I know I am. When I came away from the house where I left Annie, it seemed to me something stirred, away down the street. I waited, and listened, but nothing more moved.'

'A cat, maybe? A fox?'

Januar considered this, but shook his head.

'Something man sized. I think I was not the only one out in the burgh that night.'

'Will you come out and show me where you found the body?'

'Indeed,' said the doctor. 'I am glad to do something for her. She has been on my conscience. She was one of the women of the town, I take it? One of the town harlots?'

'She was.'

'I thought so. I could smell the clap on her.'

'*Smell* it?' Gil repeated involuntarily, holding the hostel door open for his companion. 'Wait a moment. I wanted to check these hinges.'

He leaned into the shadows behind the door and sniffed cautiously at the uppermost hinge. Socrates came back in from the street to see what he was doing, and snuffled curiously at the lower one. There was the odour of ancient wood and rust, and over it, quite certainly, mutton fat. Gil touched a finger to the iron loop and pin, and inspected more closely. There was fat smeared on the metal, recently enough not to have turned rancid.

'I'm agreed,' said Januar, sniffing with equal caution.

'So the hinges have been greased,' Gil said. 'I wonder who by? I need to check with Bessie and her man.' He stepped out into the street. 'You were saying you could smell the clap on the dead woman.'

'Oh, yes. The discharge has a very characteristic odour in the female subject. In the male, because of the difference in the way he is clothed, it is less apparent. Often the most prominent symptom to the onlooker is the choleric temper, which can go to extremes.'

'A choleric temper,' Gil said, aware that he was repeating things again.

'Indeed. In the later stages of the disease it can give rise to uncontrollable rages.' Januar paused, pointing at the wall of St Serf's almshouse, below the chapel window. 'I found her about here. I cannot be certain, but I think this was the gable. She lay with her head against it and her legs across the path, as if she was flung there and so broke her neck.'

'Hmm,' said Gil. 'No chance anyone heard anything, the almshouse brothers would all have retired for the night by the time she died.'

'I would say so,' agreed Januar. Gil looked about him, considering the distance from the Girth Cross to where they stood. Socrates joined them, carefully quartering the area they were looking at. 'She was in deep shadow,' the doctor added. 'That was why I fell over her.'

'Aye, the moon was throwing strong shadows.' Gil turned, to set off back to St Catherine's. 'My thanks, Doctor. You've given me a deal to think about.'

'The Canon's no here, Maister Cunningham,' said Canon Muir's servant. 'He's away to this special meeting o the Chapter, ye ken. It'll likely be a while.'

'No matter,' said Gil easily. 'It was just to confirm a couple o things, you'll likely be able to tell me just as well.'

'Me, maister?' said the man dubiously. 'I'm no privy to the Canon's business, it's no my place to tell things.' He glanced over his shoulder, into the house. 'And I've the Canon's dinner to get, I've no time to—'

'I'm happy enough in a kitchen,' Gil assured him. 'I'll sit by while you work, so long as you can answer me.'

Reluctantly persuaded, the man led Gil through the dark entry of the house into a large, vaulted kitchen. Light from high narrow windows showed kists and presses, two broad dusty tables, a charcoal range with no fire in it, a wide hearth where another man rose, startled, doffing his cap to the stranger.

'Here's Nory, that's servant to our guests,' said Canon

Muir's man. 'This is Canon Cunningham's nevvy from across the way, Nory, that's hunting down the lassie missing from the Cross that your maisters is hoping to wed wi.' He caught up a basket of vegetables, a knife, a chopping-board, and drew another stool to the hearth. 'Hae a seat, maister, and ask away, and you'll forgive me if I get on wi my tasks like you said I should.'

Gil sat down, the dog leaning against his leg. The servant's own name, he suddenly recalled, was William. He was elderly, though not as old as his master, and clearly set in his ways. Maggie would give a lot for a kitchen the size of this, he thought, and so would his own household, but here was this fellow ignoring its conveniences, chopping roots on a board on his knee, tossing them into a stewpot on the hearth.

'And you're caught up in the business at the hostel, aren't you no, maister?' William added. 'What was it happened last night? The Canon was right distressed when he cam home, could gie me no sensible account o the matter. Was it the Deil himsel slew the woman right enough?'

'What, in a chapel?' said Nory derisively. 'What did slay her, maister?'

Resignedly, Gil gave them as concise an account as he might of events at the hostel, while Socrates grew bored and lay down with his nose on his paws. They listened avidly, exclaiming in shock, and agreed that this was certain to have upset Canon Muir right bad, seeing as he was patron of the place. Eventually William recalled Gil's stated errand.

'Here we're channering on about this, and you wi matters to see to, maister. What was it you wanted to ken?'

He arranged his ideas, and said carefully,

'The night you and your maisters arrived in Glasgow, Nory.' Both men nodded. 'When did the household retire for the night? What time did the bar go on the door?'

The two looked at one another.

'Couple hours afore midnight,' said William definitely. 'That's when I aye put the bar up. The Canon doesny like it to be later.'

'Was later than that,' demurred Nory, 'for my maisters was out in the town, you mind, it was well after midnight afore they cam in, I'd to get up and see them to their bed.'

'I thought Canon Muir said he was still up when they came in,' Gil said.

'Oh, aye,' said William. 'He'd be asleep in his chair wi his mouth open, the sowl, thinking he was at his prayers or his books. He aye spends his evenings like that these days, maister. He wakened up when they cam in, which you're right, Nory, it was after midnight, it must ha been well after it when I put the bar up. Then he seen them to their beds and gied them his blessing, and then Nory had to get them out their fine clothes and put young Henry's shirt in the soak. That was never ale, Nory, was it?'

'No,' said Nory baldly. He was a skinny man, older than his charges though much younger than William, neatly and plainly dressed in dark blue.

'I'd never let the Canon wear a shirt like that where he was going to get in a fight,' said William, provoking a series of startling images in Gil's head.

'You think I'd argue wi them? Henry wears what he wants,' Nory said. 'The good broidered shirt, the high-necked doublet, he calls for it and I find it in his kist, and the same for Austin, if I value my skin.'

'How's his neck healing? Did that popilio unguent I gied you never work for it?'

'No,' said Nory again. 'It's right angry. Likely that collar's rubbing it, no to mention getting the grease off the unguent all ower the lining. If I could persuade him to sit wi a hot cloth, it would maybe draw it, but he'll no listen.'

'It must be hard work,' said Gil at a venture, 'keeping garments as fine as those two wear. I've never had a man to tend my garments, not since I left my mother's house, my wife sees to all. What's involved?'

Nory gave him a quick, disparaging look which encompassed his well-worn black doublet and hose and the unfashionable sleeves of his good cloth gown.

'Aye,' he said inscrutably. 'Well, it's to keep them clean,

245

which is no easy when your maisters is as careless wi their garments, and brush them to keep the moth away, and sew the braid back on when it gets torn off, and see their linen gets washed when needed, and—'

'Tell him about that satin gown,' urged William, casting another handful of chopped leaves into the pot.

'He's no needing to hear about the satin gown.'

'Difficult to clean, was it?' Gil suggested. 'When was this?'

'Just last night,' said William chattily. 'That bonnie sad red satin gown he had on, Deil alone kens what he was at wi it, for it cam home stained and stiffened, and I think he's spilled Geneva spirits all down it forbye, did you no say, Nory?'

'It's no sad red, it's marron coloured,' said Nory.

'Satin?' said Gil, thinking of remarks he had heard his sisters make. 'How do you clean satin? You'll never send that to the wash?'

'If I'd had it when it was first stained,' said Nory, 'I'd ha put oatmeal on it straight, but as it is, well! I've cut the braid off it, and put it to soak wi pearlash in the water, but I doubt it will be ruined, there's as much dye coming out the thing, the water's like blood already, and the canvas in the breast will shrink, see, and pull it in, and whose blame will it be when it canny be worn? No his, that's for certain.'

'Did he come in like that?' Gil asked. What had Henry been wearing at the pilgrim hostel last night? Not red satin, he thought, or marron coloured either, whatever that was.

'No, no, he gaed out in the marron satin after his dinner, and they were back an hour or so after, in and out the house like a whirlwind, and when I gaed up to see what they wanted I found this flung on the floor, and the other yin's murrey velvet and all, though it's no marked, Christ be thankit, and they'd took other gowns out the kist and gone out again, no thought o whether the colours consorted well or nothing.'

'May I see it?' Gil asked. 'I'd like to ken what colour that is. My wife's like to ask me,' he invented, though Nory seemed unsurprised by his interest.

'It's in thon bucket,' said William, adding a pile of shredded leaves to the stewpot. 'By the wall.'

Nory was already rocking the leather bucket, dragging a quantity of wet dark-red cloth up from its depths. The water running off it was indeed red, though whether with dye or with something more it was hard to tell.

'Course you canny tell the colour right when it's wet,' he said.

Extricating himself from Canon Muir's kitchen, Gil made his way down Rottenrow, thinking deeply, the dog at his heels. With the facts he had collected today some of what he was investigating began to make more sense, though not all of it could be fitted into the same picture. It was still hard to see how the death of Barnabas was connected to anything else, and he was dubious about the attempt to strangle the dead girl at the Cross, but the rest appeared to follow a pattern. And with what Doctor Januar had told him, he hardly needed to worry himself about a motive, a reason for the deaths.

Both courtyards of the Castle were teeming with packanimals, men in livery, clerics of all ranks, scurrying hither and yon. On the steps of the Archbishop's lodging Otterburn, looking as near flustered as Gil had seen him, and Robert Blacader himself, in grim irritation, were surveying the bustle. Behind them the Archbishop's rat-faced secretary, Maister Dunbar, was making notes in a set of tablets. Blacader's glance fell on Gil, and he raised a hand and beckoned sharply.

'Gilbert,' he said, when Gil had elbowed his way to the foot of the steps. 'What progress have you made? Have we a name for this grievous sinner yet?'

'No with any certainty, my lord,' said Gil, hat in hand, bowing over the proffered ring as he spoke.

'Hmm.' Blacader considered this, his heavy blue jowls stilled for a moment. 'I'm to read the anathema tonight after Vespers. I suppose it can be done without naming him.'

'That might be a good thing,' Gil observed. The Archbishop scrutinised him, and nodded.

'Fetch him out of cover, you mean. Aye, I suppose. We'll go ahead with *Quicunque vehementer percussit*, then, whoever violently slew this woman.' Gil, whose Latin was at least as good as the Archbishop's, bowed at this and prepared to retreat, but his master gestured to him to remain. 'Provost, you'll send the Bellman out, I hope, wi the summons to Vespers and the ensuing. They've all to be there, I want as many of the burgh as possible to hear it, we'll have no doubt what comes to any that desecrate a sacred building.'

'The Bellman's gone out already,' said Otterburn. The Archbishop nodded, and looked about him, gathering up his retinue.

'Gilbert, I want you wi me the now, I'll go up to the hostel, St Catherine's is it, and see the place. Canon Muir's no fit to make sense, I need someone that kens what's what. I need to ken whether the place is scrubbed clean, I'm no consecrating blood and brains. And as for St Mungo's,' he added, almost as an aside, 'I canny think what Dean Henderson's about, a course that chapel needs cleansing. We'll ha the full process there and all. And this lassie that's vanished and reappeared, well!'

Gil's father had been wont to say that the husbandman's best muck was on his own boots. After an hour of watching the episcopal equivalent of this, Gil was in no doubt, if he ever had been, that Robert Blacader was well fitted to be a prince of the Church.

Striding up past the Castle walls to the hostel at the Archbishop's elbow, a retinue of secretaries and chaplains hurrying behind them, he had explained as much of the situation as he dared. His master had listened without comment, but when they reached St Catherine's it was clear he had taken in all that was said. Sir Simon, Lockhart, Doctor Januar, had all been dealt with crisply and effectively, Annie had been confessed and apparently released from her vow of uncleanness on a technical detail of the original wording, her sisters-in-law and the rest of the household had been blessed. Some of the time had been spent at the bedside of the dying man, and the rest had gone on a thorough inspection of the chapel.

'Cold water, lye, hot water, your grace, my lord,' Bessie gabbled, bobbing in a sort of curtsy with every word. 'And I scrubbed and scrubbed it. And the candlestock, cold water and sand, and the hangings pit to soak or burnt, a' seen to, your grace, my lord—'

'I can see that,' said Blacader. 'You have worked very hard, daughter. Well done.'

Bessie fell on her knees, crossing herself, and Sir Simon observed,

'Bessie and Attie her man are faithful servants of the hostel, my lord.'

'You'll speak to William here,' the Archbishop said, 'about what's needed for the reconsecration. All the moveable furnishings, books, hangings, vestments, all that, to be laid out on trestles for the thurifer. Seating for the deacons. William kens what's needed.' Behind him Maister Dunbar nodded resignedly. 'We'll sort it the morn's morn after Sext.'

'The morn?' repeated Sir Simon in astonishment. 'But my lord—'

Maister Dunbar murmured something in his master's ear.

'Well, the next day then. We canny leave it longer, the King's Grace is for the Isles again and all the Court wi him. Which calls me to mind, I'll want you wi us, Gilbert.'

Turning over this startling news, Gil made now for home and his dinner. His last trip to the Isles in May had been eventful, and had brought him once again to the attention of his King. Another trip could be interesting, though he would probably have to leave Alys at home again; it certainly meant that he had to find out who killed Barnabas, and Peg Simpson, and Dame Ellen Shaw, before he left.

Lowrie was in the hall when he stepped into the house, pulling off his boots while the women set up the table and Euan gathered up plaids and saddlebags to carry upstairs. Catherine had emerged from her chamber in anticipation of the meal. Alys was just pouring ale; seeing Gil she smiled, and reached for another beaker. Socrates padded forward to greet them both, tail waving.

'Success!' the young man said. 'I've news aplenty, Maister Gil. But what's happening in the burgh? What's the Bellman crying? Did I see the Archbishop's standard at the Castle?'

'You did,' Gil agreed, taking a pull at his ale. 'Ah, I needed that. There's been all sorts happening here. I've collected a deal of news too, and Alys has found Annie Gibb safe.'

'Found—?' Lowrie stared in awe at Alys over his ale. 'Mistress, I truly believe there is nothing you can't do. Where was she?'

Over the meal Catherine listened intently as they discussed the return of Annie Gibb, and what Gil had learned from the day, and finally turned to Lowrie's errand over the second course, a dish of almond tartlets.

'I found James Bowling easy enough,' he said. 'He dwells hard by the Cross, I'd to ask no more than two people afore I found him. He's forty I suppose, stout burgess prospering well, it's clear the town supports more than one man of law in good style. I gave him your letter, which he read, and sends greetings, very civilly.' Gil bent his head in acknowledgement. 'Then I tellt him the whole tale, as I had it last night a course, and asked could he shed any light on any of it. At which he hummed and hawed a while about confidentiality and the respect of his clients, till I mentioned the Archbishop, and reminded him how much we kent already, whereupon he agreed to answer questions but no to volunteer what wasny asked.'

'I'd ha done the same, I suppose,' said Gil.

'Indeed, it shows a very proper attitude,' said Catherine in French.

'By which means I established,' said Lowrie, nodding at this, 'that William Craigie is altogether well kent in Ayrshire. It's not spoken of but widely kent that he was one of a party that burned the kirk o Tarbolton, and a course as a priest he was hit wi a heavy penance for it. He's to contribute stone for the rebuilding—'

'The quarry!' said Alys.

'Exactly. He was fined coin and all, which he's paying over a few merks at a time, and has been going the rounds of the men of law in Ayrshire, trying to get one of them to take on his case that he should ha been left the quarry you were asking Maister Mason o last night.'

'Was it only last night?' marvelled Gil. 'Aye, before Attie summoned us to the hostel. Go on, Lowrie. This is extraordinarily useful.'

'Why should he have been left it?' Alys wondered. 'Was there any reason?'

'There was. Annie's paternal grandmother was a Craigie. I think the land came to her father that way.'

'And he claimed to be unrelated to Annie,' said Gil. 'Very good. Very useful indeed, Lowrie.'

'*Maistre le notaire*, I believe you should go,' said Catherine, glancing at the windows, 'if you are to attend Vespers as the Archbishop ordered. I hope to hear an account of what passes.'

'Did you ask about Annie? Or about the Muirs?' Gil pushed back his chair, and the rest of the household took its cue to rise and begin clearing the table.

'I did.' Lowrie grimaced. 'Annie's vow is likewise well kent in the county, and the Muirs are just as notorious. It seems there's nobody willing to entertain their suit for their daughters. Not either o them.'

The nave of St Mungo's was crowded, and the people of the burgh were still pouring in by the south door. Gil led his household in and succeeded, by the use of his elbows and Euan's extra weight, in placing them all sufficiently close to the heavy stone choir screen. Vespers had already begun, and the psalms for the day were floating through the screen; Gil made out both Habbie Sim's tenor and Will Craigie's bass.

'What's to do, maister?' Kittock asked behind him. 'Are we to be kept late? For my knees isny up to a long stand.'

Vespers wound to its close. Galston and the foolish Robert led the procession, in its full panoply of brocade vestments and gleaming metalwork, out through the choir screen and down the steps into the nave. The congregation in the knave knelt with a mighty susurration as the Archbishop passed, led by crucifer, lucifers, thurifer. The thurifer's censer swung, spreading the ticklish smoke. The choir, following, divided left and right and took up position on the steps, while the two vergers led the procession of clergy away into the narrow north transept towards the vestry. On the steps the Sub-Chanter gave out a note, and the choir launched into one of the penitential psalms.

Gil looked about him. The Provost was nearby, with a small detachment of his men; they had left their weapons in the porch, of course, but their buff jerkins were conspicuous. Midway down the nave he could see Sir Simon and the party from the pilgrim hostel, and Maistre Pierre was easy to pick out even in this crowd. (Does Pierre know yet? he wondered. No, I must not be distracted.) He went on searching, and made out the Muir brothers by one of the pillars, and a number of off-duty vergers by another. Distantly down the nave he could see Peg Simpson's man, the porter Billy Baird.

The choir embarked on another psalm, and the procession returned. Once again the processional cross, the two candles on their long bearing-poles, the smoking censer went past; they must have replenished the censer, Gil thought. A junior cleric bore a bell, another held a smaller candle, the Gospel returned on its cushion. But behind them came the clergy, stripped of their brocades and embroidered vestments, robed in black and purple as if it was Lent. A murmur ran through the crowd. Archbishop Blacader, the Dean, the Chanter, Canon Cunningham, Canon Muir – Gil counted twelve high-ranking priests following the archbishop up onto the platform before the choirscreen.

Blacader turned and faced the crowd. The choir found the end of the psalm, and stopped. Without preamble, the Archbishop began to speak in Latin.

'*Quicunque vehementer percussit*,' he declaimed, in a voice

252

which carried effortlessly to the far corners of the nave, 'whomsoever violently slew the woman Ellen Shaw in the chapel dedicated to St Catherine, desecrating its stones with her blood: let him be separate, with his accomplices, from the precious body and blood of our Lord and from the society of all Christians. We declare him excommunicate and anathema, we judge him damned . . .'

As the weighty sentences rolled on, the heavy delivery and emphatic tone leaving their intent unmistakable, Gil looked about the church again. Otterburn, solemn but alert; the group of vergers long faced. Townsfolk frowning intently, trying to recognise the Latin words, one or two translating for neighbours. Many were crossing themselves, alarmed by the portentous recital. The clergy flanking Blacader watched impassively, their mourning robes in heavy dark folds, the ends of all their purple stoles stirring in the draught. *Covered all over in purple and pall*, Gil thought.

Blacader had switched to Scots.

'Let him be damnit wi the condamnit, let him be scourgit wi the ingrate, let him perish wi the proud. Let him be accursit wi the heretics. Let him be accursit wi the blasphemer. Let him be—'

On and on it went. Accursed in drinking, accursed in eating, accursed in sitting, accursed in standing. Gil could see his father-in-law frowning, Lockhart and his entourage of women crossing themselves. Some people were sobbing aloud.

' — saving only if he repent and mak amends,' concluded the Archbishop. Gil counted silently, one, two, and all twelve of the black-robed priests stirred and said in deep unison,

'*Fiat!*' So be it.

Blacader reached out and took the bell, and tolled it once. It made an incongruously sweet sound in the midst of the daunting ceremony. He closed the Gospel on its cushion before him, with a thump which made the book-bearer stagger slightly, then took the single candle from its bearer, snuffed it and threw it down. It rolled down the steps, watched by all the people around it. A child wailed, and was hushed. There was a huge silence.

'*No!* No, no, you canny!' howled a voice. Blacader looked out across the heads as Gil turned, hunting for the source. 'I'll no have it, I'll no let you!'

Austin Muir hurled himself towards the choirscreen, thrusting bystanders aside, his face contorted with fury. Behind him his brother snatched vainly at his gown and sleeves, calling for him to stop, to come back.

'You'll no snuff me out!' declared Austin, as he reached the foot of the steps. He swooped on the candle and snatched it up. 'Here, light it! Light me again!'

'Austin!' panted his brother behind him. 'Leave it, man! Leave it be! He's run mad,' he said to the nearest man, who was pushing his wife out of danger. 'Help me wi him!'

'Light me again!' demanded Austin, and sprang up the steps. The two tall candles were out of his reach, and their bearers hidden behind the ranks of the choir; he snatched the censer from the thurifer and knocked its cover off, prodding with the candle at the smoking grains of incense inside it. Behind Gil, Euan and the maidservants were attempting to drag Alys away to safety, some bystanders were pushing closer, other people were backing away, but Otterburn and his men were thrusting their way through the crowd. Gil followed Austin up the steps, elbowing bemused clergy aside, and tried to lay hands on the man.

'Austin Muir,' he said, 'leave that be and come wi me.'

'I'll no!' Austin straightened up, the chains of the censer in his hand, and backed away. 'Get away! I have to light this!'

'He's run mad,' said his brother again. 'Austin, come away, man!'

'I'll no!' Austin swung the censer now like a morningstar, scattering hot coals and smoking incense. A songman made a grab for it and was knocked aside in a smell of singed woollen vestment. Robert Blacader and his circle of clergy seemed frozen, staring appalled. Gil caught Austin's eye and said,

'Give me the candle, then and I'll light it for you.'

'Take me for a fool, do you?' retorted Austin.

'You'll never light it if you throw incense all about,' Gil said. Behind the man, Lowrie was moving carefully, quietly; the people around them were shouting, though the sound was miles away, and Otterburn and his men were at the foot of the steps now.

'You'll no get me that way!' Austin said wildly, swinging the censer again. Another of the songmen tried to grapple with him and was struck by the weapon, falling sideways against his neighbour, who fell in his turn. Incense wafted everywhere, and people began to cough.

'Put it down and give me the candle,' Gil prompted. 'Come on, man, be reasonable.'

'Never!' said Austin, shortened the chain round his hand and swung his smoking morningstar again. A huge waft of smoke billowed from it, and he choked, coughed, briefly withdrew his attention from his surroundings. Gil pounced, and Lowrie reached the man in the same moment. Gil seized the censer, Lowrie grasped his wrist and twisted it up behind his back. Gil handed the censer to the nearest pair of hands, and his uncle's voice said, 'Well done, Gilbert.' Two of Otterburn's men arrived to take a fierce hold of Austin, two more laid hands on Henry, and as Gil stepped back he finally heard the uproar in the building.

Canon Muir surged out of the black-gowned row of clergy, his purple stole awry, exclaiming in distress.

'No! Och, no, there's some mistake! Austin, Henry, you canny ha done sic a thing? Oh, my dear laddies!' He attempted to pull one of Otterburn's men away from Austin, and was firmly but politely put aside by another.

'Take them away, lads,' said Otterburn at Gil's side. 'That was well done.'

Blacader stepped forward and raised a hand for silence. To Gil's amazement, he got it, in a spreading pool of still-ness which flooded out from the foot of the steps. When the church was quiet, apart from the scuffling of Austin Muir being manhandled out of the building, his brother silent beside him and Canon Muir still lamenting behind the procession, the Archbishop scanned his flock with a minatory glare and said resonantly,

'Sic a fate lies waiting for all who commit sacrilege, ye may be sure o that. Ye ha seen God's justice done afore your een. Pray for that man's repentance and forgiveness. Confess yir ain sins, find forgiveness yoursels. And now go in peace.'

He raised his hand again, and recited a lengthy blessing, then turned and to the obvious surprise of his remaining cohort vanished through the choirscreen arch into the chancel, towards the high altar. With some milling about they collected themselves and followed him, in silence and in due order, and after a few moments, as the buzz of conversation rose in the nave, the first words of Compline floated out.

'Well!' said Alys at Gil's elbow. 'Were you expecting that?'

Chapter Fourteen

'Not entirely, I'll admit,' Gil said.

They were briefly gathered in the little solar, after an extended session with Otterburn and the Archbishop. Otterburn's satisfaction with the outcome of the anathema was as great as his master's, though with a slightly different slant.

'Two o these deaths tidied up,' he said, rubbing his hands together. 'They've confessed, the both o them, though to hear them Austin thought he was protecting Henry when he broke the one lassie's neck, and again when he took a candlestock to the other dame, and Henry reckoned he was protecting Austin when he got him away and tried to conceal it.'

'Austin has repented very completely,' said the Archbishop in Latin. 'His brother will also repent of his part in the whole affair once we have discussed it with him. A very good outcome, Gilbert, and I commend your part in it, as well as that of your servant Lawrence.'

'Aye,' said Otterburn rather drily.

'I was certain it was one of those two,' said Gil now in answer to Alys, 'but I'll admit I still thought it was Henry did the actual killing. Austin never showed any sign of a quick temper, though I suppose his brother kept him on so short a leash he never had the chance.'

'Little surprise he broke,' said Lowrie. 'I hope I never hear another anathema. The way the clauses mount up, threat upon threat,' he demonstrated a growing stack with both hands, 'must be designed to generate fear, and by Christ's nails it does.'

'It is indeed designed to be terrifying,' commented Catherine, 'and it would be a foolish person who was not struck by fear.'

'But what did happen?' Alys asked. 'Did the Provost learn why the women died?'

'They were both finding fault wi Henry, and that roused Austin,' Gil said. 'Peg was convinced it was one of them had infected her wi the clap.'

'Surely not!' said Alys. 'It would have been as likely the other way around, I should have said.'

'It could have been either,' Gil said, considering this. 'I'd ha thought both parties were equally advanced in the complaint, though Januar said the rages were a sign in the later stages of the disease, and Peg showed no such sign as yet.'

'So perhaps she was right,' said Alys thoughtfully. Lowrie was scarlet, looking increasingly awkward, and she smiled kindly at him and said, 'In any case, she was convinced of it.'

'She was,' agreed Gil, 'and demanded some reparation for it, *out in the street where all could hear*, said Austin.'

'Including the man Johnson, I assume,' said Lowrie, relief in his tone.

'Exactly. Then she went for Henry when he refused her. He marked her face the way we all saw it, but she managed to scratch his throat, and then when Austin flung her off, she struck the wall and broke her neck. That's probably no hanging matter, but at least we ken the truth now. As for Dame Ellen, it seems she'd already summoned the brothers to meet her in the chapel after the hostel dinner hour, and by the time they came she'd heard Johnson's wife and guessed who it must ha been that he heard arguing. According to Henry she was abusing him for a' things, for spoiling her plans by losing his temper, and his brother seized the candlestick and struck her down. Austin should certainly hang for that, and maybe Henry as well.'

'He did more than strike her down,' said Lowrie, grimacing.

'She was an unpleasant woman,' said Alys, 'but nobody

deserves to die like that.' She shivered slightly. 'That night when Annie was at the Cross has been a busy one. My— My good-mother,' she went on resolutely, 'spoke of crows, of shadows, about young Berthold. Indeed it seems as if the night was full of shadows, of people like crows on a wall watching and waiting for one death or another. There was the doctor moving about, and making use of Peg's death,' she counted, 'and then there was whoever it was tried to strangle her, and the Muirs swaggering through all of it after they killed her, though I suppose they are not like crows. Three crows, like the song.'

'Not entirely like the song,' said Gil. 'And those are all linked to Peg, not to Berthold. We don't know of any connection between them.'

'And has anyone spoken to Berthold lately?' she wondered. 'Now that we know more about what was happening, perhaps we can reassure him enough for him to tell us what he saw.'

'A good point,' said Gil. 'But best dealt wi tomorrow.'

Alys lifted the wine jug. 'Will you have some more, Gil? Lowrie?'

'No if I'm to go out again,' Gil said. 'There's the matter o Stockfish Tam and his customer to see to. No, I'll no take you, Lowrie, we've been over that.'

'I'll admit, I'm about ready for my bed,' said Lowrie, ducking his head in acknowledgement of this. 'Forty mile, a long discussion, and a day of Euan's conversation. I'm about done.'

'So we still don't know,' said Alys, pouring wine for the rest of them, 'who killed Barnabas and who tried to strangle a dead woman at the Cross. Do you suspect someone?' she asked Gil.

'I do,' he said, 'but I've already been wrong once. We'll see what happens in a few hours.'

'There's no a lot o cover,' said Tam dubiously to the captain of the Castle guard. 'No place to hide. Yir men's going to show up like a deid sheep on the shore.'

'I brought the best yins,' said Andro. 'No that that's saying a lot,' he added, and the three fellows behind him stopped grinning. 'So we'll hope they can lie in conceal- ment wi'out alerting the quarry. How did yir man reach you afore? Where did he wait for you?'

'Under they bushes.' Tam pointed.

'But it's a different man, mind,' Gil said. 'No telling what he'll do.'

'Aye.' Andro looked about him. The night was cloudy, and a brisk wind had got up, making sufficient noise in the trees to cover movement. 'We'll ha two o you lads in the sail shed, I think, and you and me, Richie, ahint yon bushes. Where will you lie up, Maister Cunningham?'

'I think,' said Gil, who had had time to consider the matter, 'I'll sit out by the brazier. No need for Tam to be the bait, our man has no notion of who he's to meet so far as we ken, and in the dark he'll not get a right sight of me.'

'Here—' began Tam.

'Aye, that would work,' said Andro.

'No, it's no right,' protested Tam. 'I'm no one to stand by—'

'You'll come wi Richie and me,' said Andro, 'so we'll cut off his retreat if he tries to flee that way. What time do you look for him?'

'Any hour fro now on,' said Tam, still dubious. 'Maister, I'm sweirt to let you take my place, I am that!'

'Did I hear something?' said one of Andro's men.

'Aye. Places,' said Andro, low voiced, 'and nae mair argu- ment. Bring that light, Richie.'

Sitting on a balk of wood by the brazier, Gil warmed his hands and listened. The river rippled past ten feet away, chuckling quietly to itself. He could hear small movements in the sail-shed behind him as the two men lurking there settled down, and occasional more distant stirrings which must be night birds, small animals, a hunting fox. His own lantern gave a little light; now they were in place, Andro's men had shut theirs and showed no sign.

The row of small houses belonging to the shore folk, set

well back from the strand, was silent. Beyond that, the burgh seemed to be asleep, except for the occasional barking dog; on the opposite bank Govan slept as peacefully.

The sound which had alerted Andro's man came again, a shifting of stone on stone. A footfall, or the sound of a wheel, Gil wondered. Surely he wouldn't bring the cart down tonight, he thought, he can't be certain of meeting his man. Another footfall, a scuffle, a muttered curse. A light bobbed into view on the rough ground at the foot of St Thenew's croft, came closer. Stopped by the nearest clump of bushes.

'Stockfish Tam?' said a hoarse whisper.

'Who's asking?' Gil responded in the same tone.

'I am,' said the other unhelpfully. The light bobbed forward as if its bearer had taken a couple of steps. 'Are you Tam?'

'What do you want wi Tam?' Gil countered.

'I think you ken what. You've got something for me, something that belongs to Holy Kirk.'

'And if I have?' Persuade him closer, so that Andro can cut him off. Bring him down onto the strand. 'Where's the other fellow?'

'He'll no be coming. As you well know. Come on, where's my money?'

'Yours? I thocht you said it belonged to Holy Kirk.' Sweet St Giles, Gil thought, we missed a trick here, we should have had a purse ready to tempt him wi. He reached for his own purse, and hefted it so that the contents clinked and scraped together. 'It's here. Come and get it, then.'

The light advanced another few steps, and halted. Watching tensely, Gil saw a shadow move behind it, and then another.

'Come to the fire,' he invited, 'and get your due.'

'Bring it to me.'

'It's you that wants it,' Gil returned, 'no me. It's here if you'll come for it.' He clinked his purse again.

After a long moment, the light moved forward. Boots crumped on the sand and pebbles of the shore. Gil rose to his feet.

'Now!' he shouted, and the night was full of running men and shouting. A tussle developed, people were swearing, but the dark shape Gil had his eyes on dropped its lantern, and moved to pass him with quick crunching steps, making for the bridge. He launched himself full length, and found he was rolling on the sand with an opponent who, though he was a handy fighter, lacked Gil's advantages. Street-fighting in Paris was a hard school, but an effective one. He dodged an attempt to claw at his ear, got one hand under the other man's jaw, used his knee efficiently, came out on top and trapped a flailing arm under his thigh.

'Light here,' he called, getting a grip on the throat. 'Lights, and a rope!'

'Have ye got him?' It was Andro. 'Oh, well done, maister. They eejits were fighting theirsels. I've got his arm, you can let go now, let him up. Lachie! Get ower here, man!'

The gasping quarry was hauled to his feet and held firm, crowing for breath, while Andro bound his arms to his sides. Gil lifted the lantern, and held it up to see the man's face.

'Good e'en to you, William,' he said. 'You're out ower late, for one that's to rise and sing Matins and Lauds.'

'I deny that absolutely,' said William Craigie.

'You expect us to believe you?' said Otterburn, peering at him gloomily across his desk in the candlelight.

'Killing a man in the High Kirk? Hiding his body so he canny have absolution? What kind of priest do you think I am?'

'One that would steal from Holy Kirk,' Gil said.

'That's different,' said Craigie implausibly. 'I was about St Mungo's that afternoon, I grant you that, but I never saw Barnabas till after he was dead.'

'Where were you?' Gil asked.

'I was in our hall, the songmen's hall, for a time. Then that daft Robert cam to say Dame Ellen was seeking me,' Craigie swallowed, 'and when she'd done I went back to the hall, for I'd a notion to con some of the music for the next day. I tellt you that at the time, Gil. There was one or two folks in and out,' he recalled hopefully, 'Sim and Dod Arthur for one.'

'So who was Barnabas seeking?' Gil asked. 'He went off wi a sack-tie saying *I see it now,* what did he see? What had it told him?'

'How the Deil should I ken? I wasny the man's keeper! Though I failed him in that,' the prisoner added, his voice dropping. Gil studied his bent head.

'And what about Peg Simpson? You deny that you put a cord about her neck?'

'The lassie at the Cross? Was that her name?' Craigie muttered a swift prayer in his rich bass. 'No, Gil, I wasny about that night. I was at the cards in the hall till midnight, then I gaed to my bed. Dod Arthur was there, and John Ross, and we convoyed one another home.'

Gil made a note of the names, and flicked open a different leaf of his tablets.

'What's your claim to a property called Hallrig? By Tarbolton, I think.'

'Hallrig?' Craigie stared at him. 'None whatever.'

'And yet I'm tellt you've been going the rounds o men o law in Ayrshire, looking for one to take on your claim for it. Convenient, certainly, for you to own the property, what wi the quarry.'

'I have not!' said Craigie incredulously. 'I've never— I haveny been into Ayrshire in the past year! No, no, it belongs to the Gibbs, it left the Craigies forty year since. And who goes to law over one property? It would cost more than the plot's worth by the time the bill cam in.'

'Why did you tell me you were no kin o Annie Gibb?'

The prisoner attempted to shrug, despite his bonds.

'It was easier than trying to explain.'

'Ach!' said Otterburn. 'I haveny patience for this. Take him away, Andro, and the Archbishop can question him in the morning. And the Dean,' he added.

Gil thought the departing Craigie flinched at this.

'Well, Cunningham,' continued the Provost as the door

banged shut behind prisoner and escort. 'What d'you make o that? I'd say you could accompany the King's Grace to the Isles again wi a light heart.'

'I'm less certain. Craigie's lied to me, more than once, but he was quite determined the now he was innocent o the verger's death.'

'Well, we'll get more out him in the morning when the fire's hot for the pilliwinks. I'm for my bed. It's been a long day. I hope I'll see you betimes, maister, there's the quest on Dame Ellen and the verger and I'll need your evidence, even wi a signed confession for the woman. I'm no risking another sic verdict as I had for the hoor.'

'No, I agree,' said Alys, curling warm and relaxed into the crook of Gil's arm. 'It sounds as if there is at least some doubt.'

He rubbed his cheek on the crown of her head, and stretched out his legs between the rumpled linen sheets. It was extraordinarily good to have some time alone with his wife, and she seemed to feel the same, to judge by the way she had responded when he had slipped into bed beside her.

'It would be very tidy,' he said regretfully, 'but while he denies it so firmly we must at least consider if there is another solution.'

'Who stood to benefit from the verger's death?' She was twirling her fingers in the hairs on his chest. 'We assumed his partner in the thefts had killed him to prevent some accusation being made. Could the man have set off to accuse someone else, who then killed him? Or could someone have killed him to protect Craigie?'

'Craigie lacks powerful friends,' said Gil. 'That's half his trouble.'

'And the girl at the Cross.' Her hand stilled, flat against his breastbone. 'Whoever did that to her thought he was killing Annie Gibb. Who would have benefited from Annie's death? What happens to her property at her death?'

'Likely it would have reverted to the various families,'

said Gil, 'with fat pickings for any men of law who get involved. It's always a problem when there's no will.'

'What about the property with the quarry? Was that hers outright, or was it a life interest?'

'A life interest, I think, and then I suspect reverts to her father's family.' Gil was trying to recall the documents he had seen. 'Why does one never take enough notes the first time?'

'So the Shaws would not get it. But they would get back all the lands she had from her marriage, I suppose, since there are no – no children. Could Sir Edward have ordered her killed? His daughters would benefit.'

'He seems truly fond of her,' said Gil. 'Besides, why go to this trouble and expense, not to mention the pain of the journey, when he could have ordered her killed in his own house and concealed the whole matter?'

'Lockhart?'

'He wasn't out of the hostel. That's the other thing. If whoever throttled Peg was connected with Annie's family, he must have come out of the hostel, and the doctor told us he made certain the men were all asleep.'

'And it was hardly Doctor Januar who did that,' she said slowly, 'since he knew well the girl was dead already. And then there is the door to consider. The door that went three times. Why three? Did two leave together and come back separately, or what?'

'Ah, no,' he said. 'The door has been greased. It shuts quietly now. The hostel servants know nothing about it, it's none of their doing. I suspect it was greased between the time the doctor left the hostel and the time he returned. It smells like mutton fat, and Bessie said they had mutton that night, and not since.'

'Oh!' she said. 'So anyone could have gone out and back again, at any time in the night after that, except that they were all asleep in the men's hall, and Dame Ellen was adamant nobody stirred out of the women's hall. What a conundrum it is. Could it have been someone else entirely? Annie's father's kindred?'

'Which is wide, by what I recall.' Gil grimaced into the darkness of their curtained bed. 'We need to ask more questions in the morning. I must get out to the hostel betimes, before the quest.'

'I will come with you.' She curled closer, and he rolled over to embrace her again, relishing the silky feel of her skin against his. *All of plesur she is wrout*, he thought. Her hand stirred across his chest, and halted again. 'Gil,' she began, and stopped.

'What is it?' he asked after a moment.

'Yesterday,' she said in a small voice, and then, 'I should not tell you.'

'Is it about Ealasaidh?' he prompted, after another moment. She drew a tiny breath. 'Jennet told me what she heard.'

'You know.'

'I know.' He drew her into a tight clasp. 'I'm here, sweetheart. We are together. We can weather this.'

She buried her face in his shoulder, and he felt her tears hot on his skin.

'I know,' she said, her voice muffled. 'But oh, it is hard.'

The Castle courtyard was thronged and noisy with the Archbishop's servants, making preparations for the arrival of King and court. The morning was sunny, with a brisk wind which added to the movement of the scene, snatching at plaids and gowns, sending litter whirling in corners. Otterburn, glumly surveying the bustle from the steps of his lodging, nodded to Gil as he approached, and raised his red felt hat to Alys.

'Good day, mistress. I hear we've you to thank for finding the missing heiress.' Alys curtsied acknowledgement of this. 'I should take you on the strength, you're worth any four o Andro's lot. All I need now is to learn who killed the verger, and we're done.'

'What time is the quest?' Gil asked. 'Have I time to question the Muirs, and maybe Craigie and all?'

'My lord's dealing wi Craigie right now.' Otterburn

glanced at the sky. 'It's called for after Sext, you've an hour or two. I'll ask you to go down to the cells, it's ower busy above stairs here.'

Austin Muir was in a poor state for questioning. Dragged out of his cell with his chains clanking, he fell to his knees in the passageway saying,

'Did he lift the curse, Maister Cunningham? Will you tell him to lift the curse? I'm no wanting snuffed out like the candle!'

'If you confessed,' said Gil, and took a step back as the manacled hands snatched at his gown. 'As the Archbishop said last night, if you've confessed and repented, you'll no be snuffed out, though you may hang for what you did.'

'I had to do it!' The man was snivelling. 'She kept on at Henry, I'll no let her flyte at Henry like that, I had to stop her.'

'What was she on at Henry about? What was she saying to him?'

'All sorts, she was saying, and none o it true. About he killed the lassie from the tavern and put her at the Cross, and where had he put Annie Gibb, and the like. None o it true, we was never near the Cross in the night. You'll no let them snuff me out, maister, surely?' The hands came up again, imploringly.

'D'you want him taken into the light, Maister Cunningham?' asked Andro, hauling the reluctant Austin to his feet. 'There's more light in the guardroom, and a table forbye. Come on, you. Gie's a hand, Richie, he's no for moving.'

More light did not improve the prisoner's appearance. He had a black eye and a badly grazed jaw, and his velvet gown had suffered in the struggle to arrest him as well as in the cell overnight, with loops of braid hanging loose between the greenish patches of slime from the damp stone-work. He crouched between the two men-at-arms, shivering, and said pleadingly,

'I'm no wanting to be accursit, nor any o those things. You'll tell them, maister, won't you?'

'The Archbishop said you confessed, Austin,' said Gil.

'Have you repented o what you did? Can you tell me what you ken about Dame Ellen?'

'Dame Ellen! She was a wicked woman,' said Austin. 'She'd promised us all sorts, and land and money forbye, if we did her bidding, and none of it cam about. She cheated us, and then she called Henry sic names as there was no standing for it.'

'What were you to do for her?' Gil asked. Austin shook his head.

'I canny mind. All sorts. We'd to take letters for her all across Ayrshire, to men o law, and ride in her escort when she cam to Glasgow, and make up to Annie Gibb. I didny like doing that, she wasny nice in her ways.'

'Was that all you had to do?' Gil asked, ignoring Andro's snort of amusement.

'She had us call at the hostel every day while she was there.' The prisoner began rocking back and forward. 'And then she'd more for us to do. She wanted us to go and see Annie Gibb in the night when she was tied up at the Cross, I'm right glad we never did that, we'd ha found the man that strangled her, maybe he'd ha strangled me. Or Henry. I was feart to go near it. Henry tellt her what was what about that, but she threatened him we'd never get the land nor the money.' The rocking intensified. 'And now see what's come o't all, we've neither land nor money nor Annie Gibb and I'm to be curst like a jackdaw.'

'Austin,' said Gil. He hunkered down, to look into the man's face. 'Is that all you did for her? You killed nobody for her?'

'Killed? No.' Tears were dripping onto the ruined gown. 'Who would we kill for her? Mind, she asked us to, she wanted Annie Gibb slain, seeing we wouldny wed her, so her lands would all go back to the family they cam from, but Henry tellt her no, we wereny getting caught up in sic a thing.' Austin's manacled hands came forward again in appeal, reaching for Gil's arm. 'Maister, will you tell him to lift the curse? I'm no wanting to be snuffed out like yon candle.'

'Has he seen a priest the day?' Gil asked Andro.

'No yet. There's been no word about what to do wi him.'

'He might make better sense if he was confessed again.' Gil disengaged himself and straightened up, looking down at the rocking prisoner. 'Take him away. I'll speak to my lord about a priest for him.'

Henry Muir was even less helpful. Rather more resilient than his brother, he was resentful rather than tearful, but it seemed to Gil he was frightened too. As well he might be; he faced death or imprisonment for his part in two killings, and a heavy penance from the church. He was disinclined to answer questions, nevertheless, even those relating to his signed confession.

'I can see you were protecting your brother,' Gil said at length, 'and he was protecting you. But you could help me now, at no cost to yoursel, and maybe do yoursel some good as well.'

Henry gave him a sour look, and shrugged one shoulder so that his chains clattered.

'Will I get the pilliwinks heated?' suggested Andro hopefully. 'Or the boot, maybe?'

'What's this about taking letters across Ayrshire for Dame Ellen?' Gil asked, ignoring this. 'D'you ken what she wrote in them?'

'No.'

Well, that was an answer of sorts.

'When did she ask you to kill Annie Gibb?'

Another sour look, but no answer.

'Put him back,' said Gil in resignation. 'The Provost can deal wi him later.'

In the outer courtyard of the castle, matters were being set up for the quest on Dame Ellen Shaw and Barnabas the verger. A table had been carried out to the foot of the steps from the main hall, and Otterburn's great chair set behind it, with a stool for Walter the clerk at one end. Walter himself was already standing by, clasping the worn red velvet Gospel book and directing matters crisply while the wind snatched at his long gown. The area for the members of the assize had been roped off. People were gathering, standing by in gossiping knots; Maistre Pierre was in discussion with Andrew Hamilton the joiner, other neighbours were present. The two central actors in the proceedings lay on trestles under a wildly flapping striped awning, and to Gil's surprise he saw Alys there, with the boy Berthold at her side.

As he looked, Alys raised the linen cloth from the battered countenance of Dame Ellen. Washed clean of blood the woman's face was, he knew, a less fearsome sight than it had been by candlelight in the chapel where she died, but both of them flinched from the sight. Alys gathered her resolve and looked again, and spoke coaxingly to the boy. After a moment, perhaps not to be outdone by a young woman, he also looked, visibly forcing himself to gaze steadily at the ravaged countenance. Then he glanced at Alys, apparently surprised, and said something, with complicated gestures.

Elbowing his way through the crowd, Gil reached them just as Alys laid the linen sheet down, pulling it straight, tucking the edges under so that the wind would not catch it. The boy ducked away from him, but she looked up with a troubled expression.

'Berthold has just said he has seen Dame Ellen, arguing with someone,' she said. 'Tell Maister Gil, Berthold.'

Berthold swallowed, opened and shut his mouth a couple of times, and shook his head helplessly.

'Meister Peter?' he said, craning to look about him. 'Lucas? *Ich kann nicht—*'

Alys patted his arm in reassurance.

'Try, Berthold. Try to say it in Scots.'

'Come over here.' Gil drew them both away from the two bodies, into a relatively quiet corner.

With encouragement, Berthold succeeded in explaining that he had indeed seen the woman before. He was certain it was her; he tapped his own front teeth, and gestured at the corpse under its flapping shelter.

'When did you see her?' Gil asked, thinking hard. The

boy had been kept at home since the same day that Peg had been found at the Cross; it must have been the day before, the day the Glenbuck party had arrived in Glasgow.

'After,' said Berthold, and mimed eating something in his hand. 'After food.' Gil nodded. 'In, in kirkyard. She spoke. *Verärget.*'

'Argued?' guessed Gil. Berthold nodded in his turn.

'*Sie stritt mit ihn.*'

'Who did she argue with?' Alys asked.

'A man, a man of the kirk.'

'A priest?' Gil conjectured.

'*Nein, nein.*' Berthold patted his skinny chest, below his left collarbone, then drew an oval shape like a badge there.

'One of the vergers.' Alys looked up at Gil.

'What did they quarrel about?' Gil asked, but that was more than the boy could answer; he shrugged, grinned beseechingly, spread his hands. 'Then what?'

The man had dropped something, and the woman had picked it up. '*Schnell, schnell,*' said Berthold, miming someone pouncing on the item. They had argued more. Berthold wound an invisible cord about his hand; the woman had insisted on keeping it, and sent the man away.

'Where did he go?' Gil asked.

'In kirk,' said Berthold.

'And the woman?'

She had seen Berthold watching, and threatened him, so he had run away, back to the masons' lodge.

'A cord,' said Gil. 'Berthold, come here.'

He led the reluctant boy back to the two corpses, and uncovered Barnabas' face. It had smoothed out, and was by far more recognisable than it had been immediately after he had been dragged out of the well. Berthold considered it for a few moments, then looked at Gil and nodded.

'*Es war dieser Mann.* This man.'

'I must say,' said Otterburn, 'I could ha done wi hearing this an hour or two sooner. You say the woman had words wi the man that's dead. What about?'

271

'I wonder if she knew of Craigie's thefts. She was trying to support his money-gathering, I suppose she was aware of his penance. She was certainly writing to men of law in Ayrshire, I suspect with a view to claiming property on his behalf, and without his knowledge. I need to question him, once Blacader is finished wi him. So yes, she might have tried to instruct Barnabas about the matter, which he would not have taken well.'

'And then she lifted a cord and kept it. Is that the cord she strangled him wi? Why would she strangle him, any road?'

'No, I think she used that cord on Peg Simpson. Barnabas was strangled wi the cord he had in his hand when he went off from the Almoner's store.'

'On Peg Simpson. You've still no explained why, either o them.'

'I think,' said Gil carefully, 'she had just realised that her schemes for Annie's marriage were coming to naught. So she slipped out in the night, greasing the hostel door hinges so that she could return in silence, and strangled the girl at the Cross. She was very insistent that nobody had left the women's hall, but she was our only witness for that. I suppose she could have made certain they all slept soundly, just as the doctor did in the other hall.'

'Aye,' said Otterburn, not particularly encouraging.

'I think Barnabas either recognised her part in what happened to Peg, or suspected Craigie of involvement as we originally thought. It was his misfortune to meet Dame Ellen rather than Craigie, whether it was in the Lower Kirk or out in the kirkyard as the Dean would prefer to believe.'

'She was a big strong woman,' said Otterburn thoughtfully.

'And she had done it before,' said Gil. 'Sir Edward died peacefully, a couple of hours back, but he made a deposition in his last hour, witnessed by Sir Simon and myself.' He drew the folded paper from his purse. 'It's interesting reading.'

Otterburn shot him a wary look, but took the paper and unfolded it.

'All circumstantial,' he said after a moment.

'But it all points in the same direction,' Gil observed. 'She had tried to strangle her brother with a cord when they were children, and he was never satisfied that her first two husbands hanged themselves. That detail of the bruising on the first fellow's neck is very convincing.'

'Aye, but that was twenty year or more ago. No way to tell now.' Otterburn laid the document flat and smoothed it onto his desk. 'Does it satisfy you?'

'I think it fits better than accusing Will Craigie,' Gil admitted. 'He's still swearing he did not kill Barnabas, and I'm inclined to think it's the truth.'

'Aye,' said Otterburn again. 'It would be tidy, I'll admit. It's no like you to go for the tidy solution.'

'I'm none so sure it is tidy,' Gil said. 'We still don't know just why Barnabas died, or why Peg Simpson was throttled, though we can guess, and it's still no clear whether Habbie Sim was involved or no. In some ways it would be neater if we could blame Craigie, but he swears innocence o both those crimes.'

Otterburn folded the paper and handed it back to Gil.

'Well, we'll put it to the assize, though what they'll make of it Deil alone kens. And now I'd best make a start on this quest, afore my lord sends out to know what we're up to.'

'So that abominable laddie,' said Maistre Pierre, 'had the answer to your questions the whole time?'

'Not all of them,' said Gil.

The day had been longer than he liked. The assize had accepted his evidence and brought in the verdicts Otterburn required of them, but its aftermath had included a long and difficult interview with Robert Blacader and a very painful one with John Lockhart. The Archbishop had been rather less surprised than Lockhart to learn that Dame Ellen had been malefactor as well as victim, but saddened to realise that she had died without being confessed and absolved of her crimes, particularly those against Holy Kirk.

'A lesson to us all, Gilbert,' he said in his rich Latin. 'Death can strike at any time, and without warning. That unhappy woman has died in the midst of her villainy, with no opportunity for repentance or amendment of life. I hope our two songmen, Craigie and Sim, will learn from her example and make full confession and restitution for their sins.'

Lockhart had been more realistic about the consequences.

'It falls to me, I suppose,' he said in harassed tones, 'as good-son, to order all, Sir Edward's burial and Dame Ellen's, and executing his will, and dealing wi her property, and I'll have the first hairst, the wheat field, to get in as soon as we're back in Lanarkshire. As for what to do wi these daft lassies, I'm at my wits' end. Annie will wed her doctor and be off my hands, and I'm glad of it, for she's by far less biddable than she was, but the other two, well! My wife will take them under her eye, but I've to get them to her first.'

'Maybe Mistress Forrest would mind them the now,' Gil suggested. 'She seems a capable woman.'

'Aye, maybe,' said Lockhart dubiously, and then with more enthusiasm, 'Aye, you could be right. A good thought, maister. And meantime I can get a word wi Sir Simon about getting Sir Edward in the ground, and who I should ask about whether Dame Ellen's fit to put in a kirkyard, or if she's to go out at a crossroads somewhere. I canny believe it o her, she was aye a steering argumentative woman, but you never think o sic wickedness in someone that's kin, even by marriage. I don't know, if I'd seen what would come o't I'd never ha got involved in this whole enterprise.' He rose to leave Otterburn's office, where Gil had taken him to explain his findings, and offered his hand. On the doorstep he turned back. 'At least Sir Edward's got his release now, and dee'd at peace, sic a grace as that was.'

Maistre Pierre had appeared at the back door after dinner, apparently in the hope of picking over the outcome of the case, so now they were once more in the comfortable little solar, with its windows firmly shuttered against the insistent wind, and Lowrie was handing wine. Catherine accepted her glass from him and remarked,

'The boy knew a great deal more than anyone realised, I think, including himself.'

'He's confirmed the time of Peg Simpson's death,' Gil agreed, 'which I could ha done with knowing earlier, as well as this tale of the argument in the kirkyard.'

'But what did he fear?' asked Maistre Pierre. 'What kept him silent?'

'I think,' said Alys, 'so far as Luke and I can understand him, he had hidden from the battle at the Cross, by going up the Stablegreen beyond St Nicholas'. He saw the Muirs, and described them well, going up the street and down again.'

'To call on Dame Ellen at the hostel?' interrupted her father.

'We think so,' agreed Gil.

'When they returned,' Alys continued, 'there was a woman with them, arguing, who must have been Peg Simpson. They passed him, and he didn't see what happened. But when the battle ended and all turned for home, he set off down the Stablegreen, and found the woman lying dead in the street.' She grimaced. 'He seems to have decided that some of the other prentices must have killed her, rather than the Muirs. That was what frightened him.'

'What, that they might come after him if he told anyone?' Lowrie said in surprise. 'He's no very sharp, is he?'

'No,' said Maistre Pierre with feeling.

'He is barely fourteen, and without friends in a strange country,' said Alys.

'I suppose. But when did he see these other two arguing in the kirkyard?' asked Maistre Pierre. 'Some time when he should have been working, most likely.'

'That was in the afternoon of that same day,' Gil said. 'Dame Ellen must have been newly arrived in Glasgow.'

'Then how did she know the man?' Alys wondered. 'What did they argue about?'

'I know!' said Lowrie. 'Barnabas kept saying he *tellt the woman* that he wouldny have an eye to what happened at the Cross. You mind? When we were called to the dead woman?'

'So he did,'' recalled Gil. 'I took it he was talking about Annie herself, but it must ha been Dame Ellen. Likely she accosted him, asked him to watch, and got an earful.'

'Oh, yes!' said Lowrie. 'He'd never have obliged anyone like that. *More than my place is worth,*' he quoted, and grimaced.

'And then he dropped the cord and she insisted on keeping it.' Alys was nodding. 'It fits better, Gil. It explains why he went looking for her, and why she killed him.' She made a face. 'You know, when I spoke of crows, I did not expect Berthold to be the fourth crow. The one who was not there at all.'

Gil turned his head as two figures passed the window. The house door opened and closed, and there was a scratching at the chamber door.

'Maister Gil?' It was Euan. 'There's a chiel here for you from Canon Muir's house, he was getting a crack with us in the kitchen and now he is wishing to get a word wi you. I tellt him you were busy and private,' he went on importantly, 'but he'll not listen. Will I be sending him away?'

'No, you will not,' said Gil, on a reflex. 'I'll come out. Who is it?'

It was the man Nory, neat in his dark blue garments, with his bundle at his feet, and he had come to take service with Gil.

'You've put an end to my service wi the Muirs, maister,' he said reasonably, 'and it was very clear to me when I seen you afore that you've need o a man to see to your garments. So I've heard about your household, and here I am, and I'll ha the same as you pay this fellow,' he nodded at Euan, still listening suspiciously from across the hall, 'and my keep, and a new suit o clothes at New Year.'

'Will you now?' said Gil, looking at him in amazement.

'That seems like a good idea,' said Alys, tucking her hand through Gil's arm. 'What else will you do? The garden? Sweeping the house?'

'A garden?' Nory brightened. 'I'll lend a hand to the garden, mistress, and gladly. And I can work in sugar-plate,

276

make saints and subtleties for the table, if you're so inclined. And I suppose,' he conceded, 'I can take on the household tasks the women canny manage. But my main duties would be looking after your man's clothes and himself as well.'

'It's a very different household from your last one,' Gil warned him. Nory nodded.

'Be a pleasant change.'

'Well!' said Maistre Pierre, when they reported this, returning to the solar. 'Your household increases daily, Gilbert. You will be Provost yourself before you know it.'

'Sweet St Giles, I hope not!' said Gil.